The
Promise
Girls

Center Point
Large Print

Also by Marie Bostwick and available from
Center Point Large Print:

Apart at the Seams
From Here to Home
The Second Sister

The Promise Girls

Marie Bostwick

CENTER POINT LARGE PRINT
THORNDIKE, MAINE

This Center Point Large Print edition is published in the year 2017 by arrangement with Kensington Publishing Corp.

The text of this Large Print edition is unabridged. In other aspects, this book may vary from the original edition. Printed in the United States of America on permanent paper. Set in 16-point Times New Roman type.

ISBN: 978-1-68324-377-9

Library of Congress Cataloging-in-Publication Data

Names: Bostwick, Marie, author.
Title: The Promise girls / Marie Bostwick.
Description: Center Point Large Print edition. | Thorndike, Maine : Center Point Large Print, 2017.
Identifiers: LCCN 2017003640 | ISBN 9781683243779 (hardcover : alk. paper)
Subjects: LCSH: Sisters—Fiction. | Fertilization in vitro, Human,—Fiction. | Large type books.
Classification: LCC PS3602.O838 P76 2017 | DDC 813/.6—dc23
LC record available at https://lccn.loc.gov/2017003640

For my sister, Lori,
the coolest mermaid I know

Chapter 1

The studio lights are glaringly bright and white-hot.

A disembodied voice from the loudspeaker announces, "One minute to air," in the way Joanie imagines the autopilot of a doomed spaceship might announce, "One minute to impact." Everyone in the studio—audience, host, and guests—goes instantly and utterly silent, waiting for what comes next.

Three weeks into the book tour, Joanie still isn't used to the silence of television studios, ponderous silence that feels like being closed in a concrete box with walls so thick no noise from the outside world can penetrate, just as no sound emanating inside can escape. Joanie can scream as loud as she wants and no one will hear her.

Joanie, Meg, Avery, and their mother sit in upholstered side chairs, like the ones you see in the waiting rooms of doctor's offices, motionless, waiting. Avery is so little her feet can't touch the floor, but she doesn't kick her legs or even fidget.

The audience is still as well. They stare at Joanie and her little sisters in a way that makes her think about people at the zoo staring through the glass at the reptile house, waiting for the snakes to do something interesting.

Soon they will—she will. If she doesn't lose her nerve.

The voice comes again, droning "Ten seconds." Joanie feels a bead of sweat along her hairline. She lifts her hand to wipe it away, but catches sight of her mother's eyes. She puts her hand back into her lap, feels the bead trickle down her forehead, into the crevice behind her ear, dropping onto her dress collar.

The floor director, dressed in black, counts down the final five seconds on his fingers and points at the host, whose smile appears out of nowhere.

"We're back. Today we're discussing child prodigies. We'll be meeting children and teens whose remarkable achievements in the arts, sciences, mathematics, and business can't help but make us reconsider our preconceived notions about the limits of human intelligence and even the nature of childhood itself. It also brings up long-debated questions about what matters most in tapping the depth of human potential. Nature? Or nurture?

"In her newly released book, *The Promise Girls*, our first guest, Minerva Promise, mother of three artistic prodigies, argues that nature and nurture play equally important roles in fostering genius.

Please welcome Minerva Promise and her daughters, Joanie, Meg, and Avery—the Promise Girls."

The audience, happy to have a role to play and eager to approve of anything put forth by their host, one of the wealthiest, most famous, and most trusted women in America, claps enthusiastically. When the applause begins to fade, the host asks her first question.

"Minerva Promise, most expectant parents are happy just to have healthy children, but when your daughters were born, and even before they were conceived, you made it your goal to raise three highly accomplished artists—a pianist, a painter, and a writer."

Minerva, who has been nodding in agreement while the host speaks, smiles. "That's right. My daughters were given expert artistic instruction as soon as they were capable of creating on their own. Joanie received her first piano lessons at two and a half. Meg began painting—with her fingers, of course—even before that. Avery is only five, so she can't yet write sentences, but she creates and dictates remarkably complex stories. Even as babies, my girls were intentionally and intensely exposed to great music, art, and literature to tap their natural creativity."

"And yet," the host comments, her brow furrowing, "some have said there is nothing natural in your methods. You didn't just encourage your daughters, but engineered them with the specific intention to raise prodigies in three separate areas of the arts. Is that true?"

Minerva frowns, but in a way that will not make her appear any less attractive on camera.

"I think 'engineered' makes it all sound a lot more Mary Shelley than was actually the case. I'm no Dr. Frankenstein." She flashes a maternal smile to prove it. The audience chuckles. "However, I did take advantage of technological advances to conceive and bear children with a higher likelihood of achievement in the arts.

"As a single woman with infertility issues that made conception by natural means or even by artificial insemination impossible, I feared I would never have children. But when Louise Brown was born—"

"The first test tube baby," the host clarifies, "born in England in 1978."

"Yes," Minerva says. "She was the first baby born via in vitro fertilization, in which the egg is fertilized in a laboratory and then implanted into the mother's womb. Soon afterward, I went to Europe to undergo the procedure, choosing donor sperm from an anonymous classical pianist for my first child, Joanie, and a gifted painter for my second girl, Meg." She smiles affectionately at her daughters, who smile back. "By the time Avery was born, in vitro was widely available in the U.S., so I . . ."

Joanie stops listening. The press packet prepared by their publicist and sent ahead of each interview has suggested questions written out in advance. The host has written her own questions, but Joanie knows more or less what will come next—the pseudo-serious discussion of pseudo-scientific theories, the host's gentle chiding about the social and moral implications of designer babies . . . It was pretty much the same every time.

Only a few questions will be directed toward Joanie or her sisters and those will be softballs—easy inquiries about the artists they admire most, what their average day is like, if they have time to play and have friends like "normal" kids, possibly a cheeky question about whether or not Joanie has a boyfriend—questions formulated to make them seem like other children, which they are not.

Other children don't get paraded out to perform like monkeys at the circus, stared at like snakes in the Reptile House, like freaks in a sideshow. Even now, as the grown-ups talk about the children as if they aren't there or can't hear, the audience keeps sneaking furtive glances at them. The boy in the front row, the geeky math whiz who tried to talk to her in the green room, is staring at them outright, at her, and has been the whole time.

Like the others, he probably wants to know what the big deal is about them, about her. Are they as genius as Momma claims? Joanie doubts it. Meg is different perhaps, the only true genius in the room. But they all work very hard, Momma too.

The Promise Girls—the children and the book —are Momma's life's work, the only means she had of making a living, for all of them. Having just turned seventeen, Joanie is old enough to understand about money and the need of it. That's why she agreed to go along with this, to be the one whose job it is to prove that Momma is telling the truth and has successfully and intentionally raised prodigious artists.

Avery is too little to be anything but adorable, though she absolutely is and enjoys the attention. But being adorable doesn't prove the success of the experiment, does it? Meg can't produce a painting on demand in an eight-minute television segment. Even if she could, she's too timid. She hates being stared at, being judged by strangers. Just sitting here is agony for her.

It is for Joanie, too, but she can bear it better. She must because she's the oldest. It's her job to protect the little ones, and so she agreed to this. For three weeks. It was supposed to be over by now. The publicist said that three weeks after a book is released, the public will lose interest. Unless you are on this show.

Apparently, it is a very big deal. Joanie wouldn't have known unless someone told her—they don't own a television. But because the host read

Momma's book and decided to do a show built around them at the last minute, now everyone wants them. Paula, the publicist, is booking them three months out. Three months.

Joanie hadn't agreed to that. None of them had.

Avery is turning into a brat, starting to act out because she thinks the others are getting more attention. Momma has threatened to spank her even though Avery knows her mother would never lay a hand on Avery, on any of them. Momma has a sinus infection. Joanie has a cold. All of them are exhausted. When it began they were excited because the hotels have swimming pools. Now they are too tired to use them.

Meg is suffering the most. She woke up crying this morning, has headaches every day, all day. She's anxious all the time, too nervous to eat.

Meg is suffering. Can't they see that? Someone has to put a stop to it.

The first segment is over. A stagehand comes to escort Joanie, but she knows what she is supposed to do. She gets up from her chair and goes to the piano on the far side of the stage. She will play her usual piece, Liebestraum No. 3, by Liszt. When she is done, she will go back to the chairs with the others. The host will ask the softball questions while pictures of Meg's paintings flash onto the big screen at the back of the stage.

Then it will be over. Except it won't be. Not unless someone puts a stop to it.

The commercial break ends. The cameras roll again. The host introduces her and Joanie begins to play.

How many times has she played the Liebestraum? The "Dream of Love"? Hundreds, certainly. Thousands, maybe. Yet she never tires of it. Maestro Boehm has taught her to see mystery in every note, to understand that every time she plays, no matter how familiar the notes, chords, and arpeggios become, the music can reveal something new to her, and in her, if she will release herself to it.

But today is not one of those days. She is not playing very well. Not badly, but not well. She has learned that television audiences don't know the difference; it's not like playing at a competition. But surely even they will notice the mistake she has planned, timing it to occur during the change from arpeggios to chords, where someone might easily trip up. If she goes through with it, makes this mistake on purpose, they'll see that she's not a prodigy at all, just a lazy, mediocre girl, a failed experiment, and they'll send her home. They'll send all of them home.

Will Maestro Boehm forgive her? Will Momma?

But someone has to put a stop to it; Momma should have already. When Paula started talking about booking three months out, Momma should have said, "I'm sorry, we're done. It's enough." But she didn't and now Joanie doesn't know if she'll be able to forgive her, ever, for forcing her to do this, for leaving her no choice.

Here they come, two bars away now, the chords.

Joanie's eyes shift to the far side of the stage, ignoring the suspicion she sees in her mother's eyes. Joanie looks at the keyboard and makes her fingers stumble, or seem to stumble. She frowns, pretending to be perturbed, flustered. Then she pretends to recover herself and plays the end of the piece perfectly.

The final notes fade away. Joanie lifts her hands from the keyboard and stands up as the audience applauds. Her cheeks feel hot. She knows she doesn't deserve their adulation and doesn't understand why they don't realize this, but she curtsies because that's the procedure, that's what you do after a performance. Momma always says, "It's one thing to make a mistake, another to let people see it."

The host crosses the stage to meet her. The audience claps even louder when she folds Joanie into a congratulatory embrace before leading her back to the chairs.

Momma stands up as if to greet her. Her lips are pressed into a thin line and her eyes are two cold gray mirrors. She draws back her arm and slaps her daughter across the face with such power that the sound is like the crack of wood against leather when a batter swings away and hits one into the bleachers.

The audience gasps as if they are one person and then, just for a breath, falls into shocked silence. They can't quite believe what they have just seen, can't believe that the mother of these brilliant children who has been making the rounds of all the talk shows, including this one, hosted by the empress of them all, has just slapped her daughter while the cameras rolled.

But Joanie is not surprised. She expected . . . well, not this. But something like it. She knew Momma would be angry.

Joanie totters a step, feeling off-balance. She removes her hand from her cheek, exposing the angry red imprint of her mother's hand. The crowd gasps again. They see the evidence of Minerva's wrath.

And then . . . pandemonium. It all happens so fast.

The host grabs Joanie, pulls her close, calls for security. Within seconds, two security guards grab hold of Minerva, clasping her arms, limp at the elbow. Two black-clad producers appear from the wings, swooping down on Meg and Avery. Avery is sobbing, crying for her mother and Joanie at the same time. Meg is crying, too, but no sound comes out of her mouth even though her eyes are streaming with tears and her face is contorted. There are cries and boos. People calling their mother names—terrible, terrible names. Others are calling for 911, for the police.

The floor director shouts, "Cut!" The red lights on the cameras go dark. The security guards are dragging Minerva off into the wings. Another of the black-clad strangers grabs hold of Joanie's arms and pulls her in another direction, away from her mother, away from her sisters, too, separating them like four points of a compass, to the end of the map of the world, the end of their world.

Joanie is crying now, too, louder than anyone, sobbing, "I'm sorry. I didn't mean it! Let me play it again, please! I'll do it right this time, I promise. Please! Let me play it again!"

It does no good. She can scream as loud as she wants. No one hears.

Chapter 2

2017
Seattle, Washington

March is the season of waiting in Seattle.

Rain drizzles down day after day in a dithering trickle, too hard for a sprinkle, too light for a deluge. The temperature, too, is indecisive. It's hard to know what to wear—coat, jacket, sweater, or shirtsleeves—so people tend to dress in layers, trying to prepare for anything, irritated that they need to. The skies are neutrally gray, refusing to make an endorsement or prediction. Everyone lives in suspense, waiting for the unveiling that, this year, could well pass them by, waiting for spring. Or something like it. Anything different would do, anything to break the monotony, and the tension, of waiting.

Meg Promise Hayes sat in the dining alcove that doubled as her home office, her desk heaped with papers, looking out the window. Mrs. LaRouche was tromping dutifully down the sidewalk, holding an umbrella in one hand and Punkin's leash in the other. Meg waved and then checked her e-mail, hoping there might be a message from the mortgage broker saying their new client's loan had been approved. She's unlikely to hear anything on a Saturday, but checks anyway. With Asher's winter work wrapping up, they really needed that job.

Finding nothing in her in-box, she went back to work. As usual, there were more bills than all the rest put together. It was discouraging. She sighed.

It wasn't Asher's fault that building Not So Big houses generated Not So Big profits, or that they never completely regained their footing after the recession. What bugged her was that he wasn't more concerned about it.

"We make enough to get by and can feel good about what we do. That's more than a lot of people can say. I've got no complaints."

That was Asher in a nutshell: no complaints. About anything.

After one look at those laughing eyes, Mrs. Hayes decided to name her son Asher, which means "happy" in Hebrew. It suited him. "Happy" was Asher's default mode and one of the reasons Meg fell for him so hard and so fast—that plus the dizzying, disorienting chemistry between them, an instantaneous attraction that was so thick you could have cut it with a knife.

Joanie still told the story of what happened when Meg moved to Seattle and Joanie introduced her little sister to Asher, a friend who was helping remodel her decrepit Capitol Hill bungalow. Joanie made lunch for the three of them and spent the whole time talking and talking, trying to fill the silence while Meg and Asher stared at each other across the table.

"The most awkward hour of my life," Joanie would say. "But I probably didn't need to say a word. For you two, there was nobody else in the room."

True enough. After one look at Asher, Meg was off the market. Not that she'd ever really been on the market. Until that moment painting was her only love. Asher changed all that.

His eyes were brown with flecks of gold, and his smile so bright and easy that it was impossible not to smile back. He didn't have a beard yet, but even then he wore his hair long, in a ponytail that was as thick and strong as stout manila rope. He stood six foot six and had shoulders that went on forever.

He played the guitar, read voraciously, loved hiking, skiing, and telling terrible parrot jokes. If that weren't enough, with a load of good lumber and a little advance notice, he could build just about anything you could imagine. He was sweet, funny, considerate, and incredibly masculine, a kind of urban mountain man, the perfect mix of hip and homespun, the kind of man that Seattle was made for.

What girl wouldn't have fallen in love with Asher?

They were married just six weeks after they met. She was nineteen and he was twenty-two. Nine and a half months later, they became parents of a baby daughter, Trina. They bought their first house a year later and barely escaped with their lives when it burned to the ground. Even now, Meg could close her eyes and smell the smoke, feel the heat of the flames, and remember how it felt to stand on the curb with Trina sobbing in her arms and Asher's arm heavy over her shoulders, watching the flames devour their home, grateful to be alive even as she wondered how and where they were to live.

But Asher, happy Asher, never complained, not even after realizing the insurance money wouldn't be enough to replace what they had before. He built them another house—better but much smaller —on the same lot and with his own hands.

That experience convinced them he should go

into business building smaller, smarter, quality-constructed homes. They started RightSize Homes with what little was left in Meg's trust from the sales of *The Promise Girls* and thirty thousand borrowed from Joanie.

Asher was a good builder but a bad business-man. He could construct a 600-square-foot house that was cute as a button, tight as a drum, and as comfortable to live in as one twice its size. But he couldn't keep track of scheduling, contracts, expenses, and, most importantly, income. Months could pass before he got around to sending bills for his work. Meg gave up painting entirely and became his bookkeeper, scheduler, office manager, and co-designer.

When she heard of it, Minerva left a voice mail rant about how stupid and selfish Meg was to abandon the artistic gift her mother had sacrificed so much to develop and nurture. Meg blocked Minerva's number. That worked for almost a year. Then Minerva got a new number. Meg blocked her again . . . and again . . . and again. Now, unless she knew exactly who was calling, Meg let the phone ring.

In truth, it was a relief to give up the artificial seeds of aspiration planted by Minerva upon her birth. If Meg had been braver, more realistic, she'd have scrapped it all years before, like Joanie. She'd have been happy, like Asher. For a time, she was.

It was good working alongside her husband, building beautiful little houses that people of modest means could afford, even better to build a business and family and life together, something solid that they could be proud of.

But this far in, shouldn't life be a little more certain? Shouldn't she know for sure what and who she could count on? But she didn't anymore. She hadn't for months. That was what bothered her, far more than finances.

Meg opened the Visa bill and groaned when she saw the total. The screen door slammed and she heard Asher in his work boots clumping into the kitchen.

"Hey, babe! I dropped Trina off at the Science Center and then went to the job site. They delivered an electric water heater instead of gas, so I've got to return it. I thought I'd swing by, grab some food, and say hi." He opened the refrigerator and started rooting around. "Do we have any of that leftover quinoa salad?"

"Trina finished it," she said without looking up from her work.

Asher came into the alcove carrying a container of potato salad and a spoon. He stood behind her and bent down, pressing his lips onto the curve where her shoulder became her neck.

"How's your morning going? Feel like taking a break?"

"Asher, not now. Really." She twisted her

shoulders, breaking contact. "We're either three thousand dollars under budget or six hundred over. I need to figure out which."

"Bet I know," he said with a wry smile. "And what difference does an hour make? We'll be just as broke at one as we are at noon, won't we? And since Trina's not home . . ."

He lowered his head again. Meg scooted her chair closer to the desk and sat up very straight, refusing to look at him.

"Asher. Stop. I'm not in the mood."

He was quiet, so quiet that she thought he might have left the room. But after a moment he walked around to the side of the desk. For once, he didn't look happy. He took the credit card bill from her grasp and laid it down on the desk.

"Meg, talk to me. Tell me what's going on. You haven't been in the mood for six weeks, three days, and fourteen hours. Not that I'm counting or anything." A wisp of a smile broke through his somber expression, but quickly dissipated. "We've never gone six days before, let alone six weeks. It's not just the sex. I miss you, Meg. I feel like you're a million miles away."

Meg felt her jaw set. "I'm tired, that's all. And drowning in paper. I've got to get the tax stuff organized, pull together that new bid—even though I'm sure they're going to go with somebody else—all the husband could talk about was price per square foot. I also have to write the grant application for the new computer lab at Trina's school by myself."

"Wait . . . I thought Rhonda somebody-or-other was helping you with that?"

Meg shook her head. "It's Robin. And now she can't. Her mother has cancer so she has to go to Florida. I'm fine. Just tired. Tired, overworked, and overwhelmed."

He studied her as she talked, his brown eyes searching.

"And you're sure that's all. There's nothing you want to tell me?"

"No!" she snapped, irritated by his prodding. "Anything you want to tell *me?*"

His concern turned to confusion. "Like what?"

Meg grabbed the Visa bill and stabbed her finger toward one of the charges. "Like what you bought for $478.28 at Best Buy?"

"That was the telescope. For Trina's birthday. We talked about it."

"Not for five hundred dollars we didn't. Do you know how tight things are for us right now?"

"It's her birthday," he said, as if this should be explanation enough. "You only turn sixteen once. And it's not like it's something frivolous, like a toy. You know Trina. She'll use this for years and . . ."

His voice trailed off. He stood there. Meg could see he was struggling, trying not to lose his temper. She almost wished he would.

"You're right," he said at last. "We should have picked it out together. Listen, I'm going back to work." He squeezed her shoulder and carried his dishes back to the kitchen. Meg wilted in her chair and rubbed her forehead, feeling guilty.

"Don't forget," he said, "you're picking Trina up at the Science Center. Her workshop ends at noon."

"Great. Downtown traffic."

"You want me to go instead?"

"No, no. Get the water heater. We're three weeks behind schedule already." Meg spun around so she could see him. "Hey. Sorry I'm such a witch today."

"Don't worry about it." He smiled that everything-is-fine-nothing-is-ruined Asher smile that she knew so well, then grabbed an apple from the fruit bowl and headed toward the back door. "By the way, your sister called me."

"Which one? Joanie or Avery?"

"Joanie. She called me to find out why you haven't returned her calls."

"It's spring—sort of. Bid season, tax season. I'm busy." Meg furrowed her brow as she tried to remember what she'd charged for $62 on PayPal.

"That's what I told her. She said to tell you to call back anyway and that she hates CoupleQuest .com. Oh, and something about some guy who wants to make a documentary about you and your sisters. She said not to tell you about it, so if she brings it up act surprised. Mostly I think she wanted to vent about the dating thing."

"Uh-huh," Meg said distractedly. "Tell her she's never going to meet anybody if she doesn't make an effort. It's not like some great guy is just going to knock on her door and declare himself."

"Yeah, I'll let you tell her. See you tonight. Love you."

The door slammed. Only after she heard the truck pull out of the driveway did Meg whisper, "Love you too."

Two hours later, Meg's desk still wasn't clean, but she had sorted out the accounts. Sure enough, they were already over their monthly budget. She made an online funds transfer from savings, then checked her cell phone.

Joanie had called her again. So had Asher. She didn't have time to talk to either of them now. Asher was probably calling to check on her and ask, yet again, if anything was wrong. In previous days, she'd thought his solicitousness was sweet. Now it felt stifling. Or disingenuous? Time would tell.

Meg checked the time. If she didn't leave in the next five minutes, she'd be late picking up Trina. She ran into the kitchen, plugged in the Crock-Pot, then went back to her desk to check her e-mail one last time, still hoping for some good news. Instead she saw a message that she hadn't been expecting for another two weeks, one that could allay her suspicions. Or confirm them.

For a moment, she thought about hitting the delete button and forgetting that any of this had ever happened. But it was too late for that. She had to know the truth.

She scanned the e-mail, absorbing figures and percentages, charts and graphs, until she reached the bottom and knew for certain that her suspicions had been correct. Even so, she sat there for a long moment, trying to wrap her mind around it all, feeling her heart pound but nothing more, feeling numb.

What was she supposed to do next? Whom should she talk to first and when? What was she supposed to say?

She scrolled down to read other files, the ones that were supposed to be merely diversionary, finding more figures, more charts, more evidence, a conclusion she could never have anticipated.

"Dear God," she whispered, her head dropping to the back of the chair, as if the weight of newly attained knowledge made it too heavy to hold. "I don't believe it."

She lifted her gaze to a wall filled with family pictures, eyes focused on a photograph of herself and her sisters taken at a barbecue in Joanie's backyard.

"How could she? After all this time . . ."

Meg's heart hammered even harder. Numbness

gave way to anger and she felt her fingers clench into fists. She spotted another picture, one that Asher had taken four years before, in August.

They had gone camping at Mt. Rainier to see the peak of the Perseids meteor shower, hiked the Skyline trail, and posed for a picture near Panorama Point.

Trina was shorter then. Meg stood behind her daughter, draping her arms over Trina's scrawny shoulders, looking over the top of her head. The sky was so bright, the bluest of blues, the mountain so close it looked like you could touch it. They were the only people on a trail that cut through a meadow carpeted with purplish blue wildflowers. It was a perfect day.

Meg remembered squeezing Trina, wishing she could hold on to her child and that day forever. In the photo, Trina tilted her head, smiling up into Meg's eyes. She had lifted her hand to rest it on her mother's cheek. Asher had snapped the picture, preserving the moment, in a way granting her wish.

Meg closed her eyes and took a deep breath. She couldn't give in to her emotions. Not now. She had to get her daughter, get through this day, and consider her options. It wasn't just about her.

Usually, Meg avoided I-5 when it was raining. But it was the only practical route to get downtown.

Since it was early she thought maybe she'd get lucky.

She didn't.

Meg squinted through the opaque haze left by windshield wipers that should have been replaced months ago, overwrought and anxious and late, stuck in the middle of a line of cars with red brake lights that stretched for miles. Her cell rang and she picked up without looking at the screen.

"Trina? Sorry, honey. Traffic is a nightmare. I'll be there as soon as I can."

"Meg?" The woman's voice sounded surprised. "It's me. Don't hang up."

Meg was quiet for a moment. "What do you want?"

"Can't a mother talk to her daughter? It's been more than a year."

It had been two years, but Meg didn't say so. In Minerva's hands, any contradiction or even an innocent observation could become a hook to drag others into one of her dramas. Best to say as little as possible. She thought about hanging up; she wasn't quite sure why she didn't.

"I don't have time for this today, Minerva. Just tell me what you want."

She expected her mother would now cut to the chase. Instead, Minerva surprised her by saying, and in a voice that sounded as if she really cared, "You don't sound like yourself. What's bothering you, sweetheart?"

Meg was bruised, feeling vulnerable. She had to fight back the desire to open up to her mother, like she had in the old days, and tell her everything. But that was crazy. Just crazy. Minerva wasn't trustworthy. She never had been.

The rain began to subside. The neon necklace of brake lights changed from red to pink as cars began to move, first at a crawl, then something akin to a steady walk. Meg inched her aged, rust-bucket Subaru forward.

"Nothing," she said. "Just tired. I spent the whole morning doing paperwork."

"Paperwork." Minerva puffed dismissively. "Are you painting?"

"No."

Of course she wasn't painting. Minerva knew that. Meg pressed her foot more firmly on the gas. The speedometer progressed from ten, to twenty, to forty.

"Well, there you are," Minerva said.

Meg could envision her throwing up her hands and setting her mouth into a self-satisfied line, the way she always did when she felt she'd won the argument, whether or not she actually had.

"No wonder you're tired. Who wouldn't be? Playing secretary to that handyman you married."

"Asher's not a handyman, he's a contractor."

"So? He's not much of anything if he's willing to let you waste your talent. You've got a gift, Meg. It's meant to be used. You're not tired, you're bored. And blocked, creatively blocked. What you need to do is start a new canvas. Get back to the work you were *born* to do, not shuffling around piles of papers. You're an artistic genius, Meghan. You cannot be happy unless you're creating."

I am not a genius! None of us is. Not me, or Joanie, or Avery. It was a lie, a way for you to live out your own demented fantasy through the lives of your children!

Meg drove faster now, tailgating a blue Prius. Feeling trapped, she lurched into the open left lane with barely a sideways glance and swallowed back the silent harangue in her head.

Arguing with Minerva, she reminded herself, especially about her epically bad parenting, was like trying to argue philosophy with a drunk: All you'd end up doing would be shouting the same thing over and over. And in the morning, not only would the drunk remain unconvinced, he wouldn't even recall the conversation.

"Minerva, *what* do you want?"

"I got a call from a man named Hal Seeger. He makes documentaries. He wants to make a film about the book, about all of you."

Meg frowned. This was another of her mother's delusions; it had to be.

Minerva's rise to fame had been meteoric. Her downfall had been even more spectacular, more a high-speed crash than a downfall, taking all of them with her. But no one cared about Minerva or her daughters anymore. And thank God for it.

"He's a famous director," Minerva went on, the rush of words signaling her excitement. "One of his documentaries, *Spells the End*, was screened at Sundance. You remember it, don't you? It was about homeschoolers competing in the National Spelling Bee."

Meg recognized the name of the film. She blinked, remembering that Asher had said something about a man wanting to make a documentary and that she was supposed to act surprised if it came up.

She didn't have to act. She was surprised. Especially that Minerva would imagine that any of them would go along with this.

"Hal is very enthusiastic," she said. "He wants to fly to Seattle to talk to you."

"Talk to *me?*"

"Joanie and Avery too. He wants to bring a film crew to interview all three of you and then follow you around for several weeks. He just wants to show what happened to you in the years after the book release. His concept is to—"

"His concept!" Meg cracked out a laugh and pushed her right foot down again. The Subaru sped up, practically kissing the bumper of a lumbering Chevy pickup. "His concept is a new edition of the Promise Girls sideshow! He wants to sell tickets so that people can gawk at us all over again, only this time they won't be coming to see three artistic prodigies. This time they'll be coming to see three screwed-up failures. Don't you get it, Minerva?"

"All publicity is good publicity," said Minerva. Her voice was perfectly calm, as if Meg's distress didn't even register with her. "This is a chance to restore your image, set the record straight. But *you* need to pull yourself together, Meg. You have to start painting again. And your sisters have to—"

That was it. The trigger.

The embers of anger Meg had been fighting to control all afternoon exploded into something fierce and uncontainable. She screamed into the phone, epithets pouring from her even as she pumped the gas pedal, lunging her car toward the bumper of the Chevy.

"I don't *have* to do anything! Not for you or anyone else, Minerva! Don't ever call me again. I mean it. Not ever. Forget you're my mother. Forget I was even born. I never want to talk to you, or hear your voice, or even *think* about you ever again. If I could crack open my skull and empty out every memory of you, I would!"

Meg threw the phone as hard as she could against the passenger window. The force of the blow split it into three parts. The pieces bounced off the window and fell with a muffled thump onto the passenger seat.

With hot tears coursing down her cheeks, blurring her vision, Meg smacked the heel of her hand against the steering wheel, honking at the pickup driver. Her cry of fury harmonized with the blaring of the horn. She yanked the wheel hard to the left and lurched into the farthest, fastest lane. The green semitrailer was coming up quick in her blind spot. Meg didn't see it.

After her car slammed into the concrete freeway wall, she didn't see anything at all.

Chapter 3

Joanie knelt before a wasp-waisted dressmaker's dummy, pinning the hem of an 1860s reproduction black silk mourning dress. The triple pagoda sleeves had cost her almost an entire extra day's work, but they'd been worth it. They absolutely made the gown. Placing the final pin, Joanie rocked back on her haunches to examine her handiwork, eyeing every seam, pleat, and dart.

Perfect.

Smiling, she got up from the floor and went to her desk to check her phone. There were three calls and three messages, all from Hal Seeger, an obviously insane man who kept calling and leaving messages about making a documentary about the Promise Girls twenty years later. Joanie had considered blocking his number, but a part of her was curious to see how long he'd keep after her. Apparently, a very long time.

Meg, however, had not returned any of her calls. That wasn't like her. It wasn't like any of them. Having survived one of the more publicly dysfunctional childhoods in American history, the Promise sisters tended to cling together.

Joanie had escaped LA for Seattle at age nineteen. Her sisters soon followed, each making the trip in her turn, as soon as circumstances and the California Department of Children's Services permitted. Joanie paid for their train tickets, met them at the station, took them in, fed them, and mothered them, just like she had in the old days. They'd been together ever since.

Joanie opened her laptop prior to checking her e-mail, but was interrupted by the sound of Walt's size sixteen shoes thundering down stairs.

"Mom! Mom, I got in!"

She spun around in her chair. Walt was standing in the doorway of her studio, grinning so wide you'd think he'd just found out he'd made the Olympic wrestling team, or been admitted to Harvard on a full scholarship. But college was still two years off for Walt and though he was nearly big enough for a career as a world-class wrestler, he was more of a gentle giant.

Joanie knew there was only one thing that would have gotten him this excited and propelled him out of bed before noon on a Saturday.

"The internship? You're in?"

"I. Am. In!" he exclaimed, pumping his fist in the air. "Listen! I printed it out so I could read it to you.

" 'Dear Walt,' " he recited. "Blah, blah, blah—'it is with a great deal of pleasure that we are writing to inform you that you have been chosen as the Junior Docent and Historical Interpreter for the upcoming summer season at the Fort Nisqually Living History Museum in Tacoma, Washington.' "

He paused, silently scanning the sentence a second time, and grinned even more broadly.

" 'Please fill out the attached permissions,' " he continued, switching into his don't-care-about-details voice, "blah, blah, blah. 'Training begins on June fifteenth. Very truly yours.' "

"Oh, honey, that's great. Congratulations." She came to stand beside him and squeezed his beefy shoulders, amazed as always to recall that this enormous almost man had emerged from her own body as a tiny baby. "I'm so proud of you. Did they say who you'll be reenacting?"

"Lawrence Aloysius McCormick," he read. "An eighteen-year-old fur trader of Irish descent."

"That's it? Sounds like you've got some researching to do."

"I know," Walt enthused, his eyes glittering at the prospect. "I'm going to start tonight. But, Mom? I'll need a new outfit. Early 1850s fur trader, but something a little snappy. He's young, probably trying to impress girls. I want to play him as a little bit of a peacock."

"Makes sense," Joanie said.

She loved the way Walt brought his imagination along when he reenacted a historical character.

"But I won't be able to work on a costume for you until after I get through my order backlog. You know how spring is; every reenactor on the planet wants a new costume before the start of the summer season."

"Oh, sure. I wasn't talking about right now," Walt said, though the flash of disappointment in his eyes belied his words. "Paying customers come first." He glanced toward the dress dummy, elegantly clad in silk taffeta. "Who's it for?"

"A new client who plays a wealthy Civil War widow at one of the big plantations in Virginia. Beautiful, isn't it? *So* much work."

"Hope you charged her for it."

"Not as much as I should have," Joanie admitted. "But I'm happy with how it turned out. So, what are you up to today?"

"Well, thought I'd go over and tell Mr. Teasdale about my internship and then hang out for a while—"

"I meant to get over there this week. How's he doing since the stroke?"

"Better," Walt reported. "Good enough to complain. He's really ticked about missing the encampment season. Oh, I forgot to tell you, Uncle Asher said he'll be my camping buddy this summer. Do we have a uniform he can use?"

"I'll come up with something," Joanie said casually, and sat back down at her desk. "I'm happy he's going with you. And I'm happy that you're willing to spend part of your Saturday with Mr. Teasdale. You're a good kid, you know that?"

Walt shrugged off her praise. "It's no big deal. I mean . . . it's Mr. Teasdale."

In spite of his ineloquence, Joanie knew what Walt meant. He understood how much he owed to their elderly neighbor. So did Joanie.

Walt was the product of an impulsive and completely uncharacteristic one-night stand. He was also the best thing that ever happened to Joanie. Still, even with her two sisters and a brother-in-law to help, being a single mother wasn't easy. Walt was so shy when he was little. Until he turned fourteen, shot up, and bulked up practically overnight, he'd been downright scrawny and had a voice like a cartoon character. Kids picked on him and he hated school.

Joanie never wanted to push Walt the way she'd been pushed, but she tried everything she could think of to help him get over his timidity—karate lessons, soccer camp, Cub Scouts. None of it worked. Walt's Pinewood Derby car won the race, but she and Asher were the ones who built it. Joanie even enrolled him in music lessons. It was honestly something of a relief when the trumpet teacher informed her that Walt was tone deaf and had no rhythm. But to see Walt happy, she'd even have gotten back into the music world if she had to.

When Mr. Teasdale, who played a lieutenant colonel in a troop of Civil War reenactors, recruited ten-year-old Walt as a drummer boy, Joanie was thrilled. She dove in headfirst to make him the most authentic drummer boy costume possible. Walt dove in with her. It changed both of their lives.

They spent hours researching the clothes, culture, and events of the period. In the process, Walt discovered a passion for history that spilled over into the rest of his schoolwork. Ds and Cs became Bs and then As. He was more confident, too, and started to make friends.

Happy for any excuse to spend time with her young son, Joanie started reenacting too. She enjoyed researching the lives of wives and widows, nurses and camp followers, and inventing characters to go with them. But sewing costumes was her favorite part. Hers were meticulously researched and constructed. Other reenactors noticed, and soon a brisk little side business was born. Three years in, she quit her office manager job to sew historical costumes full-time.

Now she was finally in the black, able to support herself and her son doing something creative that she truly enjoyed. All thanks to Mr. Teasdale.

"Tell the Teasdales that I'll come over to visit next week," Joanie said, scribbling a reminder to herself on a pad of paper. "I just made a batch of that lavender shortbread he likes. Take some with you when you go, will you?" Walt nodded. "So what's on the agenda after the Teasdales?"

"Thought I'd meet Joey down at Starbucks. Maybe Aunt Avery will give us free Frappuccinos."

Joanie shook her head and shot him a look.

"First of all, those Frappuccinos belong to Starbucks, not Avery. She can't give them away to you or anybody else. Even if she could, she's not working there anymore. She quit."

Walt arched his eyebrows doubtfully. "Quit? Or they fired her?"

"Quit. She just booked a six-hundred-dollar job posing for some yacht club calendar. That's enough to hold her for a month, so she finished out the shift and walked out the door.

"Two weeks," Joanie muttered in disgust, deleting unwanted e-mails. "And the sad part? That's a record. Twenty-five years old with an IQ of 152 and she can't keep a real job."

"That's not really true," Walt protested. "She babysat for the Meisners for five years before they moved to Arizona."

Walt wasn't the sort of kid who normally went around contradicting his mother, but he adored his fun-loving aunt, who was only nine years his senior, and wouldn't let anyone speak against her.

Avery literally lived in their backyard, in a tiny house she'd built with her share of the trust from the proceeds of *The Promise Girls*. It was possibly the only financially wise move Avery had made in her life. Joanie had done something similar with her trust money, used it as a down payment on her then-dilapidated bungalow. She could never have afforded a house in the Capitol Hill neighborhood otherwise. But Avery owned her place outright. She had no mortgage and few expenses.

Living in such close proximity, there were bound to be clashes between the sisters—one practical to a fault, one fanciful in the extreme. At sixteen, Walt wasn't just the man of the house, he was also the unofficial peacemaker.

"Well, maybe she doesn't need a real job," he reasoned. "She runs her own business. That's what you do." He shrugged.

"Honey," Joanie said, turning in her chair so she could see him better, "I know you think I'm picking on Avery, but I'm not. I'm just worried about her. Earning a hundred dollars a pop to dress up as a mermaid and read stories at kids' birthday parties isn't a business, it's a sideline. And that's being generous."

"Sometimes she makes a lot more," Walt countered. "When she got booked to appear at

Seafair that first time, didn't they pay her, like, a thousand dollars?"

Joanie nodded heavily and slowly. "Yes, which she spent upgrading her costume. Seven thousand dollars for a custom-crafted mermaid tail! Who does that?

"If you're putting more money into the business than you're taking out, it's *not* a business. Do you know she spent almost half of her first week's paycheck from Starbucks on seafoam green business cards that say AVERY "POSEIDON" PROMISE, PART-TIME MERMAID in blue metallic lettering? When is she going to grow up and find something meaningful to do? A real career?"

"Mom," he said with a small smile, "making mochas and foamy lattes at the neighborhood Starbucks isn't exactly a résumé booster."

"The job had benefits and a chance for advancement. It might have led to something. She could have become a manager.

"Maybe it's my fault," Joanie mused, gnawing on the edge of her thumbnail, as she sometimes did when she was anxious. "I've made it too easy on her. If I didn't let her park the house in the backyard for free . . . Maybe I should tell her that she has to find someplace else to live."

"Oh, yeah. Because that's what you're going to do," he deadpanned. "Throw your baby sister out on the street. Mom, Aunt Avery is happy, maybe the happiest person I know. Why not let her have that? Or at least let her figure it out on her own. You worry too much."

"You're right," Joanie said, and bobbed her head.

Wanting to avoid the mistakes her mother had made with her, Joanie tried to guard against confiding too many of her personal worries to Walt. She wanted him to have a real childhood. But sometimes he was the only one she could talk to, and Walt was so wise for his years. . . .

She quit gnawing on her thumbnail and looked at him squarely.

"Am I too bossy? Tell me the truth."

Walt started to laugh.

"I am *so* not going there," he said, and headed toward the door. "Love you."

"Love you too." She turned back to her laptop. "Don't forget the shortbread!"

A few minutes later, Joanie stood next to the big cutting table in the center of her sewing room, thinking about what she ought to work on next. There was plenty to choose from—two more ball gowns, a man's black frock coat, five Union blue military uniforms, an equal number of Confederate gray, and an order for a bright red and blue Zouave uniform, which could be interesting. She'd never made one of those before.

In the end, she pulled out a bolt of peacock blue

and white plaid fabric and started working on a drop-shoulder shirt for Walt, the first garment in his fur trader ensemble. A pair of trousers and perhaps a linen vest would have to wait until she was finished with her orders, but she could whip up the shirt in a few hours.

She pinned a butcher paper pattern of her own design onto the fabric and began cutting out the pieces, thinking about how happy Walt would be when she surprised him with a new shirt. She also thought about what he'd said about her—that she worried too much.

Maybe. But maybe that was because she had plenty to worry about, especially where her sisters were concerned.

Still no return call from Meg, not even in response to the funny voice mail Joanie had left about the newest round of "potentially perfect partners" that the dating Web site had recommended.

Three of them were named Lyon—apparently this was the new sexy pseudonym for married men prowling singles sites. A fourth, Gil, claimed to be forty-five, but looked seventy and wore a toupee that could have been harvested from the fur of gorillas of sub-Saharan Africa.

Joanie was not interested in Gil, or the Lyons, or anyone. She'd registered on CoupleQuest.com only because Meg had nagged her about it for months, saying she should find someone nice.

Joanie finally gave in just to get Meg to shut up about it.

Before Meg had fallen into this . . . mood . . . she would have loved hearing about Gil and the Lyons or any of Joanie's dating misadventures. And it was worth it just to make her sister laugh. Every time Meg threw back her head, brown corkscrew curls bouncing on her shoulders, to let out that snorting, surprisingly loud guffaw that seemed so at odds with her sister's petite presence, Joanie felt like she'd won a prize.

She swept her long hair, already showing a herringbone of gray threads among the brown, over her shoulder before cutting a notch into the blue plaid, marking the yoke so she'd know where to pin the shirt's upper and lower sections.

Maybe Meg's problem was hormonal. She was only thirty-six, two years younger than Joanie. But some women started the march to menopause earlier and the hormonal shifts could begin years, even decades before. Though, that would be a shame. Asher and Meg had always hoped for another baby and . . .

Wait. Could Meg be pregnant?

The only time Joanie remembered Meg ever acting like this—moody and pissy and withdrawn—was when she'd been expecting Trina. They'd delivered their babies only weeks apart. Sharing the experience of motherhood only strengthened their already intense sisterly bond, but while Joanie had a textbook "easy pregnancy," Meg had suffered from morning sickness and generalized misery up to the third trimester. She'd been *so* cranky and irritable, just like she was now. . . .

Joanie put down her scissors and pressed a hand against her smiling lips.

A baby! Why hadn't they said anything?

Meg had suffered two miscarriages in her twenties. So, perhaps she didn't want to make an announcement until she was further along. Still, the idea that Meg would keep something so important from Joanie felt strange and a little hurtful.

But a baby . . . That would make up for everything ten times over.

What fun it would be to sew little dresses, and sunsuits, and hats again, to knit sweaters and bootees and blankets. Meg had been acting like a real pill since Christmas, meaning she should be through the first trimester.

Joanie was almost tempted to drive over to their house and drop some hints to coax them into making an announcement. But, no. That would be too pushy and, in Meg's current mood . . .

She'd just have to bide her time for a few days. Meg would have to tell her soon, before she started to show. How was Asher feeling about having another baby? Probably over the moon. He loved kids and had always hoped for more. So had Meg. How great that they were finally getting their wish.

Joanie finished cutting out a sleeve and rolled her shoulders, working out the kinks. The phone rang and she ran to pick it up, smiling when she saw the number on the screen.

"Asher! I was just thinking about you guys. So how is everybody—"

"Joanie, I . . . Oh, God."

Asher choked out a strangled sob. Joanie's hand flew instinctively to her chest. Something bad had happened, she could tell. She took a deep breath, steeling herself for the worst.

"Asher? Asher, listen to me," she said sternly. "Calm down. Take a deep breath. Tell me where you are and what happened."

"The hospital." The sound of his breath was ragged. "There was an accident. Meg just . . . They just . . ."

"They just what? Asher? Tell me what's happening."

"The ambulance brought her in. There's blood everywhere. She won't wake up. Oh, Joanie."

He started to cry, to sob. Joanie hadn't heard that sound in seventeen years.

"They took her off somewhere. I don't know what to do. What if she—"

She interrupted him, her voice steady, trying to sound authoritative and calm even though her heart was hammering. "Asher, sit down and wait for me. I'll be there as quick as I can. Do you hear me? Everything is going to be fine, I promise."

Chapter 4

Avery opened her eyes a little after six and discovered she had no desire to close them again. Well, it just went to show you; even two weeks living under that Pavlovian instrument of minion mind control—the alarm clock—was enough to mess with your head.

The sun took its time getting up and so did Avery. A sunbeam crawled slowly up the quilt from her feet, to her knees, to her waist as if it meant to capture her in its net and drag her forcibly from the contented indolence of her bed. Eventually, Avery threw back the covers and climbed down the ladder from her sleeping loft.

Everything in Avery's 240-square-foot house, from the pine paneling stained Newport White, to the bathroom mirror framed with a life ring that had seen service on an actual tugboat, to the blue throw pillows with white seashell appliqués, would not have looked out of place in a Nantucket beach cottage. This in spite of the fact that the backyard of Joanie's bungalow, where Avery parked her tiny house, was more than a mile from Seattle's Elliott Bay and more than one hundred miles from the open ocean.

Avery carried her yogurt and granola to the window seat at the front of her seven-by-nine-foot "great room" and set her bowl down on a nearby stack of books. With her built-in shelves filled to overflowing, she'd taken to piling her books thirty inches high for use as coffee tables.

Avery looked out the window toward Joanie's garden. It had been damp and dreary all month. Nothing was blooming yet, but still, Joanie had been out there every damp, dank day, doggedly turning the old mulch, adding new, cutting back dead wood, raking out dead leaves.

People said Joanie had a green thumb, a natural talent for gardening. But Avery knew there was nothing natural about it. Joanie undertook the cultivation of gardens the same way she did everything else, with passionate intensity. She didn't know another way. Joanie's motto was, "If it's worth doing, it's worth doing right."

Her sister might have been surprised to hear it, but Avery agreed. That was why she invested so much money into getting the most beautiful and authentic-looking mermaid tail available, and spent so much time studying mermaid lore and honing her mermaid persona, because it was the only thing she felt passionate about. So far. She was open to other possibilities. Avery wished Joanie understood that. When she returned her sister's alarm clock yesterday, explaining that she didn't need it because she'd quit her job, Joanie had not been happy.

Avery scraped the curved sides of the bowl with

the edge of her spoon, gleaning enough for one last bite, and reached for a book. She was feeling the need for poetry, a few lines to calm the anxieties that were beginning to bubble up, and plucked a volume of Elizabeth Barrett Browning poems from the stack.

You see we're tired, my heart and I.
We dealt with books, we trusted men,
And in our own blood drenched the pen,
As if such colours could not fly.
We walked too straight for fortune's end,
We loved too true to keep a friend;
At last we're tired, my heart and I.

She slammed the cover closed—*that* wasn't helping—and reached for a slim volume with a worn leather cover and pages as thin as tissue paper. It wasn't a book Avery reached for often, but it had belonged to her foster mother, Lori, whom Avery called Mrs. Captain. Lori had been good to her. Just before they parted, she'd placed a book of the Psalms in Avery's hands.

Avery believed in God in the broad sense; creation was just too beautiful and intricate and interconnected for her to think it was all the result of some fortunate cosmic coincidence, the intergalactic equivalent of an infinite number of monkeys clattering away on typewriters until one of them, simply by virtue of sheer numbers, accidentally typed out the script of *Hamlet*. But she didn't believe in the way Mrs. Captain did. Still, the old woman's parting gift had become a kind of talisman for her, something to hold on to when she was feeling insecure about life.

Avery opened the book. She liked the way the soft, worn leather felt in her hands. She read a few lines—*"Why, my soul, are you downcast? Why so disturbed within me? Put your hope in God, for I will yet praise him."*—and felt better. Why was she so anxious? Things weren't really all that bad. She'd figure out a way to deal with everything and everyone, even Joanie.

Joanie was bossy, but she bossed because she cared. Still, what she said about Avery not even trying to make a go of it at the coffee shop hurt because it wasn't true.

Sure, she'd only filled out the application because she was down to her last hundred dollars and needed work with tips, money she could put in her pocket right away. And no, she hadn't truly gone into it thinking of making a career in coffee, but that didn't mean she wasn't open to the possibilities.

A part of her had honestly hoped it might work out. A company whose logo included a Siren, the twin-tailed mermaid of Norse legend, seemed promising. Initially, Avery had taken it as a good omen. Besides, they were local . . . or had started out that way. Now they were a huge corporate chain, but it seemed unfair to hold their success against them.

She'd never worked with adults and had been afraid that they wouldn't like or understand her. But her coworkers were good people, funny and energetic and young, and her interactions with them made her aware of how much time she spent alone. She liked the customers too.

There was something satisfying about seeing them come through the door, groggy and dour, some dreading the day to come, and being able to lift their spirits and eyelids simply by handing a paper cup of coffee across the counter. The transformation that the first sip wrought to the countenance and carriage of even the most bleary-eyed patrons was a teeny bit magical.

Avery made up a story in her head about a lost, sunken city that had been put under a spell by a Sea Witch. In this story she, Avery, was also a Sea Witch but a more benevolent sort, one who lifted the curse of her evil counterpart and released the citizens from their slumber by the administration of a magical black elixir.

When she approached it that way, with imagination and a bit of mental improvisation, being a barista was way more interesting. But as she had recently been reminded, some people don't appreciate the workings of an inventive mind.

Nearing the end of an eight-hour day spent making the same mochas, lattes, and cappuccinos,

Avery's brain felt numb. When the shift super-visor departed for the grocery store in search of almond milk, Avery decided to liven things up a little.

She erased the day's trivia question from the blackboard: *What character is the most frequently portrayed character in the history of horror movies?* Like the previous day's question, it was far too easy. Only two customers all day had answered The Mummy instead of Dracula. She picked up a thick piece of green chalk and wrote:

Mystery Mochas!!
$3.00—Any Size
Are YOU Willing to Take the Chance?

People were.

She immediately started selling Mystery Mochas to intrigued customers, refusing to tell them what she was going to put into their beverages because, until she started squirting and mixing randomly chosen combinations of flavoring into steaming cups of whatever type of foamed milk struck her fancy at the moment, she didn't know herself. Some of her inventions weren't as successful as others, it was true—key lime and cinnamon just don't combine as well as you might think—but some were delicious.

Customers definitely got into the spirit of the thing. One pointed out the similarities between

Avery's Mystery Mochas and Bertie Bott's Every Flavour Beans from the Harry Potter books. Popping a Bott's Bean into your mouth might release a delectable burst of raspberry or lemon custard or, if you were less fortunate, a gag-inducing flavor of earwax or vomit. That was part of the mystery—and the fun.

Her supervisor hadn't seen it that way. He fired her.

He told her to hand over her apron and go home immediately, even though she still had two and a half hours left on her shift. For Joanie's sake, Avery had made up the story that she'd quit because she was booked for a calendar photo shoot. She didn't want her big sister to be worried *and* mad at her.

Avery washed her bowl and placed it back on the shelf. She walked to the coat rack and got what was left of her tip money from her jacket pocket.

That was Joanie's problem; she worried too much. So did Meg. Though Meg seemed more unhappy than worried, at least for the last few months. But why? Like it said in the Psalm: What reason did they have to feel downcast or troubled? They were no more screwed up than your average, run-of-the-mill failed prodigies from your average, deeply dysfunctional family, were they? Well, not by much.

Avery dumped her money onto the counter and then reached up to the top shelf where she kept the ceramic starfish that served as her bank. The pile of bills inside was smaller than she anticipated. Frowning, she separated the bills from the coins and counted them twice, then stood staring at the meager stack of bills and little towers of quarters and dimes.

Reaching up to her forehead, Avery smoothed away the frown lines with one quick, deliberate swipe of her hand, as if literally wiping all worry and negative thoughts from her mind. She reminded herself that she would soon get a check for her two weeks of work. Of course, she'd only been working twenty-five hours a week and half of her earnings were already earmarked to pay for electricity, propane, two pairs of shoes and a skirt she'd charged because she was feeling flush, and that stack of books she'd moved off the window seat.

Living in a tiny house imposed a necessary frugality on Avery. Anytime she bought something, she had to consider where she would store it. She had no problem with telling herself no when it came to clothes and the like, but self-discipline crumbled when it came to books. She could not walk past her favorite local bookstore, Bayside Books, without going inside. And she couldn't seem to leave without buying a book. Or two. Or five.

People sometimes suggested e-books as a solution to the storage problem. She did have a few on her tablet, but there was just something so delicious about the feel of pages between your fingers, the heft of a real book in your hand, covers that were works of art. She just couldn't resist. There was always the library, but to Avery, buying books was one of life's most pleasurable and affordable luxuries, one you could keep forever and enjoy over and over again. However, until she figured out how to replenish the starfish it was a luxury she'd have to forego. No more walking past Bayside until then. She'd just have to find another route to get to Capitol Hill's commercial area. And something would turn up before she reached the end of her reserves. It always had before.

She held the starfish beneath the lip of the countertop, pushed the money into it, placed it back on the top shelf, and started looking for something to do. Should she go for a run? Hop on the bus and go to the pier? Read something? She had plenty of books, but she wasn't in the mood to sit still. Maybe she should paint? Work on the half-finished undersea landscape mural she was creating on the wall of the great room? Or glue some pieces onto the mosaic table she was making from bits of broken pottery? Or crochet some of the granny squares for the afghan she was making to give Joanie at Christmas? But she was too restless for any of that. Finally, she decided to clean the house.

Avery vacuumed, dusted, swept, mopped, and scrubbed every square inch of the house. But since 240 square feet doesn't encompass that many square inches, the project didn't take that long. After stowing the cleaning supplies, she perched herself once again on the window seat, surveying her sparkling surroundings. Her initial satisfaction faded quickly, leaving in its place an unfamiliar discomfiture.

She sat there for a full two minutes trying to put a name to it. Finally, with a jolt of surprise, it hit her. She was bored.

Bored? She'd never been bored in her life.

Avery lifted her knees and tucked her body fully into the window seat, a needlepoint sea anemone throw pillow cushioning her back, wondering how this was possible.

Maybe it was the job that had done it.

Maybe, becoming accustomed to the camaraderie and conversation of her customers and coworkers, she had lost the ability to set her own agenda, think her own thoughts, and keep her own company.

Or maybe . . . she was just lonely.

Avery wondered what was going on at the coffee shop. Had Doyle decided to dump his girlfriend? Had Cecily passed her statistics exam? And what about the guy with the wavy brown hair that flopped over the rim of his glasses—the one who made the connection between Bertie Bott's beans and her mystery mochas and said that the pineapple-peppermint latte she made for him was awesome? Had he come in for his usual three o'clock coffee fix? Had he asked where she was?

Avery looked up and saw Joanie striding across the lawn toward the tiny house. She sprung up from the window seat, happy for someone to talk to, certain Joanie would forgive her for getting fired after hearing her side of the story.

But when she opened the door and saw her sister's face, her smile disappeared. Something was wrong and somehow, before Joanie said a word, she knew it involved Meg.

Chapter 5

"Oh, come *on!*" Hal Seeger smacked the dashboard and rocked his body forward sharply, as if the sudden shifting of his weight might somehow dislodge the line of stopped cars blocking their path.

When it didn't, he twisted toward Lynn, who was humming along with the radio, a placid expression on her face.

"Can't you do something? I'm going to miss my flight!!"

Lynn Federer had worked with Hal for eight years. Starting as an intern, she worked her way up to production coordinator, but the scope of her responsibilities was basically the same as it had always been, to do whatever needed doing. Hal was the CEO of Stunted Genius Films, but they shared the same job description. Hal liked to say they ran a lean and mean, nimble organization, making it sound like operating on a shoestring budget was something they did by choice. But that was because one of Hal's unofficial titles was Company Cheerleader. Lynn was the Company Realist, the one charged with reminding Hal how things *are,* as opposed to how he saw them.

Lynn turned down the radio.

"Do something? Pookie," she said sweetly, "it's LA. It's the 405. And it's four o'clock. What do you suggest?"

Hal crossed his arms over his chest and slumped down in his seat.

"If I'd stuck with mathematics, not only would I be able to afford a car that doesn't break down every time I need to do something important, like go to the airport, but by now I'd have probably invented a retractable gyrocopter that would emerge from the sunroof at the push of a button and lift your car out of traffic jams. Straight up," he said, flattening his palm and raising it toward the roof of Lynn's car, like a rocket ship on liftoff.

"Yeah, well. Since studying math sent you round the bend once before and since I'm pretty sure you'd have had to study aeronautical engineering to be inventing gyrocopters, I don't see that working out. Would you just calm down?" she said when Hal craned his neck, searching the road ahead for signs of movement.

"If you miss the flight, you'll get the next one. There must be thirty flights a day from LAX to Seattle. Honestly, I don't know why you're going up there anyway."

"Because I've called ten times and she won't talk to me. Keeps hanging up."

"And you think showing up on her doorstep unannounced will change that?"

"Maybe." Hal slumped down again and put on a pair of sunglasses.

"Okay, but what if it doesn't? It's not too late to switch gears, pull together another project. There's that kid from Chicago, Jeremy Lao. Seventeen years old and he's starting his medical residency. I could give his parents a call. Just as a backup!" she said defensively when Hal shot her a look.

"Uh-uh. *This* is the project. I'm not interested in making another movie about another child prodigy lab rat running the maze of academia. I want to make a movie about the aftermath, about what happens when the child prodigy isn't a child anymore and their accomplishments don't seem quite so prodigious."

"I know. But if she won't talk to you . . ."

The traffic started to move, at a crawl.

"What if you interviewed the mother instead?" Lynn asked hopefully. "That'd be a fresh angle, wouldn't it? Trying to understand what motivates a parent to push her kids like that? And not only to push them, but to choose donor sperm from extremely high achievers because she wanted to raise a pianist, painter, and writer—that could be really interesting."

"Could be. Won't be. I already talked to her. I'd have a better chance of getting a straight answer from a six-term member of Congress than from Minerva Promise. A great documentary is about those rare, intimate, honest moments when the subject finally drops the veil, gazes into the camera, and says, 'Take a good, long look. Because this is who I am. And this is who you are too. This is who we all are.' "

He was silent for a moment.

"Minerva wants it too much. She sees the whole thing as a commercial, a chance to rehabilitate her public image. Plus, she might be crazy."

"Okay," Lynn conceded, "but if Joanie won't talk to you . . . And, anyway, how do you know that she's not crazy too? How do you know all three of them aren't?"

"Because I'm not that lucky." Hal lifted his sunglasses up a couple of inches, exposing his brown eyes. "Can you imagine? Three crazy failed genius test tube babies and their crazy, narcissistic mother? Now *that'd* be a movie. We'd win the Palme d'Or at Cannes. Come to think of it, forget Cannes. I'd sell it as a series to HBO, buy a Porsche, move to Malibu, and spend my life surfing and chasing women."

"Sure you would," Lynn deadpanned. "Because you're a thirty-eight-year-old frat boy. Seriously, Hal. What are you going to do if she won't talk to you? Sit on her doorstep until she does?"

"Yes."

"And if she's crazy?"

"She's not." He crossed his arms again and faced the windshield. "I met her once."

"Joanie Promise? You did? You never told me that."

"Well, I didn't meet her so much as I was in the same room with her. We were on the same talk show about child prodigies. They had me, the math whiz, as well as a fifteen-year-old girl who was already working as a programmer at Google, a thirteen-year-old boy who parlayed five hundred dollars of lawn-mowing money into one hundred and fifty thousand in the stock market, and the Promise Girls, Joanie, Meg, and Avery. And Minerva. The girls never went anywhere without her. She did all the talking."

"Hold on . . . You don't mean you were there *that* day, do you? The day of the meltdown?"

Hal bobbed his head, his lips a line. "That's how I know she's not crazy. At least Joanie's not. Can't vouch for the other two. There we all were, dressed up in the clothes we'd been told to wear, smiling the smiles we'd been told to smile, saying and doing the things we'd been told to say and do. Good little lab rats. Except for her," he said, admiration creeping into his voice.

"She made a break for freedom, right there on national television. In front of millions of people. She was the only one brave enough to try. It was a failed attempt and awkward as hell. But who gets it right on the first try? At least she *did* try. I was so jealous of her," he said softly. "And I felt so sorry for her."

Lynn let out a big breath. She was about to say something, but the traffic started to move a little and she turned her attention back to the road. A moment later Hal sat up straight, suddenly alert, and pulled off his sunglasses.

"Hey! Get off here!"

"Where?"

"Here," he said urgently, pointing down the freeway. "Exit 42."

Lynn looked up at a green sign. "Exit 42 is half a mile away."

"But the shoulder is clear all the way. Drive up there and drop me off. La Cienega will be a parking lot, but at least I can walk from there."

"Walk?" Lynn choked out her incredulity. "The airport is probably two or three miles from there."

"No, it's only one point six."

"How do you know?"

"Because I do. I used to be a genius, remember?"

"You'll never make it."

"I won't if you keep sitting here and arguing with me," he said. "Just drive."

Lynn pulled onto the shoulder and started driving. Hal unbuckled his seat belt and turned around to face the back, knees on the passenger seat, butt toward the windshield.

"What are you doing?" Lynn protested.

"Packing." He opened his suitcase, pulled out two pairs of boxers, two pairs of socks, a clean shirt, toothbrush, and razor, and stuffed them into his computer bag. "I'm going to have to run and I won't have time to check a bag."

"What are you going to do for clothes?"

"I'll figure it out when I get there." He zipped his computer bag closed and turned around just as the car reached the exit ramp. "And if she won't talk to me, then I'll figure that out too. Let me out over there."

Lynn pulled over at the corner and Hal climbed out of the car, then leaned down and looked at her through the open door.

"I'll call you when I get there."

The "good luck" she wished him was interrupted by the sound of the car door slamming, but Lynn knew he didn't need it. She watched him run down the street knowing that somehow he would make his flight, and his movie.

When Hal said that he would sit on Joanie's front doorstep until she agreed to talk to him, he wasn't kidding. If Joanie Promise and her sisters weren't willing to cooperate with a documentary about their lives right at this moment, it didn't matter.

Eventually, one way or another, the movie would be made. Because Hal Seeger had decided to make it.

Chapter 6

There was no baby. There never had been. Joanie was relieved.

Meg's face was purple with bruises. Her ribs were broken and her lung had collapsed. Any child Mcg had been carrying could not have survived the crash and that would have been more tragedy than they could bear. Definitely more than Asher could bear. He looked terrible. Worried and lost and so very tired.

For the first twenty-four hours, they'd all stayed round the clock, but then Joanie insisted that the others go home to sleep at night. There was no point in all of them staying. And Trina couldn't continue missing school.

"Aunt Joanie is right," Asher said, his eyes rimmed in red, but dry. "If . . . when your mom wakes up and she finds out that you missed your midterms she'll ground us both." He wrapped his arms around Trina and squeezed. "Really, baby. You've got to go back to school."

It made sense. Meg's most recent scan showed that the inflammation in her brain was beginning to decrease. There was every reason to hope Meg would waken and recover without surgery, but no one could predict exactly when that might happen.

And though Asher objected at first, Joanie eventually made him see that he couldn't afford to neglect his business. He was already behind schedule on his current build. If the work didn't get finished, he wouldn't get paid. Meg was unresponsive but stable. If anything happened, they could call Asher right away. They were good, logical arguments. And now, six days into Joanie's vigil at Meg's bedside, Avery turned around and used them on her.

"Joanie, this is crazy. You've got a business to run. I don't. Mermaid bookings are down right now. Why should you be the one to stay? Go home and get some work done. But first, get some sleep. You could pack clothes for a month into those bags under your eyes."

"Gee. Thanks, Avery."

Avery gave her a squeeze and shoved her out the door.

After giving her phone numbers to every nurse on the floor, Joanie drove home, leaving the window open so she didn't fall asleep behind the wheel. When she pulled into the driveway, a man dressed in jeans and a white shirt rolled up at the sleeves was sitting on her front porch. Though she didn't remember ever seeing his face before, she was sure she knew who it was.

Joanie peered at him through the car window. "Mr. Seeger?"

He nodded. She got out of the car.

"How many times do I have to tell you? My sisters and I have zero interest in participating in your documentary. Zero."

"Actually, you never said that. Mostly you just hung up on me. Then you quit answering my calls."

"And that didn't give you a hint?"

She pushed past him, yawning, relieved and a little surprised to see that the garden had not been completely taken over by weeds in her absence. The flowers were slow to bloom this spring, but the weeds were coming on hard and fast, which was starting to feel like a metaphor for everything. Weird that everything looked so good after nearly a week left untended. Maybe God was giving her a break.

Joanie mounted the porch steps. Hal was still following her. She turned around to face him.

"Go away." She was too tired for the pretense of politeness.

"I just want to talk to you for a few minutes."

"But I *don't* want to talk to you. And even if I did, which I absolutely assure you I don't," she said, fumbling for her keys, "this isn't a good time. I've spent the last six days at the hospital and I really, really need to sleep. So please. Go away." She pulled her keys from her bag.

"Why were you at the hospital?"

The key wasn't going into the lock. Joanie rubbed her eyes, turned it over, and tried again.

"My sister was in a car accident."

"You're kidding. I'm so sorry."

He sounded sincere and slightly embarrassed. Joanie's irritation toward him wavered momentarily only to return full strength when he spoke again.

"Minerva didn't say anything about an accident. Was it Meg or Avery?"

It bugged Joanie that this Hal Seeger, a man who didn't know anything about her family except that he clearly thought they were ripe for exploitation, felt like he had the right to refer to her sisters by their first names. But that didn't bother her half as much as the fact that Minerva had put him up to it, had doubtless given him her phone number in the first place.

Was she surprised? No. Mad, but not surprised. Whenever anything of this nature materialized— Minerva was always involved in some way or other.

Joanie tried the key again, shoving it in the keyhole even harder, as though the lock were a stubborn toddler and she a parent determined to wedge a spoonful of pureed peas between clamped lips.

"Minerva didn't tell you because she doesn't know about it. We don't talk to her."

She gritted her teeth, silently cursing the damned key that wouldn't go into the damned lock so she could go inside the house and close the door in the face of this damned man.

"We don't talk to her henchman either," she added.

"Joanie, I don't—"

She felt his hand on her forearm and yanked away from his grasp, jumping back as if his touch had given her some sort of electrical jolt.

"Are you deaf or something? How many times do I have to tell you—I don't want to talk to you and we don't want to be in your movie. Now go away!"

He didn't go away.

Instead, he took a step closer and took the keys from her hand.

"Try this one."

He returned her key ring, his fingers pinching a large, brass-colored key instead of the silver one Joanie had been using. It slid easily into the lock; she didn't have to force it at all.

"Sorry," she mumbled. "I . . ."

"It's okay," he said. "You're tired. Get some sleep."

He shoved his hands into his pockets and walked away.

Joanie locked the door behind her. She found a

note from Allison Gold stuck on the refrigerator door with a magnet.

White bean chicken chili in pot in the frig. Jell-O salad in the blue bowl. Try some, it's better than it looks. Weeded and watered the garden. Call me when you get a chance.

XOXO,

P.S. Do NOT send me a thank you note. I mean it.

Joanie swiped at her eyes, thinking about her full freezer and weed-free flowerbeds. God hadn't given her a break, but Allison had. Maybe that was the same thing. It was so good to have a girlfriend in the neighborhood. Joanie was close to Meg and Avery, of course, but her relationship with Allison was different. Less risky. She cared about Allison, but she didn't feel responsible for her or to her in the same way she did with her sisters. Allison knew everything about her, things she'd never shared with her sisters, but still liked her and never judged. You couldn't always say this about family.

Joanie took the Jell-O salad into the living room and reclined on the couch, eating right from the bowl. Joanie loved to cook—and to eat—but she stayed away from processed foods, believing that fresh, preferably local ingredients were crucial to a flavorful dish. But today, for some reason, Allison's salad, made with lime Jell-O, miniature marshmallows, canned pineapple, cream cheese, and Cool Whip, absolutely hit the spot.

Too exhausted to move, Joanie left the bowl on the coffee table and covered herself with an afghan. She peeked out the window. Hal Seeger was leaning against the back bumper of her car, staring out at the street and smoking a cigar.

A cigar? Yet another reason to dislike him, not that she needed one. She rolled onto her side and closed her eyes.

Hal Seeger could hang around her house until hell froze over if he felt like it; she wouldn't be in his movie. Neither would her sisters.

Chapter 7

Avery felt awkward sitting by Meg's bed, having a one-sided conversation with her unconscious sister.

But she couldn't just sit there and say nothing, listening to the beep of the monitors and watching that little green line move across the screen, trying to decide if an upward movement was a good thing or a bad thing, wondering if her sister would be the same when she woke up, or if the crack in her skull had caused permanent damage. Wondering if Meg would wake up at all . . .

She couldn't think about that. Instead, she told Meg a story. She didn't know if Meg could hear her, but it couldn't hurt to try, and so Avery told her the story of a selkie.

Selkies are mythical, seal-like creatures. According to Scottish lore, they occasionally leave the depths of the ocean and shed their skins to take on human form, wooing and sometimes even marrying humans. Because selkies are very careful to hide their sealskins, their land-born lovers might never know the truth of their identity.

Avery told her sister about a male selkie who wooed a Highland lass, then returned to the sea. When the child of their union was born to the woman, the selkie came to claim his son and bring him back to the ocean, giving the mother a purse filled with gold in exchange for the child.

Now selkies, as any Scotsman knows, possess the gift of clairvoyance. Before departing, the selkie was given a terrible vision of the future: The woman would live happily and make a good marriage, but her husband, a seal hunter, would fire the shot that ended the lives of the selkie and his son.

It was a classic Scottish folktale, a poignantly beautiful romantic tragedy. Avery made it even more so, embellishing and expanding upon the ancient story, adding a depth of detail that brought the characters vividly to life. She found the poetry in each line, spoke them with passion and theatrical skill. Sometimes her voice rose to a dramatic crescendo, at other times it fell to a suspenseful whisper. Though she spun her yarn for an unresponsive audience of one, Avery gave a brilliant performance. Her voice was hoarse with longing as she described the final scene, painting a picture of the tearful and torn woman who stood on a rocky cliff over a troubled gray sea and threw a wreath of Highland heather into the churning waves.

As Avery finished, someone behind her started to clap.

She turned around and saw a man wearing green scrubs, with a shock of wavy brown hair flopped over the rim of his glasses, standing in the doorway. It was the guy from the coffee shop, the one who liked her peppermint-pineapple latte inven-tion.

He continued clapping and Avery felt her cheeks color.

"That was awesome. I only heard the last part, but you're a great storyteller."

"Oh. Thanks. I'm not sure she can hear me, but you know . . ." Avery shrugged.

"You'd be surprised," he said. "I talk to patients all the time who wake up after days of uncon-sciousness and can repeat back everything that anybody said in their presence. I had one comatose patient whose wife thought he was dying and decided to tell him about all of the affairs she'd had during their marriage. Except he didn't die. First thing he did when he woke up was call his lawyer."

Avery tucked her legs up onto her chair, hugging her knees to her chest so he could wheel a blood pressure cart past her to the side of the bed.

"Really? Guess I'd better watch what I say."

He peeled back the Velcro from a blood pressure cuff and wrapped it around Meg's arm, calling her by her name and explaining exactly what he was doing, just as if she'd been fully conscious. Avery liked that. It was respectful, considerate. When he finished, he recorded the results on a computer tablet.

"So . . . you're a nurse?"

No, Avery. He's a rodeo clown. Of course he's a nurse! You couldn't tell by the scrubs and the blood pressure cart? See? This is why you shouldn't go out among regular people. Because you are hopelessly awkward in social situations.

"Uh-huh. I normally work in pediatrics, but they had to move people around to cover some vacations."

"That must be fun—working with kids."

He nodded. "Most of the time. I've got a patient right now, a six-year-old girl. She was in a car accident, too. They brought her in on the same day as your sister."

"Is she going to be all right?"

"She's going to live. But she'll never walk again. Six years old. Lilly Margolis. Cutest little thing you ever saw. And now . . ." He stopped in mid-sentence. "Sorry. I shouldn't be telling you this."

"I don't mind. Sometimes you just have to let it out, right?"

He shook his head. "No, I mean I really *shouldn't* be telling you this. They're really strict about patient privacy. You can get fired for violating it."

"Don't worry. I won't tell anybody."

She smiled at him. He smiled back.

"I wondered if I'd ever see you again. I go to Starbucks every day, you know. Right after work."

Avery did know. She'd noticed him on the first day and from then on had looked forward to three o'clock, hoping that—she looked at the nametag pinned to his scrubs—Owen Lassiter would come through the door again. Though she hadn't ever worked up the guts to talk to him, three o'clock was pretty much the highlight of her barista day.

But on that last day, when he struck up a conversation with *her* and they were laughing about Bertie Bott's Beans and it all felt so easy, she decided that if he came back the next day, she would try to give him her phone number . . . somehow.

How did that work anyway? Did you just give a guy your number? Or did you wait for him to ask for it? Or was there some sort of secret signal or handshake that you gave a guy so he'd *know* that you wanted him to ask for it?

If she'd met him at some seaport festival, dressed in her mermaid costume, she'd have had no trouble talking to Owen Lassiter. Avery Poseidon in her iridescent blue tail and shell-covered bra top was a true Siren—alluring, playful, and in control.

But if she had met Owen at one of those events, he probably would have been one of *those* guys—the guys who traveled in packs, called one another "bro," dropped the F-bomb every fourth word, referred to women as "females," spent their weekends either drunk or getting drunk, and their Mondays recovering—and she'd have had no interest in him. She might have toyed with him, led him on and then dropped him like a hot rock, but that was all.

And she wouldn't have felt bad about it; that's what mermaids did, used their wiles to entice and ensnare foolish, mortal men. She was playing a part and so were those bros. But Owen Lassiter seemed . . . nice. But with no persona to hide behind, playing herself instead of a part, she didn't know what to say or how to act.

Hopelessly, terminally, socially awkward.

She blamed that partly on the way she'd been

raised. Minerva had taught them at home. She said that regular school would take too much time away from developing their artistic talent. For her sisters, it almost made sense. Almost. Joanie spent hours every day practicing piano and Meg painted constantly. Avery was supposed to grow up and be a writer, so "developing her talent" mostly consisted of trying to turn her into a precocious reader—something she definitely was not, no matter how many flash cards Minerva showed her.

Later, in foster care, she did go to a regular school, but lagged behind the others academically and socially. Finally, she did learn to read and love books, but she never did master the social signals, especially the whole boy-girl thing.

It didn't matter. She couldn't hint for him to ask for her number now anyway, not when her sister was lying unconscious in a hospital bed. She shouldn't even be *thinking* about stuff like that.

Owen took Meg's temperature, tapped in the results, and put the tablet back into his rolling cart. He pushed the cart past her and toward the door.

"So, they fired you?" Avery nodded. "Well, if it makes you feel any better, I've ordered a peppermint-pineapple latte every day since. And I order loud, so the manager will hear."

"Thanks." It did make her feel better.

"He was stupid. There's nothing wrong with

bringing a little creativity to your job, right? Though, you probably *could* have charged a little more. Three bucks was a bargain."

His face split into a wide grin that made him look even cuter, if that were possible.

"Well, it was nice to see you again. And good to meet you, Meg," he said, raising his gaze to Meg's hospital bed. "I hope that you'll be up and around—"

Owen stopped in midsentence. His smile fled. He let go of the cart and crossed the room in long, urgent steps, pushing past Avery to get to Meg's bedside.

"What? What is it?" Avery jumped up from the chair.

Owen held Meg's wrist, checked her pulse again. The crease between his brows grew deeper as he stared at his watch and then at Meg's face. Avery's heart was pounding. She gripped the metal foot-board with both hands and leaned over the end of the bed just in time to see her sister's eyelids flutter, then open.

Only then did she cry.

Chapter 8

As soon as Avery called, Joanie jumped up and drove to the hospital. Her mind raced as she wove in and out of traffic, frightened about what she would find when she got to her sister's bedside.

Meg had been comatose for six days. And a skull fracture . . . who knew what the long-term impact might be? As worried as Joanie had been during the long days of her sister's unconsciousness, she now realized that the consequences they might face in Meg's awakening could be just as frightening, though in a different way.

Asher was already in the room when Joanie arrived. Either Avery had called him first, or he'd broken even more laws racing to the hospital than she had. Joanie stood beside him. Asher squeezed her hand without taking his anxious gaze from Meg's hospital bed. Meg's own eyes were clear and her expression calm. Seeing this, Joanie felt her heartbeat slow a little.

Two doctors conducted an examination. Joanie recognized the woman who was moving a penlight from left to right and asking Meg to follow the light with her eyes as Dr. Handley, the staff neurologist. The other doctor, a man, looked very young. Joanie assumed he was a resident.

"Is she okay?" Joanie whispered to Asher. "How long has she been awake?"

"Don't know," he said hoarsely. "I just got here."

Dr. Handley was asking Meg how many fingers she was holding up and Meg correctly whispered three. The doctor slipped the penlight back into the pocket of her lab coat, held out her hands flat, palms up, and told Meg to push down on them. Meg was able to force the doctor's hands down, but not very far. The young resident scribbled something on a clipboard.

"Good," Dr. Handley said. "Not bad at all. Meg, do you know where you are?"

"Well . . . the hospital," Meg replied, a lopsided grin indicating that she thought this was kind of a dumb question.

"Right. Do you know how you got here?"

Meg shook her head.

"You were in a car accident," Dr. Handley said, her voice casual and reassuring. "You broke three ribs, which is why I imagine you're finding it a little painful to breathe. You fractured your skull, too, and have been unconscious for six days.

"We'll need to keep you here for a while to run some tests. You're not going to be one hundred percent for a few days yet—expect fatigue, moments of forgetfulness, difficulty retrieving words—but it's safe to say you're through the worst of it. I think you're going to be fine."

Asher let out a whoosh, as if he'd been holding his breath for a long time.

"Thank you, Doc." Asher gripped Dr. Handley's hand and then the hand of the young resident, who looked surprised but not displeased to be included in this display of gratitude. "We were so worried," he said, the words catching in his throat.

"You're welcome, Mr. Hayes. But we didn't do all that much. Sometimes," Dr. Handley said, addressing her words as much to the resident as to the family, "the wisest course of action is to monitor the situation and wait for the body to heal itself. The human brain is the most delicate of organs, so surgery should be our option of last resort."

Asher's eyes turned back to Meg. He bobbed his head in agreement, but judging from the rapturous look on his face, Joanie doubted he'd heard even half of what the doctor had to say.

"Yes, we're all so grateful to you," Joanie said, filling in the silence.

"You're welcome," the doctor said once again, then stepped into the corner with the young resident. They huddled together, speaking in low voices as they discussed Meg's case.

Joanie and Avery stood on either side of Asher, the three of them creating a half circle at the foot of Meg's bed because the monitors were in the way. For a moment, they just stood there looking at her, unable to come up with words adequate to the occasion. What do you say at a resurrection?

"I'm so . . . I'm just so happy," Asher said finally. "You have no idea." His voice broke and his eyes filled, but he blinked back his tears. "Trina is going to be mad that she's not here, but I told her you wouldn't want her to miss her exams."

"Oh, no. I wouldn't want that."

Asher grinned wetly. "That's what I told her."

"Trina," Meg repeated slowly, as if trying to memorize the word. "Do I know her?"

Asher's smile froze. Avery looked at Joanie and her eyes went wide, as if she was asking what they should do. But Joanie was shocked too. How could Meg have forgotten her own daughter?

Calm down. Remember what the doctor said— fatigue, forgetfulness, difficulty retrieving words. Maybe it extended to names too. It's possible.

Joanie smiled deliberately, making an effort to keep her voice calm and measured. "Trina is your daughter."

"Oh." Meg was quiet for a moment. "Do I have more than one?"

"No," Asher said, unable to disguise his dismay. "Trina is our only child. We wanted to have more, but we—"

"Oh!" Meg's lips stretched into a smile and her eyes grew brighter, the expression of a student who has just found the solution to a difficult math problem or a crossword puzzle aficionado who has just thought of a seven-letter word for *seismic anomaly*. "So you're Trina's father. And I'm her mother," she said, putting it all together. "And we're . . . married?"

"Yes," Asher said hoarsely, and looked over his shoulder. "Doctor? Can you come over here, please?"

A few minutes later, Dr. Handley stood next to Meg's bed.

"Let's just pick up where we left off," she said

calmly as the family looked on. "Can you tell me your full name?"

Meg pressed her lips together, an expression of intense concentration on her face. After a moment she shook her head.

"Do you know what city we're in?"

Another head shake.

"Do you know who this is?" she asked, pointing to Asher.

"My husband?" Meg said uncertainly.

"We already told her that," Joanie said.

"What about this lady?" the doctor asked, pointing to Joanie.

"No, I'm sorry."

Meg looked very young and vulnerable, like a child who has been caught misbehaving and is disappointed to be such a disappointment.

"It's okay," Joanie said, and laid her hand on top of the light blue hospital blanket, patting Meg's leg. "You're doing fine."

Avery moved closer. "Do you know me?"

Meg's face lit up, the transformation from despair to elation so instantaneous that Joanie was reminded of a child, someone who hasn't yet learned the trick of filtering her emotions or wearing masks.

"Yes!" Meg exclaimed, looking at Avery with dancing eyes. "You, I remember! That beautiful voice! You told me a story, didn't you? About a lovely girl. And a selkie who came from the sea.

"Oh, it was sad," Meg said, her expression of happiness melting into something more poignant and tender, the place where joy is outlined by shadows of suffering. "So terribly, terribly sad. And you told it so beautifully."

Chapter 9

In spite of Dr. Handley's warnings about fatigue, Meg didn't feel tired. That was a good thing because although everyone kept urging her to rest, in the four days since she'd regained consciousness, no one let her sleep, even the curious collection of family members who had been issued to her upon her awakening.

Now that she was out of immediate danger of losing her life, the family no longer took turns spending the night sleeping in the uncomfortable upholstered vinyl recliner, keeping watch in case Meg should suddenly breathe her last (really, what had they supposed they could do to prevent it?). But they continued to stay on a steady rotation of visitors throughout the day, arriving at six in the morning and finally departing at eleven. She was never alone.

Had she actually known any of these people, remembered them or the stories they kept telling of their supposedly shared past experiences, it would have been fine. It would have been sweet.

It really *was* sweet, they were all so incredibly devoted.

But it was hard to know quite what to do with the love and devotion of people who profess to know you intimately but whom you remember not at all, like stumbling into someone in the grocery store whom you do not recognize by name or feature, but who calls to you with familiar affection across the produce aisle and uses your first name to catch you up on the outcome of events that you have not the slightest recollection of. It's all very confusing, but you don't want to embarrass this stranger or yourself, so you smile benignly, nodding as they speak, hoping that they'll soon remember the time and some appointment they're late for.

That morning she'd had another visit from Asher, the very tall man with the brown eyes and ponytail who she'd been told was her husband. He'd come to see her almost every day, not staying too long at any stretch because he owned some sort of construction business and this was the beginning of the building season. But today, for the first time, he was bringing along Trina, who she'd been told was her daughter, her only child.

When they arrived, Asher was smiling, as usual. A grin seemed to be his default expression. Meg had decided just the day before that she liked that about him. But the girl's expression was more somber, a mélange of anxiety, distrust, and studied but unconvincing indifference.

Meg didn't remember the girl any more than she did the rest of her newly minted relatives, but she could see her own features reflected in Trina's face—short nose, full lower lip, brown eyes set a little too far apart and topped with thick brows, hair that couldn't make up its mind to curl or frizz. For the first time, Meg started to think that what everyone was telling her might be right, that all these people really did belong to her, that this was her family and this girl was her daughter. Watching Trina take a seat in a side chair, pulling up her knees and hugging them tight to her chest like a hard-shelled beetle curling into a self-protective ball, Meg thought it must be true even as she struggled to believe. It looked like Trina was struggling, too, and for much the same reasons.

If Asher was aware of the tension in the room—and over the previous couple of days Meg had decided that he was much more tuned in than he appeared at first glance—he gave no outward indication of it. Instead, he made breezy conversation about what was happening with the house he was building, occasionally asking Trina a question, getting one-word responses in return.

After a few minutes of this, he launched into a series of parrot jokes. He knew a lot of them. He started with riddles, asking and answering his own questions.

"What do you call an escaped parrot? A pollygone.

"What do you call a parrot in a raincoat? Pollyunsaturated.

"What do you call memory loss in parrots? Pollynesia."

Meg laughed out loud at that one. Trina smiled a tiny bit even as she let out an anguished groan. "Dad, that's so lame. We've heard all these a million times."

"Hey, it's all new to her," Asher countered, pointing at Meg.

"Pollynesia," Meg said, and laughed again.

After the riddles, Asher launched into proper jokes. Starting with: "This parrot walks into the pharmacy and buys some ChapStick. The pharmacist says, 'Will that be cash or charge?' The parrot says, 'Just put it on my bill.' "

And ending with: "A guy goes to the movies to see the summer blockbuster, but gets there late and sits down in the first seat he can find. He keeps hearing this munching sound next to him and when his eyes adjust to the light, he looks over, sees a parrot sitting next to him, watching the movie and eating popcorn, and says, 'What are you doing at the movies?' And the parrot says, 'Well, I really liked the book.' "

That one made them both groan. Looking at each other with pained expressions, Trina and Meg were momentarily joined in a bond of affection and anguish for this hopelessly goofy man. The moment was brief but nice. Meg thought Trina felt the same way, but she couldn't be certain.

When it was time for Asher to get to work and Trina to school, Avery showed up for the changing of the guard—Joanie, apparently, had worked out all the schedules in advance. He stood next to Meg's bed, his fingers wrapped around the bedrail. Meg thought he looked like an overly friendly retriever who was thinking about jumping his fence, but Asher stayed on his side of the railing, said good-bye and that he'd see her tomorrow. Then, addressing Trina, he said, "Don't you want to kiss your mom?"

Trina pressed her lips to Meg's forehead and muttered a farewell. For a full hour after they'd left, she could feel the imprint of the girl's lips on her brow, a gentle branding. It felt warm.

Family members weren't the only ones who couldn't leave Meg alone. Nurses and orderlies constantly woke her up in the night to take her temperature, pulse, and blood pressure, or to administer medications. During the day it was worse.

She was continually being wheeled off for X-rays, scans, and the like, and spent much of her time lying on some table or inside some tube, trying to obey the technician's instructions to remain perfectly still as the machines looked through walls of bone, blood, and brain in search of her lost memories. Meg kind of enjoyed these times, the only time she had to herself. Having no active role to play in these investigations, apart from the occasional demand to hold her breath, she let her imagination wander.

The metallic *knock-knocking* of the imaging machine became the drumbeat of an undiscovered tribe in an Amazonian jungle. Closing her eyes, she envisioned tropical forests, humid and verdant and humming with life, trees populated by troops of chattering monkeys and brilliant plumed parrots. Mental pictures of parrots opened up a cache of parrot jokes.

Some were the jokes that Asher had told her recently, but there were scores more and she couldn't recall ever hearing them before. Reciting them to herself and making up new ones kept her entertained during part of the thirty minutes she spent flat on her back inside a metal can that took pictures of slices of her brain that were beamed to a darkened room to be examined by sober-faced physicians.

When she exhausted her supply of jokes, she started conjuring images of her absent memories, Casper-like creatures, naughty ghost children playing hide-and-seek with the doctors. She imagined them scampering about, wispy and impish, clamping translucent hands over giggling mouths, shushing one another into silence and invisibility as they insinuated themselves into the shadow of an eye socket or the curve of a frontal lobe.

It seemed like a lot of fuss over nothing, as far as Meg was concerned. If everyone would just calm down and quit paying them so much undeserved attention, she felt sure the memories would emerge in their own good time, tiring of the game once they realized no one was looking for them. That was what naughty children always did, wasn't it?

Though Meg couldn't remember having given birth to Trina, she somehow knew the ways of children.

She knew a lot of things.

For example, she knew that she hated broccoli and was allergic to strawberries before having taken a bite of either. Also, upon watching the opening credits, she found she already knew the entire plot of a multiseason PBS series set in England in the 1920s, a farfetched but nonetheless riveting melodrama with heroes and villains both upstairs and down.

She could describe the plot and characters in detail, but not the circumstances of having watched it. Asher said it was one of her favorites and that they never missed an episode.

Though he always kept his words and demeanor light and encouraging, she knew he was upset that she didn't remember that, or anything else about him. Had the tables been turned, she imagined she'd feel the same. Maybe that was why, even though he was so kind and patient, she still felt uncomfortable around him. He was obviously a very nice and good man, a man who clearly adored his wife, but Meg wasn't sure she wanted to be adored.

She very much liked her younger sister, Avery, the mermaid storyteller. She was easy to be around.

And then there was Joanie. She had no memories of her either, but after spending five minutes with her, Meg could easily have pegged her as the big sister. Either that or the mother. Joanie was very motherly, concerned for the well-being of everyone and willing to take on their problems as her own, but also . . . well, a little bossy. Not in an overbearing way, but she was clearly the leader, the sister who took charge and to whom others came for advice. Even Asher deferred to her.

When Joanie came to visit the day after Meg first woke, she brought a denim tote bag filled with photo albums. She perched on the edge of Meg's bed, her right leg resting at an angle on the bed and the left bracing the floor, and started flipping through the pages of the album, pointing at faces and scenes, demanding answers.

Did Meg remember this person? That place? That day?

No, none of them.

But there was one picture of a pretty woman dressed in a polka dot dress with a wide belt that emphasized her trim waist that got her attention. She stopped turning the pages, stared at the woman with the porcelain smooth skin and slate-colored eyes.

Meg sensed Joanie's eyes boring into her, felt her posture stiffen and her neck lengthen, like a cat stalking an interesting insect with its eyes.

"Do you recognize her?"

"No." She closed the album and pushed it away. "But I don't think I like her."

"Yeah, well . . ." Joanie smiled bitterly. "You're not the only one."

Meg thought about asking why Joanie, or any of them, should harbor such strong feelings toward the woman in the picture—their mother, Minerva —but decided she was happier not knowing.

And that was the strangest thing of all. Though she was in a hospital, with the skin on her face and body mottled with formerly blue bruises turning yellow, and minus her memories, most of the time Meg experienced a kind of happiness that bordered on elation. The most simple, ordinary objects and observations sparked her to wonder and delight.

She took joy in the brilliant colors of the flowers Avery picked for her and placed in a Mason jar on her nightstand and the velvet softness of the petals when she stroked them with her fingertips. She was delighted by the way the sunlight glinted against the jar's clear curved glass and the water inside, creating diamond bright pinpoints of light that skipped about the walls and ceiling if she moved the jar from side to side. She laughed because the skipping lights reminded her of water sprites from one of Avery's stories.

Apart from the occasional discomforting awareness that came from not remembering the people who remembered her, Meg delighted in everything. She noticed everything. She experienced life in a manner that adults usually don't—that is to say, fully. She couldn't recall being unhappy before her awakening, but somehow knew that she had been.

And though this lightness of mind and spirit was entirely new to her, Meg wanted to hold on to it. She wanted to very much.

Chapter 10

In April, Seattle plays hard to get.

Just about the time it's been so gray for so long that people start thinking about sticking a FOR SALE sign in the lawn and moving to Tahoe, the sun breaks through just long enough to give you a taste of what might maybe perhaps be in store for you if you stick around a little longer. On those rare, fleeting, surprisingly sunny days in April, anybody who can possibly find an excuse to go outside does.

With orders backed up three deep in Joanie's sewing room, fertilizing the roses was far from an urgent matter. Even had it been otherwise, she could certainly have borrowed some bonemeal from Allison, or driven down to the hardware store in the Pike/Pine neighborhood to buy it and been back home in fifteen minutes. But when she looked out the window and saw that it was a beautiful day and that—at last—Hal Seeger was nowhere to be seen, she decided to make the trek on foot.

Before she left, she was tempted to call Allison and tell her that her plan had worked and that Hal had finally given up and gone home.

Just the night before, she'd gone over to offer her opinion on carpet samples for Allison's master bedroom redecoration. They sipped glasses of Pinot Noir while they considered the plusses and minuses of pile versus shag and caught up.

"So Meg still can't remember anything?" Allison asked as she topped up her glass. "Doesn't that seem weird to you?"

"Yes, but the doctor says it's early days and that we shouldn't be too worried. There's still some swelling in the brain. I'm just grateful she's alive and getting better."

"What about that movie guy? Hal whoever-he-was. Did he finally shove off?"

"Nope," Joanie said. "Still hanging around like a stray dog looking for a handout."

"Still? It's been days! Joanie, you should call the cops and have him charged with harassment or trespassing or something. Or go to court and get a restraining order. He's got some kind of weird obsession with you. He's obviously crazy. Probably dangerous."

Joanie was tempted to ask Allison why she felt that any man who was obsessed with Joanie must be, by definition, not only crazy but dangerous. Instead she said, "Don't be so dramatic. If I ignore him, he'll go away eventually."

And finally, he had, she thought, putting on her sunglasses and slipping some money into the back pocket of her jeans. Now, if they could get Meg home and better, everything would be fine and back to normal.

Joanie took a circuitous route to the store, skirting the edge of Volunteer Park where people who had called in sick at work that morning had spread out a patchwork of blankets on the brilliant green grass and were lying on top of them with eyes closed, exposing as much pasty, winter-white skin as was possible in public, basking in the sun like harbor seals on a rocky shore. A lot of the people who weren't sunbathing were walking or playing with their dogs.

Recently, Walt had made a joke about her getting a dog to replace him after he went away to college. "After all, you're going to need somebody to talk to when I'm gone." Maybe he wasn't joking after all. Maybe he had a point.

On the return trip, Joanie took a different route through residential streets, enjoying the creative and varied ways that her neighbors turned Capitol Hill's postage-stamp-sized yards into a personal urban oasis. No two were alike. Some were Japanese influenced, with tiny concrete pagodas, bonsai trees, and an occasional koi pond. Others, like Joanie's own, leaned more toward the English style with picketed garden gates, bare branched rosebushes not yet in bloom, and close-cropped patches of lavender that would shoot up suddenly in summer, blossoming into fragrant purple mounds. There were Zen-influenced rock gardens with white, black, and gray pea gravel raked into tranquil patterns and teak benches for seating and contemplation. There were Pacific Northwest gardens with rhododendrons, fir trees and pine trees, and native plants bedded in bark dust. There were typical suburban American gardens, too, with orderly rectangular swatches of bright green grass bordered by straight-edged flower beds planted with crocuses, daffodils, and tulips just beginning to bloom to be followed by pansies, geraniums, and mums as spring gave way to summer and then summer to fall. There were high-, low-, and no-moisture gardens and even a few urban farmscapes with raised beds devoted entirely to the cultivation of vegetables and fruits.

In every third or fourth yard, Joanie saw someone was weeding, trimming, mulching, or mowing. And very nearly to a person, whether she knew them or not, the gardener in question looked at her with a smile of delight and surprise that bordered on shock and called out, "Isn't it a beautiful day?" to which she would respond, "Beautiful!"

And it was.

Until she turned the corner onto her own block and saw Hal Seeger sitting on her porch holding a flat of somewhat wilted yellow flowers on his knees. This was getting ridiculous. Maybe she really ought to take Allison's advice and call the police.

"What are you doing here?" she asked, her voice weary rather than angry.

"You mean aside from employing my charm and devastatingly good looks to win you over and convince you to cooperate with my documentary?"

She nodded, silently giving him points for honesty. Well, about most things.

She wouldn't have described him as devastatingly handsome; his jaw was a little too heavy for her taste and his eyebrows were kind of bushy. But his smile was nice, teeth straight and very white, in spite of the often-present cigar, which gave off an aroma like leaves burning on an autumn evening that she didn't find as unpleasant as she had expected. In fact, it was kind of a nice smell, earthy.

He was a nice-looking man. No denying it. But *devastatingly* handsome? No.

"Yeah, aside from that."

He set the flowers down on the porch and stood up.

"Waiting for you. The old man across the street . . . What's his name? Mr. Teasdale?" Hal lifted his arm over his head and waved at Mr. Teasdale, who was out with his walker, getting the mail, and waved back. "He's a nice guy. Thinks the world of you and Walt."

What? Now he was stalking the neighbors too? Joanie raised her arm over her head and smiled at Mr. Teasdale, pausing to be pleased at seeing him out of the house before turning her attention back to the problem standing in front of her, Hal Seeger. Hal wasn't short on nerve, was he? Well, Mr. Teasdale was one thing, but he'd better steer clear of Allison. If he set one foot on her property she'd probably call in a SWAT team.

"Anyway, you've been pretty busy, going back and forth to the hospital, taking care of your sister, of everybody really. I just thought it might be nice if somebody took care of you a little bit. Or at least did something nice for you. You like flowers, right?" he said, glancing down at the flat filled of scraggly, slightly limp coreopsis.

"True. But I usually prefer them alive."

Hal frowned.

"They're dead?"

"Almost. Not quite." She squatted down, plucked one of the plastic rectangular containers, each with six little plant pots, from the flat and held it up. "See this?" she asked, pointing to a clump of sinuous threads. "They're root bound—too big for these teeny containers. They need to be transplanted into better soil with plenty of space for the roots to spread out and take hold."

"Right," he said, nodding as if he was following her completely even though she could tell he wasn't. "Well, looks like I brought them to the right place."

"Not really. Coreopsis isn't a great choice for Seattle, not unless your garden has a lot of direct sunlight. Mine doesn't. Plus, it's early in the season for them."

"Oh." Hal pushed his fists into his pockets, as if he was trying to break through the seams. "Sorry."

She got to her feet. "It was a nice thought."

"I know you've been going through a hard time," he said, shifting his shoulders in a kind of don't-mention-it gesture. "But Meg's doing better now, right? Except for the memory thing. And the doctor thinks a full recovery is just a matter of time? Till the swelling in her brain goes down?"

Joanie narrowed her eyes.

"Who told you that?" He clamped his mouth shut. "Avery! When I see her I'm going to—" She stomped the ground with her foot. "She should know better. And so should you! What is it about the word *no* that you don't understand, huh? Why won't you leave us alone?"

Hal spread out his palms, as if to show her that he had nothing to hide. "Because I think you've got a fascinating story that deserves to be told. That *needs* to be told. A documentary about what you and your sisters went through, how you survived it then and are dealing with it today, could help a lot of people—"

"Oh, I'm sure it could. You especially." She pushed past him and mounted the steps, shoving the flat of flowers aside with her foot. "Save the speech for somebody else. I've already been to the puppet show before, remember? I know how this works. If you think I'm going to let you exploit my sisters so you can put a bigger pool in your mansion—"

"I make documentaries, Joanie, not block-busters. I do what I do because I love it and I'm good at it. Not because I think it'll make me rich. Just so you know, I live in a two-bedroom condo in West LA. No pool. No yacht. No private jet. I don't even have a 401(k)."

"Me neither," she replied. "What I do have is this house and my family. That's *all* I have. And I've had to work very, very hard to hold it together and find a little peace for all of us. So when I tell you that there is nothing in the world that would

100

make me put that at risk, you should believe me."

She turned her body to face him squarely.

"I'm sure you are good at what you do, Hal. But you're going to have to do it somewhere else, with someone else." She bent down, picked up the flat of flowers, and held them out to him. "Go home. Please."

Hal gave her a long, appraising look, so long that it started to make her feel uncomfortable. Finally, to Joanie's surprise, he simply said, "Okay," and walked away. Just before getting into his car he looked at her and said, "Try not to overdo it, Joanie. I meant what I said before. Somebody really ought to be looking after you."

"Seriously? He said *that?*" Allison asked, handing Joanie a glass of iced tea when she walked over to see her friend a little later that day. "He said, 'Somebody really ought to be looking after you'?"

Joanie nodded, took a sip of tea, closed her eyes, and tilted her face toward the sun. Allison poured a glass for herself and plopped down into the patio chair opposite.

"So now what are you going to do?"

"Do? Worry about Meg getting better and coming home, about Asher and Trina not starving to death before she does, about Avery finding a job, Walt getting through the year carrying three AP courses, and about how I'm going to catch up on my order backlog. You know, just go back to my normal thrilling and deeply fulfilling life."

Joanie opened her eyes. Allison was staring at her.

"You wish he'd stayed, don't you? He was starting to grow on you."

"He was not!" Joanie exclaimed, aghast. "Are you crazy? He was a complete pain. And totally nuts. Practically a stalker. If I never see him again, it'll be too soon. But I just . . . well, I hope I didn't hurt his feelings."

"What did you do with the flowers?"

"What?"

"The flowers he brought you—the coreopsis. What did you do with them?"

Joanie furrowed her brow, wondering why she cared.

"I planted them. What? I couldn't just let them die."

"I thought you said they would anyway."

"Well, they will. Probably. They're meant for a sunnier, warmer climate. I doubt they'll survive a week, let alone take root. But what could I do? They're living things, right?"

Allison shook her head slowly from left to right. The cloud passed, flooding Allison's patio with sunlight once again. As if on cue, both women closed their eyes once again and turned their faces skyward, drinking in the sun's warmth while it was yet to be found.

"You are a mess, Joanie Promise."

"I know," she sighed.

Chapter 11

Hal stopped by the Capitol Hill Public House, original home of Elysian Brewing, a micro-brewery he had come to appreciate during his pointless quest to Seattle.

It was happy hour. Given how much this trip had cost him and how little had come out of it, even happy hour stretched his budget, but a guy had to eat. And drink. Especially today.

He'd spent six months on this project and even more on Joanie Promise. That wasn't counting the times he'd spent unsuccessfully pitching the idea over the years. Finally, after the relative financial success of *Spells the End*, he decided to go ahead on his own, trusting that the money would come on board once the project was rolling. It almost worked. A producer he'd met at Sundance had shown some serious interest. But now . . .

A wasted week. A wasted month. Just a waste.

Who could count the hours he'd spent in the years since he'd talked to Joanie in the green room at the talk show—or tried to talk to her. At the time he was a seventeen-year-old boy, which by definition made him an idiot. His cause wasn't helped by the fact that he'd spent most of those seventeen years eschewing humans for the company of numbers—thinking, dreaming, and doing nothing but math.

He'd been a full-blown, scientific calculator-carrying math nerd and totally fine with it. In fact, he'd been proud of it. He tacked pictures of famous mathematicians on the walls of his bedroom—Albert Einstein, Emmy Noether, John Nash—the way other kids put up posters of their favorite rocks bands. Most people didn't understand how beautiful math can be. And how comforting.

Equations couldn't lie. They never pretended to be something they weren't. And they didn't change—ever. The solution today was the solution tomorrow. Equations were dependable that way. And the most complicated ones could be so elegant, so sublimely beautiful, that unlocking the secret to the solution will make you feel like the King of the Universe, a god among the lesser mortals.

But by the same token, the solution that evades you, that refuses to be unlocked no matter how many hours, days, or months you spend fumbling for the answer, can make you feel like a rejected lover, a failure, a total loser. If you give yourself up to it, math can make you crazy. Literally crazy.

He didn't know that when he was seventeen. Back then, math was still his only love. But when he saw Joanie Promise standing next to a table in the green room, pouring apple juice for her little sister, Avery, a strange, wholly unfamiliar sensation came over him. It was impossible for him to say why, then or now. It may have been something about the way she behaved with her baby sister, so kind and patient, her eyes shining when she looked at her. But maybe not.

She was pretty, but there are plenty of pretty girls in the world. And she was smart, naturally, or she wouldn't have been there. But he doubted she was the smartest person he'd ever met, probably not even the smartest person in that room—yes, he'd been that arrogant back then—but still, he wanted to know her. He wanted to talk to her, this girl his own age, a thing he'd never done before.

He'd strolled over to the table, stood next to her, poured a glass of juice, trying to give himself time to think of something that would impress her.

"Do you know about the Euler line?"

She turned toward him. "Excuse me?"

"The Euler line."

He started to explain, trying to keep his tone deliberately casual, but before long he was talking faster and gesturing excitedly with his hands. He couldn't help it.

"Start with a triangle. Any triangle. Draw the smallest circle that contains that triangle and find the center. Then find the center of mass of the triangle—the point where the triangle, if cut out of a piece of paper, would balance on a pin.

Draw the three altitudes of the triangle and find the point where they all meet. All three of the points you just found will always lie on a single straight line, the Euler line. Always. Isn't that awesome!"

By the time he finished, her eyes were wide, but with something closer to confusion than amazement. She opened her mouth to say something and—

"Joanie! What are you doing over here?"

Minerva pushed her way between them, becoming a human barrier. She plucked the juice cup from Joanie's hand.

"You shouldn't be drinking this stuff. Too much sugar. It'll flood your bloodstream and make you nervous, ruin your timing. Plus, it's fattening. No wonder the waistband on your skirt is so tight. Come sit down with me and your sisters. You should be concentrating on your performance, not flirting with some boy."

He never got a chance to hear what she was going to say to him. But it probably would have been pretty similar to what she'd said today— something brief and dismissive and firm, making her lack of interest crystal clear.

What an idiot. What a waste of time.

Hal sat at the bar and asked the bartender for a plate of wings with Death Sauce and an Elysian Loser Pale Ale. It seemed like an apt order. Then he called Lynn.

"How's it going?" she asked. "Have you worn her down yet?"

"Nope, she's worn me down. I'm flying home tomorrow. Can you pick me up?"

"Sure," she replied slowly, her voice revealing a note of disbelief. "But . . . you're really giving up? Abandoning the project?"

"Afraid so."

The bartender put the wings down in front of him. Hal jutted his chin out a bit, signaling his thanks.

"Wow. That's a first. I can't remember a time when—"

"Yeah. Can we talk about something else?"

"Sorry," Lynn countered. "I'm just surprised, that's all. You're usually so good at getting around people's objections."

"That's because most people don't usually have objections to letting somebody make a movie about them. They might want to be coaxed a little bit or courted, especially after they realize that you don't get paid for being the subject of a documentary, but they cave in the end. It's just a matter of figuring out what they want—attention, approval, fame, self-justification—and then convincing them that the movie will give it to them. But Joanie Promise is not most people."

"Meaning you weren't able to figure out what she wanted?"

"No. She was very clear about that, right from the first."

"So? What does she want?"

"To protect her family and be left alone," Hal said. "That's it. I didn't believe her at first, but today, when I was over at her house, I saw a look in her eyes. . . ." He shrugged, picked up his glass. "Anyway, she's not the kind of lady who plays hard to get. She tells you what she thinks and that is that. And that is all. You can't get around it. Well . . . I couldn't anyway. I shouldn't speak for all mankind."

"I'm sorry, Hal. I know how much you wanted this one."

"Yep."

He picked up one of the wings and tore the meat off the bones with his teeth. His eyes started to water. They weren't kidding about the Death Sauce. It was lethal.

"So, what do we do now?" Lynn asked. "You want me to pull out the research files on Jeremy Lao? Put in a call to his parents?"

With his mouth practically on fire, Hal coughed, blinked a couple of times, and tried to speak. "Uh-uh," he rasped. "I want to take—"

"What? I can't understand what you're saying, Hal. You okay?"

He took several big gulps, trying to put out the flames on his tongue.

"I'm fine," he said, his voice still raspy but audible. "Hot sauce."

He cleared his throat.

"Let's hold off on the Lao kid for a little while. I'm going to go to the beach for a few days, work on my tan, and lick my wounds."

"Okay. But just for a few days, right? We need to pull something together pretty soon. I was going over the books last week . . ."

"How bad are they?"

"Do you really want to know?"

"Probably not. Listen, I'll be back soon. I just need some time to recalibrate my brain. You're right. We should probably start working on the Lao kid project. It'll be easy to find backing for it."

"You think?"

"Absolutely," Hal assured her. "Because it's almost exactly like the last two projects we did—both of which were profitable. We'll contact the kid, pull together a pitch, take a few meetings. People will be falling all over themselves to fund it. You know why? Because it's been done before and there's no real risk involved. Hollywood can't resist that combination. Which is exactly why I couldn't care less about it," he said morosely, and tossed back another swig of Loser ale. "But . . . we've got bills to pay, right?"

"So, I'll pick you up tomorrow. Twelve thirty-five?"

"See you then."

Hal ended the call and waved to the bartender.

"Can I get another Loser down here?" he asked. And then he laughed.

Chapter 12

Meg was asleep when Avery returned from lunch in the hospital cafeteria,

Moving quietly, Avery picked up a pad of drawing paper she'd left on the nightstand and sat down near the window. She'd slipped the pad and a box of watercolor brush tip markers in her bag that morning, thinking it would be a good way to pass the time, and a good distraction from her worries.

She was worried about Meg, of course, and frustrated that the doctors hadn't been able to come up with a means to restore her sister's lost memories. Also, she was increasingly concerned about the dwindling stash of cash in the purple starfish.

Plus, she was confused about this . . . whatever-it-was she had going with Owen Lassiter. Friendship? Relationship? Test-drive? Mission of mercy? It was hard to tell.

Owen dropped by Meg's room every day to say hello. He spent as much time talking to her sister as to her, so it was hard to know which of them he was coming to see, her or Meg. Probably the latter. But Owen was a nice guy. She could tell by the way he talked about his patients, especially Lilly Margolis, the little girl who had been paralyzed in the car accident. He really worried about her.

Avery flipped through the pages on her drawing pad, assessing her work. She had always doodled a bit and thought of herself as artistic, but not really an artist. She loved perusing the crafty mommy blogs. Recently she had begun watching online tutorials on using brush markers to make greeting cards and so, after an orderly wheeled Meg off to one of the labs, Avery broke out her art supplies and began reproducing the flowers, vines, honeybees, and heart motifs she'd learned online.

She was definitely improving. The hydrangea had turned out especially well. Thinking it might be good enough to mount and frame as a Christmas present for Joanie, Avery carefully tore it from the pad. But instead of finding a blank piece of paper underneath the hydrangea, she discovered something finer than anything she could ever dream of drawing.

It was a picture of a mermaid swimming through a magical underwater landscape with banks of pink and orange corals, schools of tiny silver and yellow fish, and a huge olive- and sage-colored sea turtle who looked very old and wise.

It was more a painting than a drawing, with colors blending one into another, creating subtle shading that added depth and life to the scene. Each animal and element was skillfully drawn, but the thing that most caught Avery's attention was the sense of movement within the entire scene.

The silvery yellow fish darted and flashed through the water, the sea turtle lumbered along at his own pace, and the mermaid undulated sensuously among them all, coppery tresses floating above and around her head.

Avery moved her head slowly from side to side, amazed by what she saw. "How did you do this?" she whispered, her voice hushed with awe.

"Q-tips."

Avery jumped.

"Sorry," Meg said. "I didn't mean to scare you."

Avery took in a quick breath. "It's okay. Did you say Q-tips?"

"Uh-huh. I drew the outlines with the markers and then took a wet Q-tip to move the color around the paper and blend everything in. A paintbrush would have been better." She yawned. "But I think it turned out all right."

"More than all right. Meg, this is amazing."

"I hope you don't mind that I borrowed your markers. There was some scheduling mix-up in the lab so they brought me back to the room early. I was thinking about your story, the one you told me yesterday, about the sea turtle and the mermaid. I decided to draw it."

"It's beautiful, Meg."

"I drew it for you."

"Really? Thanks."

Meg yawned again and shifted her body downward in the hospital bed so her head was resting against the pillow.

"Avery, can I ask you something?"

"Sure."

"Am I an artist? I mean, was I before I woke up?"

Avery paused for a moment, not sure how to answer.

She'd been so young when it all happened, she wasn't quite sure where the line lay between what she knew and what she'd been told. To Avery, the facts surrounding Meg's short-lived career as a painter were, like so much of her past, a story she'd been told, one that began the way all truly good stories did.

Once upon a time, a few months before the publication of Minerva's book, Meg's canvases had been photographed, appraised, and insured for thousands of dollars. After the publisher pulled her book from the shelves, the paintings were sold to pay the bills, earning only fractions of those appraised figures. So, were they ever worth as much as the appraiser claimed? Or was that all part of the hype? If Joanie had played the Liebestraum perfectly that day, or if Minerva had been able to restrain herself, might those pictures have attained higher values? What would Meg's paintings have been worth had they been judged simply as the work of a painter, not a prodigy?

It was impossible to say. The pictures of those paintings, prints in a book that was no longer in print, were the only remaining evidence of her sister's talent.

Should she tell Meg that?

"That's right," Avery said at last. "You are an artist, a great painter."

"Yes. Yes, I thought so," Meg said in a drowsy voice, then closed her eyes and fell asleep.

When Owen dropped by for his daily visit, Avery tiptoed into the hallway and showed him Meg's picture.

"This is really good. She painted the whole thing while you were at lunch?"

Avery nodded. "With brush markers and a wet Q-tip," she said.

"Wow. So she's an artist?"

"Was. She packed up her paintbrushes a few years ago."

"Huh. Maybe it's like riding a bicycle," he said, lowering his head to examine the picture more thoroughly. "One of those things you never really forget."

"But for Meg, it seems like forgetting is the thing that helped her remember. It's kind of weird, don't you think? Have you ever seen anything like this before?"

"No, you should probably show this to her

doctor." He changed the subject, clearly not as fascinated by Meg's painting as Avery was. "Hey, listen, I just came up here on my break and—"

"Oh, right!" she said, quickly pulling the drawing back. "I didn't mean to keep you. Sorry."

"You aren't keeping me. I wanted to drop by to see if you had time to go with me and grab a snack. I mean, if you're hungry. You said you already had lunch."

"No, no! That'd be great!" Hearing the sound of her own transparent enthusiasm, she felt her cheeks turn pink. "I mean . . . sounds good. Let me just peek in to make sure Meg is still asleep and grab my bag."

"You won't need it. My treat."

"Yeah?"

He grinned and pushed a hank of hair from his eyes.

"Well . . . sort of."

The pediatric department was having an un-birthday party, to honor all of the young patients who weren't having birthdays that day, which turned out to be all of them. Volunteers from a children's theater company attended, dressed as Alice, the Mad Hatter, White Rabbit, and other characters from the Wonderland books.

Keeping in character the whole time, the actors circulated through the playroom among the pint-sized patients, some in wheelchairs or on crutches, others wearing paper masks to ward off germs, and offered them slices of un-birthday cake and plastic teacups filled with lemonade. Most of the kids were laughing and interacting with the performers, but one little girl in a wheelchair, with sienna-colored skin and dark brown eyes, sat off by herself in a far corner of the room. When the White Rabbit hopped over and pulled an oversized watch from the pocket of his red-checkered waistcoat, then asked in a lisping voice if she knew the time because he was sure his watch was running slow, or fast, or perhaps not at all, she turned her face to the wall and wouldn't speak to him.

The rabbit pulled something else from another pocket, a miniature plush rabbit, about six inches long, and left it in her lap, wishing her a happy un-birthday before hopping away. The toy fell onto the floor. Avery walked to the corner to retrieve it, crouching down beside the wheelchair.

"This is a nice bunny," she said. "He's got really soft fur. Do you want to hold on to him?"

The little girl said nothing, her face still toward the wall.

"I can give him to one of the other kids, I guess," Avery said with a shrug. "But it might hurt his feelings. He might think you don't like him."

Without moving her head, the child moved her arm to her lap and opened her hand. Avery laid the rabbit in her palm. Small fingers closed around one of the toy's plush arms and then pulled the bunny closer to her body. She turned her head, enormous brown eyes taking in Avery's hazel ones, looking at her unsmilingly for a moment before turning away once again.

Avery crossed the room to stand next to Owen once again.

"That's Lilly?" she whispered. "The one you told me about?"

He nodded. "She barely says a word to anybody, not even the other kids."

He took in a long breath and let it out slowly. "This isn't always an easy job. Sometimes you see stuff, really hard stuff, and it makes you wonder about . . . well, a lot of things. How life can be so unfair to little kids who never did anything to hurt anybody? After a while, though, you learn to shake it off and box it up, do what you need to do. But this one . . . There's just something about her. Even when I'm at home, I can't keep myself from thinking about her."

Avery looked toward Lilly with her useless legs and sweet face, and two huge brown eyes that seemed to hold all the sadness in the entire sad world.

"Yeah," she said. "I get that."

Chapter 13

Asher hated meetings. Yet, he was the one who had called this meeting with Dr. Handley and Dr. Simon Patel, the head of the hospital's psychology department. When they were seated in the hospital's family conference room, Dr. Patel started the conversation.

"Mr. Hayes, I've spoken with your wife. I didn't detect any signs or symptoms of depression. Can you tell me what leads you to think otherwise?"

"I didn't say she was depressed," Asher clarified. "I just thought she might be. I thought it might help explain why she can't remember anything, and the way she was behaving before the accident."

"And how was that?"

"Moody, crabby. She and Trina were always getting into it. Though Trina is really good at pushing Meg's buttons. But it wasn't just Trina. Some days she'd barely speak to me. It'd been that way for three or four months. I had started to think that maybe . . ."

"Maybe?" Dr. Patel prompted.

"I thought she might be pregnant. I hoped she was." He shrugged. "We wanted more kids, but had a couple of miscarriages. It was tough on her, on both of us. After a few years, we stopped trying. But she's still young enough and, you know . . . Accidents happen. I thought maybe she wouldn't want to tell me about it until she was pretty far along. Just in case something happened. But, obviously, I was wrong. They ran a preg-nancy test in the ER. So now I'm wondering if her moodiness could somehow be related to the memory loss. Maybe there's a psychological explanation."

"It's the swelling," Dr. Handley interjected. "That's the explanation. As I told you and your sisters-in-law, swelling to the brain can cause—"

"Memory loss. I know what you said. You also said that it's very unusual for someone to completely lose her memory, like Meg has. And you said that it would be temporary."

"Mr. Hayes, it's only been a few days."

"Seven," he said, his voice even but firm. "Have you ever had a patient who totally lost their memory and still hadn't gotten it back after seven days?"

Dr. Patel leaned closer and spoke in a friendly tone as if addressing someone he'd known for some time.

"Mr. Hayes, I can certainly see why you'd be looking for a psychological cause to explain your wife's condition. But I didn't see any sign of that. Of course, it's possible that she was trying to put up a good front for me, but it's pretty hard for a patient to fool me. From a psychological standpoint, she appears to be fine. Actually, she seems quite happy."

"I know. And I think that maybe losing her memory is the reason why."

Dr. Patel nodded slowly. "Ah. You think your wife has unconsciously suppressed memories of her past because they're too painful?"

"That can happen, can't it?"

"Well . . . in cases of severe psychological trauma, memories can be blocked. It's a sort of survival method, a means of protecting the mind from something too painful to endure. We sometimes see it in children who survive physical or sexual abuse, and occasionally in adults, as a response to extreme emotional stress. It's not impossible, but highly unlikely that—"

Dr. Handley interrupted. "I still say that it's the swelling. The most recent MRI still shows some brain inflammation, particularly in the left temporal lobe, one of the areas that affects memory. We should be focusing on neurological causes."

Dr. Patel looked at Asher, his voice gentle in contrast to Dr. Handley's strident tone. "I'd be happy to conduct a more thorough interview with your wife, Mr. Hayes. But I tend to agree with Dr. Handley. Unless Mrs. Hayes has undergone some traumatic event that you haven't shared with us, it doesn't seem to me as if—"

Asher cut him off. "What if I told you that her

maiden name was Promise, Meghan Elizabeth Promise? And that her sisters are Joanie and Avery Promise, would that convince you?"

"Your wife is one of the Promise sisters?" Dr. Patel looked taken aback. "Really," he said, sounding almost impressed.

Dr. Handley frowned. "I don't understand. What's a Promise sister?"

"You never read the book? *The Promise Girls*? It came out about twenty years ago."

"Twenty years ago I was in medical school," Dr. Handley said defensively. "I wasn't reading anything except organic chemistry textbooks."

"It caused quite a sensation. Especially after the author, the girls' mother, had a meltdown and struck one of the daughters on national television," Dr. Patel informed his colleague. "They replayed the tape over and over again on all the daytime talk shows. I was doing my residency at the time and I remember discussing it with the other residents. We diagnosed the mother as having narcissistic personality disorder. But," he added quickly, "that was just medical resident hubris based upon one sensational video of a person at her very worst. It wasn't a complete picture."

"No," Asher said, "that sounds about right. Meg told me all kinds of stories about Minerva when we first met. After a while, she stopped talking about it. She said that thinking about it just made her feel bad.

"The state took all three girls away from Minerva. Meg was separated from her sisters because they couldn't find a foster family that would take all of them. Joanie was in foster care for less than a year, but Meg spent almost three years in the system."

"And then what happened?"

"She came to Seattle and moved in with Joanie. That's how we met. I was doing some remodeling for Joanie on weekends, helping fix up her house. When Meg moved in, I fell for her pretty fast. We got married six weeks after we first met."

"Six weeks? That was fast."

Asher smiled. "When you know, you know. And the first time I laid eyes on Meg, I *knew*. So why wait?"

"How did her sister feel about that?"

"Joanie hosted the wedding, baked a big cake and everything. Meg was always close to Joanie, more like a mother than a sister, and Joanie was happy that Meg was happy. She'd been through an awful lot up to then.

"The lady Meg was living with, the foster mom, was really a witch. She'd tell Meg that she could see Joanie, but then, if Meg did anything wrong— say even if she didn't put away the dishes in the dishwasher the right way—she canceled the visit." Asher's fingers curled into a fist and he clenched his jaw. "If I ever run into her."

Dr. Patel said, "Sounds like you felt pretty

protective of Meg. Do you still feel that way? Like it's your job to protect her?"

Asher drew his brows together into a small frown. "I'm her husband," he said, as if that should answer the question. "I just want her to get well and be happy."

"And she wasn't happy before," Dr. Patel said, a confirmation rather than a question. "Not until she woke up after the accident."

Asher pushed his body slightly back from the table, addressing both doctors.

"Listen, I just want her out of here. She needs to go home, to be in familiar surroundings and spend time with the family. Once she's home, she'll start remembering again. Don't you think?"

"It couldn't hurt," Dr. Handley said. "Barring any complications, she should be ready to go by Monday." She looked toward her colleague. "Unless you can think of any reason we should keep her longer?"

Dr. Patel shook his head. "No, I agree with Mr. Hayes. Going home may be the best thing for her. However, Mr. Hayes . . . Asher . . . I know how anxious you are for life to return to normal. But keep in mind that Meg may feel differently."

Asher's frown became a scowl. "You don't think she'll want to come home?"

Dr. Patel took off his glasses and laid them on the table.

"I'm saying, go slowly. Give her space and time.

The Meg who woke up in the hospital is not the same woman you knew before the accident. It might be good for you to think of her that way, as someone you are just beginning to know. Last time when you wooed and won your wife, you were in a hurry, impatient for life to begin. This time, go slowly. Reveal yourselves to each other bit by bit, as if you were meeting each other for the first time. Because, for Meg, it will be."

Chapter 14

As the car approached Asher and Meg's house, Joanie spotted Trina kneeling next to a planter, angrily tugging at tufts of grass and dandelions from the beds and then throwing them into a plastic bin.

"Looks like Trina is in a bad mood," Joanie said to Walt.

"Trina's always in a bad mood."

It was hard to disagree with him. Whatever happened to that sweet, sunny, adoring little girl who used to cling to her mother so closely that Meg had nicknamed her "Velcro-Child"?

Naturally, Trina was upset after the accident, but the incessant moodiness had been going on for a couple of years now. Meg was always talking about it, trying to figure out what had happened.

"I'm serious," Meg told Joanie a few months

back. "One day, I was scrambling eggs for breakfast and a completely different person climbed down the loft ladder than the one who'd climbed up the night before. Like some kind of alien entered her body. If Trina slept in a real bed instead of on a mattress on the floor, I'd have looked under it to check for the pod."

Still. Poor Trina. This had to be so hard for her.

"Just be nice, okay? Maybe you could give her a hand with the weeding?"

The look on Walt's face told Joanie he'd rather eat the weeds than spend time helping his cranky cousin pull them, but he didn't say so.

"How about mowing the lawn?" Joanie suggested.

"Fine. At least I won't be able to hear her talk."

"Hey!" Joanie called to her niece as they got out of the car. "Looks like you're getting everything in shape for your mom's homecoming."

Trina tugged at a dandelion. "Dad wants everything perfect for the return of The Amnesiac. You'd think the president was coming to visit or something."

"We brought dinner—lasagna, a Caesar salad, and an apple cake," Joanie said cheerily, ignoring Trina's grumbling. "Walt, can you put all that in the refrigerator? And then why don't you get out the lawn mower?"

Walt went inside. Joanie knelt down next to her niece and reached for the nearest weed. "It'll be easier if you get your hand down close to the ground before you pull. And if you shake the dirt off the roots before you throw them away, it'll leave more soil in the flowerbeds."

Joanie demonstrated the technique. When she looked up again, she saw two tears rolling out from beneath Trina's sunglasses.

"Oh, sweetie," she said, and quickly brushed the dirt from her hands, ready to hug her niece. "Don't cry. Everything's going to be okay."

"No, it's not," Trina sniffled. "Justin Able asked Taylor MacLean to the spring formal. I just read it on Facebook."

Trina removed her sunglasses and rubbed at her eyes with a dirty hand. Joanie silently thanked God for giving her a son. Girls could be so self-absorbed. But maybe it was better for Trina to be crying over a boy than her mother's illness.

"I don't care," Trina mumbled, which Joanie knew was what she said when she did care. "I don't have money to buy a dress anyway."

"I could make you a dress. When's the dance?"

Trina's big brown eyes filled with a new flood of tears. "Sometimes I wish you were my mom," she said in a choked voice.

"Oh, Trina. Stop. You know you don't mean that."

"I can't talk to her the way I can to you. Now she doesn't even know me," Trina said bitterly. "Or Dad. How can a mom forget her whole family?" Trina collapsed onto Joanie's shoulder, sobbing silently, her lithe, little body quaking.

"It's the accident, honey. She can't help not being able to remember."

"How do you know?" Trina sniffled. "Maybe she wants to forget us. She and Dad weren't getting along before. Every time he'd ask her something she'd just cut him off, like she didn't want to talk to him. And the two of us are always arguing about something. I'm usually the one that starts it," she admitted. "I don't know why. If I had me for a daughter, maybe I wouldn't want to remember me either."

Joanie pushed Trina to arm's length so she could look her niece in the eye.

"Listen to me," she said. "Your mom and dad are crazy about you. Did you know that, after you were born, your mom sold her bicycle so she'd have enough money to buy a camera to take pictures of you? You were the most photographed baby in Seattle. She'd stop people on the street to show them pictures of you."

Trina blinked. "Really?"

"Really. It was actually kind of obnoxious," Joanie said with a smile. "Look, maybe you're not getting along with your mom right now, but if you check with your girlfriends, I bet a lot of them would say the same thing."

"I don't have friends. Everybody thinks I'm some kind of a freak, a loser."

"Yeah, well, I bet most of the girls at school feel the same way about themselves. Take a poll sometime. Look, Treenie-Bean. Of course it hurts that your mom doesn't remember you, but it isn't because she doesn't want to. Really. What if you looked at this as a chance to get to know her all over again? And to let her get to know you? You know, a fresh start."

Trina bit her lower lip, looking doubtful, but finally said, "You think?"

"It couldn't hurt to try."

"I guess . . ." Trina shrugged.

Joanie smiled. "Good girl. Now, let's get back to the formal. How much time do I have to make you a dress?"

"End of May. But it doesn't matter, Aunt Joanie. Nobody wants to go to the dance with Freakazoid Science Geek Girl. It was winning the freshman science fair that did it. I should have just made a stupid volcano model like everyone else instead of a computer model of the 'Location and Characteristics of Brown Dwarf Stars.' Social suicide," she mumbled, shaking her head.

"Walt could take you," Joanie said. "I don't think he has a date yet. At least he hasn't said anything about it. I doubt he even knows there is a spring formal."

"Go with my cousin?" Trina's eyes grew wide with horror. "No way! That's like announcing to the entire world that I am un-dateable!"

Walt came around the corner of the house, pushing an aged lawn mower. "Honey, do you have a date to the spring formal yet? Would you like to take Trina?"

Trina groaned and buried her face in her hands. Walt's eyebrows lifted into an anguished arc. Joanie gave him a pleading look and silently mouthed the words, "I will make you a pie. TWO pies," exaggerating the movement of her lips.

There was almost nothing Walt wouldn't do for a homemade marionberry pie, which was why she made them only on special occasions, reserving them for times when Walt had done something really good or if she was asking him for a huge favor. Taking Trina to the formal definitely qualified as the latter.

"Uh . . . sure. I guess."

Trina lowered her hand from her face.

"I wouldn't have to buy her a corsage or anything, would I?"

"No," Trina said quickly, answering for herself. "That would just be creepy. And if we go out to dinner, we can split the bill."

"Okay. Sure. Why not?" Walt's face brightened. "Hey, can I wear my general uniform?"

Trina clutched her aunt's arm. Joanie felt fingernails digging into her flesh.

"You have to wear a suit. Or a tux. Whatever the other boys will be wearing."

"Tux," Trina said.

"I don't own a tux," Walt countered.

"We'll rent one. So, that's all settled?" Joanie asked, looking from her son to her niece and getting two somewhat hesitant nods in response. "Good."

She peeled Trina's fingers from her arm and got to her feet.

"Where's your dad?"

"Out back, trying to finish up Mom's house."

"*Your* mom's house?"

"Yeah," Trina replied, a touch of snark creeping back into her voice. "Since Mom doesn't remember either of us and we don't have a guest room, Dad is giving her a tiny house in the backyard, just like Aunt Avery's."

Asher was hammering shingles onto the roof of a tiny house that did look very similar to Avery's. He had his earbuds in and was humming with the music. Joanie wondered it if was The Ramones.

When she met Asher for the first time, they were standing in line for mango empanadas at a summer street fair. "Rockaway Beach" was playing over the loudspeaker. The line was long. They started talking.

Joanie had moved to Seattle just a few months before, about the same time Asher dropped out of the University of Washington, where he'd been studying English. He told her he'd grown up outside of Spokane, in a family of modest means.

Faced with taking out another round of student loans and realizing that, even should he graduate, the market for sixty-page papers on Beat poets was fairly limited, he decided to leave school, stay in Seattle, and get a construction job.

"Don't feel sorry for me," he said when Joanie expressed her regret about his choice. "Carpentry is great, very satisfying. I get to create something tangible that people can use and at night I get to go home and read anything I want. I only majored in English because I love books. But reading them isn't the same as studying them. I'd rather put my eye out with a drill bit than read one more page of Milton. What a blowhard!" he said, then laughed and laughed.

That was what attracted her to him initially, that ability to accept himself as he was and life on his own terms, to find the best in every situation.

Having grown up surrounded by a particular brand of academics and artists, Joanie knew that a certain segment of the world delighted in mocking those who make lemonade from lemons. For those ivory tower types, the mark of intelligence lies in recognizing and expounding upon the extent of life's misery with extra credit for glorifying humanity's hopelessness and inability to alter its pathetic condition.

Joanie didn't buy it. She'd already figured out that choosing happiness was harder than it looked, no matter who you are. It was a trick she was still trying to learn. Asher showed her how.

After so many years devoting herself entirely to her music, Joanie went a little crazy after she moved to Seattle, going through several short-lived and mostly unhealthy romantic relationships with a series of boyfriends—Steve, Vincent, Mark, and two different Jeffs. But Asher was her friend.

When she told him about the house she'd bought, a fixer-upper that some said ought to be a tear-down, the only house she could afford in Capitol Hill, Asher offered to help. When she said thanks, but she couldn't afford him, Asher said he'd work for food. But he warned her that he liked to eat. A lot.

Every Saturday, Asher showed up with his tools and spent the day working on the house while Joanie cooked. Around four, he'd clean up his mess and sit down to eat. If Joanie had a date that night, she'd sit and watch him, saving her appetite for later. If she was between boyfriends, they'd eat together.

They went on like that for close to a year. And then Meg moved to Seattle. Joanie had never seen that kind of chemistry between two people. You could have lit up a city with the sparks that flew.

Two weeks later, Asher and Meg were engaged. They wanted to get married immediately, but Joanie talked them into waiting a month so she could pull together a proper wedding for them.

They didn't have many friends, so Joanie walked door-to-door, introducing herself to the neighbors and inviting them to the wedding. They all showed up—Mr. and Mrs. Teasdale, Allison and Will Gold, Bruce Lydell and Thomas Gray, Jeanne and Sam McCullough—everybody. They brought gifts, too, even though Joanie had told them not to.

It was a lovely little wedding, if she did say so herself.

When Asher and Meg returned from their honeymoon they moved into the bungalow with Joanie. That's when she told them she was pregnant and planned to raise the baby on her own. She didn't say anything before the wedding because she didn't want her news to overshadow their big day. Soon, Meg was pregnant too. The babies were born just ten weeks apart.

For three years, they lived together as one big family. Joanie loved having them there and was happy that Walt had a man in his life. It was one of the best times of her life. But the house was definitely crowded and she knew they couldn't live like that indefinitely. When Meg and Asher found a 1700-square-foot rambler in Wedgewood at a price they could afford, they snapped it up. It wasn't a pretty house, but there was plenty of room and the lot was fairly big for the area. Asher figured he could fix it up. As it turned out, he didn't have time.

When the house caught fire it went up so fast that they were lucky to get out with their lives. They lost everything. That's when Joanie really saw what Asher was made of, even more than she had before.

Meg, Asher, and Trina, now five years old, moved back into the bungalow. They didn't have enough insurance to replace the house or buy a new one. For a week, they seemed a little shell-shocked, uncertain about what to do. One day Joanie was roused before dawn by the sound of someone rattling around in the kitchen. She went downstairs and found Asher standing at the stove, making bacon and pancakes and whistling.

"I figured it out," he said when he spotted her in the doorway. "We're going to build smaller. But better. Much better!"

And that was it, the disaster took Asher's business in an entirely new direction, placed him squarely in the forefront of the Not So Big house movement, and helped him find his true calling in life.

Asher kept his business small, never taking on more work than he could supervise personally, with Meg keeping the books and managing the office. Most of his work was custom, houses of 800 square feet or less. But he also built tiny houses on trailer platforms like the one he'd constructed for Avery. He did these in his spare time and on spec, beginning a new one as soon as he found a buyer for his current project. Asher and Meg earned enough to live modestly, but not more. They seemed to be fine with that.

Asher didn't talk about his childhood back in Spokane much, but when he did he spoke of a loving and gentle mother he adored and an angry father who used religion as a yardstick to show his son how far he fell short. Asher's faith in organized religion had been shaken by his experiences, but he still kept a plaque on the wall of his workshop with a Bible verse from 1 Thessalonians, "Aspire to live quietly, and to mind your own affairs, and to work with your hands."

Asher lived by those words. He was a good and decent man. Joanie hadn't met many of those.

Asher reached into his carpenter's apron for the final nail, hammered it in, and pulled out his earbuds. "What do you think?" he asked. "Tomorrow, I'll hook up the water pump, bring in some furniture, and we'll be all set."

"It's nice. But . . . are you really planning on having Meg live out here? Why?"

Asher slid backward to the eave of the tiny house and climbed down the ladder. "The psychologist at the hospital said I ought to go slow, give Meg a chance to get to know me again. Then I was thinking, she might feel nervous about sharing a room right off. Don't get me wrong, I'd much rather we were in the same bed, but I don't want to rush her."

Wiping the sweat from his brow with the back of his hand, he said, "You know, maybe this will all turn out for the best. We hadn't been getting along too well. But I bet you knew that already."

Joanie didn't say anything. Asher snorted out a short laugh.

"That obvious, eh? Well, fair enough. Anyway, a part of me thinks that this really is a chance for us to start over, get to the bottom of whatever was bothering her and get our marriage back on track. Be happy again, the way we were before."

It was hot up on the roof and Asher was thirsty, so they went in the house to get something to drink. Joanie was surprised by what she saw inside.

A pair of muddy work boots was lying in the entryway. Unfolded laundry lay mounded on the sofa. Though there were two beautiful built-in bookcases flanking both sides of the ceramic-faced fireplace, half a dozen books lay scattered haphazardly on the floor. Plates, cups, and glasses, some holding the remains of partially consumed food or beverages, were sitting on the coffee and side tables.

Joanie closed the front door, stirring the air. A dust bunny emerged from under a chair and tumbled across the wood floor like sagebrush rolling down a windswept plain. The house wasn't filthy, just untidy. In a larger space it wouldn't have given the impression of things being such a mess, but in such a small room . . . Joanie picked up two plates and a coffee cup and carried them to the kitchen.

"You don't have to do that," Asher said, sounding embarrassed. He grabbed two glasses from a side table and followed her. "We've been at the hospital so much . . . I was going to get to it tomorrow."

"Don't worry about it." Joanie turned on the faucet to rinse dried ketchup from one of the plates. "That's why I came over, to see if I could help."

Joanie got a clean glass from the cupboard and opened the refrigerator, searching for a pitcher of filtered water. Inside she found a partly empty six-pack of beer.

Asher didn't drink anymore. He'd never been much of a drinker but, after his mother died, right before Meg moved to Seattle, he'd shown up on Joanie's doorstep with a case of beer and a buzz on. She sat up with him into the wee hours, listening to him talk and watching him drink, finally putting him to bed in the guest room. The next morning, humiliated by his behavior, unable to remember much of what happened, and wincing from the mother of all hangovers, Asher vowed to stop drinking. Apart from the occasional brew on the Fourth of July or at a football game, he kept that vow.

Joanie pulled the six-pack from the refrigerator and looked at him.

"I had some beer," he said, shrugging but clearly embarrassed. "It's not that I can't drink, you know. It's just that I don't."

"I know. I'm just worried about you. You don't normally have two beers in a year. Now you're having four in a week?"

"Ten," he admitted. "That's my second six-pack. It's hard to sleep without Meg next to me. A couple of beers before bed helps. You're right. Throw it out."

Joanie poured the beer down the drain, set the empty bottles on the counter, and handed Asher a glass of water. He gulped it down.

"I brought dinner."

Asher wiped water from his lips. "Lasagna?"

Joanie smiled. Everybody loved her lasagna. She was famous for it. "I thought we could all eat together. Why don't you go and shower while I set the table?"

Joanie shooed Asher away to the bathroom, then turned on the oven. Walt was only about half-finished with the lawn. She had plenty of time to tidy the house and prepare the meal. She made a loop around the house, gathering up the abandoned dishes. The dining room table was covered with bills, invoices, ledgers, and unopened mail. Asher must have tried to tackle the paperwork himself. He hadn't gotten very far.

Twenty minutes later, Asher had yet to reappear. Joanie went looking for him and found him lying facedown on the bed, snoring softly. She decided to let him sleep a little longer.

A delicious smell of meat and melting mozzarella was coming from the oven. Joanie couldn't set the table while it was still covered with papers. She pulled up a chair and got to work, separating papers into more or less logical groupings before placing them into labeled file folders so Asher would be able to find what he was looking for.

She went through the mail, throwing out the junk. Near the bottom of the stack she found an envelope from the hospital, probably a bill. Judging from its thickness, it was a big one. She held it in her hands, trying to make up her mind.

Under normal circumstances, she'd never dream of opening an envelope that wasn't addressed to her, not even junk mail. But these were not normal circumstances. Meg couldn't remember who her husband was, let alone advise him. Asher was exhausted and under so much stress, trying to juggle all of his work and Meg's too. She wasn't sure how much more he could take.

Joanie turned toward the kitchen. The sight of those empty beer bottles sitting on the counter made up her mind for her. She slipped her fingertip beneath the flap, tore the top, and took out the hospital bill, flipping through multiple pages until she found what she was looking for, the total.

She gasped, refocused her eyes, recalculated the part owed after insurance, hoping that she'd miscounted the zeros. She hadn't.

"Thirty-three thousand dollars," she breathed, so shocked that her hushed tone might have been mistaken for reverence.

The bill slipped from her fingers, sheets of white paper covered with numbers dropped and scattered over the floor like a fall of dried leaves.

Joanie stood up, tiptoed down the hall, and opened the bedroom door a crack. Asher was lying on his side now with his knees to his chest and his fisted hands tucked under his chin, curled up like a comma. She closed the door and stood with her back to it, eyes cast toward the ceiling, wracking her brain for a way to raise thirty-three thousand dollars quickly. Nothing even remotely feasible came to mind.

At first.

She'd have to get the others to sign off on it—her sisters as well as Asher. After all, it involved him too. It might take some persuading, but she knew that, in the end, she could get them to agree.

There was no other way. None. If there were, she wouldn't even be considering this. But she had to. She'd seen all the red ink in those ledgers. She couldn't sit by and watch Meg and Asher lose their business, possibly even their home. Not if there was anything she could do to prevent it.

She owed it to Meg. And Asher. She owed it to everybody.

Chapter 15

"He's not picking up," Lynn said. "Hang on. Let me see if I can find him."

Lynn jogged down the short hallway that led to Hal's office. She twisted the doorknob and found it locked. "Hal?"

"What?"

"You've got a call. I tried to transfer it in, but it kept bouncing back to me."

"I'm not taking calls right now. I've got a meeting with Larry Ketcher in two hours and I need to have the treatment ready."

"Yeah, I know." Lynn laid her head sideways against the door so she could hear him better. "But, trust me, this is someone you're going to want to talk to."

She heard a grumbling, the shuffling of footsteps on carpeting, and stood back. The door opened. Hal looked as annoyed as he sounded.

"Who?"

"Joanie Promise wants to know if it's too late to say yes to the documentary."

Hal took in a sharp breath. "Really?"

Lynn tipped her head to one side. "That depends. She has conditions. But I figured that her coming to you is a good sign. Maybe she was playing hard to get before."

Hal shook his head. "She's not like that."

Lynn didn't know how Hal could be so sure of that, but this wasn't the time to argue. Joanie was still on hold.

"Well, I thought maybe if you talked to her—"

"What kind of conditions?" he asked, cutting her off.

"Unreasonable ones. She wants thirty thousand dollars." Lynn rolled her eyes.

"Okay, fine. Put her through."

"Hal? We can't afford to pay her," she said in a doubtful voice, seeking confirmation. "Not thirty thousand dollars. Not anything like that."

Hal sat down at his desk and started shoving papers aside.

"Yeah, yeah, I know. Just put her through."

Lynn wasn't the sort of person who listened at keyholes. But the combination of Joanie Promise's demands and that look on Hal's face—as though he might actually agree to something so utterly impossible—had her worried. In the interest of protecting the company's future and, by extension, her job, she felt compelled to try and eavesdrop on Hal's conversation with Joanie.

But Hal had an odd habit of turning his chair away from his desk and resting his feet flat on the opposite wall when he was involved in a long conversation. Lynn could hear only the low rumble of his voice punctuated by long silences when, she supposed, Joanie must be talking.

After a few minutes she went back to her own desk and tried to work. Finally, Hal emerged from his office, loudly calling Lynn's name as he walked down the hall. She jumped up from her desk and met him halfway.

"You don't need to yell. I'm right here. How'd it go?"

She needn't have asked; his face said it all. Hal Seeger had gotten his way.

"We're a go!" he said, smacking his fist into his palm. "But I want to get up to Seattle and start filming right away—end of next week if we can swing it. I don't want to give her a chance to change her mind.

"I need you to find me a cameraman and sound guy who're willing to travel on short notice and can stay up there for a couple of months."

"What about Brian Lutz? He moved to Seattle last year."

"Perfect. Call and see if he's available and if he knows of anybody local who can do the sound. Oh, and you'd better get in contact with the Laos. Tell them the project has gone back into development. And get hold of Larry Ketcher and postpone our meeting until the day after tomorrow. Better call Larry first."

"Hang on, hang on. I'm going to need to write this down," she said, walking back to her desk. Hal followed her.

"Don't tell Larry why I want to postpone. Say I'm having some emergency dental work or something. That'll buy me a couple of days to work up a new treatment. He was hot for the Lao project, but if I can pull together a good presentation, maybe I can get him to back The Promise Girls project instead.

"Have you still got the old research? Pull that out for me, will you? Minerva's book summary, that memo we did on the family history, all the interview clippings, all the editorials that came out after Minerva's meltdown, any articles that came out after the book was shelved—especially the ones with quotes from psychologists and child development experts."

Lynn scribbled furiously. "You want the video clips too?"

"Yeah, all of them. I've already got the talk show clip, but they were on a lot of other shows. Anytime they stepped in front of a camera, I want the video."

"Anything else?"

"I need a phone number for Gerhardt Boehm."

"And he is?"

Hal rolled his eyes. "Don't you listen to anything besides Pearl Jam?"

"Not if I can help it."

"Gerhardt Boehm—world-renowned concert pianist. He retired from touring in the seventies, but he taught Joanie and a lot of other musicians too. Some of them very, very famous. I think he lives in Pasadena. I need to interview him before I fly to Seattle."

Hal started heading back to his office, but then remembered something else.

"And I'll need some temporary housing in Seattle. Something clean, but cheap. We've got expenses of thirty grand to cover before we even start, so the production budget is going to be tight, especially if I can't get Larry to back us."

"And if he won't? Then what?"

"I haven't figured that part out yet. Call Deborah Munoz and ask her to come over here," he said, striding down the hallway toward his office.

"Your Realtor? Why?"

"In case I have to sell the condo. If I can't find anybody to back me, then I'll back myself."

Lynn's stomach hurt. She thought about the fifteen hundred dollars she'd just spent on a new refrigerator and the fact that she owed the IRS thirty-three hundred dollars.

"Hal, maybe we should slow down and talk about this. Are you sure this is a good idea?"

"Nope," he said before closing his office door. "But I'm doing it anyway."

Joanie and Allison stood in the bedroom, looking at the wall.

This is it, Joanie thought to herself, *the supreme compliment that one woman pays to another, trusting her girlfriend with the task of choosing what kind of room she'll wake up in for months, probably years to come.*

Joanie had never been shy about offering advice or opinions to her sisters. With Meg and Avery, she inserted herself, gently she hoped, but a mild intrusion was still an intrusion. Allison had invited her in and Joanie loved her for it.

Joanie took another step back, carefully studying three patches of paint color.

"The yellow," she said finally.

"You're sure? I like the lavender too."

"So do I. Lavender is great on a sunny day in April, but think about how it's going to make you feel on a gray day in February. And the yellow will be easier to work with when you're picking fabrics."

Allison pursed her lips, staring at the patch of yellow.

"You're right. Thanks," she said, sounding so much like she meant it that Joanie felt happy all over again.

Allison squatted down to clean up and Joanie

squatted down next to her to help, putting lids back on the pint-sized paint cans.

"When does the movie crew show up?"

"Week and a half," Joanie said. "I want to give Meg a little time to settle in. I mean, physically she seems to be recovering, but still . . . she was unconscious for so long. And after more than a week's worth of incredibly expensive tests and scans, no one seems to be able to give us a concrete answer about when or if she'll start remembering, or if there might be any hidden problems that might crop up later. I'm still worried about her."

"Well, I'm worried about you," Allison said pointedly. "Are you *sure* you want to do this movie?"

"Want to?" She gave Allison a you-gotta-be-kidding sort of look.

"So this isn't about Hal?" she said, looking for confirmation. "It isn't because he was starting to grow on you?"

Joanie laughed. "Are you serious? No, absolutely not. Look, I don't think he's necessarily a bad guy. For whatever reason, he's got his heart set on making this movie. And, yes, I did feel a little bit bad about telling him to shove off. But that was his problem, not mine.

"Except now it *is* my problem, because Meg and Asher are really, really broke. Even more than I knew. The client they were counting on to get them through spring couldn't get financing. Asher's building a house on spec."

"On spec? So they'll use their own money for construction and then hope they can find a buyer when they're done?"

"Their money and the bank's, but yes. But if they've got over thirty thousand dollars of debt to the hospital, the bank won't loan them the money and they can't stay in business. Bottom line is, we have to do the movie. We *have* to. I'd rather poke my eyes with a chopstick than reopen the whole *Promise Girls* can of worms, but it's the only way."

"Joanie," Allison said, her tone sympathetic but chiding, "why is everything *your* responsibility?"

Joanie was about to say because it always had been, but that wasn't quite true.

Until her mother got pregnant with Avery, Minerva had definitely been the adult in charge. That was when things started to change.

Minerva was terribly sick during her pregnancy and so Joanie stepped up, taking care of the house and her little sister. Someone had to. And Joanie discovered it felt good to be needed. She became Meg's surrogate mother, her protector, counselor, and cheerleader. After Avery was born, Joanie was there for her youngest sister as well.

After the birth, Minerva was more demanding than ever, pushing them even harder, Joanie especially. No matter what she did or how hard she worked, it wasn't enough.

Joanie spent countless hours practicing for her first major piano competition, which was not long after Avery was born. When the prizes were announced and she was awarded the bronze medal, third place, Joanie was thrilled. So was her new teacher, Maestro Boehm.

But bronze wasn't good enough for Minerva. On the drive home, she berated Joanie, called her careless and ungrateful for the opportunities she'd been given. She said it was a shame to see talent wasted on a lazy and mediocre mind.

That was the first time Minerva spoke to her that way, but it wouldn't be the last. Before long, Joanie started to believe it.

But oddly, as Joanie came to accept her label as the daughter of lesser promise, Minerva became more dependent on her, bringing Joanie more and more into her confidence, especially when it came to their financial situation. Until then, Joanie had never thought about money. It was always just there even though Minerva had never worked outside their home. When people asked her what she did for a living, Minerva would say, "My girls are my life's work, my masterpieces." Now Minerva explained that, for all those years, they had been living on an inheritance that was running out.

It was a lot to unload on a child, but Joanie,

anxious for love, was honored by her mother's trust. For the year when Minerva was writing her book, Joanie took on even greater responsibility for the house and her sisters. Later, when Minerva explained that the success of the book and their financial security depended on the success of the tour, she had gone along with it. For three weeks. And then . . .

But Allison knew all of that. Allison knew everything about her, things she never had told or would tell anyone else. And even before she asked the question—*Why is everything your responsibility?*—Allison already had to know the answer.

Chapter 16

Meg sat in her hospital bed, drawing a picture of her sister. The bruises around her eyes had nearly disappeared and the stitches along her jaw had been removed, leaving a reddish scar that would eventually fade into a shiny but nearly imperceptible ribbon of white that would show only when the light hit her chin just so.

Avery sat in a borrowed wheelchair, gazing out the window. Her perfectly coiffed hair sparkled, sprinkled with silver glitter. She had on full makeup, raspberry pink lipstick, and iridescent turquoise eye shadow the exact same color as the scales on her mermaid tail.

When Owen entered the room, his face split into a grin.

"Meg! You look great! Rumor on the ward is that you're ready to go home."

"I guess so. That's what everybody says."

"Everybody's right. You look way too healthy to be hanging around here. But I can see why you'd want to stay. I *know* how much you'll miss the food."

Owen winked and turned his attention to Avery. "Thanks a million for doing this. You ready?"

Avery nodded, but didn't speak. She was concentrating.

It was early. The playroom and halls of the pediatric ward were mostly empty. The young patients were still having breakfast and being readied for the day. But a nurse manning the ward desk, a tall woman in her early fifties, dressed in a purple smock with yellow and pink flowers and with a nametag reading SHARON GARRETT, looked up from her computer and smiled as Owen wheeled Avery down the hall.

"What have we got here? A mermaid?" She stood up. "I thought mermaids always stayed in the ocean."

"Normally, that is true. But on special occasions, assuming an appropriate means of ambulation is available," Avery replied regally, her hand gliding slowly to the left, as if the speed of her move-ments was impeded by the weight of water, "we make exceptions. We've come to see Lilly Margolis."

"She's awake and in her chair. Not in a very good mood, but I bet a visit from you will perk her up." Sharon looked at Owen. "This is great."

He smiled. "It was all Avery's idea."

"Well, if a visit from a mermaid doesn't cheer her up, I don't know what will. Poor baby." Sharon sighed and looked to Avery. "The father died five months ago, cancer. Now this. The mom is all alone, trying to take care of Lilly and hold down a job. But you're awfully nice to do this. I sure hope it helps."

Owen entered the room first, holding open the door. "Lilly? There's someone here to see you, a friend of mine. Her name is Avery."

Avery wheeled the chair through the door herself, smiling at the little girl with the brown braids whom she'd seen at the un-birthday party and hadn't stopped thinking about since. But this time she was struck by Lilly's legs, long in proportion to the rest of her body, the legs of a little girl who had once loved to run and never would again.

Avery pushed the thought from her mind. Feeling sad and sorry wouldn't help Lilly. The child was paralyzed; Avery could do nothing to change that. But she might be able to cheer her up and perhaps rekindle the flame of joy and imagination that was natural to children but sadly absent in so many adults.

Avery was a stubbornly notable exception. In feeding her imagination, she had smothered the bitterness, despair, and hopelessness that often mark those who know life's cruelty acutely and at too young an age. Imagination had saved her. Maybe it could do the same for Lilly Margolis.

Avery wheeled her chair close. Lilly stared at her with wide and wondering eyes.

"Are you a mermaid for real?"

Avery tilted her head to one side. "What do you think?"

The little one pressed her lips together. Her brow furrowed and her dark eyes grew darker still. In them, Avery saw a battle between disbelief and desire.

"I thought mermaids could swim."

"Of course. But I can't swim without water, can I?"

Lilly shook her head, assenting to the logic of the statement.

"My friend," Avery continued, casting her eyes to Owen, "told me he knew a little girl named Lilly who he thought might make a fine mermaid. Is that you?"

"I'm not a mermaid. I can't swim. I can't even walk."

"I can't walk either. That's why I'm in this," Avery said, glancing down at the wheelchair.

"As far as swimming, I couldn't do that either. Not until I learned how."

"Mermaids don't have to learn to swim. They just *know*."

"Some know. Mermaids who were born mermaids. Others, those who become mermaids, have to learn."

Lilly shook her head, doubt crowding out the faint flame of hope. "You can't just decide to be a mermaid."

Avery reached up and swept her hair over her shoulder, made a show of arranging her luxuriant locks. "Of course, you can," she said nonchalantly. "I did."

"How?"

"Just like you start doing anything, by deciding. First you decide and then you learn. I learned how to swim, how to talk to fish and sea creatures. Dolphins are the easiest to understand," Avery said informatively, "and the most interesting to talk to. Urchins are awfully dull. They just sit there like lumps, complaining about the weather and trying to prick passing seahorses with their spines. It's very rude."

Avery clucked her tongue in a scolding sort of way. A smile tugged at Lilly's lips.

"Mermaids have to learn to sing too. That's part of how we attract handsome seafarers." She glanced toward Owen once again, looking up at him briefly beneath the fringe of her lashes. "But it can't be just any song. It has to be all your own."

"Like something you made up?" Lilly asked uncertainly.

"Exactly. Would you like to hear mine?"

Lilly nodded and Avery began, lifting her voice to a clear and lovely middle-range soprano, singing in a melodic minor key that was full of mystery and longing for things just out of reach.

I float to the surface, drawn by the lights,
Of the worlds of men and the stars at night
I frolic with seals and surf on the waves,
In search of a soul mate, a sailor to save,
With a heart that is pure and a love that is free,
A man among men, with eyes that can see
To the depths of deep, to what's wondrous and
     strange,
Whose heart speaks to mine, who won't ask
     me to change,
Who wants me as I am, which is how I want
     him,
With a love that endures till the stars shall
     grow dim

It was a new song for her, composed in the moment, definitely not her best. As she sang, she kept her gaze fixed fully on the child. But she could feel Owen's eyes on her and the knowledge made her heart beat just a little faster.

"That was pretty," Lilly said. "What else do mermaids know?"

"Oh, a lot of things—how to identify the different kinds of kelp, how to bite through fishermen's nets to free trapped sea turtles, how to explore sunken shipwrecks while avoiding angry sharks, that sort of thing. How to imagine and to dream—that's very important, probably the most important of all. And how to grow your hair."

Lilly looked skeptical. "That's silly. You don't have to learn that. Everybody knows how to grow hair. It just happens."

Avery shook her head. "Not everybody. Haven't you ever seen a bald man?"

"My doctor is bald."

"See? But I'm not just talking about regular hair. Mermaids have long hair."

"I have long hair."

"You do?" Avery said, feigning surprise. "Let me see."

Lilly pulled the elastic bands from the ends of her braids and combed through her hair with her fingers. Avery gasped.

"Oh my! You do! You have beautiful long hair! No wonder my friend thought you had mermaid potential. But there's just one thing missing."

Avery reached beneath her sequined mermaid tail and withdrew a little glass vial with a silver cap. She opened the vial, shook a small mound of silver glitter into her hand, and sprinkled it carefully over the child's long brown hair.

"Much better," she said, taking out a small,

mother-of-pearl hand mirror and holding it up to the little girl's face. "Don't you think so?"

Lilly examined herself, moving her head from left to right to see how the movement made her hair sparkle. The door opened and Sharon stuck her head into the room, pretending to be surprised when she saw Avery in her wheelchair.

"My goodness! What do we have here?"

"A mermaid," Lilly reported.

"Really? I don't think we've ever had a mermaid at the hospital before. How exciting! Lilly, I hate to break up the party, but it's time for your physical therapy."

"I want to stay here," Lilly protested.

"I know," Sharon said sympathetically. "But Cindy will be waiting to help you with your exercises. You want to get stronger, don't you?"

"It doesn't matter. I'm never going to walk again anyway."

Lilly's tone was matter-of-fact, resigned rather than wheedling, the voice of a person who had given up. The fact that it came from a child who had yet to blow out seven candles on a birthday cake nearly broke Avery's heart.

"Feel this," Avery said, placing the little girl's hand on the upper part of her arm, bending at the elbow, making her bicep bulge under Lilly's little fingers.

Lilly's eyes went wide with surprise. "You've got ginormous muscles!"

"Mermaids have to. You can't swim if you don't. Or push yourself up on coral reefs or rocky shores to wave at passing ships. Mermaids have to be strong."

Lilly thought about this for a minute. Finally, she sighed. "Okay. I guess I'll go. Will you come to see me again?" she asked.

"Of course. Until then, I've got something for you."

Avery pulled out a blue hardback book she had tucked in the wheelchair and handed it to Lilly.

"Can you read yet?"

"Not very good," Lilly admitted. "I'm only in first grade."

"You'll get better. It takes practice, like anything else. And this book has lots of pictures of fish and other sea creatures. See?" Avery flipped to a two-page layout of an underwater seascape, teeming with life. "You can learn the names of the different fish, read about where they live and what they're like. And then, when you're asleep, you can dream of being there yourself, swimming far and free under the waves, having conversations with dolphins—"

"Or lumpy, grumpy urchins," Lilly added, bowing her lips into a smile that was spontaneous and sunny and wide, like any normal six-year-old.

"Exactly," Avery said with a laugh.

"Maybe you could come back and read that book to all the children," Sharon suggested.

"I bet the kids would love to meet a mermaid. Don't you think so, Lilly?"

Lilly bobbed her head, still grinning.

"Yes? Well, I think I'd like that too," Avery said, and matched Lilly's smile with one of her own.

Traveling in her full mermaid regalia presented a number of logistical challenges. Owen made it easier by offering to drive Avery home. As he wheeled her from the main entrance of the hospital and through the parking lot toward his car, drawing many stares from patients, staff, and visitors during their progress, Owen couldn't seem to stop talking about their successful morning.

"Seriously, Avery, that was amazing!" Owen enthused yet again as they approached the car. "Nobody on staff has been able to make Lilly smile, let alone make a joke. And you made her believe you; she absolutely believed you were a mermaid. For a minute there, you made *me* believe it! You were fabulous!"

He looked at her with momentarily shining eyes, then clicked a button on his key and busied himself with opening the door. Avery's face felt hot. She put her palm to her cheek and smiled, flushed with pleasure under the warmth of his admiring glance.

"Oh, well . . . People want to believe in what's magical. Even adults. But it's easier with children. They still remember how to pretend. Kids have faith. That's our natural mind-set, the thing that makes poets pen verse and inventors invent. But somewhere along the way, most grown-ups default to doubt. It's still in there, though—the need to believe. That's what I try to tap into."

Owen checked the passenger seat, making sure it was pushed back as far as it could go. "Well, I don't know how you do it, but it's pretty awesome, whatever it is."

Avery scooted forward in the wheelchair, trying to figure out how she was going to get into the car without falling.

"Hold on," Owen said. He bent his knees, slid one arm behind her back and the other beneath the crook of her knees, and lifted her up. Avery looped her arms around his neck. She felt her cheeks get even hotter.

"Awesome," he said in a softer voice, holding her captive in his arms and the heat of his gaze. "Amazing, and wonderful, and absolutely gorgeous," he murmured; then he kissed her.

Avery had known only two love relationships in her life; one unrequited, the other heartbreaking. She had been kissed but a few times in her life. And never like this.

Owen's lips were soft. His kisses were anything but. There was nothing tentative in the way he pressed his mouth to hers, as if he had no question about what he wanted and no doubts that Avery wanted it too.

As he pulled her body even closer against his chest, Avery did want it. Or thought she did. As a mermaid, Avery was a sensual being, fully cognizant and in control of her own sexuality, a Siren. That was a part she played.

But beneath the makeup and glitter, the persona she had honed so skillfully that she wore it like a second skin, Avery was a vulnerable and almost wholly inexperienced young woman trying to sort out urges that were simultaneously exhilarating and alarming.

Owen lifted his lips from hers. His breathing was heavy and ragged, matching her own. "I have the rest of the day off," he said, searching her face with hungry eyes. "Come home with me."

Avery opened her mouth to answer and closed it again. There were all kinds of reasons for her to decline his invitation. She hadn't known Owen for very long or very well. Until this moment, he'd given no indication that he wanted to be anything more than friends. Either he'd been playing it cool or she'd misread the signals. Entirely possible. She hadn't had much practice at this.

Still . . . A handful of conversations, a shared sympathy for a wounded little girl . . . Was that enough for her to know if he was the kind of man to whom she could entrust her heart? Was she ready to take that risk? On the other hand, was she ready to miss her chance?

"Kiss me again," she said.

He did, without hesitation, and though Avery could scarcely have believed it possible, his second kiss was even better than the first. He was so sure of himself, so unapologetic in his desire. His confidence was both arousing and reassuring.

Avery let the weight of her head drop back onto his arm and parted her lips, feeling like she had fallen from a great height and landed safely, caught up in the sure embrace of a man who might, just might, turn out to be her hero.

Chapter 17

Meg looked out the passenger window of Asher's truck. The neighborhood was busier than she had thought it would be, more urban. She didn't know why she had formed the impression that they lived out in the country except that Asher looked like someone who spent a lot of time outdoors. And since he'd told her that he owned—that they owned—a home construction business, he probably did. But somehow she had imagined something with more trees and less traffic.

They passed a building that looked like it had been a gas station in a former life, with café tables out front and a huge ceramic doughnut perched on the roof.

"What's that?"

"Top Pot. Great doughnuts. You hardly ever let

me take you there because you say you love them too much. That's Grateful Bread," he said, pointing to a storefront with brown siding. "Another of your guilty pleasures."

"Does the doughnut place have the old-fashioned kind?"

"That's right!" Asher enthused. "Maple glazed old-fashioned is your favorite! I knew you'd start to remember once we got home."

Meg didn't remember ever having eaten a maple-glazed doughnut, but she smiled anyway. He wanted so much for her to remember. She hated to disappoint him.

A couple of blocks farther on, they took a left and then a right. "This is our road," Asher said. This street was considerably less busy, with trees and grass, spring flowers blooming in gardens, and people walking their dogs along the sidewalk. One of them, a gray-haired woman wearing a navy blue jacket and walking a schnauzer, waved.

"That's Mrs. LaRouche and Punkin," Asher informed her. "They go for their walk twice a day, rain or shine."

"Punkin's the dog, right?"

Asher barked out a more enthusiastic laugh than her joke deserved. It occurred to Meg that he was just as nervous as she was.

"Here we are. Home sweet home." The narrow driveway was occupied by a silver sedan. Asher pulled the truck to the curb.

"You have company?"

"You didn't think your sisters would let you come home without a welcoming committee, did you?"

He hopped out of the truck, then jogged around to open her door, as if they were on a date, trying to make a good first impression on each other. In a way, she supposed they were.

"It's cute," she said, looking at the house. And it was.

The story-and-a-half house was built in a cottage style. The vertical siding was painted a soft sage green with wood-cased windows trimmed in white. The simple rectangular footprint was made more interesting by the addition of an alcove that jutted from the front of the house with four windows at the front and two on each side.

"Really cute," she said again. "It's like a dollhouse."

"But it feels like a house twice its size," Asher said with obvious pride. "We make use of every square inch."

The lot could easily have accommodated a much bigger house, but Meg was glad that the little cottage sat so far back from the street, with flowerbeds and a big lawn in front and just as much space in the back. There was no foyer, just an entry door on the side. But a covered porch extending to the right and flanked by two white pillars gave the impression of a grander entrance and was roomy enough to accommodate two white wicker chairs.

Stepping onto the porch, Meg experienced something strange, something between an impression and a vision.

She saw herself sitting in one of those chairs, wearing a T-shirt and pajama pants, knees pulled to her chest, cold fingers wrapped around a hot cup of coffee, staring blankly at the garden in the half-light of early morning. The picture was so vivid that, for a moment, she thought it might be a memory. But she felt detached from the woman in the chair, as if she was watching a movie or a reflection in a mirror, an exact replica of someone who looked just like she did. She couldn't tell what the woman was feeling, or indeed if she had any feelings at all.

"Meggie? You okay?"

The sound of Asher's concerned voice startled her.

"It's a nice porch."

"Your favorite place to sit when you're trying to think something through."

Asher opened the door. Meg took a deep breath and passed over the threshold of the sweet and unfamiliar house she'd been told was her home.

Her sisters meant well; everyone did. She'd known that from the first moment of her awakening in the hospital. Everyone wanted her to be happy and whole and well. That was why she tried so hard, because their intentions were so good. They were trying just as hard as she was, perhaps harder. But it was an awkward home-coming just the same. Of all those people present—her sisters and nephew, her husband and her own daughter—she felt truly at ease only with Avery.

But she tried. They all did.

Meg smiled deliberately in response to the chorus of welcomes and hugged them back when they hugged her first. She initiated an embrace with Trina, who hung back from the rest, hesitant, looking the way a cat does when it stands by an open door and can't quite make up its mind to go through or stay put.

While Joanie and Avery fussed over food in the kitchen, Trina and Walt set silverware on the dining table in the sunlit alcove. Meg was still in some pain from her broken ribs, so Asher helped her to the sofa and made sure she was comfortable. She listened as they talked about the documentary, which would commence filming in a little over a week.

Avery was excited about the prospect, joking that this might be their first step on the road to stardom, or at least a reality show on cable TV.

"Really, I can't believe it's taken this long for us to be discovered. Those shows specialize in oddball families. Who's odder than us?"

Walt and Trina shared her enthusiasm; Trina

wondered aloud if the crew included a hair stylist and, if so, would they give her some highlights. Joanie was cautious to the point of suspicion, but resigned to the financial necessity of their cooperation. Asher was mostly silent, but when he did speak, it was to thank Joanie for negotiating the fee and the sisters for going along with it; he seemed both relieved to be getting help dealing with the hospital bills and embarrassed that he needed it.

Meg felt . . . uncertain. She wasn't excited about the prospect of being followed around by cameras and microphones like Avery. Nor did she dread it like Joanie. Maybe because she was convinced that the filmmaker, this Hal person, would quickly lose interest in her.

Over the previous days she'd been told all about her childhood, the test tube genius father and the narcissist mother, the book that catapulted them to fame, the day it all came to a crashing halt, and everything that came after. But to Meg, it was just a story about three characters with whom she felt no more connection than she did to the reflection who sat huddled on the porch, drinking coffee and staring at nothing.

She felt badly for Asher. She, too, was embarrassed that other people were stepping up to help take care of her bills, and relieved that they had. When Joanie had named the figure owed at the family meeting, Meg's jaw dropped. It was a staggering sum. But what bothered her most was that Asher felt saddled with the responsibility of settling the bill. He wasn't the one whose car had slammed into the cement wall and racked up tens of thousands of dollars in medical bills. Why should he have to carry that load?

She posed the question when they met to discuss and vote on doing the documentary and had been met with a simple answer: "Because we're married."

Right. She had to keep reminding herself of that.

She was married, to Asher. She had been married to him for seventeen years. They had a daughter. They'd built a house and a business together. Everything they did, they did together. Everything that happened—sickness, health, good times and bad—was something that happened to both of them.

But if they were as married as everyone said they were . . . why did it feel so awkward between them? Especially after the dinner was done and the Capitol Hill contingent went home and Trina climbed the ladder to her loft, leaving them alone? Why did Meg wish he'd quit staring at her when he thought she wasn't looking?

And why was she so relieved when he took her to the door of their bedroom but not through it, then escorted her outside to a miniature, perfectly appointed house in the backyard that was to be hers alone?

On the other hand, unless they really were married, how could he have read her tangled thoughts when he said good night, leaning forward and kissing her on the forehead and saying, "I know. It's confusing. But give it time. Give us time."

And why, after she crawled into the bed built for one and turned out the light, did she lay awake so long, looking out the window and seeing nothing, crying about nothing, feeling like nothing?

Chapter 18

Approaching his ninetieth birthday, Gerhardt Boehm still cut an imposing figure. He was tall with a full head of white hair that shone like spun silver and was nattily dressed in a crisp white shirt, a linen sport coat, and toffee-colored trousers pressed to a knife-edge crease.

"Very good," Boehm said, standing in the doorway of his 1928 Spanish Revival bungalow as Hal came up the walkway. "I tell my students that if they come late, they should not bother to come at all. But you are most punctual. Come in. Come in."

It was one of the more modest houses in an expensive neighborhood, but elegant and well cared for. Following Mr. Boehm through the formal living area, Hal made a comment about the beautiful barrel ceilings and arched doorways.

"Ah, yes," the old man replied. "All original. I haven't changed a thing since I bought it in 1975, a gift to myself. I had just completed a successful but exhausting concert tour and recorded an album of the Mephisto waltzes. Very difficult."

"That's right. You like Liszt."

Boehm looked over his shoulder. "Yes. Doesn't everyone? I was tired of traveling and had a bit of money in my pocket. It seemed a good time to retire. I came to America in search of someplace sunny, found Pasadena and this house. I couldn't afford it now, though; the neighborhood has gotten so expensive. Not a month goes by without a Realtor calling to say they have a client willing to pay a lot of money for my house. But of what use is money to me now? I have no one to leave it to. And where would I go? This is my home. And this," he said as they entered a large, open room at the back of the house, "is my studio. May I get you a cup of tea?"

Hal accepted the offer. Boehm went to the kitchen.

Hal had decided to film the interview himself with a single stationary camera. He quickly set up his equipment and started investigating his surroundings.

The room was a good size, but seemed smaller owing to the presence of a massive grand piano placed near a set of French doors that overlooked the garden planted with pink bougainvillea. The piano, lid lifted high, was a thing of beauty, shining as brightly as a pair of new patent leather shoes, showing not a speck of dust. The same could not be said for the rest of the space.

Stacks of sheet music were piled on every flat surface and in every corner, as well as on the seats of chairs. The wall shelves opposite the piano held papers, memorabilia, and many, many haphazardly stowed books. One of the shelves was so overloaded that a bracket had fallen under the weight, causing books to slip and heap at the lower end, like children left unsupervised on a playground slide. Everything except the piano was covered in a thin veil of dust, including the framed photographs hanging on the back wall. Hal walked closer to examine them.

Some of the photos showed Mr. Boehm alone as a much younger man, his hair as black as the swallowtail tuxedo he wore, playing the piano on stages of different concert halls, his hands on the keyboard, his expressions intense, displaying passion, fury, rapture. Most, however, showed him with other people.

Some had been taken in that very room as Boehm leaned over a student to give an instruction, pointing at a particular spot in the music or reaching out to correct a hand position. Others, taken in various concert halls or theaters, showed him with arms draped protectively over the shoulders of beaming students who were obviously relieved at the completion of successful performances.

There were also pictures of Boehm standing next to musical peers, formally dressed men and women with faces as lined and heads as gray as his own, familiar faces of famous musicians, conductors, and composers. And there were younger famous faces, too, of Boehm's former students, people who were unknown commodities when they began to study with him but who went on to brilliant futures in classical music. Of course, many of his unknown students continued to remain unknown, had careers that either never took off or fizzled before they began.

What would it be like, Hal wondered, to enter this room as a young student of the legendary Gerhardt Boehm? To wait alone while the maestro prepared you a cup of tea and look at these photographs, the famous alongside the failed? Would you feel inspired? Or intimidated?

Hal found Joanie's picture among all the scores of other photos.

Her hair was long then, reaching the waistband of her long black skirt. She was a child when the picture was taken, or a young teenager, probably not long after she began studying with Boehm. Her white lace blouse lay flat and smooth over her then-nonexistent chest, but her hands were the same, fingers long and slender. The expression on her face was the same, too, determination and earnestness overlaid by anxiety, the face of someone who was afraid to be afraid.

"Ah. You have found her, I see."

Boehm entered the room, carrying a silver tea tray.

"Clear a space for this, will you? Take those papers off the ottoman. Oh, and off the chair as well. Lay them anywhere. The floor is fine. Yes, that's right."

He poured tea for Hal and himself, then took a seat on the piano bench. Hal clipped a small lapel microphone on the maestro's jacket, started the camera, and sat down. Boehm raised the teacup to his lips before setting it delicately back down on the saucer.

"So . . . you want to talk about Joanie Promise. What do you want to know?"

"How old was Joanie when she began studying with you?"

"Twelve. She was talented. There was no mistaking it, even then."

"Is that usual? For you to take on a student who is so young?"

"No, but a friend asked me to give her an audition."

"A friend?"

"A fellow musician. He heard her play and thought that she might benefit from studying with me."

Boehm set his teacup down on the piano bench and sprung to his feet with the enthusiasm of a much younger man. He went to a shelf loaded with CDs.

"I used to have a big, old-fashioned tape player. What do you call them? Reel to reel. But a few years ago I put all of my tapes onto discs. Much more convenient," he said, placing the CD into a dusty black player. "I was listening to this again before you arrived. It was recorded on that day, when she auditioned for me."

Boehm pressed a button on the CD player. He stretched one arm over his head, resting his hand on one of the upper shelves, and leaned forward, eyes closed, his body swaying slightly to the strains of a lovely and familiar melody.

"That's the Liebestraum," Hal said, his voice registering surprise. "She was already playing this when she was twelve?"

Boehm nodded his head deeply, eyes still closed. "Yes. Not as well as she would play it later, but very well indeed. Do you hear that?" he asked excitedly.

Boehm cocked his head to one side, listening intently to an especially fluid phase of the music, the notes flowing one into the other with grace and purity, like clear water tripping over stones in a mountain stream.

"That is what I was talking about. That spark. That brilliance and bravura! Even at twelve, the music flowed through her freely, without inhibition, like blood coursing through the body. That's why I decided to take her on, because this is something you cannot teach. It is also something that often disappears with age. The doubts and worries of adulthood squash it.

"And the mother . . . already she was putting too much pressure on the girl. I believe in holding my students to a high standard, the highest. I encourage them to push themselves beyond what they believe they can do. But there is a difference between pressuring and encouraging. Encouragement lifts. Pressure smothers. I feared this was what the mother would do to Joanie in another year or two, extinguish her spark. I hoped to protect her from that. I failed."

The old man fell silent, listened. So did Hal.

It was strange for Hal to hear the melody he had come to know during the course of his research simply as a piece of music. Before, he'd always heard it while watching the infamous talk show tape, more tuned in to the visual than the music itself, looking for that crucial moment. Joanie's eyes shifting toward Minerva, showing a gleam of rebellion. A breath later, her fingers stumbled on the keyboard.

It was an act of deliberate defiance. Even at the time, he knew the error was intentional, a purposeful declaration of independence. But he only knew it because he had been watching her face so carefully. Otherwise, he wouldn't have noticed her mistake; most of the people in the audience didn't. The fact that they believed Joanie had given a flawless performance made Minerva's response all the more shocking.

That episode never aired. The other prodigies, including Hal, were ushered from the set and back to their hotels and regular lives with no discussion of rescheduling. But somehow the videotape of Joanie's performance and Minerva's attack was leaked and played, over and over again. The publisher pulled *The Promise Girls* from bookstore shelves within days of the incident, but people kept talking about it for weeks afterward.

On the surface it seemed so small, the sort of thing that happens at any given hour on any given day: teenage rebellion and parental over-reaction. If it had taken place in private, no one would ever have known about it. But people *had* known about it, all kinds of people. The public outcry became an explosion that, rightly or wrongly, splintered a family and irrevocably altered the course of four lives.

No. Not four lives. Five. Including mine.

Liebestraum No. 3 was nearing its end. Hal's ears were practically twitching in anticipation, waiting for the mistake. He'd heard it that way so many times before that he'd almost come to think of it as part of the original composition.

He closed his eyes, pictured twelve-year-old

Joanie, sitting at Boehm's piano, with lanky limbs and hair hanging to her waist. Her nimble fingers fluttered up the keyboard and down again, conquering arpeggios as easily as if she was born to do that very thing, which she was. When it came to the fateful moment, the tricky transition from arpeggios to chords, a juncture at which any pianist might easily muddle her fingering, the spectral presence of the younger Joanie played flawlessly.

The final chord faded away and for a moment the two men sat silently, as if wishing for its return. Boehm poked a button on the CD player. The silence brought Hal back to the present, reminding him why he was there.

"She played it perfectly," Hal said, still surprised. "Is that when you realized she was a prodigy? A genius?"

Boehm returned to the piano bench and reclaimed his teacup.

"I don't believe in genius, not in children. Joanie had a great love of music. She had stamina and the right physique for a pianist—strong arms and hands, long fingers. And she had desire—to learn, to please, to prove herself. And, of course, she is very intelligent. Capable of mastering things which others would find difficult. She had that spark. That thing no teacher can teach.

"But genius is more than this. Genius requires maturity, an emotional sensitivity that comes from experiencing life fully, in all its divinity and devastation, and having not only the skill but the courage to express this through art. Genius is the willingness to stand on the stage, drop the kimono, and let the world have a good long look, to allow oneself to be completely vulnerable. You see the difference?

"A child may be vulnerable, yes. Vulnerability and youth are inexorably tied. Children by their nature lack the ability to protect themselves. But to be a genius is to consciously forgo that right of self-protection, to express your full humanity through your art, in all its glory and all its shame, holding nothing back.

"No matter what Ms. Promise claimed in her book," he said, lifting his chin to a haughty angle, "geniuses are not born. They become."

Hal continued the interview. Boehm was forthright in his answers, but after a half hour Hal noticed that Boehm's posture was not as erect as before. Looking more closely, he saw that the old man's clothes hung loose on his body and realized that what he had taken for the fading glow of a California tan might be yellowing of the skin. Hal wrapped up the interview.

Boehm rose slowly from the piano bench. "Will you do something for me? Will you give this to her?"

He took the silver CD from the player, slipped it into a white paper sleeve, and handed it to Hal.

He shuffled to the wall and removed the photograph of himself and his former protégé. "And this?"

"Are you sure? It leaves a big hole in your collection," Hal said, tilting his head toward the vacant space on the wall.

"I'm sure. I won't be able to keep it much longer in any case. I had hoped," he said, gazing at Hal with eyes that said everything, "I might see Joanie again. If that is never to be, I hope this will remind her of who she was and is. And of the time we spent together. Happy times, I think. Will you do this for me?"

Hal accepted the photograph from Boehm's now-trembling hand.

"I'll tell her everything you said."

Sitting in his car, Hal took another look at the photograph of Joanie and her teacher and noticed something he'd missed at first glance.

Joanie stood in the foreground of the photo, on a stage and near a grand piano. Boehm stood next to her, beaming. Joanie was smiling too. On her neck she wore a bronze medal hung on a bright blue ribbon. Standing in the wings of the theater, far in the background, Hal saw a woman. Her face was turned slightly away from the camera and her mouth was open, talking to someone, but even from that distance he knew it was Minerva.

She was standing next to someone, a man. His

hair was iron gray and he wore a black suit. His face, partially hidden behind the black velvet stage curtain, looked like it had been cut in half. Minerva was talking to him. Nothing unusual in that. Joanie had just won a prize and Minerva was always eager to brag about her daughter's accomplishments to anyone who would listen.

What was strange was the way she was looking at him, fixedly, and with a kind of desperate determination. And that she had hold of the lapel of his suit, almost as if she was clutching at him.

Hal picked up his cell phone, dialed Lynn at the office.

"Do you have Minerva Promise's number? I want to see if she's still willing to give me an interview."

"Why? I thought you said letting her tell her story would be a waste of time and that anything she'd say would be self-serving and predictable."

"Still true. But what I care about is what she's not willing to say, the stuff she's never told anybody."

"And you think she's suddenly going to tell you about it?"

"Maybe she'll drop a few breadcrumbs."

"Okay, but I don't think you have time. She's probably at work already and your flight leaves for Seattle tomorrow morning, remember?"

"Right." He clucked his tongue a couple of times, thinking through his options. "What's the name of that restaurant she works at? Wildfire . . . Wildwood?"

"Wildfish Seafood Grille. Hal, you're not going to drive all the way to Newport Beach tonight, are you? It's rush hour. The traffic will be terrible. Plus, she'll be at work. She might not have time to talk to you."

Hal turned the key in the ignition. "Don't worry. If it means a chance to get her daughters in front of a camera, trust me, Minerva will figure out a way to make the time."

Chapter 19

With bleached-blond hair and eyebrows that had been tweezed into two perfect arches, then outlined with a dark brown eye pencil, and wearing a gold choker with chains thick enough to restrain a Doberman, Minerva Promise was definitely not Hal's type. But she was an attractive woman, no doubt about it. Looking at her flat stomach, tanned and toned arms, relatively unlined face, and curvaceous figure, no one would ever have guessed her age as sixty-three.

Minerva pulled aside one of the restaurant's younger assistant managers and asked if she could take over for her at the hostess station for fifteen minutes. Hal, she explained, was her only nephew, a photojournalist who was about to leave on a three-month assignment in a very dangerous part of Syria, and he had come to say his good-byes. Her performance was convincing and confirmed Hal's earlier impressions of her. Minerva was not only manipulative, she had a flexible, possibly nonexistent relationship to the truth.

The tables were full so they grabbed two stools at the bar. Minerva gave a high sign to one of the bartenders, who brought over two cups of coffee.

"Thanks, Joey," she said with a wink, then turned her attention to Hal. "Is this all right? Unless you want something stronger?"

"No, I'm driving. Coffee's fine."

He took a drink and started to cough. Minerva smiled.

"Irish coffee."

"Yeah," Hal said, choking his response. "With how much whisky?"

"As much as it takes." Minerva took a ladylike sip from her mug and sighed. "I never thought I'd be back doing restaurant work at my age. But with Jerry gone . . ."

"Jerry was your boyfriend?"

"Fiancé. We had a beautiful condo near the beach, a million-dollar property. His son sold it right out from under me. Jerry hadn't changed his will yet. Story of my life. So . . . here I am, working my tail off, trying to make rent on a one-bedroom apartment in Costa Mesa with a view of the parking lot and the manager's Winnebago.

"But," she said in a deliberately cheerful tone, "this is just a temporary setback. Things are starting to look up." She leaned closer, resting her chin in her hand. "You know, I talked with Meg just a few weeks ago. I think she's getting ready to start painting again."

"She told you that?"

"We talked about her work and getting around creative blocks. She's ready to make a change, I'm sure of it. She got sidetracked for a while, but what woman doesn't? It's hard to balance family and a career. No one knows better than I do. But I have no regrets. When Meg starts painting again, people will finally see what she's really capable of and that I was right all along. And once Meg is back on track, maybe the other girls will follow." She paused and took another sip from her cup. "Anyway, you're here to talk about my girls. Go ahead. Ask me anything."

Hal pretended to take a drink, giving himself time to think.

Joanie hadn't been kidding when she said she didn't speak to her mother anymore. From the way Minerva was talking, it was clear she still hadn't heard about the accident or that Meg had lost her memory and only recently been released from the hospital.

If she didn't know, he wasn't going to be the one

to tell her. Nor would he tell Joanie or the others that he'd come to see Minerva. He'd seen the look on Joanie's face when he'd mentioned his previous phone conversation with her mother.

"Actually, I'm here to talk about you. I read your book for my research, and watched every television interview I could get my hands on—"

Minerva sat up straighter, increasing the distance between them. Her smile disappeared. "That was the only time I ever hit Joanie. Or any of the girls. It was one terrible mistake that I'll always regret. Joanie was deliberately trying to push my buttons and it worked. But I was under a lot of pressure. And exhausted.

"If you've never been on a national book tour, a new city every day, interview after interview, never sleeping in the same place two nights running, and constantly having to be 'on' and to keep your cool and hold your tongue in the face of those so-called psychological experts they kept trotting out to say that I was a bad mother, selfish, making up for my own failures and inadequacies by pushing my children to achieve the things I couldn't . . ."

She picked up her cup, drinking a little deeper this time.

"I just wanted to give them the opportunities I never had, to do something meaningful with their lives, to contribute something important. . . ." She drank a little more. "If I was as

184

selfish as all those quacks claimed, I would never have had children at all. I'd have focused on my own career—"

"Exactly." Hal nodded deeply as he interrupted her tirade, which Minerva seemed to take as an expression of support. Her posture relaxed and her expression softened.

"That's what I want to know about—your career, *your* past. In the book you didn't really talk about what you brought to the mix. Half of your children's DNA came from you, right? I'd like to know more about that half and how it influenced your children's artistry."

"Well, I really think it was my day-to-day presence that had the greatest influence. From the moment they were born, I made certain they were exposed to great art." She smiled. "When I was pregnant with Joanie, I bought the biggest pair of headphones I could find and put them on my stomach. Even before she was born, Joanie was listening to Mozart, Bach, Rachmaninoff. . . ."

"Yes, I remember that story from your book. But you grew up in the South, right?"

She narrowed her eyes and gave him a sly, almost flirtatious smile, then lifted her cup to her lips again.

"How did you know that?"

He looked past her toward the bartender, Joey, lifted his eyebrows, and pointed to Minerva's now-empty cup, silently requesting a refill.

"You've still got just a touch of an accent. I had a girlfriend once upon a time; Meliss Claypool Jensen. She was a Tennessee girl, a Tri-Delt from Vanderbilt. You?"

"A Tri-Delt from Vanderbilt? Lah-di-dah! But I can't tell you how disappointed I am that you've found me out. Three years of elocution lessons right down the drain."

Joey replaced Minerva's empty cup with a fresh beverage. She left it sitting on the bar while she examined Hal's face.

"But you're not going to talk about me in your movie, are you? This is just for background? People have always accused me of being out to elevate myself through my children's accomplishments, but it's always been about the girls. Everything I've done, I've done for them."

"Just for background," he echoed. "Your personal history influenced the choices you made, which, in turn, influenced your daughters. I can't understand them unless I understand you."

Minerva pulled her cup closer, studying the caramel-colored contents for a long time. Finally, she looked up. "All right. What do you want to know about me?"

"Everything," he said. "As much as you're willing to tell me."

186

Chapter 20

When the doorbell rang Joanie didn't get up from her sewing machine. Instead, she pressed her foot harder on the pedal, the needle racing down the seam. The bell rang again.

"Answer the door, will you? I'm in the middle of something."

A couple of minutes later, Walt, his backpack slung over one shoulder, poked his head into the sewing room.

"Mom? Mr. Seeger is here."

Hal walked in, dropped two black duffle bags on the floor.

"Big day, huh? You ready to get started?"

Joanie looked at Walt. "You better get going or you'll be late. Are you ready for your calculus test?"

"Ready enough." Walt shrugged. "Can we go driving tonight? I'll never pass my license test if I don't get more practice."

"Oh, honey," she said wearily. "Not tonight. I've got two more uniforms to finish, then a ball gown with cartridge pleats and six rows of piping in the skirt. I'm just so far behind. I'm sorry."

Walt shrugged again. "Okay. Maybe this weekend? Or we could ask Uncle Asher?"

"Maybe. He's framing a house and needs to get

the roof on before it rains. Let me see how far I get today with all of this, okay? See you tonight."

She pursed her lips and made a kiss noise. Walt hurried off, his big feet thumping across the wooden floor. The front door slammed behind him as he raced to make his bus. Joanie went back to her sewing.

"Bull in a china shop," she muttered.

"I could take him driving."

Joanie lifted her head and looked at Hal, almost as if she was surprised to see him there.

"I'm just saying, I wouldn't mind. The place I'm staying makes my old college dorm room look palatial. I'd just as soon have something to do in the evenings."

"Oh . . . that's nice of you, but I—"

"Never mind." Hal waved off her excuse. "Just wanted to help if I could. You did remember that we're supposed to start filming today, right?"

"How could I forget? I woke up thinking about it at three this morning. Couldn't go back to sleep so I decided I might as well get some work done. I wasn't expecting you this early."

"Yeah, well . . ." He shrugged. "I couldn't sleep either. I'm always wound up on the first day of a shoot. The crew will be here later, but I thought it'd be good if we talked before they showed up. I brought you something."

He bent down, unzipped one of the duffle bags, and started digging around inside. "I saw

Gerhardt Boehm before I left LA. He asked me to give you these."

Hal handed her a big padded envelope. Joanie reached inside, pulled out the picture frame, and felt her breath catch in her throat.

"Oh . . . I'd nearly forgotten . . ."

But that wasn't true. She remembered, all of it.

She remembered wanting to win so badly that she was afraid she wanted it too much. Boehm said there was no such thing. He convinced her that it was right to feel so passionate, to strive, to grasp at the extraordinary, but that she could only do so by *being* extraordinary and to do this she had to be willing to immerse herself completely in the music.

She remembered his studio, always such a mess, and the shining black piano by the French doors, the sunlight and the pink bougainvillea. She remembered the thousands of miles her fingers had traveled up and down the keyboard playing scales and arpeggios, chords in combinations that sometimes seemed impossible, the tears of frustration at her failure, the heights of ecstasy at her mastery.

She remembered her elation at winning the bronze, and how Minerva had crushed it, calling her lazy and an embarrassment, saying she spoiled everything. And she remembered believing her.

But she also remembered coming into the studio for her next lesson and seeing that Boehm had placed her photograph on his wall along with his other students. That was the maestro's way of saying she'd done well, that he was proud, and that she belonged.

And now, he had removed it.

"Is he all right?"

"I don't know," Hal said slowly. "I don't think so. I think he wanted to make sure you got it before he goes. He said that he hopes it will remind you of the happy times you shared. And of who you are."

"Who I was? Or who everybody thought I was supposed to be. It was a long time ago." She slid the picture back into the envelope. "Well . . . thank you."

"There's something else in there; a recording of your audition for him," he said, even as the question was forming on her lips. "Do you remember what you played for him?"

"Liebestraum Number Three. It was always my party piece. People recognize it, even if they can't name it. And it's flashy, sounds like it's difficult to play."

"Isn't it?"

"Not as difficult as it sounds." She shrugged. "I was playing it at eleven."

"But you were a prodigy."

Joanie picked up her embroidery scissors and carefully snipped the slit for a buttonhole. "And now I sew pants for a living." She could feel his

190

eyes on her. "I need to finish this. There's some coffee in the kitchen if you want it."

"You're not going to listen to it?"

She shook her head. "I already know every note. I could play it in my sleep."

"Even today?"

"I don't know. Probably."

She pulled a length of dark blue thread from a spool, ready to stitch the buttonhole.

"Why don't you have a piano anymore?"

Joanie dragged the blue thread across the surface of some beeswax.

"No room."

"There's plenty of room. Not in here maybe, but the living room is—"

"Hal, if the reason you're interested in making this movie is to try and figure out why I don't play anymore, I can save you a lot of time and tell you right now—I was sick of it. The piano was my mother's idea, not mine, and I'd had enough of it. So I sabotaged my performance on national TV, knowing that Minerva would react exactly like she did and that would be the end of it. And it was. Maybe I didn't think through all the consequences of what I was doing, but I put a stop to it. To her."

He looked as if he was about to speak again. She didn't give him the chance.

"I wanted a life. Just a simple, regular, ordinary life. Is that so hard to understand?"

"Okay. But what I don't understand is why you wouldn't—"

"Wow." Joanie let out a hollow laugh. "You don't know when to quit, do you?"

"I just want to get a clear picture of what happened and why."

"And I just gave it to you. You can ask me questions all day long and I'm going to tell you the same thing. But, hey, it's your money. And your time, which extends between the hours of nine and four. Like. We. Agreed."

She lifted her brows and stared at him, just in case he'd missed her meaning.

"Right," he said, and shoved his hands in his pants pockets. "I'll go into the kitchen and get some coffee until the guys show up. Oh, and speaking of money . . ."

He pulled a folded check out of his pocket and gave it to her. Joanie opened it.

"A personal check?" She looked at it again. "This is only fifteen thousand."

"Yeah, I'm producing it myself, at least for the moment. I'm still working on bringing in some investors. But, you know. It was pretty short notice."

"We had a deal for thirty. The only reason we agreed to this was because we needed money to pay off Meg's medical bills. If you're not going to be able to come up with it . . ."

"I will come up with the rest. I swear. I just need a little more time."

His eyes begged her to trust him. Joanie wasn't sure if she could. Or should. But what else could she do?

"Coffee's in the pot," she said. "Cream is in the refrigerator if you use it. I think there are some bagels in there, too, if Walt didn't eat them."

"Thanks. I'll go get out of your hair for a while." He grinned. "See you at nine."

Joanie stabbed her sewing needle into the blue wool.

"And not a minute before."

Chapter 21

Joanie sat in a ladder-back chair they'd placed near the picture window in her sewing room, fidgeting as Hal tinkered with the placement of the studio lights.

"Is this going to take much longer? I have work to do."

"So do I," Hal muttered, looking at his light meter. "Hold still." He shifted a light three inches to the right, took two steps backward, checked the light meter again, then moved the light back one more inch.

"There we go," he said at last.

Brian Lutz, the cameraman, frowned. "You don't think it's too dark? You're going to have some shadows."

"Yeah, but they work. Look for yourself."

Brian peered into his lens. "Wow. I was worried about her eyes being so deep set, but you're right. This works."

Hal shrugged. "See? You've got to trust me on this stuff."

Joanie twisted in her chair. "You know I'm here, right? And that I understand English? What's wrong with my eyes?"

"Nothing," Brian said, still looking into the camera. "Not a thing. You're going to love the way you look. Like a goddess. Or the Mona Lisa. That's why Hal's the boss. He's got an eye."

"Okay, okay. Enough sucking up. You ready to go to work?"

Brian bent down and fiddled with his camera. Simone Alcott, a film student they had been able to hire cheap to do the sound, put on her headphones. Hal took a seat off camera and smiled at Joanie.

"Relax. You look great. Just forget about the camera and talk to me."

Joanie looked better than great. She looked beautiful. Hal really did have an eye, that gift for seeing what people couldn't recognize in themselves. But she wouldn't talk to him.

She went through the motions of talking to him, fulfilling her obligation and answering his inquiries, but she revealed nothing. Her responses were stiff and over-rehearsed, like a politician who has settled on what to say before the question has even been asked. She didn't trust him.

Hal tried not to take it personally, reminding himself that she didn't trust anybody. After an hour, he gave up.

"Okay, cut. Thanks, everybody."

Joanie unclipped the microphone from the waistband of her pants. "That's all? That wasn't so bad."

"That's all for today," Hal corrected. "We'll be doing more of these."

"How many more?"

"As many as it takes."

The interview with Meg was different, but no better. Her answers were monosyllabic rather than evasive, consisting primarily of "yes," "no," and more often than not, "I can't remember." They also shot some footage of her sitting on the porch steps of her tiny house, sketching a bird.

It didn't add up to much and Brian told him so as they drove back to Capitol Hill to catch up with Avery.

"Will you give me a break?" Hal spat back. "It's only the first day."

"I'm just saying. People aren't going to pay to watch some lady say 'I don't remember' ten times in one interview. You've got to find a way to loosen them up."

"Thanks. I'll keep that in mind."

Hal wasn't worried. The first few days of film almost always ended up on the cutting room floor. It was part of the process. It always took time for people to open up. They had to get to know him, and vice versa. Often, in spite of all his research, it wasn't until filming started that he discovered who he was really dealing with and what the film would be about.

Still, time was money. And this time the money was his. All told, this day was going to cost him around a thousand dollars. Hopefully, the time they spent with Avery would give him a better return on his investment.

Avery was only five years old when *The Promise Girls* was published and so the book focused less on her than Joanie and Meg. Minerva claimed that her youngest, fathered by an unnamed sperm donor who was also a gifted writer, displayed an extraordinary gift for narrative. In Chapter 5 she presented evidence of that claim, a story that Avery had dictated and her mother had transcribed.

It was the tale of three dragon sisters, each with her own distinct personality, whose flames had been extinguished by the spell of an evil sorceress. They went on a quest to regain their incendiary powers, enduring many trials before facing their final test, solving a riddle that would unlock the door of an enchanted lighthouse, ascending the stairs to the eternally illuminated beacon, and then swallowing some of the magical lamp oil to ignite their flames once again.

But upon arriving at the sea, the oldest dragon, entranced by the beauty and peace of the waves, decided that she preferred the idea of life as a leviathan to that of a dragon. She waded into the surf and beckoned her sisters to do the same. Knowing that to do so would be to extinguish their flame forever, the other dragon sisters hesitated, but ultimately followed their sibling, disappearing into the depths, never again to be seen by human eyes.

It was a remarkable creative effort for a child so young and, as things had turned out, eerily allegorical. If Avery truly had authored that story, Minerva had some basis for her claims as to the girl's genius. But two decades later, Avery still wasn't a writer. Or much of anything else.

Hal found Avery was winsome in her way, but with a demeanor that made her seem younger than her years. He theorized that the mermaid thing was a way for an otherwise unremarkable baby sister to gain some notice among her more gifted siblings. Avery was nervous on camera, something Hal hoped was just a product of first-day jitters, but at least she was willing to talk to him.

"Tell me more about how you decided to become a mermaid," he asked.

"Well, I didn't exactly *decide*," Avery said,

corkscrewing a piece of hair around her index finger. "I mean, not consciously."

Hal reached out, gently, and touched her elbow, hoping to contain her fidgeting.

"Oh. Sorry." She blushed and lowered her hand, clutched both hands together in her lap.

"It's okay. We can edit it out. Let's try again. Tell me about becoming a mermaid."

"Well, when I moved to Seattle I needed some kind of job. I didn't have any real work experience. So, you know . . ."

Her giggle sounded more like a product of nerves and embarrassment than amusement. It was hard to know for sure from a first impression, but Hal was starting to wonder if Avery's lack of interest in a serious career was more a reflection of a lack of faith in her own abilities and experience than a conscious choice to remain unencumbered by the demands of adulthood. Of one thing he was certain, Avery suffered from a genuine lack of confidence. He'd need to go gently with her.

"Anyway, this family in the neighborhood, the Meisners, needed a part-time babysitter. I figured even *I* could take care of one five-year-old girl, right?" She giggled again. "And they were pretty desperate. They'd gone through four sitters in a year."

"Why so many?"

"Sarah was autistic. She had a hard time interacting with people, even her parents and especially

198

babysitters. But she loved the Disney movie *The Little Mermaid*. She watched it over and over. Whenever anyone turned it off she'd throw a tantrum.

"So, I had this idea. Kind of crazy," she said, rolling her eyes to emphasize just how crazy. "I bought this cheap mermaid tail on discount at a Halloween store. It was pretty terrible. Nothing like a real tail, just this tight, horrible, shiny green skirt with a purple bodice that had a bunch of seashells sewn to it. Really tacky.

"I felt like a total idiot when Mrs. Meisner opened the door for my interview, but Sarah turned away from the television and said, 'Do you know Ariel?'"

Hal laughed. "What did you say?"

Avery smiled and, for the first time since he'd met her, it looked like she actually meant it.

"I just went with it. I said, 'Oh, sure. We're old friends. Would you like to hear about the time we were swimming with a school of porpoises and got caught in a tuna net?'"

"Next thing I knew, Sarah turned off the television—which was a very big deal—and sat down next to me to listen to the story. Mrs. Meisner started to cry and I got the job."

"That's great," Hal said. "So you took a chance and it worked out."

"Oh, I don't know. I think it was just more of an . . ." She shrugged. "I don't know."

She started to reach for her curls once again. Hal touched her on the elbow and Avery clutched her hands together tight in her lap, as if she were afraid they might suddenly fly off her wrists.

It took some time, but eventually he teased out the rest of Avery's story, how she came to adore little Sarah Meisner and to be adored in return. But what Sarah loved most were Avery's stories. If she became belligerent or started to throw a tantrum, all Avery had to say was, "Well, I guess you're too upset to listen to a story today," and the girl would calm down. Over time, Sarah's ability to connect with other people improved. So did Avery's storytelling skills. Parents in the neighborhood started hiring her to entertain at birthday parties. And that was how Avery Promise became Avery Poseidon, Part-Time Mermaid.

It was a neat story. But considering she was the sister who supposedly possessed a gift for words, she had a hard time explaining it. Avery was a nice enough and very pretty young woman, but overall, she seemed unremarkable to Hal and pretty inarticulate.

He asked her what she thought it was about mermaids that captured the imagination of so many people, even adults, including herself, but she couldn't seem to come up with any straight-forward answer and kept stumbling over the response.

The second time she said, "I'm sorry. I'm not

explaining this very well," Hal interrupted her.

"Don't worry about it. Let's try something different. Why don't we film you getting into your mermaid costume? That might be a good place to start."

"It's not a costume," Avery corrected. "It's a persona."

It was such an unexpectedly definitive response, delivered in such a haughty and almost pretentious tone that Hal had to fight to keep from rolling his eyes.

Ten minutes later, he understood what she was talking about.

Avery tapped a makeup brush into a pot of loose, sparkly pink powder and swept it across her eyelids and then her cheekbones before dipping her fingers into another jar filled with a substance that had the texture of sand but the shimmer of glitter. She sprinkled it sparsely over her hair, then moved her head left and right, observing the effect. Light sparkled on her hair like the sun on the surface of a wind-swept sea.

She twisted her body around, the mirror behind her now, and slid her hands very slowly down the shiny blue-green length of her mermaid tail, then lifted her head and smiled straight at Hal.

"I'm ready."

"Don't look at the camera," he said. "Forget we're here and just be yourself. It'll be easier after a couple of days, but it's going to feel weird at first."

Avery's smile softened into an expression that was sensuous and knowing. She lifted her arm, arching it above her head with a movement that was almost balletic.

"Oh, I don't know about that," she murmured, sweeping her auburn mane over her shoulder, then looking at him through the fringe of her lashes. "I can think of worse things than being followed around by you."

Her voice had changed. It was lower, but almost lilting, like the deepest notes on a flute. Her demeanor changed too. Avery was confident, in control.

She fixed him with her eyes for a moment, then raised and lowered her knees, flipping her tail fin with an undulating, sinuous movement before reaching for a pearlescent-colored comb and brushing it through her shining hair, humming to herself in a low and longing vibrato.

Avery wasn't quite young enough to be Hal's daughter, but was close enough so he'd felt no attraction to her; that wasn't his thing. But looking at her, hearing her voice, he experienced a physical stirring that took him by surprise. At the same moment, he felt the hair on the back of his arms stand up. Both signs of danger.

He stepped behind Brian and peered over his shoulder and into the viewfinder, not because he needed to check the shot, but because he felt the need to put some distance between himself and Avery.

She let out a low laugh.

"Do you feel safer there? Standing behind your friend?" Her voice was hushed, almost a whisper, like she was sharing a secret. "You're right to be afraid. Mermaids have a deservedly dangerous reputation. The stories of sailors lured to watery graves by songs of the Siren are legion."

Ignoring what he'd told her, looking directly into the lens of the camera as if she were gazing into the eyes of someone she knew well, Avery told the story of one such ill-fated seaman, a tale of unobtainable desire, tragic consequence, and destiny, the inborn weaknesses that lead us to make the choices that leave us no choice.

It was a compelling story, but what was more compelling was how she told it.

Avery was a dancer. She used her hands and arms to heighten the drama, choosing just the right gesture, movements that seemed simultaneously choreographed and completely natural. She was a Kabuki. Her eyes widened with delight, narrowed in suspicion, hooded with desire. She was a musician. Her voice was her instrument, rising and falling like a wave, calm one moment and tormented the next, yet always under her control. She was a composer and conductor, knowing what she wanted the listener to feel, when she wanted them to feel it, and how to make certain they did.

She's an artist, Hal thought.

Not like any artist he'd ever seen before, but there was something undeniable about her. She held him completely in her thrall, riveted. What she'd said before was true; Avery Promise didn't put on a costume, she put on a persona. She inhabited it.

Wouldn't it be something if Minerva was right?

Just a few hours before, Hal had been certain he knew what this movie was about. Now he wasn't so sure.

The story ended. The sailor drowned beneath the depths. The mermaid returned to the surface, singing her song again, searching the horizon for sails.

Avery lowered her eyes slowly from the camera lens, drawing the curtain between herself and the audience. She turned back to the mirror.

"You should go now," she said, her words a warning as well as a command.

Chapter 22

After the film crew left, Meg sat down on a stool at the kitchen counter of the tiny house, started drawing, and didn't stop for hours. She sketched a bird, a car with a crumpled hood, an all-seeing eye, a bottle of pills, a man standing in profile wearing a hat that obscured his features, a baby swaddled in blankets, two ducks standing at the edge of a pond, an envelope, a garden gate that stood ajar, a clutch of daffodils in bloom, and filled the spaces between with abstract patterns of squiggles and squares, bubbles and pebbles, filling the paper from edge to edge.

This was something she'd started doing while she was still in the hospital and did more frequently since she'd left; it calmed her. When there was no more white space on the paper, she crumpled it tight in her fist and threw it away. That was the most calming part of all.

Meg tore the paper from the pad and was about to crush it into a fist-sized ball when someone knocked at the door. She looked through the front window of the tiny house and saw Trina standing on the stoop.

"Hi. Dad thought you might want to come over for dinner?" The tenor of her tone lifted a little at the end of the sentence, turning a statement into a question. She glanced at the paper Meg held in her hand. "But . . . maybe you're working?"

Meg smiled. "Furthest thing from it."

"Oh. Well. Dad's making tacos."

Meg's plan for the evening had been scrambled eggs, a shower, and maybe a book—assuming she could manage to stay awake long enough to read. The interview with Hal was more tiring than she'd expected. Being the guest of honor at a taco dinner with the family she didn't remember would doubt-less be more so. But how could she say no?

"I'll put on my shoes."

Meg sat down on the window seat to put on her tennis shoes. Trina peered through the doorway before stepping tentatively over the threshold.

"It's just like Aunt Avery's. Without the beach theme."

"At least she has a theme. I haven't gotten around to decorating yet. But I was thinking about wallpaper." Her comment was greeted by silence and Meg looked up from tying her shoes, surprised by the stormy expression on Trina's face.

"So you're going to stay out here? You're not moving back in with us?"

"Oh, Trina . . . I'm sorry. I was just joking around."

"So you *are* moving back in. When?"

"I don't know. I don't know what I'm going to do. Or when I'm going to do it. This must be really weird for you. It's weird for me too."

"Well . . . Maybe it would be less weird if you just moved back home and tried to act normal." Her tone was practical rather than accusing. "That's what you always tell me to do when I'm in a bad mood or something—pretend I'm not. 'Act as if and pretty soon you won't be acting.' "

"Does it work?"

A smile tugged at Trina's lips. "No, it's actually pretty stupid advice."

"Sounds like it."

"It's because of Dad. You don't want to have sex with him, right?"

Meg's jaw went slack. She wasn't prepared for the intimate nature of Trina's question, or the whiplash swing of the girl's emotional responses. Meg paused, trying to figure out how or even if she ought to respond, finally deciding that she had to.

"It's not that I don't like your father; it's just that I don't know him. And sleeping in the same bed . . ." She waited, hoping the girl wasn't going to make her spell it out. Trina just stared.

"It would be really weird. Even weirder than this," Meg said, spreading her hand to encompass the tiny and separate house. "And, yes, it is about sex. At least partly. You wouldn't want to go to bed with someone you didn't know, would you?"

"The way things are going, I'll never have a chance to find out. I can't even get a date to the spring formal."

Meg felt her lips bow into a smile; she couldn't help it. The girl was a bundle of contradictions, joking one minute, serious the next, deeply concerned about her family and, in the next breath, thinking only about herself.

"But I thought you were going. Joanie's making you a dress."

"I'm going. With my cousin." Trina slumped into the chair across from Meg.

"Walt seems like a nice guy."

"My cousin," Trina repeated slowly, as if Meg hadn't quite understood her the first time. "Even if he wasn't, Walt's idea of a fun weekend is hanging out with a bunch of fifty-year-old men who are dressed up like the cast of *Gone With the Wind* and reenacting the Battle of Gettysburg. The only good thing about having Walt for a cousin is that it means I'm not the biggest nerd in this family."

"So, you're going with him because . . ."

"Because I just have to go!" She grabbed a throw pillow and hugged it to her chest. "They're going to have this amazing indie band, Quartz Collective. They're *super* famous. And the only reason they're coming is because the lead guitarist is Stephanie Zinmeister's cousin. Why can't I have a cousin like *that?*" she moaned. "Somebody famous and cool? But, no. I've got Walt. The only thing worse than going to the formal with Walt is not going at all. I think. I might turn out to be wrong about that."

She pushed her face into the pillow, screamed her frustration, and then lowered it and started talking again.

"If I go with Walt, everybody is going to know I couldn't get a real date. But if I stay home, I'll have to spend the whole rest of the year listening about how great it was, and listening to them make jokes about how I stayed home and spent the night with my telescope, staring at the Cassiopeia constellation instead of dancing to the best indie rock band in Seattle."

Trina threw out her arms and flopped back into the chair, limp as a rag doll. Meg felt pretty certain this was her cue to say something.

"Personally, I think looking at constellations sounds like a fabulous way to spend an evening."

Trina glowered at her.

"Okay, maybe not. And going by yourself isn't an option?" More glowering. "Well, then, I say you go to the prom with Walt, wear a pretty dress, dance to the best band in Seattle, and make up your mind to have a really great time."

"That's all you've got? Act as if?"

"That's it. Sorry."

"Okay." Trina heaved another dramatic sigh and got to her feet. "Are you ready? Dad's tacos are super spicy. He uses a ton of chipotle chili powder."

"Thanks for the warning."

Meg grabbed the pencil sketch from where she'd left it on the window seat, stood up, and started to crumple the paper in her hand.

"Hang on! Can I see it?"

Meg handed over the paper. Trina examined it carefully.

"Cool. What does it mean?"

"It's just doodling. It doesn't mean anything."

"So, why did you draw it? You've got two ducks here and a prescription bottle here. They don't relate somehow? And who is the guy in the hat? Why is his face hidden?"

"I don't know. I started drawing and that was what came out. It's just something I do to relax."

Trina didn't look convinced.

"I read this book on Jungian dream theory . . ."

Meg's eyebrows shot up. Sixteen years old and she was reading Jung?

"For a class?"

"No, just for fun." Trina looked down at the floor for a moment. "Don't tell anybody. Anyway, Jung says that dreams are how we try to communicate with the unconscious and that everything in them means something, no matter how weird or unrealistic it might seem once you wake up. He said that dreams are like clues that the unconscious mind gives to the conscious mind to help it find the solution to a problem.

"It's kind of like when you go on a scavenger hunt and you have to solve these really ridiculous riddles so you can figure out where it is you're supposed to go. I said that part, not Jung," she explained. "But see what I mean? Maybe, instead of dreaming, you draw."

"Maybe."

Meg smiled to herself, thinking what a brilliant and very strange girl Trina was. A child-woman who knew all about brown dwarfs, constellations, and Carl Jung, but had yet to master the basics of male-female relations.

Meg liked Trina a lot. She could see that, when she put her mind to it, the girl could be a major league pain in the butt, but she liked her anyway, liked the way she wore her heart on her sleeve and wasn't afraid to ask questions.

"So you think I should save it?"

"Definitely. Besides, it looks cool," Trina said, and handed the paper back to Meg. "Is it nice, living here by yourself? Having a space that's just yours?"

"It is," Meg admitted. "But it's lonely too. Hey, should we go? I'm getting hungry."

Trina nodded and walked ahead of her. When they reached the doorway, she turned to face Meg.

"Mom?"

The sound of the word, applied to her, together with the look in Trina's eyes, pulled her up short, hitting her with something akin to a jolt of static electricity—not painful, but surprising and momentarily disorienting.

"Yes?"

"Can I come out here sometimes? Just to see you, I mean?"

Meg looked into the face of the woman-child, *her* child, who hadn't yet learned to hide her feelings or her fears, and felt something crack inside her.

"Sure. Anytime you want."

• • •

Entering through the back door, they were greeted by the sound of rattling of pots and pans and Asher grumbling about a missing box grater and people not putting things away where they belonged.

Trina called out, "We're here!" and let the screen door slam. Asher emerged from the kitchen, wiping his hands on a towel printed with a picture of a rooster.

"Hey! Come on in! I was beginning to wonder what happened. Hungry? Shouldn't be too much longer; the taco fillings are all ready."

"It smells good," Meg said.

Trina went into the kitchen and lifted the smaller of two skillets that were sitting on the stove. "Is this one mine? No meat, right?"

"Soy chorizo and black beans."

Asher looked over his shoulder while addressing his daughter, giving Meg a good look at the ponytail that hung to the middle of his shoulder blades. A lot of men were wearing ponytails, she'd noticed, but most of them looked scrawny or scraggly or, worst of all, dirty. But long hair looked good on Asher. So did the beard, heavier on the chin, but carefully trimmed, fading to stubble along his jawline.

Asher turned back toward her. Meg's eyes shifted reflexively from his face, embarrassed to be caught studying him so closely, but he didn't seem to notice.

"Last week she decided to go vegan," Asher informed her in a conspiratorial tone. "We'll see how long it lasts. Two months ago, it was raw food."

"I heard that!" Trina called out, putting the lid back onto the skillet. "The only reason I gave up raw food is there was *nothing* I could eat at school."

"They have a salad bar," Asher reminded her.

Trina put her hand on her hip. "Iceberg lettuce, shredded carrots, radish roses, and croutons. That's it. Can we eat now?"

"Hang on. I want to give Mom her welcome home present first."

As surprised as she was to hear herself referred to as Mom once again, this time by Asher, she was twice as surprised to hear that he'd gotten her a gift. He swept his hand toward a corner of the dining/office alcove and a large object covered with a light tan sheet.

Meg looked at Asher with a confused half smile. "What is it?"

"Go see."

He followed her into the alcove and Trina came close behind, bounding across the room like an excited puppy, taking up a place next to her father and grabbing his hand.

"Go ahead!" she urged.

Meg reached up and tugged. The sheet slid down and pooled onto the floor, revealing a wooden easel with brass fittings, a thick tripod of adjustable legs, a slim adjustable mast to hold the canvas, and a thicker wooden ledge on which to rest brushes or paints. It smelled clean, like new wood shavings, and had a rich, dull sheen to it. Someone had rubbed it with oil to bring out the reddish tint of the wood.

Meg reached out, slid her hand down the mast and across the brush ledge, feeling the smooth texture beneath her fingers.

"I wanted to have it ready when you came home from the hospital, but it took a little longer than I thought. Work's been kind of backed up."

"You made this?"

Asher smiled a little and shrugged. He was clearly proud of his handiwork, but not the sort of person to say so. He didn't have to; the quality of his work spoke for itself.

"It's beautiful."

"I used solid oak," he said matter-of-factly. "Should last a lifetime. And I rubbed in a little bit of oil-based stain, just a single coat, to bring out the color. Now that you've started drawing again, I just thought you might be ready to give painting another try."

"We got you some painting stuff, too," Trina reported. She ducked down and pulled a cardboard box out from beneath the easel.

Meg knelt down and lifted the lid. Inside, she found watercolor, acrylic, and oil paints, a mixing palette, a dozen paintbrushes of varying size and styles, and all kinds of other tools and supplies, everything an artist could possibly need.

The painting supplies were wonderful, but the easel . . . She lifted her eyes to look at it again. Asher must have spent hours on it, and at a time when she knew he was trying to catch up on the work he'd missed during her illness. How had he found the time?

She remembered the whirring sound of power tools coming from his garage workshop long after dark and the light that shone through the back window and into her own bedroom window, making it hard for her to fall asleep or stay asleep. She remembered waking up to the sound of hammering at one in the morning and feeling annoyed at his lack of consideration for others. And all the time, after a full day of physical labor, he'd been working into the wee hours, making her this gift.

Asher was many things, she was sure. Inconsiderate wasn't one of them. What else could be said of her husband? Looking at him and seeing the way he looked at her, she realized that she wanted to find out.

"Thank you. I . . . I don't know what else to say."

"You don't have to say anything," he said, and held out his hand. She grabbed hold and he helped her up from the floor.

"Can we eat now?" Trina asked.

"Sure," Asher said, smiling again, his voice hardy. "Treenie-Bean, you start heating up the tortillas. I'll finish getting the toppings ready."

"What can I do?" Meg asked him.

"Nothing. Just sit down and relax."

"I want to help. At least let me set the table."

The three of them headed off to the kitchen. The space was tight, but the layout was efficient and they moved past and around one another without colliding, falling easily into the work without need of conversation or instruction.

Asher cut two avocados in half, scooped the soft green flesh into a bowl, and mashed it with the back of a fork. Trina took a packet of flour tortillas from the refrigerator and started heating them in a skillet. Meg opened a drawer to the right of the dishwasher, took out forks, knives, salad tongs, and serving spoons, then opened a lower drawer for napkins, carried them to the table, and set three places. Returning to the kitchen, she opened a cupboard to the left of the refrigerator and took out water glasses from the lower shelf and plates from the upper.

Asher was squatted down near the floor, rifling through the lower cupboards.

"Where is the grater? I can't find it anywhere."

Trina slid a platter of tortillas into the oven to stay warm. "Don't look at me."

"I can't shred the cheese without it. Why can't people just put things—"

Meg opened the second drawer under the stovetop, reached far into the back, pulled out a stainless-steel box grater, and set it on the counter. Asher hopped to his feet like he had springs in his calves and gave her a strange look.

"How did you know where to find that?" He looked toward the alcove and the neatly set table. "And the dishes? How did you know where those were?"

"I don't know. I just . . . knew."

Meg knew only a few things about Asher: He was considerate, valued deeds above words, family above all, and smiled easily. Now he smiled wider than ever before. Seeing his happiness, she smiled, too, feeling that she had in some small way returned the gift of his kindness.

They sat down at the table. Trina reached automatically for Meg's left hand. Asher took her right. Meg gave Asher a look, wondering what this was all about.

"I know," he said, giving her a goofy smile as if he realized that this must look a little ridiculous to her. "But when you were in the hospital and we didn't know if you would wake up or if . . . I didn't know what to do, Meg. There wasn't anything I *could* do except pray, for the first time in years, since my dad threw me out. And I was pretty rusty, I've got to tell you. All I could really come up with was, 'Please. Please, God. Let her stay.' And here you are." His voice hoarse even though he was smiling. "And I am so, so grateful. So grateful for everything."

He squeezed her hand and lowered his head. Meg did the same as Asher recited:

For food and health and happy days,
Receive our gratitude and praise,
In serving others Lord may we,
Repay our debt of love to thee.

Once again, Meg just knew. This was her home, the place she belonged.

The meal commenced. Trina grabbed the tacos, took two for herself, and passed the platter. Asher handed Meg the guacamole. "Should I have invited your sisters?"

"No, not tonight," she said. "It's nice with just the three of us. Just the family."

Chapter 23

Coming to the end of a curve that had to be precisely sewn so the bodice of the gown would lie smooth, Joanie snipped the emerald green threads that matched the emerald taffeta and examined her work, smiling until she saw the too-tight threads on the back of the seam.

"Idiot! How could you forget to adjust the tension when you went from wool to taffeta?"

She grimaced and grabbed a seam ripper, slicing the threads one by one, careful of the delicate material.

When Joanie fell into the rhythm of it, when the machine was humming and the needle flashed a silver streak through the layers of wool, satin, or silk, and the loose pieces of the pattern were coming together seam by seam into the garment she'd pictured in her mind, she found sewing satisfying and almost meditative. But doing it properly required tremendous focus. There was so much to think about.

She had to be aware of her tools and materials—the thickness or delicacy of the fabrics, the ease or difficulty with which they would feed into the machine, and how the different types and weights of thread and even the size of the needle would impact the finished product. She had to be aware of her body as well. Sewing on a machine with the tension set too loose or too tight could ruin the garment. And because she was, in some sense, an extension of the machine, the same was true of her physical tension.

She had to pay attention to her posture, the set of her shoulders, the way the fabric fed through her fingers, not too loose and not too tight, keeping it under her control even as she allowed it to slip from her grasp, becoming all that she'd planned and sometimes more than she'd hoped. She had to be in the moment mentally as well, clearing her mind of distraction and completely giving herself over to the process. And finally, while she was doing all that, she had to let go and let it happen. She had to trust herself.

In the broadest sense, sewing beautiful garments had much in common with playing beautiful music: Both required discipline as well as freedom. And a certain amount of faith.

The difference was that when she was sewing she made her mistakes in private and corrected them the same way. A snip of the scissors, a tug of the thread, a bit of re-sewing, and no one ever had to know she hadn't done it perfectly the first time. There was no audience looking on or listening in, no teacher to judge, no mother to disappoint. Small wonder Joanie had taken to sewing so naturally and enjoyed it so thoroughly.

But now she did have an audience, Hal Seeger and his crew. And not only were they watching her, judging her, they were recording her words, actions, and answers so that other people, strangers in untold numbers, could do the same, putting every part of her under a microscope. Why, oh why, had she agreed to this?

For Meg. And for Asher. Because they need you. Because you owe it to them. So suck it up and quit being so selfish.

As Joanie ripped out the last of the stitches, she heard Avery's voice coming from the kitchen, calling her name.

"In here!"

A moment later, Avery was standing in the doorway. "Hey. How'd you like your first day as a movie star? Wasn't that cool!"

Joanie glanced up and then continued placing silk pins into the bodice pieces, making sure the two curves matched perfectly. "I guess that's one way of putting it."

"I gave them my full-on mermaid," Avery enthused. "You should have seen the looks on their faces. Hal actually cowered behind the camera guy. I think I scared him."

"See if you can scare him enough so he'll pack up and go back to LA."

"Didn't you have fun? I thought it was cool."

"I thought it was a waste of time."

Avery's eyes scanned Joanie's usually tidy sewing room, taking in the piles of fabric, pattern pieces, and projects in progress. "Sorry. You want me to come back later?"

"It's okay. I don't mind you. I just mind *them*."

"Are you sure? I want to make a mermaid tail, a kid-sized one. Lilly's really started to cheer up since I've been visiting and I thought it would be fun to surprise her."

Joanie smiled. "I've never sewn scales, but they can't be any harder than this bodice. Do you have a pattern?"

Avery bounded into the room. "Sort of. It won't be a swimming tail, nothing complicated. It's just so she can play dress up." Avery unfolded a piece of paper and pointed to a drawing she'd made of a tail with rows of multicolored scales, shaped like Us and layered one upon the other, like shingles on a roof.

"I was thinking I could use scraps from your ball gowns, sew them onto some kind of lining, and then stitch the two halves together."

Joanie examined the sketch. "Muslin would work for the lining. You can sew the scales right onto it. But make the fin separate from the tail and then sew them together. It'll lay better. Elastic to the waist will make it easier to get in and out of."

"So you'll do it?"

"*You'll* do it," Joanie clarified. "I don't have time. But I'll help you. It shouldn't be that hard. The scraps are under the table."

"Thanks!"

Avery took a big plastic bin from under the sewing table, sat down cross-legged on the floor, and started sorting through scraps, setting aside bits of taffeta, satin, damask, and brocade, anything that was colorful and silky, humming while she worked.

Avery had always done that, hummed to herself. Joanie remembered how, when Avery was hardly more than a toddler with ginger-colored ringlets lying on her round baby cheeks, she would stand at the door while Joanie was studying, observing her with wide and silent eyes, then take her thumb from her mouth and say, "You lonely. Want me stay with you?" And then, without waiting for an answer, walk into the room and flop down on the rug.

The strange part was that Avery only appeared when Joanie really *was* feeling lonely. Even then, she had a great sensitivity about what people needed and what it took to make them happy. Unfortunately, she was less insightful about her own needs. Avery always made a big show of living "in the moment," free from the restrictions of every sort of commitment. But Joanie knew her easygoing ways had as much to do with fear as freedom. It's hard to be disappointed, or hurt, if you never allowed yourself to care in the first place.

And now, at long last, it seemed like Avery was willing to make a commitment, at least a small one. She went to the hospital twice a week and couldn't stop talking about Lilly and the rest of the kids. That part seemed like a good idea. Joanie was less convinced about the fact that, after her visits to the hospital, Avery never came home until the next morning.

"I need more blue. Something bright." Avery frowned and examined her pile of scraps. "Can I have some of that?"

She pointed toward a sky-blue polyester crepe that was sitting on the sewing table. Joanie shook her head.

"That's for Trina's prom dress. I'm going to need all of it. Try some of this." She balled up a piece of emerald green satin and tossed it to Avery.

"Pretty. Thanks. Hey, where's Walt?"

"Upstairs studying. He's got this sadistic teacher for AP Economics who likes to assign big papers at the last minute." Joanie laid a towel over the green bodice piece and pressed it carefully, using just a touch of steam. "Ten pages on the aggregate demand curve, with footnotes and graphs, by Thursday morning."

"Aggregate demand curve? What does that even mean?"

"No clue. But Walt knows."

"It's kind of funny, isn't it? Minerva went to so much trouble to find just the right sperm donors to birth and raise genius children. You and Meg just bed down with the first studmuffins who come through the door and boom! Brilliant babies."

Joanie shot her a look.

"Sorry. I didn't mean for that to come out like it sounded. But it is weird, isn't it? That you both produced genius kids practically by accident?"

"Walt is not a genius." Joanie got up from the sewing machine and placed the bodice onto a curvaceous dress form that stood in the corner. It fit perfectly.

Avery gave her a "sure he's not" look.

"Aggregate. Demand. Curve," she repeated.

"Not to mention that he's acing three AP courses. Then there's Trina, with her computer mapping of brown dwarves, whatever that means. The way things are going, she'll be able to skip college and go straight into the astronaut training program."

"Okay, fine. They're both smart, very smart. But let's not slap them with the G-word. It leads nowhere good."

"I'm just saying—what are the chances? Kind of makes you wonder about the whole nature versus nurture argument, doesn't it?" Avery grabbed a pair of scissors off a nearby table and started cutting the emerald satin into U-shaped scales. "I mean, maybe none of that matters. Maybe it's attraction that counts, lust and passion and pure animal instinct. Maybe that's the way to go."

Joanie turned around to look at her little sister. She didn't like the way this conversation was headed or the expression on Avery's face. She looked . . . practical, as if she was weighing her options. She couldn't ever recall Avery looking like that before. What was going on between her and Owen?

Avery put down the scissors. "Did you love Walt's father?"

"I've told you before, it was nothing, a hookup. A stupid mistake."

"You don't think Walt was a mistake, do you?"

"Walt was a gift. But that doesn't mean I wasn't stupid. And wrong."

"You didn't answer my question—did you love him?"

Joanie turned back toward the dress form, gazing at a spot on the wall beyond the headless torso.

"He wasn't mine to love."

"He was married? You never told me that!"

"Not married. But not mine. I didn't know at the time, but that's no excuse."

She pushed a pin through a spot of emerald green, deep into the shoulder of the dress dummy, and turned to face Avery again. "Are you going to the hospital today?"

"Yes. In fact, I need to get going," she replied, gathering up the fabric and getting to her feet. "Owen is working until seven so I decided to go in later. That way I don't have to wait so long."

Joanie pressed her lips together, nodded. "Listen . . . I'm the last person in the world who can sit in judgment or tell you what to do—"

Avery raised her hands, cutting her off. "I know what you're going to say, but it's okay. It is. Owen is a great guy."

"You've only known him a few weeks."

"I know. But you should see the way the kids look up to him, Lilly too. He's like a hero to them."

"I just don't want you to get hurt."

"I won't," she said, the confidence of her tone making a promise of her words.

Joanie sighed. How could she make her sister understand? Looking at Avery's face, she realized she couldn't. Some lessons you have to learn for yourself.

Joanie finished the bodice, made dinner, and brought a tray up to Walt's bedroom. He was hunched over his desk, working on his paper.

"Why don't you take a break and eat something?"

He looked up, blinking, so absorbed in his work that it took a moment for her words and the smell of seasoned beef and melting cheese to penetrate his brain.

"Enchiladas?" His face brightened. "You said we were having salmon."

"Well. You're working so hard. I can always start my diet next week."

She put the plate down on his desk, gratified to see his scowl disappear and the way he fell onto his food. Walt was so easy to please. Was that just a boy thing or did he simply possess a gift for happiness? Either way, making him happy made her happy too.

She ruffled his hair and nodded toward his laptop. "How's it coming?"

"Meh." He shrugged. "I'll be so happy not to have Mr. McKnight next year."

At that moment, Joanie wasn't too crazy about

Mr. McKnight either. She hated watching TV by herself. But she'd have to get used to it—two more years and he'd be gone.

Walt shoved nearly half an enchilada into his mouth and went back to the computer, tapping the keyboard while he chewed.

"Well," she said after watching him for a minute. "Guess I'll leave you to it. *NCIS* starts in half an hour, you know. Just in case you finish up in time."

"Uh-huh." He hit delete several times, staring at the screen. "Sounds good."

She did watch TV for a bit, stitching buttons and officer's insignia on the jackets of blue and gray uniforms while investigators from *NCIS* tried to clear a sailor wrongly charged with a crime.

Normally, doing handwork helped her focus, but not tonight. She felt so unsettled that she accidentally sewed a Union Army major's insignia onto the shoulders of a Confederate jacket. Finally, she gave up, switched off the TV, and went to the sewing room, knowing she wouldn't be able to sleep until she dealt with the thing that was bothering her, that had been bothering her all day.

She switched on the overhead light. There it was, the envelope Hal had given her. She carried it back to the living room, pulled out the CD, and slid the flat silver disc into the slot of her stereo and pushed play. Perched on the armrest of the sofa, leaning in, she listened to her twelve-year-old self play the Liebestraum No. 3.

It began softly, as softly as an echo in a far-off canyon, so faint that it was hard to be certain if you truly heard something or if the notes might be a musical mirage. And then, at the moment when it seemed it must be so, that you'd imagined the sound and there was no music, only the memory of something lost and found and lost again, the soft phrases swelled and burst into something precious and lovely, petals unfurling in pink and purple glory.

Joanie closed her eyes and lifted her hands. Her fingers curved, an almost involuntary reflex, and began traveling up and down an imaginary keyboard, fingertips pressing and lifting and floating as she played spectral arpeggios. Tears seeped out from beneath her closed eyelids.

This was it, the music that had changed all of their lives. And it was so beautiful, so achingly beautiful. In all this lonely and weary world, she had forgotten there was such beauty to be had. She had made herself forget because remembering what she'd had and lost hurt too much.

She felt a presence in the room, someone watching her, and opened her eyes to find Walt standing in the doorway. She hadn't heard him come downstairs, his elephant feet treading softly for once.

"That was you, wasn't it? Mom, you were so good. Why did you stop playing?"

There were a dozen reasons she could have given him, none of them quite complete, but each valid in its own way. She could have rattled off the list easily because she'd been rehearsing them all day, thinking about how she would answer the question when Hal asked it, as he inevitably would.

Prior to the release of *The Promise Girls*, the publishing house hired a media coach to prep them all for television interviews. Karen, a thin brunette, had eyes that always looked distant, even when she was smiling.

"Unbiased journalists are mythical creatures, like unicorns or the Tooth Fairy. Before their first question, they've already decided on their story angle, the more sensational the better. So you've got to beat them at their own game. Decide ahead of time how you want to appear to the public and stick to that. No matter what questions they ask, stick to your script. Remember: You can't trust a guy with a camera. Ever."

As far as Joanie was concerned, Hal Seeger was just another guy with a camera. But Walt was her son and she owed him the truth.

"I was good. But not great and I never would be." Joanie tilted her head toward the stereo as the final notes of the piece faded away, a dream of love that ended in silence.

"That's why I stopped playing, because that was all I had, my peak. It took me years to figure that out. But the truth is, at twelve years old, I was the best I was ever going to be. And that wasn't good enough."

Chapter 24

Sunlight crawled over the windowsill and caught the sequins of Avery's mermaid tail, lying crumpled in the corner on the floor of Owen's studio apartment in the busiest section of Capitol Hill, a place where counterculture thrived and Seattle's youngest, hippest inhabitants gathered in bars, pubs, and clubs at night and in coffeehouses, bookstores, and boutiques during the day. A garbage truck drove up the street and stopped under the apartment window. The rumble and crash of the truck and the shouted conversation of the trash collectors, as well as the sound of water rushing from the bathroom faucet and the *boom-chick-hiss* of Owen beat boxing to himself while he was shaving, made Avery stir in her sleep.

She pointed her toes and extended her arms, stretching, blinking to get her bearings, then pulled Owen's pillow from the tangle of sheets and clutched it close, anxious about the day to come.

In the previous two weeks, she'd filled out more

than twenty online job applications. She'd gotten two phone interviews for her efforts, but no offers. Today she was going to try going door-to-door through Capitol Hill's commercial district to fill out applications in person, giving potential employers the chance to reject her to her face rather than via the anonymity of the Internet.

And in case that wasn't humiliating enough, Hal and the crew would be trailing along, capturing it all on film.

For a while, being followed around by a camera crew had been kind of glamorous. She imagined herself as a movie star with an entourage, a starlet pursued by a pack of paparazzi. But maintaining that illusion was harder when the camera was recording the day-to-day events, or small failures, of her oh-so-ordinary life.

He documented their every move. There was Meg sitting at her new easel outside her tiny house, painting in plein air and stealing glances at Asher who was sawing boards outside his workshop. There was Joanie working, always working, stitching Union blue and Confederate gray uniforms on her sewing machine, baking bread or cookies, saying she made them only for Walt but consuming at least a third of them herself, trimming shrubs and pulling weeds, wearing a straw hat with an eight-inch brim. The hat was new. Avery thought she had bought it just to make it harder for the camera to see her face.

And of course he filmed Avery, as a mermaid, but also as herself, hand-sewing silk scales to the mermaid tail she was making to celebrate Lilly's upcoming release from the hospital, filling out applications for jobs she never got. . . . Sometimes he filmed her just sitting on the window seat in her house, twirling her hair around her finger, staring out the window, doing absolutely nothing.

The crew came along for the more interesting stuff, too, like when she went to the hospital to read to the kids and when Owen got the idea of taking her to Volunteer Park for a picnic/photo shoot.

It was a beautiful, sunny day and the park was full. Avery was in costume so even while they were sitting quietly on the grass, eating cheese and crackers and drinking hard cider, they'd drawn more than a few curious glances. When lunch was over, Owen got out his camera and started snapping pictures, telling her how to pose, speaking with a very bad French accent.

He was just being goofy; no one who actually heard him speak could seriously have believed Owen was a real photographer, but when Hal and the crew moved in closer to get a good shot of Owen trying to get a good shot of her, a crowd gathered and gawked, thinking she must be "somebody."

After Owen finished taking his pictures, people who had been watching wanted to do the same.

Avery posed for at least forty photos. She enjoyed it. On camera or off, being a mermaid was easy. Being a human came harder.

The longer Hal and the crew followed her, the more she realized that her life didn't add up to anything meaningful to her. Avery started to think about how moviegoers would see her—like a loser, somebody who had to invent an alternate reality in order to appear even marginally interesting.

And now, to confirm their suspicions, they'd watch as a twenty-year-old assistant manager in a clothing boutique told Avery she was under-qualified to sell T-shirts.

Avery buried her face in Owen's pillow, shouted into the polyester and foam depths to muffle the sound. The bathroom door opened. Owen, shirt-less but wearing a pair of blue surgical pants, stepped out of a cloud of steam, rubbing his wet hair with a towel.

"You're yelling again?" he asked. "Why?"

"Again? When was I yelling before?"

Owen sat on the edge of the bed. He looked tired, really tired. And annoyed? But maybe not. Maybe she was reading too much into his expression.

"Last night. You were yelling in your sleep. You don't remember?"

"Uh-uh."

"Well, you were."

The way that he said it confirmed her suspicions. He was definitely annoyed with her.

Owen pulled on a blue scrub shirt. Avery sat up, swung her legs out over the side of the bed, and reached down for the paper grocery bag that held her things.

After that first intimate encounter, she'd learned to bring a change of clothes along whenever she visited the children's ward. It was one thing to have Owen pick her up and drive her to the hospital in costume and another thing entirely to slink home in loose sequins, tangled hair, and no makeup.

Now the paper bag suitcase just seemed like a symbol of everything about her relationship with Owen as it stood now—something temporary and easily tossed away.

After that first fabulous night, a night so magical that it met and exceeded any fantasies she had ever had about what romance could or should be, she'd invented a new fantasy. This one was far more ordinary, a dream of sharing a bed and life permanently, about knowing somebody so intimately that you could talk about anything in the world or nothing at all, about being completely accepted by someone else and being real for him and there for him, no matter what, and knowing that he would always be there for you, just the same way.

She was getting way ahead of herself, she knew

that. She'd only known him for a few weeks, and marriage . . . that was a big step, one she was miles from being ready to take. But maybe, in a few weeks or months, they might try moving in together? Even though Owen's apartment was a studio, it was big, probably three times the square footage of her tiny house.

But it was too soon for that.

She had been thinking about asking him if it'd be all right for her to leave a few of her things here, maybe claim one of the drawers in the dresser as her own. But seeing the way he yanked his scrub top down hard over his head, made her reconsider.

Avery pulled on a pair of jeans, careful to keep her back to him. It still felt a little weird, dressing in front of somebody else. Not that Owen was watching. He was always in a hurry in the morning.

He had a lot on his mind, thinking about his patients. She liked it that he cared about them. But it would have been nice if he could spend a little more time with her in the morning, lingering, just talking. They hardly knew each other. What would have been even more of a good thing would be for them to go out on a regular date, to the movies or dinner, and not always just tumble into bed together. But that would come soon enough, she told herself. And maybe she should just enjoy the passionate part while it lasted. She didn't want to lose it all by pushing for too much, too soon.

"Sorry about the yelling," she said. "There's this dream I have sometimes. About when the Children's Services people came and took me away. They came to the house and a lady was in my room, helping me pack a bag. She said that my mom needed a break and that my sisters and I needed to go stay somewhere else for a while. I wasn't too freaked out because there'd been some kind of investigation after the whole talk show thing and the police in Chicago let us fly home to LA together the next day. I thought that maybe this was just more of the same, that we'd be together after a couple days.

"But when we got out onto the street, there were three cars. I realized that I wasn't going with my sisters. I screamed. The social worker grabbed me and I started kicking and biting and screaming louder. Joanie was yelling for her to leave me alone, to let me go. But she didn't. She just shoved me in the car and slammed the door closed."

Owen was lacing up his tennis shoes. His head was down. He made a sound, something halfway between a sigh and a grunt. Avery couldn't tell what it meant.

"I used to have that dream all the time," she said. "But when I moved up here with Joanie, it stopped. I think it's all this stuff with the documentary that's bringing it back. Hal keeps asking questions, dredging up stuff I haven't thought about in a long time. Anyway," she said, and put her hand on his thigh, "I'm sorry I woke you up."

Owen stood up and walked across the room toward the little galley kitchen.

"Want some tea?"

"Sure. That'd be great."

He filled two mugs with water and put them in the microwave, then opened the refrigerator, took out two containers of yogurt, and handed one to Avery. They ate their breakfast standing in the kitchen, waiting for the tea.

"Looks like I'm going to have to trade in my tail for tennis shoes and find a real job," Avery said, trying to keep her voice light. "Mermaids just can't make it in the gig economy."

"What about the lady we met in the park? She wanted you to do her daughter's birthday party."

"She could only pay me fifty dollars." Avery shrugged and scraped the last bite of yogurt from the cup. "And the party's not until next month. I really do have to find a job soon. Like today. The starfish is empty."

"The starfish?"

"Never mind. Let's talk about something else."

Avery tossed the yogurt container into the trash and boosted herself up onto the counter, bare legs dangling off the edge.

"What are you doing over Memorial Day weekend? Joanie's throwing a barbecue to celebrate Meg and Asher's anniversary—she does it every year. The whole family will be together—

always entertaining," she added, smiling even as she rolled her eyes. "But it should be fun. And Joanie is a great cook. You want to come?"

"Whoa." Owen raised his hands and took a step back. Avery frowned.

"Whoa, what? What's that supposed to mean?"

"Just that . . ."

He took another step back and his butt bumped against the stove. Avery had the feeling that if he could have backed up farther he would have.

"Job troubles and money problems. Hearing you yell in your dreams and then listening to the story of how you were torn away from your family when you were little . . ."

"Yeah?"

"It's just a little too much reality for a Thursday morning, Avery."

"Too much reality? What's that supposed to mean? I'm just telling you about my life, Owen."

"I know. That's what I'm talking about. Look, Avery . . . I lost two patients this week. Two sweet little kids who didn't do anything to anybody. Ramona, a little girl I've been taking care of on and off for two years, died of cancer. Another one, a nine-month-old baby, died because his mom's boyfriend kicked him, broke three of his ribs, and shook him until his brain bled. I've got all the reality I can take right now."

Owen looked like he was going to say more, but didn't. Instead, he clenched his fist and drove it hard into his thigh, like he wished there was somebody around he could punch. Avery hopped off the counter and touched his arm.

"Hey," she said softly. "You saved a lot of lives too. Don't forget that. How many kids did you send home healthy last week? Thirty? Fifty? How many next week? Including Lilly. She'll be home in a few more days and happy, dealing with her disability and living her life, because you cared about her, *really* cared."

"I guess. But the thing is, Avery . . . you and me . . ."

He rubbed hard at his forehead, his expression determined, as if he'd made up his mind about something that had been bothering him.

"This isn't working. When I met you, I thought you were gorgeous, really a knockout. And smart too. Creative and sweet. But most of all, fun. You seemed so playful. Almost like one of the kids, you know? That's what attracted me to you.

"So many things I have to deal with every day are just so hard," he said in a voice that sounded almost surprised. "Cruel and hard. But you seemed to live in this fantasy world. That first time you came to the ward and did your thing for the kids? They believed you really were a mermaid. For a second, so did I. And it made me so happy, getting caught up in the story. And I wanted more of that. Just to have some fun. And we did. But the thing is . . ."

His words trailed away, as if he was suddenly embarrassed by what had been about to come out of his mouth. Avery finished the sentence for him.

"Then you woke up one day and figured out there was a real person in your bed. A woman. Not a fantasy. Somebody with a real life. With problems and a past."

"And expectations."

"What expectations? When did I ever say anything about expectations? All I did was ask if you wanted to come to a barbecue!"

"And get to know your family."

He gave her a look and Avery felt her cheeks color.

"That's way more than I'm looking for, Avery. I just thought we could have a good time together, that's all."

He reached for her hand, but she pulled back.

"So you brought me home and took me to bed?"

"Well, yeah. That was part of the fun, for both of us. Don't try to pretend it wasn't. Oh, come on. Don't look at me like that! It was just sex, Avery. It's not that big a deal."

"Not to you, maybe. I'm not like that."

"Like what?"

"Never mind." She walked back to the bed, started stuffing her things into the grocery bag. "It's my own fault. I should have listened to Joanie."

"Avery. Come on. Don't spoil it. We had fun

241

together, didn't we? And I like you. I really do."

She rolled up her mermaid tail and shoved it in the sack. Two of the sequins came loose and dropped onto the wooden floor. She didn't bother to pick them up.

"I like you, too. You're not a bad guy. Actually, you're a pretty good guy. But you're not my guy. Deep down, I think I knew that, but I tried not to. Like you said, I'm really good at pretending."

She walked to the door and he followed her.

"Avery. I didn't mean to hurt you."

"I believe you. But do you think that doing it by accident makes it hurt any less?"

Avery kept it together as she walked down the stairs and then around the block, in case Owen, or anyone else, might be watching from a window. But after she turned the corner, she ducked into the alley that ran between the rows of apartments. Her eyes began to fill and her shoulders started to shake. She gave herself over to it, the disappointment of dashed hopes, the embarrassment of being rejected, and vulnerable, and foolish, the fear that she was unlovable and that no one could ever understand or care for her.

She cried for a long time, shedding so many tears that she felt literally drained. But she cried rather than sobbed and in doing so began to wonder if her grief was less for Owen personally than for what he might have become.

Maybe. After all, she really didn't know Owen. But she'd gone to bed with him because she *wanted* to know him.

Why didn't he love her? What was wrong with her? Was there anyone out there who would ever be able to love her for who she was? Or was the cost of togetherness pretending to be something she wasn't? The way she'd been pretending with Owen?

She needed to talk to someone, sort out her feelings, and get a little sympathy. Even if she didn't deserve it. But it was too early to call her sisters.

Sniffling, Avery fished inside her purse and pulled out her cell phone. She knew she shouldn't call her. Look what happened last time. And if Joanie found out, she'd be furious. But still . . . she needed to talk.

After four rings a groggy-sounding voice came on the line.

"Hello?"

"Mom? It's me. Avery."

Chapter 25

Joanie couldn't keep from yawning as she pulled into Meg and Asher's driveway. She'd been up all night, sewing, far from the inquisitive gaze of Hal and his camera crew.

243

She hated the feeling of being constantly under surveillance. That was why she'd started working late at night, sometimes into the wee hours of the morning. To be fair, the previous night's stitching marathon wasn't really Hal's fault. She started working on Trina's dress for the formal and got so involved that she just kept going.

The dress Trina asked for was simple, strapless with a short skirt and a petticoat of blue tulle to make it flare. But around one in the morning, Joanie decided it was a little *too* simple. She added an inch-wide swath of rhinestone beading to the waistband and an overlay of blue peekaboo lace to the bodice, providing a stylish covering to the previously bare shoulders.

It was a darling dress. She couldn't wait to show it off. But since Avery hadn't come home last night—again—and since Walt had already left for school, Joanie hopped in the car and drove to Meg's. Maybe she would be up for a lunch date? It would be good to catch up. She'd been so busy with work she hadn't seen Meg or Asher all week.

Meg didn't answer when she knocked. Maybe she was in the shower? The house was unlocked. Joanie opened the door, calling for her sister, and gasped.

Paintings! There were dozens of them hanging on every wall from floor to ceiling. They were beautiful and unlike anything Meg had ever painted before. Joanie examined her sister's work with open-mouthed amazement.

Joanie could discern no patterns of subject or theme. Meg had painted landscapes and streetscapes, abstracts and geometrics, portraits of people, animals, and objects, as if everything she saw or thought about had simply spilled from her brain to the bristles of her paintbrush.

And the colors! So vivid! The hues were fanciful and flamboyant, almost gaudy—lollipop purple, peacock blue, chartreuse green, candy-apple red, cotton-candy pink—the colors of a carnival midway, of confetti tossed in a parade, of glorious abandon and unfettered celebration.

Meg's brushwork had always been precise, applied in small and careful strokes, layer upon layer. Joanie, who appreciated precision in all its forms, had admired Meg's painting for that reason, because she understood exactly what the piece stood for and the response it was meant to elicit.

But with these big, brilliant canvases, colors that bordered on garish, applied in bold, thick strokes, creating textures and layers that had such movement and life, she wasn't sure what it was she was supposed to feel. It was a little intimidating, but also exciting, like trying to solve a riddle, one for which there might be ten correct answers or none at all.

It occurred to Joanie that another word for precision, the quality she had always admired, was control. Before, Meg was controlled. Reined in. Not anymore.

These paintings were almost shockingly joyous, unabashed and unashamed, free. Yes, that was the word. Whatever it was that had been holding Meg back before had been released.

Joanie took her time, looking at each and every canvas, turning in a slow circle. When she reached the place where she'd begun, she looked down at the dress she was holding, an inconsequential pouf of satin, tulle, and rhinestones.

"Good for you, Meg," she said to the empty room. "Good for you."

Now it was time to find the artist. Joanie walked across the yard to the big house. Asher's truck was in the garage and the back door was unlocked. "Hey, guys!" Joanie shouted as she sat down on the mudroom bench to slip off her shoes.

A strange, low sound was coming from the living room. She paused, tilted her head to one side, listening. There it was again, a little louder, a little sharper, higher pitched, a human sound, as if the person making it might be in pain. Joanie jumped up. Wearing only one shoe, she limped quickly through the kitchen like a race walker with a leg cramp, following the sounds, which grew in volume and intensity the closer she got to the living room.

"Meg? Asher? Are you okay? Did something hap—Ack!" Joanie screamed.

So did Meg. So did Asher.

"Holy . . . ! I didn't realize you were—" She clamped her hands over her eyes. "I'm so, so sorry!"

Joanie heard movement, the sound of feet, Asher gruffly mumbling something as he pushed past her in the doorway, and laughter. Her sister's laughter.

"It's okay, Joanie. You can look now. He's gone."

Joanie lowered her hands from her eyes, but slowly. Meg was grinning, wrapped in a blue and green crocheted afghan.

"I'm so sorry," Joanie said again, her tone and bright pink cheeks making her mortification obvious. "I should have yelled louder."

Meg laughed again. "Don't worry about it. You could have fired a cannon and I doubt we'd have heard you. We were pretty involved."

Joanie's cheeks went from pink to crimson.

"Well . . . I'm really, really sorry," she repeated. "I don't know what to—"

"Joanie, it's okay. Awkward, but okay. We're married, remember?"

"Right. Still."

Meg was walking toward the bathroom, retrieving a trail of abandoned clothing along the way.

"So, what are you doing today?" Meg asked, her voice casual, as if this wasn't the most awkward situation in the world. "Want to go to lunch? Maybe do a little shopping? I need to go to the art supply store."

"Uh . . . sure. Sounds good."

"Great. Wait while I get dressed. Won't be ten minutes."

Joanie started inching toward the front door. "Oh, that's okay. Take your time. I'll just, you know . . . wait in the car."

"Suit yourself," Meg said, and closed the bathroom door.

They stopped at the art supply store, fabric shop, and consignment shop. By the time they stopped for lunch, Joanie was over her embarrassment and laughing about catching Meg and Asher in flagrante delicto. They were also laughing about the hat Meg bought in the consignment shop, a frothy creation with a tall tangerine-colored crown and hot pink, extra-wide organza brim, decorated with huge pink lilies.

"Where are you ever going to wear that thing?"

"I'm wearing it now," Meg said primly, touching her fingertips to the brim.

"Okay, but where else?"

"To picnics. And royal weddings. Possibly to my box at Ascot," she said, lifting her nose to a haughty angle. "If you play your cards right, I might let you borrow it."

"I don't have a box at Ascot. Maybe I could

wear it during filming. Nobody would be able to see my eyes. It'd make Hal crazy."

"I could loan it to Asher," Meg added. "So he'll have something to hide under next time he sees you."

Joanie choked on her iced tea, sputtering with laughter, and Meg joined in.

"Poor Asher," Joanie said after they calmed down. "Will he ever be able to look me in the eye again?"

"Oh, he'll be fine. But I bet he locks the door from now on."

Joanie chuckled. "When did you move back into the house?"

Meg speared some chicken and a lettuce leaf with her fork. "I didn't. We're just dating."

"Dating?"

"It was Asher's idea. To give me time to feel comfortable with him and to remember."

"Oh. That makes sense, I guess. And it seems to be working. You're obviously feeling more comfortable with him." Joanie smiled. "Are you remembering him too?"

"Some things. I remember that we rented a canoe on Lake Washington and it tipped over. You were there too."

"I remember that! Just a few weeks after the wedding. Our picnic went right to the bottom of the lake—"

"So we went out for pizza instead," Meg said,

249

finishing for her. "We were absolutely soaked, left a big puddle of water next to the booth. Asher found a mop and wiped it up so the waitress wouldn't have to. He's a sweet man."

"He is," Joanie agreed. "What else do you remember?"

"A lot of things. More every day. I remember sitting at a kitchen table covered with butcher paper and finger painting with vanilla, chocolate, pistachio, and butterscotch pudding."

Joanie nodded. "You were three and I was five. One of Minerva's early attempts at artistic indoctrination. Sometimes it was actually fun."

"I also remember getting off the bus in Seattle and you being there to meet me, and bringing Trina home from the hospital, and signing the loan papers on our house, and making a cake for Asher's thirtieth birthday, and cheering when Trina won first place at the science fair. Seems like every morning when I wake, there's a new crop of memories there, like they sprouted in my brain while I was sleeping."

"Do you remember the fire? Or anything about the accident?"

Meg shook her head. "No, I don't remember the big blowup on the talk show either. Hal showed me the video."

Joanie dropped her fork. "What! Why?"

"Calm down," Meg replied evenly. "I asked him to. Everybody talks about that day like it was this pivotal moment in my life . . . in our lives, so I wanted to see it. But I don't remember it, even after watching the tape.

"It was so awful. People were shouting and Avery was crying and so was I. But I didn't recognize me as me. But I felt sorry for that little girl. And for you and Avery. It was terrible for everybody. I even felt sorry for Minerva."

"Oh, please," Joanie huffed.

"I'm not kidding. Have you watched that tape?"

"Everyone in America did, twenty-four seven, for two straight weeks."

"But I mean recently, now that you're a mother. The look on Minerva's face as those security guys step in to separate her from her kids is heartbreaking.

"When they hand you off to the guy in the black shirt, the one with the headphones around his neck, and you turn away as they take you off on the opposite side of the stage, Minerva was watching you. Right at that moment, you can see she's doubting every decision she's ever made, that she wishes she could roll back the tape, and time, and do it all differently. But she knows it's too late. And as she watches you being taken away, she wants to tell you she's sorry, for everything."

Joanie rolled her eyes. "Somehow I doubt that. You don't know her like I do, remember?"

"Well, maybe that's why you can't see it. Don't

251

you think it's possible to know someone too well? So well that we can't make space in our brain for the fact that people change, or that we might not have the whole picture?"

Meg's philosophical tone, as if she was discussing some rhetorical question, removed from reality, was getting on Joanie's nerves. Minerva's personality and motives were not abstract concepts to Joanie; she *knew* their mother. She hadn't enjoyed the luxury of forgetting.

Joanie pierced a cherry tomato with her fork.

"One of the fascinating things is the way my memories are returning," Meg said, reaching for a second roll and spreading it with butter, "not as consecutive events but more like snippets of history. When you live life day to day, and year to year, the people, situations, and feelings around you change so gradually that you're not so aware of it."

Joanie frowned. "What do you mean? How have things changed for you?"

"Now, I'm happy. Before, I wasn't."

"What makes you think that?"

"Because every memory that's come back to me is a happy one. And because I don't have a single memory of anything that happened for a year and a half before the accident. Not one. That seems like a pretty good clue that, for the last eighteen months or so, I didn't have any happy memories. Another clue is the sex."

Joanie swallowed fast, almost choking on her tomato. "Yeah?"

Meg leaned closer, lowering her voice. "Joanie, it's incredible! Completely amazing. And constant. He's voracious, can't get enough. Which leads me to believe he's been doing without for a very long time."

"Leads you to believe?" Joanie frowned. "You haven't asked him?"

Meg shook her head. "It's too soon to be delving into all the personal stuff."

Joanie put down her fork. "Hang on. You know him well enough to have sex, but not well enough to talk to him about *not* having sex? Meg, that makes no sense. Zero."

"You don't understand. Everything is going great right now. I have my own life, time to paint, to think my own thoughts and do my own thing, but I also get to spend time with my family whenever I feel like it. I get to have all the benefits of marriage and family without any of the burden.

"Plus, I'm having the greatest sex of my life," Meg said, then stopped her fork midway to her mouth and frowned. "I think it is. I don't remember that either. But it's hard to imagine it could be any better. This morning, he actually—"

Joanie held her hand out flat. "Okay, sis. Stop. Too much information. Plus, you're making me jealous. You do remember how long I've been single, right? Always."

The waiter came to refill their glasses. Joanie and Meg sat in silence, working to suppress their mutual grins, until he finished and left.

"Listen, Meg, I'm happy for you. Jealous but happy. But I'm still not convinced things are as good as you think they are. Don't you want your life to get back to normal? Don't you want to have a relationship with your daughter?"

"I do have a relationship with her. Trina comes over to see me every day after school. She is so, so smart," Meg said, her voice simultaneously amazed and amused. "One big bundle of hormones—but also absolutely brilliant. Yesterday, in the space of half an hour, we discussed why the lacrosse players make bad boyfriends and hedgehogs make bad pets—pretty much the same reasons, by the way—the proper use of emoticons in text messages, wave particle duality, the theory of quantum consciousness, and why Sleeping With Sirens is the most overrated band in America."

"It is? Don't tell Avery. She'll be crushed," Joanie deadpanned. "But seriously, it's terrific you and Trina are getting along now."

"Aha," Meg said, raising a finger. "You said we're getting along *now*. Which implies that we weren't getting along so well before. Am I right?"

Joanie shrugged in assent.

"See? That's what I am talking about. Before the accident, I wasn't happy and neither was

Trina. Or Asher. Maybe we were taking each other for granted, getting so wrapped up in the day-to-day garbage that we couldn't appreciate each other. Who knows? Now we're starting from scratch. No agendas. No baggage. We enjoy each other's company.

"Last night Asher made eggplant parmesan for dinner and we sat around the table playing Settlers of Catan. And as soon as Trina went to bed, he jumped me. He does that every night. Never says a word. Just grabs me and . . ." Meg looked away for a moment and put her hand over her mouth, briefly covering her smile.

"It's fun, Joanie! It's fun, and sexy, and passionate. And," she said, letting out a little laugh, "it feels just a tiny bit wicked. But it isn't because I barely know him—we're married! How great is that? Why would I want to risk messing up something this good by talking to him about why things weren't working before?"

"But . . . Meg, you can't go on like this forever. At some point you're going to have to talk to him, really talk to him. You can't just go around pretending that nothing bad has ever happened and that life is one big party."

Meg's smile flattened. She removed her hat and laid it on a chair, as if sensing the festive flowers and carnival colors didn't match the look on her face.

"Why not? I mean it, Joanie. Why do I have to

remember everything, the good *and* the bad? Life is good for me now, for Asher too. If we weren't happy before and we are now, why would we want to go back to that?"

"Because it's not real. Because you'd be ignoring half of your life, an important half. The hard times shape us just as much as the happy ones, maybe more. You can't just wake up one day and decide to be somebody else."

"You did."

"*I* did?" Joanie's hand went to her chest. "What are you talking about?"

"About you. You were a budding concert pianist with a brilliant career in front of her and one day you woke up and decided you'd had enough. And now you're here," Meg said, spreading her hands. "You didn't like the reality you had so you made a new reality. Simple."

"It wasn't like that." An argumentative edge was creeping into her voice. "First off, I didn't have a brilliant career in front of me. That was all Minerva. Don't you get it? She invented me. I didn't come up here to escape my life, but to find it. And, believe me, nothing about that was simple. But I'm here now and this is my life. It's not exciting, but it's good. And I'm happy."

"Then why can't you let *me* be happy? Why do you have to keep pushing?"

"What? Meg, I'm not . . ."

Joanie was startled by the vehemence of her

sister's tone. Meg turned her face away, clamping her lips tight together and screwing her eyes shut.

"Meg?"

"I'm sorry. I'm sorry," she murmured, leaving her eyes closed for a moment longer. "I don't want to argue with you, Joanie. I really don't. You've been incredible. The hospital bills? They were astronomical!" She shook her head in amazement. "I don't know what we'd have done without you. Or how we can ever repay you. I know how much you hate doing this movie."

"Stop. What are you talking about?" Joanie waved her hand dismissively and smiled, relieved that Meg had regained her composure. "It's not me. We're all in this together. It's not like any of us were excited about the movie. Well . . . except for Avery. But even she's kind of over it now. Anyway, there's nothing to repay. I'm just glad your memories are coming back."

"Yeah, I'm especially happy I remembered that you're my sister. And that I love you."

Meg reached across the table for Joanie's hand and gave it a squeeze. Joanie blinked, feeling her eyes fill.

"You know what we need?" Meg asked, laughing and swiping at her own eyes. "Dessert! I saw the daily special when we were ordering— peach cobbler with cinnamon ice cream."

"Oh, I can't," Joanie protested. "I was going to start my diet today."

"We'll split it. You can diet next week." Joanie said nothing. Meg waved at the waiter, who was delivering orders to another table.

"Listen, I had an idea for something fun we could do together. Kind of a sisters' night thing. Have you heard of painting parties? Apparently it's a thing now. Trina was telling me about it. Friends go to these art studios and paint together. Simple things—a landscape, a vase of flowers, whatever. They use the same image for inspiration, but everybody's painting comes out a little different."

Joanie winced. "I'm not sure I want to expose myself to that kind of ridicule. I can barely draw stick people."

"Oh, come on! It'll be fun! I'll help you. And you won't be in public. We'll do it at my place. And the other thing about painting parties? They serve wine."

"How much? Because I think I'd need a lot."

Meg looked at her, waiting.

"Oh, all right. I'm in. I guess. Where's our server?" Joanie asked, craning her neck. "I've been sitting here so long that I'm hungry again. You know, that was a pretty small salad. Maybe we'd better get two cobblers."

Meg lifted her brows. "With two scoops of ice cream? Each?"

"Definitely. I'm starving."

Chapter 26

Hal and the crew were standing outside the clothing boutique where Avery had promised to meet them. It was starting to rain.

"If she's not coming, I should get the equipment in out of the wet," Brian said.

"Yeah," Hal answered irritably, looking up at the gray sky. "You and Simone go sit in the van. I'll try to track her down."

He took out his cell phone. "Avery? Hey, it's Hal. You said we should meet you on the corner outside of the boutique. Did I get the wrong one?"

"Oh, crap. I forgot. Sorry. I'll be right there."

Hal frowned. Something about her voice didn't sound right. And Avery wasn't the sort of person who blew off appointments.

"What are you doing?"

"Spending my last four dollars on a cupcake," she muttered. "Hang on a sec."

Hal heard a rustling sound, as if Avery had put down the phone. Though her voice was fainter, he could still hear what she was saying. He also heard a clattering sound, like somebody was pouring coins onto a table or countertop.

"Three dollars and fifty-six cents. That's all I've got," Avery said.

"Sorry," said another voice.

Hal raised his voice, almost shouting into his cell, trying to get her attention. "Avery? Avery, pick up." A moment later, she did.

"Sorry. I'll be there in a couple of minutes."

"Where are you?"

"Just up the street at Cupcake Royale."

"Stay there," Hal said. "I'll come get you."

"No, don't," she protested, her voice almost pleading. "I don't want the whole crew invading the place."

"Just me. Don't move."

Hal jogged two and a half blocks south to Cupcake Royale, his tennis shoes splashing over the wet sidewalk. Inside, he found Avery sitting slumped in a pink painted chair.

"Where's your cupcake?"

"Cupcakes make you fat." She sniffled.

Her eyes were red and puffy from crying. He felt like hugging her, but settled for a squeeze on the shoulder.

"Something happen with you and Owen?"

Avery shook her head. "Nothing's happening with me and Owen. Or anything else in my life. I don't have a boyfriend, or a job, or plan, or enough cash in my pocket to buy a cupcake. Everything sucks right now, Hal. *Really* sucks. I just . . ." She propped her elbows on the table and dropped her head into her hands. "I don't think I can deal with the cameras today."

Hal looked at her. Avery was emotionally

vulnerable, wounded and raw. In his experience, that kind of vulnerability generally made for compelling, sometimes dramatic video. And though she'd been holding back so far, Hal knew that Avery was a verbal processor. Talking aloud was how she sorted out her feelings.

Avery was open, trusting, and eager to please, which was why she'd gotten her heart stomped on. After watching her with Owen over the last few weeks, observing how much more engaged Owen was when Avery was in mermaid mode than when she was trying to be herself, he could have predicted that this would happen. Just as he could predict that if he pushed a little harder, she'd let him bring in the camera and tell him everything. . . .

He sighed inwardly. He couldn't do it. He didn't want to be that guy.

"Okay, sure. I get it. You need a break."

Avery lifted her head, swiped at her nose. Hal took his phone from his pocket.

"Who are you calling?"

"The crew. They can head over to Asher's place. He said he's installing some cabinets in the spec house today. They can get some B-roll of him working."

"Aren't you going with them?"

"Naw, they don't need me for that. You hungry?"

Four cupcakes—whiskey maple bacon and

tiramisu for Avery, salted caramel and triple-threat chocolate for himself—set Hal back $17.04, including tax. After taking a bite of the salted caramel confection, he decided four bucks was a bargain.

"Oh, wow. This is just . . . Wow. But gourmet cupcakes? These are a thing now?"

Avery nodded. "Oh, yeah. For years and years."

He took a smaller but no less appreciative bite of the triple-threat cupcake and groaned with pleasure. "Oh, man."

"I know, right?" Avery wiped a smear of whiskey bacon frosting from her lip and looked at him. "Hal? I'm really sorry about backing out today."

He waved off her apology. "We had to get some B-roll of Asher at some point. We'll pick up with you tomorrow. What will you be doing?"

"Probably still looking for a job," she sighed. "Can I ask you something? Why do you have to spend so much time following us? It's not like we're doing anything interesting. What are you going to do with ten hours of video of Meg painting? Or Joanie weeding and sewing button-holes? Or me filling out job applications?"

"Throw it away mostly. I'll probably end up using fifteen minutes of the stuff we've filmed in the last three weeks."

"That's crazy. Why not just do some interviews, set up some scenes in interesting locations, and focus on the highlights? Wouldn't that be easier?"

"Sure," he said, pausing to lick the edge of his cupcake, making the frosting even. "I could do that. Come in with some preconceived idea of what I want to have happen and the story I want to tell, ask preprogrammed questions to get the answers I'm looking for. But that's not how I work.

"I don't make a movie because I have answers, but because I'm searching for them. Remember, I started life as a mathematician. In a lot of ways, I approach a movie the same way I would an equation. I begin with a theory, but consider all the variables, all the possible combinations and proofs. That's what I'm interested in: proof. And facts. Not what looks real, but what *is* real—the truth."

"Okay. But why?"

"Why the truth?" He raised his brows, surprised by the question.

"Why us? What's so interesting about *our* truth?"

Hal tilted his head to the side. "You know, I don't really have a good answer to that. I mean it," he said, responding to the look of doubt on her face. "Hey, just because I spend my time examining the lives and motivations of other people doesn't mean I have a clue about my own. I'm sure it has something to do with my own experiences. But I've always been interested in prodigies. In genius."

"But we're *failed* geniuses."

"Not the way I see it. I think people will find you inspiring."

"Inspiring?" Avery choked out a laugh. "Joanie purposely flushed her whole career down the drain. She could have traveled the world, giving concerts and being famous. Instead, she sews uniforms for people who want to pretend the Civil War never ended. Is that your idea of success?

"Is Meg a success? Am I? Can't even scrape up enough money to buy myself a lousy cupcake," Avery said, sniffling as she peeled the paper off the tiramisu cake.

"Hey, now. I won't sit here and listen to that kind of talk." Hal frowned and Avery rolled her eyes. "I mean it," he said, keeping his voice artificially low and stern. "That is a *fantastic* cupcake."

Avery smiled weakly and shook her head.

"Really, Avery, I think you're being too hard on yourself. I think you're incredibly interesting. I mean it!" he protested when she shot him a look. "That first time we filmed you putting on your costume and you told that story . . . I've never seen anything like it. You made me *believe* you. You're an artist. Maybe not in the conventional sense, but you're one of the most creative people I've ever met."

"It's an escape," she said. "That's all."

"From what?"

Avery pressed her lips together and looked at him, as if trying to decide how much she should say.

"Hey. This is just you and me talking. No cameras. I won't bring it up again unless you do. Promise."

After a moment of silence, she turned her head away and began to talk, as if telling her story came easier when she wasn't looking him in the eye.

"Joanie and Meg are smarter than me. I can't remember a time when I didn't know that. I don't know the name of the sperm donor Minerva picked when she decided to have me—I don't think Minerva did either—but he was a writer, somebody famous, and had published a lot of books. And so, according to Minerva's plan, I was supposed to become a writer too. She engineered the whole thing, decided our future before we were even conceived, like God. Or a god—little g. Minerva is the name of a goddess of Roman mythology."

"The goddess of wisdom and patroness of the arts," Hal replied.

Avery nodded. "Right. Anyway, she set out to live up to the name by hatching three little artists. It worked, for Joanie and Meg. I was *supposed* to be a writer. But it's hard to write if you can't read."

Hal leaned closer. His brows drew together,

becoming a line of doubt. "But you can read. You read to the kids at the hospital. You read all the time."

"Now," she said. "Not when I was a kid."

"But Minerva's book has stories that you wrote."

"Minerva's book has stories that I *told* her. It's not the same thing."

"But how old were you when Minerva's book came out? Five? Nobody expects a five-year-old to be able to read and write."

"Minerva did. She spent hours and hours and hours showing me flashcards, making me copy letters. I hated it. Well, not all of it," she admitted. "She read to me a lot, told me stories. After a while, I started telling stories back to her and she was thrilled. So I kept doing it. But I couldn't read until I was nine.

"Once I was in the foster care system I went to public school. But it took a while before anybody realized I couldn't read. I wasn't causing any problems so they left me alone."

"But one of them figured it out?"

"No, it was my foster mom, Lori Raisch. She was a retired teacher. Her husband, Keith, was a sailor. He retired from the Coast Guard and then captained a charter boat out of Long Beach, taking tourists on whale-watching tours. Captain Keith," she said softly. "He was a good guy. They both were. And big into church. They didn't do what they were doing out of obligation or anything. It was just who they were. They were the kind of people who are always looking for a chance to give back. When they retired, they started taking in foster kids. I was their last."

"So Lori taught you to read? And Keith taught you about mermaids?"

"Keith taught me about stories," she corrected, turning toward him at last, her countenance brighter. "Oh, he had some good ones! Sailors have always been storytellers and Captain Keith was one of the best. It's part of the maritime tradition. Back in the days when a sea voyage could take months, storytelling was a way for sailors to pass the time, and confront the things that frightened them.

"Stories of shipwrecks with tragic endings helped them come to grips with the possibility of death. Stories of miraculous and heroic rescues gave them courage to go on in the face of fear and the torment of a storm. Fantastical myths of gods, and monsters, and mermaids explained the unexplainable natural phenomena around them, strange animals, fish, and birds, hurricanes, the aurora borealis. Stories are how we make sense of a world that seems senseless, a way to protect ourselves from feeling overwhelmed by forces we can't control. At first, I just listened to Captain Keith's stories. After a while, I started to study the way he told them.

"I saw how he used just the right word at the right moment in the right way, turning a story about untangling a shark from a fishing net into poetry. I saw how he chose his themes, transforming a story of shanghaied sailors battling a storm into a tale of good versus evil, man versus nature, an epic drama. I paid attention to how he used his eyes and hands and voice to build the action, then dropped back and built it up again, like a pulsing tide, like music, until his listeners were on the edge of their seats.

"And then, when the tension was so tight it felt like they might snap in two, I saw how he brought the crisis crashing over them like a wave, a thing of power and beauty that knocked them back and made them gasp. And after it passed, they just stood there, shocked, shivering with cold, and strangely alive, tingling, trying to make sense of what just happened, to sort fact from fiction, watching the waters recede and grow calm. Waiting. Wishing the wave would return."

Avery finished speaking. Hal looked at her for a long moment.

"And you say you're not a writer?"

"Writing is different. I tell stories."

"Better than anybody I ever heard."

"That's because you never met Captain Keith."

"So if he wasn't the reason, why did you get so interested in mermaids? What's the attraction?"

"Because of Sarah, the little girl I babysat for.

She was obsessed with mermaids. Only a few of Keith's stories were about mermaids, though, so I started doing research so I could make up my own stories. Soon, I was just as obsessed with them as Sarah was. I didn't just want to know about mermaids, I wanted to *be* one. Who wouldn't?

"Mermaids are beautiful and magical, seductively feminine, but also powerful. Sailors are afraid of mermaids, even while they are drawn to them. If you study the body of mermaid myth and lore, you'll see that many of the legends paint them as strong and potentially malevolent creatures, to be approached cautiously, with fascination as well as fear. Obviously, this was before Disney made them all perky and playful. Until then, mermaids were seen as mysterious and dangerous, witches of the sea. Scholars theorize that this is a result of the fear that men have when faced with powerful women, especially those who are comfortable with their sexuality. It gets back to what I was saying before, about how people use stories to frame their fears."

"Hold on. There are mermaid *scholars?*"

"Oh, yeah," Avery said earnestly. "Mermaids are a thing."

"Like cupcakes?"

"No," she said pointedly. "Not like cupcakes. You mess with a mermaid at your own peril. Mermaids are in control. And when I am dressed in my costume, inhabiting that persona, that's how

I feel—beautiful, powerful, mysterious, and in control of my destiny. Of everything."

It all made sense to him now. As a helpless little girl, Avery had been torn from her family. Then she was shuttled between strange families and schools for years. And after she finally found a stable home with loving foster parents, she was bounced back to unstable Minerva. No wonder the idea of mystical creatures that controlled their own destiny was appealing.

"What happened to Captain Keith and Lori?"

Avery looked down at the table, examining the crumbs that clung to the white paper liner of her now-devoured cupcake.

"One Saturday, Captain Keith took me roller skating and had a heart attack. He died right there in the roller rink."

Hal's throat tightened.

"I'm so sorry, Avery. That must have been terrible."

She dipped her head, acknowledging his statement without expanding upon it. "Lori died a couple of years later, but I was back with Minerva by then. She regained custody when I was twelve. Joanie tried to get custody of me before that, but she was young and broke, plus she lived out of state, so the judge wouldn't allow it."

"So what was that like, living with Minerva again?"

"Not that bad. Joanie and Meg and I share the

same mother but, in a lot of ways, our upbringings were totally different. When I came back she didn't push as much. I think she was afraid they'd take me away again if she did. She was still Minerva—always cooking up some crazy plan. In a way, I actually liked that about her. Sure, she's nuts. And completely unreliable. But she's tough and resourceful. She truly believes that, someday, one of her schemes will pay off and we'll all be propelled to fame and fortune. Look, Minerva screwed us up in all kinds of ways. I get that. But doesn't every parent? There are worse fates than being raised by an overly optimistic mother who thinks you're a genius."

"But if you feel that way about her, why did you leave?"

"Because she's toxic," Avery replied regretfully, as if she hated to admit it but couldn't deny the truth. "For every plus there's a minus, a big one. Like so big it creates a vacuum. And if you stick around long enough, eventually you'll get sucked into the void."

"What do you mean? Give me an example."

"Okay. So you remember how I said Minerva is resourceful?" Hal nodded. "That's a plus, it's what makes her a survivor. The minus is that she thought of her children as resources to be tapped.

"It sounds awful when I say it like that, but in a way, you can't blame her. She was all on her own. Who else could she turn to? And no matter what people think, she wasn't just out for herself. She was trying to make a life for us, an extraordinary life. That's the thing about Minerva. She really wants the best for everybody. But, somehow, she always manages to go about it in the worst possible way. So, I left. I had to. But that doesn't mean I don't love her."

He'd misjudged her. Until now, he thought of her as immature. But at twenty-five, she'd mastered a skill that a lot of people twice her age never would: the ability to step back emotionally and weigh people's intentions alongside their actions, showing others compassion while still protecting herself.

"You know something, Avery? I think there's a lot of your mother in you. The good parts," he assured her. "You're tougher than you think you are, a survivor. You're also optimistic, resourceful, and just crazy enough."

"Crazy enough? For what?"

"To be interesting. To find your own path in life, and on your own terms."

"Right now I'd settle for finding a job."

"You will," Hal said confidently. "You just haven't found your niche yet. When you do, it'll be something you love and that you're really good at, something that'll surprise even you. You're going to be fine, Avery. You'll see."

"Yeah?" Avery smiled and glanced at her phone, checking the time. "Well, then I guess I'd better get on with it. Thanks for the cupcakes. And the pep talk."

Hal was still eating, but when Avery stood up he did the same.

"Anytime. It was fun talking to you. And for the record? Owen is an idiot."

Avery laughed, really laughed, and headed toward the door with a bit of a bounce in her step, the paper sack that contained her mermaid garb and cosmetics swinging at her side. But before she got halfway across the room she stopped and spun around to face him.

"Do you want to know how to get Joanie to talk to you? I mean, really talk?"

"Well . . . yes," he stammered, surprised by the question and that Avery should be the one asking it.

"Do what you just did with me—turn off the cameras."

Hal didn't quite roll his eyes, but almost. Avery seemed to have forgotten that he was trying to make a movie. Heart-to-hearts were all well and good, and he was glad he'd been able to cheer her up, but he was a filmmaker, not a life coach. And for a filmmaker, anything that didn't happen on film might as well not have happened at all.

"I know, I know," she said. "You want to capture everything on tape, but stop and think about it. Cameras turned Joanie's whole life upside down. She *hates* cameras. If you want her to open up to

273

you when the cameras are rolling, you've got to show her that she can trust you when they're not."

"You think that'll work?"

"Maybe, maybe not. But it's got to work better than what you're doing now."

"Why are you telling me this?"

"Because you seem like a really good guy. Because, as I'm learning, those are really hard to find. And because, in spite of your moving speech about the search for truth through cinematography, I think there's only one reason you wanted to make this movie: Joanie. You got a crush on her when you were seventeen and never recovered."

He coughed out a laugh. "A crush? That I've supposedly been nursing for twenty years? Come on. You don't seriously—"

Avery cleared her throat and raised her eyebrows, daring him to contradict her. He said nothing further.

"Just don't tell Joanie I told you what to do, okay?"

"It's our secret," he promised.

"Good. Now, can you do me a favor? It's hard to look for work when you're carrying a grocery bag with a mermaid tail. Not a good first impression. Would you mind dropping this off at my place? Better yet, leave it with Joanie. It's too expensive to leave sitting on the porch."

"Sure," Hal said, taking the paper bag from Avery's hands. "No problem."

"Thanks. Oh, and as long as you're going over there, you might want to bring some cupcakes. Joanie loves desserts."

"Anything else?"

"Yeah." She lifted herself onto her toes and kissed his cheek. "Don't screw this up."

Chapter 27

Avery left Cupcake Royale feeling much better than when she arrived. But after four hours of filling out applications, the closest thing she got to an offer was when the manager at Urban Outfitters said they might have some openings in July and to check back then.

If she was so tough, and resourceful, and interesting—all the things Hal said—then why didn't anybody want to hire her? And why didn't Owen want her? What was wrong with her anyway?

Feeling discouragement drop over her like a too-heavy blanket, Avery stopped in the middle of the sidewalk, closed her eyes, and took a deep breath, trying to conjure what Joanie might say if she was there.

Stop. Is whining going to help? No. It's like Hal said, you've just got to find your niche. So, suck it up, Buttercup. Life is tough, but so are you.

She stood there for a moment, waiting, hoping

this sound advice would take root and make her feel better. It didn't.

"Why, my soul, are you downcast? Why so disturbed within me? Put your hope in God, for I will yet praise him . . ."

As the words entered her mind, Avery's face and chilled cheeks were suddenly bathed in warmth. With her eyes still closed, she saw bright spots of red, yellow, pink, and orange, like colors in a stained glass window. She opened her eyes, blinking, and found herself standing in bright sunlight that had broken through a hole in the cloudy, rainy, completely gray sky and was beaming directly down on her. The street sidewalk five feet in front and in back of where she stood remained in shadow.

"Well, that was impressive."

Casting her gaze upward, she caught sight of a street sign almost directly above her head that said BOYLSTON AVENUE.

Boylston was the home of Bayside Books, her very favorite Capitol Hill haunt. She hadn't allowed herself to go into Bayside, or even walk down this street, for weeks, afraid she'd give in to the temptation to spend her dwindling funds on books. Looking up at the street sign, it occurred to her that the upside to having only three dollars and fifty-six cents to her name was that the temptation was now removed—she couldn't buy a book if she wanted to. And browsing was free.

Five minutes later, Avery was standing in the nonfiction section, reading the opening chapter of an autobiography written by a woman who left behind a high-powered job to open an orphanage in Malawi.

A bookseller squatted down next to Avery and started placing books on the lower shelves, but she was so absorbed that she didn't notice him. She read on to the end of the chapter and then reluctantly closed the cover and slid it back on the shelf.

The bookseller got up from the floor. "That's a really good one," he said.

"Seems like it."

Avery sighed and turned away from the shelf, finally noticing him. He was about her age, perhaps a couple of years older, tall, a little on the skinny side, with a ginger blond beard and wavy hair that hung halfway to his shoulders.

"Excuse me, but . . . haven't I seen you somewhere before?" He gave his head a quick shake and laughed. "Sorry. Oldest line in the world, right? But I mean it; you look so familiar. I'm sure I've seen you before."

"I used to come here pretty often. But I haven't been in for about a month."

"No, it's not that," he said. "I'd have remembered. And I only started working here a couple of weeks ago. I've definitely seen you somewhere before." He narrowed his eyes for a moment, examining her face, then snapped his fingers. "The hospital, right? You're the mermaid. My nephew had an operation for a brain tumor."

"Oh, no! I'm so sorry. Is he okay?"

"Doing fine now," he assured her. "The tumor was benign. But that's why I moved to Seattle. My sister's husband is in the navy, so I came out to give Amy a hand during Cory's surgery. I only planned to be out here a couple of weeks, but I liked it so much that I decided to stay. Lucky for me there was—

"Sorry," he said, stopping himself in mid-sentence. "I didn't mean to tell you the story of my life. Side effect of a Midwestern upbringing; we're overly friendly."

He gave her an awkward, sort of goofy grin. He wasn't as handsome as Owen, but he was definitely cute, in a farm boy kind of way. She could imagine him playing the part of Huck Finn in the school play when he was little. Or out in the garden hoeing sweet corn in the summer . . .

No! Do not go there! Do. Not. So what if he came halfway across the country to help out his sister and nephew. That doesn't mean anything. Owen seemed like a sweet guy, too, remember?

"Anyway," he went on, "I saw you at the hospital one day when I was visiting Cory. You were reading the kids a story."

"That's just some volunteer work I do."

"Well, you're really good at it," he said, bobbing

his head. "Do you always go as a mermaid or do you have other characters?"

"Nope, I specialize in mermaids."

Avery reached into her purse and handed him her business card.

"Funny, but you don't run into a lot of professional mermaids in Minnesota, even part-time ones. Another reason to like Seattle," he said, looking up with that same goofy grin and holding the card back out to her.

Avery hesitated for a moment, rehearsing in her head how it would sound if she casually said, "Oh, that's okay. You can keep it." Would he think she was just being friendly? Or obvious?

Obvious, she decided and took it back.

"Well, I hope you like it here."

"Thanks. I do already." He tilted his head toward the bookshelf she'd been perusing before. "You really should get that book. I finished it last week and could hardly put it down. Best biography I've read all year."

"You read a lot of nonfiction?"

"I read a lot of *everything*. Lucky for me, I get a store discount. Couldn't keep up with my habit otherwise. Seriously, you need to read that. Everybody should. Tell you what," he said, pulling the book off the shelf and placing it in her hands, "take it home and give it a try. If you don't like it, bring it back and I'll refund your money."

"Oh. Well . . . The thing is, I don't have any money right now. Like none. I'm looking for work. But so far . . ."

Avery shoved the book back toward him and felt her face go crimson.

"Sorry," he said. "I didn't mean to be so pushy. Professional hazard. When I get excited about a book I want everybody on the planet to read it. But you said you're looking for a job? Have you applied here?"

Avery's eyes went wide. "No. Are there openings?"

"One. In the children's department. It's only part-time and doesn't pay much. . . ."

"I don't need much," she said excitedly. "I'd love to work here! And the children's department would be perfect. I love kids."

"Great. Let me see if I can find you an application."

He walked toward the front of the store to the information desk. Avery followed, feeling almost dazed by the way that this day, which had started out so badly, had taken a 180-degree turn to the good. She hoped. Putting in an application was only the first step. How many had she filled out in the last couple of weeks and not even gotten an interview, let alone been offered a job? Even so, remembering the way the sun had beamed down just on her when the Psalm popped into her head, she couldn't help but feel hopeful. Maybe the sunbeam was a sign, a signal that things were finally going to get better.

Avery fidgeted nervously while he ducked his head under the counter and grubbed around before popping up and handing her an application. She filled it out while he went to the checkout counter to help some customers.

"Thank you *so* much," she said when he returned, giving him a brief but grateful glance before taking up the pen again. "Really. I've been looking for a job forever. I was a babysitter for five years and I've got my mermaid business on the side, but I don't have any serious retail experience. Well. I was a barista for a while. Two weeks. But I'm not putting that down because I got fired. The manager was kind of a jerk, no sense of humor. Sorry," she said, still writing furiously. "I'm babbling. I'm just really excited! Working in a bookstore would basically be a dream job—I read three or four books a week. And they give you a discount?"

"Twenty percent off."

"Wow. That'd be fantastic." She giggled, giddy with excitement. "You know, this day started out so incredibly crappy. My boyfriend dumped me. Then I called my mom—always a mistake and if my sister finds out she'll kill me. And I got to be the one who told my mom that my other sister was in a car accident and lost her memory— she's fine now and it's starting to come back. Then

I had to calm her down and make her promise not to call either of my sisters. Or come up here. It was a mess. Plus, it was pouring rain. And I'm down to my last four bucks. Really, that's the only reason I let myself come in here today. There was no risk of me overspending because I'm so broke that I can't afford to buy a cupcake let alone a book.

"And *then*," she said, head still down, adding Hal's name and number to the references section because she was sure he wouldn't mind, "when I was feeling so depressed I felt about ready to eat a bug, I was standing up there on the corner and I closed my eyes and said this . . . Well, it was kind of a prayer. Not exactly. But kind of. The thing is, I believe in God—I mean, look at the mountains, right? And the trees and the ocean. Do you know there are two thousand different species of starfish? Oh, sure. Evolution and everything. But still, two thousand kinds of starfish! They had to come from somewhere, right? And—" She stopped herself and blushed. "Sorry. I'm doing it again, aren't I? I'm just pumped about this."

She signed the application and handed it to him. "Thanks. I appreciate this."

"No problem," he said, reading over what she'd written. "So . . . Avery. Do you have time for an interview?"

"When? Oh, you mean now? Sure." She craned her neck, looking around the store. "Is there a manager around?"

He thrust out his hand. "Adam Malinowski. Assistant Manager."

Avery felt the rush of adrenaline and hope that had been pumping through her veins drain from her body.

"Oh, you're kidding," she said weakly. "You're so young. And you said you just started . . . I didn't . . . I had no . . ." She covered her face with one hand.

"Avery?" He waited for her to respond. He stepped closer and peered through the lattice of her fingers. "So, is this *not* a good time for an interview?"

Avery lowered her hand. "You're serious? After the way I yammered on? And all the stuff I said? You really want to interview me?"

"The stuff you said is why I want to interview you." He started ticking her comments off on his fingers. "I love books. I love kids. I don't care that the pay isn't great. I read three or four books a week. This is my dream job. I'm pumped about this."

"It is! And I am!"

"Then you're somebody I want to talk to. I do wish you had a little more retail experience, but enthusiasm is important. And you know how to run a register, right?" Avery bobbed her head. "Good."

"You don't care that I got fired from the barista job?"

"I won't say I don't care. But it depends on what happened. Let's get a cup of coffee and you can tell me about it."

Bayside Books didn't have a full-service café, but sandwiched between the fiction and reference sections was an area with a half-dozen tables and chairs and a pine sideboard painted French blue that held urns for coffee and hot water for tea.

Avery and Adam sat there for about twenty minutes, discussing the job and her past work experience. Avery was nervous, especially when he started to frown while she was explaining the whole Mystery Mocha debacle.

"I know. It was stupid," she said, thinking how very true this was after having heard herself tell the story aloud. "I completely get that now, but . . ."

Her voice trailed off. What was the point of trying to explain? It was stupid. She was stupid. Mystery Mochas. Who *does* that?

"Yeah," he said slowly, staring at a spot past her shoulder.

Avery felt her heart sink. She'd blown her chance. No way was he giving her this job. He was just trying to think of a nice way to tell her that.

"That probably wasn't the best idea you've ever had," he said. "Well, not the idea itself—it actually sounds pretty cool. Might have been a good way to drum up some business on a slow afternoon. But you should have checked with your manager first.

"Bookselling is tough. My parents owned a bookstore in St. Paul. I practically grew up in the business, so I know what I'm talking about. We need all the creative ideas we can get. Just talk to me before you put them into practice, okay?"

Adam looked down, scanning some papers he'd brought to the table.

"Now, about the hours—twenty a week to start. You'll have to work a full shift on either Saturday or Sunday. As I said, the pay isn't great, but—"

Avery raised her hand like a first grader asking permission to go to the restroom.

"Wait. So . . . you're offering me the job?"

"Yes, if you want it."

"I do! Absolutely!"

"Great. You can start Monday morning. Just one thing," he said, his suddenly serious expression bringing a little knot of anxiety to Avery's stomach. "And I hope this won't be a problem for you. But we have a strict dress code. No fins. No scales."

He was trying to make a joke and she got that. But his comment made her think.

"Okay. But what if it was in the line of duty? What about a Saturday story hour? With costumed characters? I could start with the mermaid, but there's no reason I couldn't do other characters."

Adam laughed and got to his feet.

"See you on Monday."

Avery hopped up from the table. "Right! Yes. See you then!"

"Avery? For the record," he said before walking away, "you're going to be really, really good at this."

Chapter 28

Though she spotted the bag from Cupcake Royale right off, this did nothing to lessen Joanie's irritation when she answered the door and found Hal on the other side. "Why are you here? I'm supposed to have the day off, remember?"

She was purposely rude. Hal and his crew had invaded her privacy for nine days out of the last ten. Plus, he still owed her fifteen thousand dollars.

Joanie's phone rang before he could respond. By the time she hung up and went back to the door, her expression and attitude had softened. "That was Avery. She got a job at the bookstore."

His face split into a grin. "She did? That's great! Good for her."

"Whatever it was you said to her this morning really did the trick. Thanks."

"It was all her," he said even as he ducked his head to acknowledge Joanie's appreciation. "She just needed a pep talk. She asked me to drop off her stuff with you," he said, lifting the grocery bag that held Avery's mermaid tail. "I was hoping we could talk. Do you mind if I come in?"

"Where's your crew?"

"Over at Asher's job site, packing up their gear. I sent them home a couple of weeks early."

"What do you mean? They won't be back?"

"Not for a while. Maybe not at all. That's what I wanted to talk to you about. I was thinking it might be best to take a break from the cameras, take some time to get to know each other and then see where we stand in, say, three weeks? If you're not more enthusiastic about the project by then, then it might be better for everybody if we just called it off."

Joanie made her eyes into slits. What was he up to? He'd bet his business on making this movie. She couldn't imagine him "just calling it off."

"It's not a trick," Hal said, as if reading her mind. "I know how much you hate all this. I honestly thought I could get you to come around, make you comfortable enough with the process so you'd actually enjoy telling your story, maybe even find some relief in it. You'd never have agreed to it if you didn't need the money, but if that's your only motivation, this is never going to work—not for you or me.

"So, I'd like to take a new approach for a couple of weeks—just you and me talking, like people do. If we get to the end of it and you're still not ready to talk on camera then, fine. I'll go back to LA and you'll go on with your life. No hard feelings. What do you say?"

Joanie relaxed her tense expression. She figured it out. She knew what this was all about.

"It's the money, isn't it? The fifteen thousand. You said you'd have it this week and you don't. What happened? Did your condo buyer back out?"

Hal put his bags down on the porch and reached into his wallet.

"Nope, everything went through. The seller's check was deposited into my account last night. Here you go," he said, and handed her a check. "And before you ask, that belongs to you and your sisters no matter what. At the end of three weeks, if you're not willing to continue with the project on camera, I won't ask for a refund."

Joanie opened the check, read the amount, and looked at his signature. She lifted her head and stared at him.

"Is that from Cupcake Royale?" she asked, nodding toward the bag.

"I wasn't sure what kind you liked so I bought one of each." He smiled. "Just in case you were up for a late-afternoon snack. Or maybe an early dinner? I'm buying."

Joanie pressed her lips together, thinking over his offer and what he'd said about the sale of his condo going through. So it was done. Presumably anything he'd made on the sale of the condo—and perhaps even his capital—had gone into the movie, the thirty-thousand-dollar fee Joanie had demanded plus the rest of the production costs.

How much could that be anyway? Another thirty thousand? More?

And he really expected her to believe that, after hanging out with him for a couple of weeks, she could just walk and keep the money?

"Thanks, but no. I'm still full from lunch and I already made dinner—shepherd's pie. I'll just heat it up later."

Hal's hopeful expression was replaced by one of defeat.

"Shepherd's pie. Right. Well, okay then. It was worth a try. I'll give you a call on Monday and we'll . . ." He shrugged. "Well, we'll just have to see."

He turned and started to leave. But when he got to the top step, he turned around once again to face her.

"You don't trust me," he said. "And you know something? Maybe you shouldn't. I haven't been one hundred percent straight with you. First off—and promise you won't get mad—"

Joanie felt her jaw set. Somebody warning you not to get mad is usually a pretty good indication that you should do the opposite.

"—but this wasn't just my idea, it was Avery's.

So were the cupcakes," he said, jerking his chin to the bakery bag he'd left behind.

"What! If she thinks . . . If *either* of you think—"

He raised his hands. "Just let me finish before you tell me to shove off, okay? Avery was just trying to help me out. And possibly you, too, but I'm pretty sure I'd have more to gain from this than you.

"Anyway, what I was trying to say was that I wasn't completely truthful with you. Or with myself. After Avery told me what was going on, I went for a long walk to think about it and realized she was right. Avery is really very perceptive. Either that or I'm really obtuse . . ."

Joanie furrowed her brow. "Hal. What are you talking about? What did Avery tell you?"

"Hang on, I'm getting to that. Avery said that the real reason I wanted to make this documentary was you."

"Me?"

He nodded. "You. She said that when I met you that day, twenty years ago in that green room, when we were both seventeen—Do you even remember? Because I've never forgotten it— Avery said I developed a crush on you and that my obsession with making this project is because I never got over it."

"Wait . . . What? Is that true?"

Hal was quiet for a moment. He twisted his lips

with a kind of weird, corkscrew motion, doing that thing Joanie noticed he did when he was thinking hard about something.

"Yeah. Maybe. At least partly. I know it's hard to believe, seeing as I grew up to be such a Casanova and everything, but you were the first girl I ever really talked to. Up until then, the only figures I found interesting were numeric, not female." Joanie made a face. "Yeah, sorry. That sounded a little pervy, didn't it? My point is, I did have a crush on you and, yes, in a way, I never really got over it."

"Okay . . ." Joanie said slowly. "But you've liked other women since, right? I mean, you've had girlfriends and everything?"

"Yes," he said, his tone purposely patient. "Girlfriends and everything. I'm not *that* big of a nerd. Even a couple of long-term relationships, including a short-lived engagement I was very lucky to slip loose of. But I gotta tell you though, after a couple of dates, or occasionally a couple of months, those women bored the hell out of me. But, Joanie . . . you?"

He turned his head to one side and let out a frustrated laugh. Joanie couldn't tell if he was laughing at himself or at her.

"Since I came up here you have irritated me, aggravated me, and occasionally infuriated me. When I'm trying to come in for a close-up and you purposely drop your scissors under the table for the third time, do you seriously think I'm not going to figure it out? For the last four weeks, you've made me ten kinds of crazy! But what you have *not* done, not once, is bore me. For reasons I'll probably never completely understand, I find you endlessly fascinating.

"So, yes. Avery's right. Part of the reason I've been so fixated on making this movie stems from my unrequited personal interest in you—a schoolboy crush. But it's not just about you," he said, looking her in the eye at last, a thing Joanie didn't realize she wanted him to do until he did it. "It's about me too. About what you did for me.

"If it was just that encounter in the green room, I still would've had a crush on you, but I'd have gotten over it. It was what you did after that stuck with me. When you sat down to play the Liebestraum and I saw it—that defiance in your eyes . . . When you made a break for freedom and the right to determine your own future, you changed my life.

"It's true," he said, responding to the doubtful look Joanie gave him. "If not for you, I'd probably be holed up in some moldy math department today, rehashing other people's research and trying to pass it off as original and my own. That's the best-case scenario. Worst case is I might have gone round the bend and stayed there, the Ludwig Boltzmann or Alan Turing of my time."

He smiled.

"Okay, now I'm flattering myself. I wasn't good enough to become a full-blown Mad Mathematician. So, there I'd be, miserable in the math department, fighting for tenure, publishing and perishing. By inches. One thing is certain; I'd never have become a filmmaker. And that would have been a waste because, as it turns out, I'm much better at making movies than I ever was at doing math.

"So. There it is," he said, taking in a big breath and letting it out in a whoosh. "The truth. I wanted to make this movie more than anything because, from the moment I saw you, I couldn't get over you. I've been waiting twenty years to finish that conversation that never really started back when we were teenagers.

"And then, after I solved the puzzle, understood your story, understood *you,* I wanted to share my findings with the world. Because that's what I'm good at. Because I'm convinced there is something in your story that the world needs to know. Maybe even something that you need to know. Who knows?"

He shoved his hands into his pockets, looked down at his feet. Joanie ducked her head, trying to see his face. She thought he was doing that thing with his lips, making the corkscrew face, but she couldn't be sure. He popped his head up again.

"Sorry. I seem to be making a lot of speeches these days. I'll call you on Monday," he said, and started down the steps.

"Hal! Wait!"

He stopped at the bottom stair, looking up at her.

"You said I'd get a chance to talk. Are you done?" He nodded. "Good. What I was going to tell you was . . ."

She stopped herself, frowned.

"Let me start over. If you're being honest, then I should too. I was going to say exactly what you thought I would—shove off. But that was a pretty convincing speech.

"So here's the deal—I'm really *not* hungry right now. I wasn't making that up. I had this huge bowl of peach cobbler and cinnamon ice cream at lunch. I should have split it with Meg. Anyway," she said, seeing his look of confusion and realizing she needed to get to the point, "I'll be hungry in a couple of hours—I always am—and I have a shepherd's pie ready to go into the oven later. So if you'd like to come inside and talk until then, you're welcome to stay for dinner."

Joanie opened the door wider. Hal climbed the steps, two at a time.

Chapter 29

"You don't have to do that," Joanie shouted from the dining room.

"I know," Hal shouted back, opening and closing kitchen cupboards. "You already told me twice."

"I did?" Joanie's voice sounded surprised. "Guess I had too much wine."

"We both did. That's why I'm making tea. Hey, where do you keep your trays?"

"China hutch. Breakfast nook."

"Found them."

Hal placed two mugs of hot tea, cream, sugar, spoons, and a plate of cupcakes on the largest wooden tray and carried it into the dining room. Joanie was sitting at the table, resting her chin in her hand, staring sightlessly into the flame of a beeswax taper, now half the height it had been at the beginning of the meal.

"Listen to that!" she exclaimed when the piano concerto coming through the stereo speakers began a new, faster, and more vibrant movement. "Edvard Grieg. Concerto in A minor, Opus 16. So beautiful. Did you know that Liszt was the first person to play this? Not on the stage. The two composers met in Rome; Grieg wanted an opinion on the new concerto and Liszt sat down and played it, even the orchestral parts. Sight-read the whole thing! Can you imagine? Me either.

"Listen," she said once again, more reverently. "So lovely. A waterfall."

She closed her eyes, enraptured, her face bathed in candle glow, her features soft and her skin luminous. Hal placed the tray on the table, pulled out a chair, and sat down across from her, moving quietly, giving himself time to study her face.

An angel's visage, he thought. She swayed ever so slightly along with the music. The flickering flame caught the highlights of her hair and deepened the blush of her lips. For a moment, he let himself imagine what it would be like to kiss her, to hold her, to . . .

No. He'd had a lot to drink, but not so much that he couldn't see that getting emotionally involved with Joanie would be a really, really bad idea. He was a documentarian. His job was to observe objectively and from a distance, not to insert himself into the scene.

It was a fine line he was trying to walk and he knew it. He had to be open and honest enough so that Joanie would trust him with her story, but not so involved that he was unable to maintain his status as dispassionate observer. If he didn't, then he couldn't make this movie, and if he didn't make the movie, he'd end up losing his home and his business for no reason.

Joanie opened her eyes and smiled, as if she was happy to see him.

"Thank you."

"For what?"

"For bringing music back into my life. I didn't realize how much I missed it."

"You're welcome. Dessert?" he asked, shoving the plate in her direction.

"Oh. I shouldn't."

She bit her lip, then reached across the table and plucked a coconut cupcake from the pile. He chose a chocolate one with green mint frosting, peeled off the paper, and broke it into pieces, eating them one at a time.

"Do you know why I decided to let you in? It's not because of what you said about having a crush on me. Or the part about never having the guts to give up math for moviemaking if you'd never met me. That was sweet, but that wasn't the reason," she said, moving her head slowly back and forth.

"No? Then what was it?"

"Hang on," she said, tipping her head to one side and lifting her hand to silence him, listening intently as the Grieg concerto ended and another piece began.

The first notes were hesitant and darkly ominous. Hearing them, Hal pictured someone standing outside a closed door, fingertips on the knob, heart racing, afraid of what was waiting on the other side. A few measures later, it was as if the door burst open, releasing the fearful thing. As the notes raced and rippled over the keyboard, Hal could imagine that same someone, a woman, running down corridors that led to other corridors, lined with door upon door, chased by the thing she feared most.

"*That* is why I let you in," Joanie declared, pointing toward a speaker in the far corner. " 'Gaspard de la Nuit,' by Ravel. Specifically, the third movement, the Scarbo. One of the most technically challenging solos ever written for piano."

She was about to reveal something important. Hal could tell. He'd seen that look on the faces of other subjects over the years. There was a way that people had of leaning forward, fixing you with their eyes, and choosing their words when they were about to share a secret they'd kept hidden for a very long time. Whatever it was she was about to say, Hal was sure she wouldn't be saying it if she hadn't consumed three quarters of a bottle of Pinot all on her own.

For a moment, he wondered if that was quite fair and if he should stop her before she revealed anything she would later wish she could retract. But she was inebriated, not drunk, consuming enough to relax her tongue, but not so much that she didn't know what she was doing. And he hadn't forced the wine on her. She'd filled her own glass, not once but three times. Perhaps on purpose? Joanie obviously wasn't a drinker, but maybe she became one that night so she would have the courage to unburden herself to him.

He sat there quietly, saying nothing, part of him wishing he'd brought his small video camera, another part relieved he hadn't.

"Everybody thinks—the world thinks, my sisters think, and *you* think—that I quit playing at seventeen, that the talk show was my last public performance." She shook her head. "Not true.

"After I aged out of the foster care system I stayed in Los Angeles for almost a year. Actually, I lived in Pasadena. Maestro Boehm took me in. I didn't have any money, or a job, or anything. But he housed me, fed me, and taught me. Or tried to teach me—that. The Scarbo.

"I wanted to go to a conservatory, the Curtis Institute of Music in Philadelphia. Julliard is the name everyone recognizes, but Curtis is excellent as well, one of the best in the country, but has fewer students. Also, tuition is free.

"The competition is incredibly tough. The most gifted musicians in the world apply, but only four to ten percent are accepted. It was always going to be a stretch and I hadn't played a note for the seven months I was in foster care, so I was rusty. Plus, I'd muffed a piece of only moderate difficulty on national television. There was no way the admission committee wouldn't know that.

Everyone in the country did. The only chance I had of getting in was to tackle a famously difficult piece and perform flawlessly—the Scarbo.

"We worked on it for months, all day, every day. Even now, if you gave me staff paper and a pen, I could copy out every measure, every note. The maestro put a piano in the guest room and extra insulation in the walls so I could practice on my own, seven or eight hours a day, not counting the hours studying with Maestro Boehm. He worked with me every night, even though he'd already spent a whole day teaching. He even paid for my plane ticket to the audition."

Joanie lifted her chin, looking at the ceiling, blinking back tears. "He's such a good man. And I let him down. He wasted months on me, years."

Hearing her words, Hal had to battle to keep still and stay silent. He wanted to reach across the table, grab her hand, and tell her it wasn't true, to hold her in his arms and tell her about that day in Boehm's studio, the affection he'd seen in the old man's eyes, that her old teacher had marveled at her resilience and strength, that he was and always would be proud of her.

But he was there to observe, not intervene. And even had it been otherwise, Joanie needed to speak. You can't wrestle a demon that stays hidden in the shadows.

"I didn't get in. You probably guessed by now," she said, laughing mirthlessly and swiping at her eyes. "And it wasn't because I froze. Or because I got flustered and muffed the piece. That would have been some comfort, thinking I was just too nervous and had a bad day.

"The truth is, I played it as well as I ever had. Getting up from the bench and bowing to the audition committee, I remember feeling very good about how it had gone. I'd given a solid performance.

"I waited in the wings while the committee conferred, then was called back onstage for their verdict. The director of the program congratulated me on having taken on such a challenging piece and performed it admirably. That should have been my first clue. If you've truly done well on something as difficult as the Scarbo, you should be hearing adjectives like 'brilliant' and 'stunning,' not 'admirable.' In that situation, telling someone they've done admirably is like awarding an A for effort but a C for execution, which was pretty much what they were saying.

"They'd seen the video—just like everyone else in the country—and told me that they'd had doubts about even letting me audition. But a personal letter from Maestro Boehm persuaded them to give me a chance, explaining my 'extenuating circumstances.' The letter, he informed me, was very heartfelt. It was clear that my teacher had a very real affection for me.

"The director said I was a capable pianist and

technically skilled, but lacked the emotional sensitivity that is the mark of a world-class musician. 'You are a very, very good pianist,' he said, 'and you can certainly make your way as a professional, teaching or perhaps playing with a regional orchestra. But the gap between the craftsman and artist is a vast chasm that cannot be crossed by any other means than God-given genius. We feel that Mr. Boehm's fondness toward you has blinded him to this fact.' "

Joanie's eyes were dry now. Her speech was clearer and her posture less relaxed. Perhaps the wine was wearing off. Or perhaps the cold draught of memory had shocked her back to sobriety. The dull edge in her voice touched Hal more deeply than tears. He didn't know why.

"What did Boehm say when you went back?"

"Nothing. I was too ashamed to face him. When I got back to LA, Maestro was teaching. I snuck inside, gathered my things, snuck out again, and headed to Seattle. I found a job, a place to live, and a new life. As soon as I had enough money, I sent him a check for my expenses and a letter saying how sorry I was to have let him down."

"Did he write back?"

"I didn't put a return address on the envelope. He never cashed the check, though." Joanie paused, took a long drink from her barely warm tea. "He still had my picture on the wall?" she asked doubtfully. "Even after all these years?"

Hal nodded. "He was proud of you."

"Blinded by affection still. But there are worse things to be blinded by. And it's good, thinking someone can care even after you've disappointed them."

"You should write to him, Joanie. Or call. I don't think he has a lot of time left and I'm sure he'd like to hear from you before it runs out."

"I should," she murmured, but the furrows in her brow revealed her apprehension. "I wouldn't know how to begin, or what to say."

"Start with hello," he advised. "And see where it goes from there."

"Maybe," she said softly. "Maybe I will."

She lifted her head, gazing frankly at Hal. "So, now you know the story, the real story, of how I stopped playing and why I don't now. It wasn't Minerva's fault, not really. Her only sin was trying to convince the world that her oh-so-ordinary daughter had the spark of genius. Mine was believing her, or wanting to."

"Is that what you think you are? Ordinary?"

She tipped her head to one side, shifted her shoulders, a grudging admission. "Maybe not ordinary. I mean, I was conceived in a test tube, which practically makes me a human lab experiment. And my mother is crazy."

"*Pfft.* Big deal. Whose mother isn't?" Hal said, smiling, responding to the touch of sarcasm that returned to her voice.

"Darn. So I struck out there too? Okay, but my sister *is* a mermaid."

"Sure, but only part-time," Hal said.

"Good point. Okay. So I'm not ordinary, but I'm not extraordinary either. I'm just . . ." She lifted her gaze upward and then around the room, as if searching for a word. Finally, she found it.

"I'm that." She pointed to a framed photograph sitting on the sideboard, the old picture of herself and Gerhardt Boehm. "I'm a third-place finisher. Better than most, not as good as some.

"And *that's* why I decided to invite you to dinner. When you said that thing about ending up as a math professor in some middling liberal arts college, I knew we were kindred spirits." She lifted her tea mug and held it out to him. "You, sir, are a bronze medalist."

"And happy about it," he said, clinking the edge of his mug against hers.

"You are, aren't you? Really happy."

"Yes, and I never could have done it without you. You were my role model."

"Huh. Well, that's good. Now maybe you can be mine."

They talked for a while about happiness, what it was and wasn't, and how Joanie had tried to convince herself that "happy enough" was enough and having no comparative cause for complaint meant she was content, or should be.

"It was the music," she told him, "that helped me realize I'd been kidding myself.

"It was incredibly hard to make myself listen to my old audition CD that first time. You have no idea. But once I started I couldn't stop. I must have played it thirty or forty times. I was obsessed. It started to feel like that was the moment, even more than the talk show, when I could have made a turn to the left or right and changed everything.

"I started to fantasize about the CD as some kind of magical time portal, like in one of those time-traveler novels." She gave Hal a wry smile. "See? Avery isn't the only one with an overly active imagination.

"I spent a lot of time imagining what I would say to twelve-year-old me, how I could warn her without robbing her of hope. Finally, I realized that was impossible. She wouldn't have listened to me anyway. She wanted it too much. And was that such a bad thing? Wanting? And I wouldn't just have been robbing her of hope, I'd have taken the music from her too. The more I listened, the more I knew I could never, ever do that. It meant too much to her. To me.

"Once I was able to separate the memory from the music, I realized what I'd been denying myself all these years—that incredible joy—the exhilaration, and ecstasy, and unfiltered happiness I experience when I listen to a great piece of music.

"It makes me wonder," she told him, "if I

haven't been stifling joy in other parts of my life too. I'm not sure. It's possible. Maybe it's time to go back and take another look at . . . well, at a lot of things."

They talked for a long time. Hal could have talked longer. But when the beeswax tapers began to sputter, he knew it was time to go.

Hal felt sober-ish, but decided to take an Uber back to his apartment anyway, just to be safe. Pulling his phone from his pocket, he saw that Lynn had called several times.

"It's about Minerva," she said when he asked what was up. "I've been working through some of the background information you gave me after you met with her and . . . something's just not right."

"What do you mean, not right?"

"I wish I knew. Look, some stuff checks out—she was born in Georgia, moved to the UK, then LA, raised the girls here. She says she came to California in 1982, but I can't find any records and it's all kind of vague. And that music academy she told you she graduated from? They don't have any record of her."

"So, you think she made it up?"

"I don't know. Probably. But there could be more to it than that. I just have this feeling."

"That's it? A feeling? We're going to need more than that."

"I know. That's why I'd like to go out to Georgia and do a little sleuthing."

"Sleuthing?" he chuckled. "What are you now, Nancy Drew?"

"Hey, don't dis Nancy Drew. She was my childhood hero. But, seriously, the only way I'll be able to figure out if I'm right or wrong is to go out there."

"So? Go out there."

"Have you looked at the bills lately? Shooting on location is expensive, especially since you're funding the production. And I'm just not sure—"

"Oh. I forgot to tell you. The expenses are about to take a dramatic decrease; I sent Brian and Simone home for a couple of weeks."

"What? You mean you suspended filming? You're kidding. Why?"

"Because I wasn't getting anywhere!" he snapped, irritated by her tone. "I'm never going to get Joanie to talk honestly on camera until I earn her trust off camera. So I sent the crew on hiatus. No point in paying them if we're not getting anything usable, is there? I'm going to spend the next couple of weeks just getting to know her better, talking off the record."

"And you think that will work," Lynn said, her words a statement rather than a question.

"It's already working. I'm on the sidewalk in front of her house right now."

"Which is exactly where she left you cooling

your jets for weeks before you ended up coming back to LA with your tail between your legs. So how is this progress?"

"Because," he said, matching his sarcastic tone to hers, "she invited me to dinner. We talked for hours and she really started to let me in, told me some things I'm not sure she's ever told anybody."

"That sounds good, but if you didn't get it on tape—"

"I will, okay! It takes time! Why does everything have to be so black and white with you? We've been dead in the water for weeks and now, at last, we're getting a little wind in the sail. Plus, I'm saving a ton of money. Can't you at least give me credit for moving this thing in a better direction?"

"Hooray," she deadpanned. "Good for you. I'll send you a medal."

"Make it bronze," he muttered.

"What?"

"Never mind." He sighed. "Go to Georgia, Miss Drew. You have my blessing."

Chapter 30

When Avery got to work on Saturday morning, only her second Saturday on the job, she arranged ten pint-sized plastic chairs and four beanbag cushions in a half circle in front of an adult-sized wingback chair, then stood back to examine her handiwork.

Maybe it was a bad idea, putting out every chair they had. This was the first meeting of the Saturday Shenanigans Society, an idea she'd pitched to Adam. What if he came to check on her and saw that only a handful of kids showed up?

She put four of the plastic chairs and two of the beanbags back into the storeroom. Twenty-five minutes before they were due to start, she had to bring them out again.

"I didn't think there'd be so many kids," she said, turning to Elsa, a coworker in the children's department. "I'm not supposed to start until eleven. Where are they going to sit?"

Elsa scooped chocolate pudding into a plastic cup, topped it with a spoonful of crushed chocolate cookie crumbs, and handed it to Avery, who shoved three gummy worms halfway down into the mixture. The cups of "Dirt and Worms" would be the post-story snack, a fitting accompaniment to the first day's theme: "If You Were a Bug." After eating, the children would make insect antennae from pipe cleaners, keeping them occupied while their parents browsed and, hopefully, purchased some of the bug-themed books Avery set up on a nearby display table.

"They're kids," Elsa said, and started filling another cup. "They'll sit on the floor. Would you quit being so nervous? Geez."

"I can't help it. I'm not sure Avery Promise is as good a storyteller as Avery Poseidon. Maybe I should have gone with an undersea theme. What if I suck?"

"So what if you do? You're reading bug books to a bunch of four- to eight-year-olds, not auditioning for a movie. It's a free event with food. It's not like they're going to ask for their money back."

"I know, but if I do a good job, then the parents might want to actually buy the books. Adam ordered twenty copies each of *The Very Hungry Caterpillar* and *Diary of a Worm*. What if we only sell five? What if we don't sell any?"

"You're sure getting yourself worked up over a minimum wage job," Elsa said. "You haven't even been here two weeks. I've worked here for four months. You don't see me volunteering any ideas."

"I just want to be good at this."

Elsa glopped pudding into another cup. "Yeah? Well, I'd rather be good at something that pays. The second I find a job that does, I'm out of here. Oh, good. More urchins," Elsa muttered as another group of kids arrived. "I'll go to the break room and get more cups."

Avery kept shoving gummy worms into cups. She knew Elsa thought she was a sap for caring so much about a job that was, to her, just a job, and not a very good one. She got it.

Only the day before, Avery Poseidon had

booked a TV commercial for a local seafood restaurant. That gig would pay more in one day than she'd make in two weeks at the bookstore. If that had happened a few weeks earlier, Avery knew that the manager at the coffee shop wouldn't have had to fire her, she'd have quit. But the bookstore was different. She loved this job and was working hard to be good at it. Sometimes she even used her lunch break to read children's books.

"Why?" Elsa asked the first time she saw Avery sitting in the break room with a copy of *Who Broke the Vase?*, a picture book by a new author, Jeffrey Turner.

"Because when a customer comes in looking for a suggestion on what to read or give as a gift, I want to be able to recommend the perfect book."

Elsa rolled her eyes. "Please. Just sell them something based on a cartoon or TV show. They won't know the difference."

Elsa didn't like her. She thought she was a suck-up. But Elsa was one of those people who lived to pee on other people's parades. Who cared what she thought?

Avery could only imagine what her disgruntled coworker would say if she knew Avery had spent her whole day off reading *The Very Hungry Caterpillar* and *Diary of a Worm* aloud in front of a mirror, practicing with different gestures, facial expressions, vocal delivery, and even accents.

(Worm, she decided, needed to have his adenoids out and sounded like he had a head cold.)

But what was so wrong with wanting to be good at something you loved doing anyway? After all, Avery thought as she stuffed another gummy worm in the last cup of dirt, if something was worth doing it was worth doing right!

Wait . . . Had she really just quoted her big sister? Thankfully, it was only her inner monologue. But she'd have to watch herself. If she ever said that within earshot of Joanie, she'd never live down her sister's "I told you so's."

"Wow! You've got quite a crowd here. How'd you get the word out so fast?"

Startled by the sound of Adam's voice behind her, Avery accidentally jerked her arm, knocking over three of the dirt cups. Cookie crumbs and chocolate pudding spilled all over the white tablecloth.

"Oh, no!"

She grabbed a napkin and tried to wipe up the mess, but that only made it worse. It looked like a St. Bernard had wiped his muddy paws on the table after taking a romp in a mud puddle.

"Hang on," Adam said, "try this."

He quickly unfolded four of the green paper napkins that were sitting on the table and used them to cover up the stain. It wasn't wonderful, but it was better.

"Thanks," Avery said.

"No problem. Really, this is a great crowd, Avery. I don't know how you did it, but I'm impressed."

"I don't either," she admitted. "All I did was print up some flyers and put a notice in the online calendar. I pulled it together pretty quick. There wasn't even time to get an article into the newsletter."

"Well, good job. I've been thinking we should start a book club for middle-grade readers, nine- to eleven-year-olds. Would you be interested in leading it?"

"Really? I'd love that."

"Good. Let's talk about it next week. What time are you supposed to start? Your audience seems a little restless," Adam said, looking across the room.

He was right. The squirmy children were getting squirmier, and louder. A little girl was trying to shove a little boy off a chair. Another little boy, whose mother was too involved in conversation with another mother to notice, was pulling book after book off the shelves and piling them on the floor.

"Not for ten minutes. Maybe I should start reading now?"

"No, it wouldn't be fair to the people who arrive on time. But I think you'd better do something to keep them entertained or we're going to have to re-shelve the whole department. Do you know how to make balloon animals?"

"Uh . . . no."

Balloon animals? Was that part of the job description?

"That's okay. I do." Adam reached into his pocket and pulled out a handful of long, skinny balloons. "Something I picked up to impress my nephew. And girls."

Grinning, he bounded up to the front of the room. "Hey, gang!" he shouted to make himself heard over the din of chattering children and a crying baby. "Welcome to the first Saturday Shenanigans Society at Bayside Books! In a few minutes, Avery, our newest management trainee, will be here to read two creepy, crawly bug-a-riffic books. But right now—let's make a balloon stegosaurus. What color should it be? Orange? Or red?"

Little hands waved in the air, voting for their favorite color. Elsa, carrying a sleeve of plastic cups, came up and stood next to Avery.

"Wait. Did he just say he's moving you into management? I've been here four months and you've been here two weeks, but now you could be my boss? You've got to be kidding me." She swore, dumped the cups onto the table, and stomped off.

Avery was too stunned to say anything, almost too stunned to move. In fact, she hadn't really heard what Elsa said, or Adam's surprise announcement. The only thing she heard were the words Adam said just before he ran up front, now playing over and over in her mind. . . .

Something I picked up to impress my nephew. And girls.

Girls? As in girls in general? Or did he mean . . . No. That was just something he'd said to be funny. He wasn't flirting with her.

Was he?

She didn't have time to decide. Adam finished making his balloon stegosaurus and introduced her. The sound of applause broke her concentration. Hearing it, she shoved aside every stray thought and focused on the only thing that mattered at that moment—doing her job. Doing it right.

As thirty children and their parents put their hands together, Avery Promise, costumed with nothing more complicated than a pair of black jeans, a white blouse, and a smile, walked confidently to the front of the room, picked up a book, and began her story.

As soon as she started to read, the children stopped squirming and started listening, laughing, and sometimes—as *The Very Hungry Caterpillar* was well-known to so many of them—jumping up in the middle of a line to tell the others what was going to happen next. Avery didn't mind; it meant they were so engaged with the story that they needed to participate in it. That's what she'd hoped would happen.

She looked at the faces of her young audience.

Some were familiar. In fact, most were. Probably three quarters of them were children she'd read to before, at the hospital. How had they found out she was working at the bookstore? There was some movement near the back of the crowd. Parents standing in the back stepped to one side or the other, parting ranks for the late arrival.

Lilly gave a little wave as her mother pushed her wheelchair nearer to the front so she could see. Avery winked, turned the page, and kept reading.

The event was a success. Avery knew that even before she finished reading. That didn't mean there weren't improvements to be made. For one thing, if they decided ever again to serve a goopy snack—and she wasn't sure they should—she needed to have plenty of wet wipes on hand. For another thing, she needed more help. Or maybe just better help.

Elsa had returned, but brought her attitude along with her. She was putting in her time, doing what she had to, but that wasn't the same thing as being helpful. It occurred to Avery that, even at minimum wage, a person could be overpaid. The minute the kids finished their snacks, Elsa went off to get an extra trash bag and disappeared for an eon, leaving Avery to coordinate the crafts for nearly thirty kids all by herself. Fortunately, some of the parents pitched in, but still . . .

With the chaos finally starting to subside, Avery

was able to break away and talk to Lilly and her mother.

"I'm so glad you came!" she exclaimed, looking first to Mrs. Margolis and then squatting down next to Lilly's wheelchair so she'd be at eye level with the little girl.

"I am sorry we were late," Mrs. Margolis replied in good but not perfect English, her lilting accent giving away her native Mexican roots. "I did not see Owen's e-mail until this morning."

"Owen sent you an e-mail about my event?"

"Yes, I think he sent it to many hospital parents. I don't think they know about it otherwise. I didn't. But I am glad we came. Lilly is having fun. Aren't you, *Hija*?"

Lilly bobbed her head deeply and deliberately, making the googly eyes glued to her blue and purple pipe cleaner antennae bounce. "Miss Avery? Why aren't you a mermaid anymore?"

"Oh, I'm still a mermaid. Just not today." Avery reached into her back pocket, pulled out one of her business cards, and placed it in Lilly's hand. "See? What does that say?"

" 'Avery "Poseidon" Promise. Part-time mermaid.' "

Lilly read the words, slowly but surely, only needing help to sound out Avery's made-up middle name. Avery looked up toward Mrs. Margolis, arching her eyebrows to silently tell her how impressed she was by Lilly's progress in reading. Mrs. Margolis gave a quick nod, smiling to show she felt just the same.

Lilly lowered the card. "So you're only a mermaid part of the time?"

"That's right. Sometimes it's fun to be a mermaid. Sometimes it's fun just to be yourself. Or sometimes," she said, flicking one of Lilly's antennae with her fingernail to make it bounce and bobble, "it's fun to be a ladybug."

"I'm a spider," Lilly corrected.

"Sure. I should have known that. Multiple eyes, right?"

Lilly nodded solemnly. Avery got to her feet so she could talk to the girl's mother more easily.

"Thank you so much for coming. I think about Lilly all the time. It's great to see her doing so well."

"She is. The doctors helped her body to heal, but you healed her spirit. You show her the power of her mind, that she can travel the world without taking a step.

"Sometimes," Mrs. Margolis said, her hand rising to finger the crucifix she wore around her neck, "when life feels too heavy to bear, God sends a beautiful angel to help carry the load. I think you are Lilly's angel. I think maybe you are mine too."

Mrs. Margolis's brown eyes were swimming with tears. She took Avery's hand and squeezed it hard before looking down at her daughter.

"We must go now, *Hija*. I will be late for work."

"Nooo," Lilly moaned. "I want to stay with Avery."

Avery squatted down again. "Don't worry. I'll see you again soon. Guess what? Mermaid me just got hired to make a commercial. We're going to shoot it at Pier 66. If it's okay with your mom, you can come and watch."

Lilly hinged her neck up so she could see her mother's face. "Can I, Mami? Please?"

"I will have to check my work schedule. But, yes, *Hija*. And now we must go."

Avery gave Lilly and her mother a quick hug and got to work putting away the chairs and tables. Elsa was still nowhere to be found. After a few minutes, Adam came looking for her.

"Hey, I thought you'd want to know—we sold eleven copies of *Caterpillar*, thirteen copies of *Worm*, and six other titles. Nice job."

"Eleven and thirteen? Is that all?"

"What do you mean is that all? That's great!"

"But you ordered twenty copies of each book."

"Because I didn't want to risk running out, also because I knew we'd be able to sell any leftovers later. Those are popular titles. They'll be gone by the end of the month, you'll see."

"So. Adam," she said slowly, not quite sure how to bring this up. "Were you kidding about moving me into management?"

"Nope, not kidding."

"I've only been here a couple of weeks. Are you sure that's a good idea?"

"Very," he said. "With some training, you'll be a great manager. You're creative, you care, and you work hard. Speaking of which, I'm a little short-handed. Can you pick up a couple of extra shifts next week?"

"Sure, anything you need."

"Good. Because I just fired Elsa."

Chapter 31

May is the month when, having had your hopes raised by the sight of newly sprung, lush green grass that turns to mud and straw beneath your feet when storm clouds gather and split into deluge on the next day, mucky enough to build bricks with, you are tempted to give up on Seattle entirely.

It is exhausting, waking up each morning, uncertain if this day will be good or bad, or even really, really good and really, really, *really* bad. You've sampled it all in recent days, but the pattern is impossible to predict and you're simply worn out with trying. You truly do think about giving up. But you don't. Because this is where you are, and where else could you go? So you stay put, hang on, and soldier through, left-right, left-right, hoping that, eventually, it all leads to someplace good.

Or at least familiar.

Meg moved furniture and set up card tables, humming some pop diva single that Trina insisted on playing whenever they were in the car. It was bouncy, upbeat, and stuck in her head, an ear-worm, the perfect soundtrack for a sisters' paint party, and it perfectly matched her mood.

Someone thumped on her door.

"It's open!" she shouted, and put a bottle of wine in the refrigerator. Asher came inside, carrying a platter with chicken wings, veggies, and dip.

"I was just going to microwave a bag of popcorn," she said when he put the tray down on the kitchen counter. "Are they here yet?"

"Joanie called. They're running late. We have twenty minutes before they get here. Maybe twenty-five."

His eyes sparked with that hungry, now-familiar flame that never failed to melt her. A smile tugged at the corner of her mouth as he stepped toward her and she stepped back, advancing and retreating together, until she backed into the wall and there was nowhere for her to go, not that she wanted to. He lowered his head and kissed her, pressing his body into hers, and she kissed him back, reveling in the sensation of being so willingly entrapped, reaching up to encircle his neck with her arms so they were even closer.

He reached down, sliding his hand up her thigh,

raising the hem of her skirt. She pulled her mouth from his and laughed. "Whoa! Slow down there, cowboy. My sisters—"

"Eighteen minutes out," he murmured, burying his lips in her hair and reaching higher. "Possibly twenty-three. Plenty of time."

"Asher!" She squealed with laughter and pushed his hand back from beneath her skirt. "Seriously, we don't have time. And even if we did, we can't do it here. There's no curtains on the front window."

He raised his head, looked at her blankly for a moment. "Right. Bedroom," he said, then grabbed her by the wrist and started pulling her down the hallway.

"Asher, no! We can't!" She laughed some more and pulled in the opposite direction, digging in with her heels like a reluctant Labrador at bath time. Asher was stronger, though, and eventually managed to drag her to the bedroom, only to find the narrow bed was heaped high with paintings.

"I had to put them somewhere," Meg said, grinning when he glowered at her. "I needed room for the card tables."

Asher released his grasp on her wrist and wilted against the wall, dropping his head forward, groaning.

"I'll come see you tonight," Meg promised. "After everybody's gone."

"Oh, fine. Another booty call. I feel so cheap."

Meg moved closer, wedged her body between his legs. "Most men like booty calls," she said, and kissed him. "Don't they?"

They kissed and caressed, more slowly than before, more gently, but with no less passion or intensity. Feeling her desire increase and resolve waver, Meg finally took a step back, placing her hands against his shoulders and taking in several deep gulps of air, trying to slow her heart and catch her breath.

"We have to stop. Really. I don't want to, but we have to. My sisters . . ."

Asher groaned again. "Okay. You're right. But you're coming over later?"

"Yes."

"And staying?"

"Asher . . ."

Meg's insistence on getting up and returning to her own house after their trysts had become a bone of contention between them in the last few days. Every time she came to his bed, he begged her to stay.

"I just think it's better if I go back home. How will it look to Trina if she gets up in the morning and I'm there in your room?"

"How will it *look?*" he asked, his jaw going slack. "It'll look like we're married. You know why? Because we are. It's not my room, Meg. It's our room. It's our house, yours and mine. Your name is on the deed right next to mine—Meg and

Asher Hayes. Same last name. Why? Because we're married."

"I know, I know," she said, walking down the hallway and into the great room with Asher following. "But, right now, I don't feel married. I feel like we're having one long, fabulous date. Or maybe a torrid love affair." She opened a cupboard, pulled down three wineglasses, and turned toward him. "And, really, what's so bad about that? Why can't we just go on like this for a while?"

"It's not bad," Asher replied. "In fact, it's been great. But it's not real. Look, I've got nothing against dating. Dating is fantastic. But it's not supposed to be a permanent condition. I married you because I wanted to *stop* dating you."

Meg put the glasses on the counter and tipped her head to one side, giving him a look. "You married me because you wanted to have sex with me. You were a good Christian boy from a good Christian home and you couldn't sleep with me unless we were married. *That's* why you married me. You told me so yourself."

"No," he said slowly, in a correcting sort of tone, "that's why I married you so fast. Six weeks was as long as I could wait and I wanted to do it right, without compromising anything. If Joanie hadn't been so set on throwing us a wedding, I'd have married you sooner. But sex wasn't the only thing I couldn't wait for.

"Don't you get it?" he asked earnestly. "I couldn't wait for *you*. I wanted us to be together forever. Every night, every morning. For always. I love you." He grabbed her hands. "Come to me tonight. Come to me and stay with me."

Asher's eyes pleaded with her just as intensely as his words. Looking into them, thinking about all the things she had learned about him over the last weeks—that he was kind, considerate, hard-working, handsome, funny, playful, creative, a good father, a good man, a gentle and generous lover—she couldn't understand why she couldn't say yes to his request. It didn't make sense, not even to her. And yet . . .

"I'm just not ready yet, Asher."

He dropped her hands, almost pushing them away. "When will you be ready? It's been a month. And that's not counting all the months before the accident when you'd hardly talk to me. But we've finally gotten past all that. We're good now. Can you blame me for wanting my wife and life back? What are we waiting for?"

"Your life? Your wife?" she barked, incredulous. "So this is all about possession?"

"Oh, come on! You're not being fair. That's not what I was saying and you know it. I just want to get our lives back to normal. I want us to go back to being married again."

"Why? So we can spend more time arguing?"

She knew she wasn't being fair even before he

pointed it out, just as she knew he didn't mean his words to sound the way she'd taken them. But she was annoyed at him for cornering her on a subject that she wasn't ready to deal with. She'd been in such a good mood when he came in, looking forward to a fun night with her sisters and a steamy tryst afterward. What more did he need? Why couldn't he just let it be, let *her* be?

Someone coughed.

Meg and Asher turned toward the sound. Meg didn't know how long Trina had been there, but judging from the look in her eyes, it had been long enough.

"Looks like you're getting your wish, Dad. The two of you are definitely back to normal. Way to go, guys."

Asher turned to her. "Honey, you don't understand. We're not fighting—"

"We were just talking and it got a little heated," Meg interrupted when she saw that smoldering look in Trina's eyes and knew she wasn't listening to him. "Really. Everything's fine."

"Whatever. I don't care," Trina said, dropping an unconvincing curtain of indifference. "I just came out to tell you that Aunt Joanie and Aunt Avery are here."

She stomped off across the yard to the big house.

Asher watched her retreat. "If people came into the world as teenagers, the world would be filled with nothing but only children. . . ."

Meg slipped her arm around his waist, the indignation of a moment before dissipating into guilt. Trina slammed the backdoor so hard that the two of them jumped. Asher looked at Meg with an expression of feigned desperation.

"Couldn't I stay out here and paint instead?"

She smiled with relief. The moment had passed. She was right. They were good now.

"Sorry. Girls only. You still want me to come over after? It might be late."

"I'll wait up." He gave her a peck on the lips. "Have fun."

"We will," she said.

Having fun comes easier to some people than others.

"I can't do this. I told you," Joanie said, pointing at her canvas and what should have been a field of flowers but looked more like a pile of regurgitated jellybeans, then to Avery's canvas, which looked even better than the inspiration photo Meg had pinned on the wall for them to work from, a mountain landscape with blue sky above and wildflowers at the base. "Look at Avery's. It looks exactly like it's supposed to."

Meg looked at her sister's easel and frowned. She truly believed the old saying that inside every person there is an artist waiting to get out, that all human beings are born with a natural talent and urge to express themselves through art. But if that was true, then why did so few adults do so?

The answer was perfectly illustrated by Joanie's pointing finger, first at her work, then at Avery's. Comparison, competition, and perfectionism—the toxic trifecta that is certain to corrode and, in time, destroy one's God-given, joy-filled, natural desire to create. Among other things.

"Don't pay attention to what Avery is doing," Meg said, nudging her younger sister's easel to an angle so the older one couldn't see. "It's not a contest. Just have fun and enjoy the process."

"How can I when Avery's is perfect and mine sucks?" Joanie put her paintbrush into her water cup and left it there, pouting.

"It *is* perfect, isn't it?" Avery said, frowning as she studied her own canvas. "It looks almost exactly like the picture. No wonder I'm so bored."

Avery dropped her paintbrush, crossed her arms over her chest, and stared unhappily at her painting. Meg made an exasperated sound and got to her feet.

"Okay, this isn't working," she said, then plucked her siblings' canvases from their easels and put them aside. "Time to try a new approach."

"Like what?" Joanie asked.

"Like wine," Meg answered, going into the kitchen and pulling a bottle of white from the refrigerator.

"Nope." Joanie lifted her hand like a defendant taking an oath. "I swore off it after I invited Hal to dinner. Makes me too loose."

"Tonight you could use some loose," Meg replied, pulling out the cork. "You're thinking way too much. What you need to do, dear sister, is kill a few brain cells. Here."

Meg held out a glass of wine and kept holding it out until Joanie, finally and reluctantly, took it from her hand and took a sip.

"Better," she said, and filled a glass for Avery.

"Hey, how come Joanie gets more?"

"Because she needs it more." Meg poured some wine for herself. "All right, now that we're all provisioned, let's give this another try."

Glass in hand, she marched back over to the painting tables, laid a big piece of white butcher paper at each place, then put three aluminum pie plates in the middle of the table. Joanie lowered her glass from her lips.

"Meg. This is pointless. It doesn't matter how many times I try, I'm never going to be able to paint a mountain that looks like that," she said, pointing to the inspiration photo that was still tacked on the wall.

Meg ripped down the picture and then picked up a big bottle of yellow acrylic paint and started pouring some into one of the pie pans.

"Good to hear. Because I can't think of anything less fun than trying to copy somebody else's painting. Forgive me. I don't know what I was thinking," she said, pouring out a pool of blue. "Now get over here. Bring your glasses."

Chapter 32

Looking at the stars always made Trina feel better. She wasn't exactly sure why. Maybe it was because she could count on them no matter what.

She understood logically that, over the course of time and millennia, even constellations change and move, but she liked knowing that they were up there, where they were supposed to be. Sometimes, when she was having a bad day, she liked to look up to a certain spot in the cloudy or sunny day and think, *I can't see it now, but the Andromeda Galaxy is right there,* and then, when night came, she'd train her telescope on that same spot and see that she'd been right. Even when you couldn't see the stars, they were there. Always. It was comforting. She wished the rest of life could be so reliable.

Trina bent down low and adjusted the telescope lens, bringing everything into focus—stars, planets, and constellations. She began searching for Cassiopeia, moving the scope very slowly, a fraction of a degree at a time, in the direction where she thought it ought to be.

Why did they have to start fighting again?

Trina had thought her mother was going to die when she was in the hospital. It was awful and scary, especially when she then recalled all the times she had thought about, not exactly in a wishing sort of way but more just considering, what life would be like if she didn't have a mother. At least not *her* mother.

But when Meg came home, it seemed like the thing Trina never quite dared to wish for had actually come true—she had a new mother. One she liked a *lot* more.

This mother listened, laughed, painted, and understood. She was fun, cool, and available. The way her dad looked at this mother made Trina know that he was happy now, too, and that everything was good, for all of them.

But after a couple of weeks, it occurred to Trina that this wasn't a new mother after all.

As Meg regained memories, so did Trina. She remembered the mother she had adored, her best friend, the mother who had organized art projects, games nights, and camping trips. The mother who listened, laughed, painted, and understood. She remembered the way that her mother and father used to look at each other, like they were sharing a secret without uttering a word. She remembered the sounds, late at night, when they thought she was asleep, coming from their room, sounds of soft laughter and whispered words, of unintelligible urgencies that Trina could paraphrase but not translate, not understanding the details, only knowing it meant that her parents loved each other, and her by extension, and that everything was safe and she could count on them always.

In the last few weeks, it seemed that they were headed back to that safe place, that everyone was where and how they were supposed to be—her mother, her father, herself.

Where had they been before that? She couldn't say. Maybe nowhere. Maybe it was like the stars, more visible on some days than others, but always, always there. She liked that theory best. It was comforting, for a time.

But now they were fighting again. And she couldn't find Cassiopeia.

Trina stood up, straightening her spine and lifting her face to the night, searching the skies and blinking back tears. She couldn't see it.

She heard something, a squeal followed by laughter. It was coming from her mother's house. Lamplight on the shades backlit the windows of Meg's tiny house like a scrim, illuminating a crazy pantomime of female figures, dancing, twisting, and leaping like witches roiling round a caldron.

As that first squeal and ripple of laughter was followed by others, becoming louder and more sustained, voices separate in cadence and pitch overlapping into a single hysterical howl, Trina walked toward the house, drawn by curiosity and her inability to picture what was going on behind the curtain.

No one answered Trina's knock. There was so

much noise coming from inside that probably they hadn't heard her. She opened the door a few inches and stuck her head inside, jaw dropping at what she saw.

The walls were covered with paintings, at least a dozen of them. These weren't her mother's canvases but big rectangles of white butcher paper covered with pictures of birds and bunnies, owls and alligators, flowers, squiggles, and shooting stars, all executed with quick, broad swipes of paint in bold, vibrant colors—red, blue, yellow, pink, purple, and neon green—the same colors she now saw on her mother's and aunts' fingers, faces, and even their clothes. Crazy!

But not as crazy as the way that Meg and the others were chasing one another around that tiny room, dodging and weaving around chairs and tables, sometimes knocking them over, roaring with laughter in a raucous game of tag that had no discernible rules and only one goal, to catch somebody and mark their face or body with streaks of paint without being marked yourself, like a pack of preschoolers counting coup.

"Mom?" Trina called as her mother pirouetted past the door with Avery in hot pursuit, too bent on escape to see or hear her daughter. Trina tried again. "Mom!"

Still no response.

Trina opened the door completely, stepped into the room and into the path of her aunt Joanie, who leapt off the window seat, howling a war cry as she attempted to ambush her sisters. She landed on Trina instead, leaving a big pink handprint on Trina's T-shirt.

"Aunt Joanie! Are you insane? I just bought this!"

The sound of Trina's indignant cry startled the sisters, freezing them into momentary silence and immobility as they stared at Joanie's pink handprint on the belly of Trina's Forever 21 tee, before collapsing into gales of hysterical laughter and one another's arms.

"What is wrong with you guys? Didn't you hear me say this was a new shirt?"

Trina spun around to face her mother. "Mom, seriously! What's going on? Have you guys been smoking weed or something?"

This question brought forth a fresh wave of hysteria. Meg, one hand covered with orange paint and the other with green, approached her daughter, gasping to catch her breath even as she blinked tears of laughter from her eyes.

"Oh, honey! No weed. Just wine. A couple of bottles. That's all. We're finger painting."

"Finger painting?"

Avery started to giggle. Meg pressed her lips together, struggling to regain her composure. "Yes. But . . . well . . . things kind of got out of control."

"You think?" Trina threw out her arms and

looked down at her stomach. "I paid sixteen bucks for this shirt!"

"I'm sorry," Joanie said, grinning even as she apologized. "I'll get you a new shirt. Although, personally, I think it looks better this way." She started to laugh again, giving herself up to it so thoroughly that she could barely choke out her words.

Joanie's laughter was a contagion. Her sisters quickly succumbed. Trina, hungry for justice but surrounded by madwomen and derision, stamped her foot impotently and started toward the door.

"Trina! Don't go! We're sorry." Meg walked toward her daughter, arms open wide. "Don't go away mad, honey. Let me make it up to you. Come on and paint with us."

"Paint with you?" Trina gasped. "Are you kidding? I'd rather—"

Before Trina could finish, Meg clasped her in her arms and held her close, leaving two more handprints, one orange and one green, on the back of Trina's shirt.

She squealed and wriggled from her mother's grasp, mouth gaping as she realized her mother had done it on purpose. Avery, with tears tracking down her cheeks, swept her arm to the right, dipped her fingers into blue paint, and wiped a line down Trina's nose and twin thunderbolts on her left and right cheeks.

"War paint!" she cackled.

Trina howled, thrust her fingers into a pie pan of purple, and chased Avery around the table and into the kitchen. Meg and Joanie came right behind them, laughing.

The noise from the tiny house was loud enough that Asher heard it over the baseball game he'd put on for company while paying bills. He went outside to make sure everything was okay.

Standing just a few steps from the back door, he looked across the yard, saw shadows projected onto the window shades, heard the hoots of laughter. He couldn't see precisely what was happening but he understood what it meant.

His wife was making memories, new ones, to replace the lost and augment the found, something to share with people she loved. What a good idea.

He stood there for some long minutes, looking toward Meg's house, picking out his wife's and daughter's voices from the rest, letting the sound wash over him, and thinking.

When he made up his mind, Asher put his hands in his pockets and hinged his head high, his face bathed in starshine. He turned his gaze to the northern sky, searching the heavens for something familiar.

There it was. Cassiopeia.

He lifted his hand skyward and traced the constellation's distinctive "w" shape, touching each star with the tip of his finger, then went inside.

It was past midnight when Meg finally padded quietly across the lawn toward the darkened house and her husband's bed. When she got inside she found the bedroom door was locked. She jiggled the knob and called Asher's name, but softly so as not to wake Trina. When he didn't answer, she gave up and went home, supposing he must have fallen asleep after all.

Alone in her tiny house, her narrow bed, Meg tried to sleep, but couldn't. A piece of her was missing. And so she lay there for a long time, staring into the darkness, waiting for morning.

Chapter 33

Until it started to buzz in the dark, Hal didn't realize he'd forgotten to turn off his cell phone. He cursed groggily as his hand explored the nightstand, then put the phone to his ear.

"Who and what?" he growled.

"It's Lynn. Did I wake you?"

"It's okay," he said sarcastically. "I had to get up to answer the phone. What time is it?"

"Oops. Only five-thirty your time. I forgot about the time difference. Sorry."

He rolled to his side and lifted the shade on the bedroom window. It was just as dark outside as in. "You are not forgiven. Ever."

"Think of it this way, you've got a jump on the day. The early bird and all."

"Lynn. You know the only thing worse than being woken from a sound sleep by a phone call at five-thirty?"

"When the person calling is a morning person and you're a night person?"

"Bingo." He dropped the shade, rested his head back on the pillow, the phone still held to his ear, eyes still closed. "So? What's wrong?"

"How do you know something is wrong?"

"Because you never call with good news."

"That's not true. I told you last month that my mechanic replaced my bad muffler for free. And the last time we talked I told you that the guy I met down in Venice Beach called and invited me to go to see Eli Young at the House of Blues when I get back to LA."

"I meant good news for *me*."

"Oh. Right."

Hal yawned. "So? What's the disaster du jour?"

"Well, it's not a disaster exactly. And it's not just one thing. Hang on, let me get my list."

He clapped his hand over his eyes. She had a list. A *list* of not exactly disasters. And she wanted to discuss them before the sun was up.

"Okay. Got it," she said. "First, have you looked at the bills lately? Or the books?"

Of course he hadn't. That was part of why he'd hired Lynn in the first place, because the sound of calculator keys clicking was music to her ears and a well-balanced budget made her go weak in the knees. Which was great. Every small business needs that person. As long as it didn't have to be him.

"Nope. How bad are they?"

"Bad enough that you'd better have a movie in the can by the end of the year. And it better be good enough that somebody will pay to watch it."

For all the urgency in Lynn's voice and message, Hal wasn't overly concerned. She could have been describing their financial position in any given year. Stunted Genius frequently teetered on the brink of financial ruin. Then they'd finish the project, enter some film festival, build the buzz, find a distributor, and everything would be fine. Until the next time it wasn't. Lynn was a worrywart. What she was describing was just the normal business cycle, at least for them.

"So, we'll finish the movie by the end of the year. Next?"

"Are you sure? Because that brings me to my second point. After you've exhausted the barbecue and mini-golf options, there's not a whole lot to do in rural Georgia after the sun goes down. So I've been spending my nights with my computer, looking over the footage you shot so far. I'm just not seeing it, Hal."

"Seeing what?"

"The movie. The only really interesting stuff is

of Avery—can't go wrong with a mermaid. Apart from that, you've got forty hours of tape and no story."

"Yes, I know," he said in a sarcastically patient tone. "That's why I suspended filming, remember? There was no point in going forward until I could convince Joanie to cooperate."

"And is she?"

He draped it over his head and smiled, thinking about Joanie.

"I'm making progress."

"How much progress?" she prodded.

Hal hesitated, twisted his lips, thinking. "She'll be ready to bring the cameras back in soon. Maybe another couple of weeks."

"Okay. Will *you* be ready to bring the cameras in by then?"

He shifted himself up on the pillows. "Of course," he said, a little annoyed and more awake now. "I've put years of my life and every dime I have into this project. Why would I want to keep the cameras away?"

"Because this isn't just another movie for you, Hal. I can tell by the way you've been talking about her since you sent the crew home. And not just Joanie—all the sisters. The son, too. You talk about them like they're family."

"It's just because I'm getting to know them better. But I'm not emotionally involved, if that's what you're asking. Not to that degree. I'm up here because I want to make a movie, not because I need new friends."

"Just wanted to make sure that we're still on the same page. And we are," she said, though she didn't sound completely convinced. "We're making this movie no matter what, documenting the facts and putting them on film without holding anything back. Because that's what we do."

"Lynn, what are you talking about? It's too early to be mysterious."

"Well, it's like I told you before I flew out here—everything Minerva told you is sort of true—or at least has some seed of truth to it—but there's always more to it than what she told you. Or less."

"Like what? Give me specifics."

"For example, her birth name was Melanie Ann Weldon, just like she told you. And, she was a singer. Apparently a pretty good one—sang solos in the school choir and such. But nobody remembers anything about her being discovered at a radio station talent show, or getting a scholarship to study voice in Atlanta and then taking Minerva Promise as her stage name. In a town this small, you'd think somebody would have remembered.

"I could confirm that she was raised by a single mother, Betty Jean Weldon, but Betty Jean was a barmaid at the local nightclub, not a singer like Minerva said. Sounds like she might have done a little business after hours, if you know what I mean, but I can't confirm that. People aren't too keen to talk to strangers around here, especially if they're from Los Angeles.

"But I've combed through every issue of the local paper from the beginning of the Korean conflict to the end and couldn't find an obit notice for a Daniel James Weldon, or anybody else with that last name."

"So," Hal said. "Maybe Minerva invented a war hero father to cover up the fact that she was illegitimate? She wouldn't have been the first one to do that, especially if she was born in the early 1950s."

"Which brings me to my next discovery. Minerva was born in 1959, not 1954. She's five years younger than she claims to be."

"What? Are you sure?"

"One hundred percent. The only person I was able to win over in this town was a lady named Nancy. She started working as a secretary at the elementary school when she was eighteen. Now she's seventy, doesn't ever plan to retire. She's amazing, Hal, remembers every single student who ever came through the door, including Minerva, who started first grade in 1965. That was the same year Nancy started working at the school. Which means Minerva is only fifty-eight years old, not sixty-three like she's been telling everyone."

"But why? Who tacks an extra five years to their age?"

"Nobody I know," Lynn said. "I've been celebrating the anniversary of my twenty-ninth birthday for the last four years."

Lynn chuckled at her own joke, but Hal didn't hear her. He was too busy trying to poke holes in Lynn's theory. Nothing she was telling him made sense.

"How can you be sure she didn't mix up Minerva with somebody else?" he asked. "Or get the year wrong? Even if she's as sharp as you say, who could remember every kid who came through the door for the last fifty-odd years?"

"Nancy can," Lynn said confidently. "I tested her. They didn't start printing yearbooks at the school until about forty years ago, but I showed her pictures of a couple of dozen kids picked at random and she was able to name every one of them and tell me the year they started school. I'm telling you, Hal, she's got a photographic memory.

"And get this: I asked Nancy if I could see Minerva's school records. She said she couldn't let me see them personally or make any copies, but she said she'd take a look in the archives and tell me if she saw anything strange. But when she went to look, she couldn't find Minerva's records, not for 1965 or any other year.

"Here's something else that's weird; Joanie was born in England in 1979, but I found a source that swears they saw Minerva on a street in Atlanta in 1978 and that she was very, very pregnant."

"Case of mistaken identity? A crowded street in a big city—could have been somebody who looked like her."

"I don't think so. This person says they got close, maybe ten feet away, and that Minerva turned away and ducked into the nearest office building when she spotted her."

A sliver of sunlight was showing on the horizon. Hal stared out the window, trying to make sense of all this new information.

"So, if she was pregnant a year before she had Joanie . . . That would mean there was a fourth Promise sister."

"Or brother," Lynn offered. "It could have been a boy. The big question is, what happened to that baby?"

"Maybe she gave it up for adoption. Or to a relative?"

"I couldn't find any adoption records or any relatives. Minerva was an only child. After her mother died, she had nobody."

"You're kidding. So what happened to her?"

"I'm not sure. I found somebody who she went to high school with who told me that Minerva left town the summer between her freshman and sophomore years—the same year her mother died. Minerva was placed in some kind of foster situation for a while, but then she disappeared.

Maybe ran away. Anyway, that's the last anybody around here saw of her."

"Do you think she could have gone to Atlanta, like she claimed?"

"Possibly. But if she did, she was only sixteen at the time, not twenty-one. And if she actually did study music there, I sure can't find any record of that."

"But there wouldn't be, would there? She said she studied privately, with . . ."

"Cornelia Armstedt," Lynn said when Hal couldn't immediately supply the name. "A former opera star. She retired to Atlanta in the early fifties and taught privately. There's only one problem with that part of the story; Armstedt suffered from dementia. She moved into a nursing home about a year after Minerva claims she began studying with her and died three years later. So, if Minerva studied with her, it couldn't have been for long.

"Bottom line is, Minerva's story has enough holes in it to sink the *Titanic*, but there's nothing I can absolutely prove. When it comes to actual printed documents, I can't find anything about Minerva or Melanie Anne before 1979. It's almost like she didn't exist before then. I'm no private eye, but it looks to me like somebody wiped out her records on purpose."

"Minerva?"

"Maybe. But I'm starting to wonder if she had help. Whoever did it was very, very thorough."

Hal shook his head. "Then why didn't the media find out? There were a zillion stories out there, especially after the talk show video was leaked."

"Yes," Lynn said, "but those stories focused on the girls, not Minerva. She was very good at deflecting attention from herself and back to her daughters. If everything hadn't blown up the way it did and the book hadn't been pulled, the inconsistencies in Minerva's story might have come to light eventually. But once the tape was out there, the past didn't matter. There was plenty of pay dirt to be mined from the Promise Girls story without bothering to do any actual investigative journalism. Why schlep all the way down to a centrally isolated town in south Georgia trying to dig up facts from people who don't want to talk to you when you can just play that juicy video over and over and get better ratings with less work?"

"Makes sense," Hal mused. "Even if anybody had tried to do any real reporting on Minerva, the story would have been old news by the time they got to the bottom of it. It was tabloid stuff, the kind of thing people love to watch and get outraged over because it gives them a chance to feel better about themselves by looking down on somebody. After a few days, people would get tired of watching and move on to some new outrage."

"Exactly," Lynn said. "So. Can I come home now? I miss my cat. And California cuisine. I'd pay fifty bucks for an In-N-Out Burger right now."

"But there are still so many unanswered questions. Can't you just—"

"No," she said firmly. "I've done all I can here, Hal. Every lead I've followed has turned into a dead end. And after all this time, the only thing I know for sure is that Minerva went to a lot of trouble to fabricate a new past for herself."

"I know, but why?"

"That's what you have to figure out. But you're not going to be able to do that playing nice. You're going to have to dig deeper, start asking the hard questions, and be willing to expose the truth about Joanie and her sisters, the truth they might not even be aware of. If you're not up for that, then we don't have a movie. And if we don't have a movie—"

"Stunted Genius goes under."

"Right. So should I go back to LA and start trying to cut these forty hours of tape into a usable fifteen minutes? Or should I go back to LA and start writing my résumé? Because, either way, I'm going home."

"All right," Hal said finally. "Book a flight to LAX. I might join you in a couple days. It may be time for me to make another visit to Minerva. I'm not convinced that Joanie or the other sisters know anything about this."

"But you're going to ask, right? You're not just going to let them off that hook? If you don't have the stomach for this, tell me now."

"I'm on it. Joanie invited me over for lunch this afternoon. I'll talk to her about bringing the cameras back in and then start asking questions about Minerva and a fourth Promise sibling."

"You think she trusts you enough to let you?"

"Maybe. We'll find out soon enough, won't we? Hey, good work out there," he said, getting to his feet and adjusting the angle of the window blinds. "I mean it. As soon as you land in LA, drive to the nearest In-N-Out, order a shake, fries, and burger, and charge it to the company expense account. In fact, make the burger a double-double."

"Wow. Big spender. Is that what I'm getting instead of a raise?"

"Afraid so," Hal said. "You know better than anybody how busted I am."

"True. But that might be about to change. I don't know if it occurred to you, but if Minerva's lies end up leading to some kind of scandal, our quiet little documentary might end up being the kind of tell-all that big studios or cable channels would be willing to pay big bucks for."

Chapter 34

Meg woke to the sound of someone knocking on the front door. The insistent sound became a prop in her dream. It took some time for her to separate dream from day and get out of bed.

"I made pancakes," Asher said when she opened the door, tilting his chin toward the tray in his hands. "They might be a little cold by now, but the coffee's hot."

"Breakfast in bed. You're sweet."

Threads of the dream still clung to her, like sticky filaments of spider silk when you walk inadvertently into a web. Now she brushed them away, replaced by a surge of affection and desire. There was something flattering about a man whose first thought upon waking was to concoct a plan to lure her to bed; seduction is just so seductive. She opened the door, inviting his entrance.

"What time is it?"

"Almost ten. I wanted to let you sleep for a while. You had a late night."

A little crease of confusion appeared on Meg's forehead as he set the tray down on the kitchen counter before pulling out one of the stools and sitting down, wondering why he didn't bring the tray into the bedroom. But then, it probably made sense. Pancakes and syrup were less than ideal aphrodisiacs. All fantasy aside, there's nothing sexy about sticky sheets. But the no-nonsense way he tucked into his food without waiting for her made him look more like a man fortifying himself for a day of work than one setting the stage for a midmorning tryst. Was he upset with her? She pulled a stool to the opposite corner of the counter and sat down, facing him.

"Sounds like you had a good time," he said, pouring more syrup onto his pancakes. "I could hear you guys laughing from inside the house."

"Yeah." She smiled and sipped her coffee. "Things got pretty wild. We're probably lucky the neighbors didn't call the cops. It was a lot of fun, though."

"I could tell."

She rested her fingers on his forearm. "When I said I'd be late, I didn't realize how late. I'm sorry. Hope you didn't wait up too long."

"No problem. I worked on the books for a while and then went to bed. They're still a mess, though. I've got to meet up with a building inspector at eleven, then install some countertops, so I guess the books will have to wait until tonight."

"Why don't you let me do that? Now that I'm recovered, it's time I quit acting like a guest and start to do my part."

He lifted his brows to an uncertain angle, but she saw the relief in his eyes.

"Are you sure? I don't want to get in the way of your work. I'm really happy you're painting again."

"So am I, but really, I want to help. I can paint and help run the business too. Avery's a part-time mermaid. No reason I can't be a part-time artist, right?"

"If you don't mind, that would be a huge help. I can hammer nails and saw lumber all day long.

But paperwork?" He shook his head and took another bite. "That just wears me out."

"Well, I've got no objection to you wearing yourself out, but not on paperwork." Meg's fingers found their way back to his arm; she stroked a line from his shoulder to his elbow, lightly but not so lightly that he could miss her invitation.

"I missed you last night. I don't like sleeping alone."

He smiled, lifted her hand from his arm, and raised it to his lips, kissing that soft spot on the interior, where her palm met her wrist.

"Neither do I. In fact, I hate it. But I think we should, at least for a while." She frowned and he answered the question in her eyes. "I didn't lock my door by accident last night, Meg."

Stung by rejection, she tried to draw back her hand, but he wouldn't release it. Instead, he tightened his hold on her.

"Listen to me," he said, moving his head when she tried to escape his gaze, locking his eyes onto hers. "The accident . . . every time I think about what could have happened, I feel sick, terrified. Then I feel grateful because what could have happened didn't happen. We got another chance and it's helped me remember what it was that made me fall in love with you in the first place. It wasn't just the sex, Meg, not then or now.

"Though," he said with a bad-boy smile, "the

sex is pretty spectacular. I've missed that a lot. But I've missed you even more. So, knowing all that, can I ask you to do me a favor? Marry me."

Meg rolled her eyes. "Very funny. Where would you like to have the ceremony? St. Paul's Cathedral? Oh, wait . . . How about Disney World? Daisy Duck can be my bridesmaid."

"This isn't a joke, Meg. I'm asking you to marry me."

"We're already married, remember? That's what you keep telling me."

"I remember," he assured her. "We've made so many good memories over the years that I could never forget. In time, I hope all those memories come back to you, including our wedding day. But whether they do or not, it's time for us to move forward. Because the thing I remember most about you is what I knew the minute I laid eyes on you and remember fresh with every new day: You're the only woman I ever have or ever could love.

"Marry me, Meg. Make me the happiest man in the world, again."

Meg felt her throat thicken and she averted her eyes, saying nothing, knowing the next word she spoke would bring her to tears, remembering with absolute clarity something she hadn't been certain of until just that moment, that she loved him. Yet, as much as she wanted to picture herself as the woman he was describing, the only woman for him, a piece of her resisted the idea. She didn't want to believe it unless it was true.

Asher got to his feet, still holding her hand.

"You say you need time and space and I'm willing to give it to you. As much time as you need. But, I'm not going to make it easy for you, love. Not anymore. I'm just as impatient to make you mine as I was at twenty-two. And I want to do this right.

"So until you know for sure that you want to marry me, live with me, and hopefully grow old with me, I'll be sleeping alone. It won't be easy, but I'll do it, for you. You're worth the wait."

He bent down and kissed the top of her head, letting his lips rest in the softness of her hair for a long moment before lifting his head.

"I gotta go to work," he said, and walked to the door.

She watched him go, still fighting a battle inside herself.

"Asher?"

He turned to face her. Those brown eyes, flecked with gold, and the hope she saw in them vanquished her. Just as she feared, the next word she spoke, she spoke in tears.

Chapter 35

Avery stood at Joanie's back door and hesitated. Though she'd never done so before, she felt like she ought to knock, announce herself in some way. Or maybe she was just putting off what was going to be a very unpleasant conversation that, quite possibly, might end with Joanie never speaking to her again.

Joanie was standing at the kitchen counter, holding the phone to her ear with one hand and cracking eggs into a bowl with the other. Avery stood in the doorway, waiting for her to finish her conversation, fascinated that her sister could crack eggs single-handedly without managing to crush the shells.

"Of course!" Joanie exclaimed to the caller. "Are you kidding? I'm thrilled to do it here. No, no. You're *not* having it anywhere else."

Joanie turned around to throw the eggshells into the trash and saw Avery. She smiled and gave her head a little upward tilt by way of greeting, then went on to wrap up the call.

"It's no trouble. This will be as much fun for me as for you. Okay, sure. We'll discuss the details later. Congratulations!" She paused to listen, then laughed. "Well, I know, but still. This is exciting!"

Joanie ended the call and turned to Avery with a

huge smile. "That was Asher. You won't believe this! He proposed to Meg this morning and she said yes!"

"Proposed? They're already married."

"I know, but Meg doesn't remember the wedding. So they are going to renew their vows. We're going to do it at the Memorial Day barbecue, just like the first time. I want to make it as close to the original ceremony as possible."

Joanie's eyes glazed in thought. "Too bad Meg and Asher's wedding album got lost in the fire. I still remember a lot of the details, but it would be a lot easier if I had some pictures to work from."

"That's so romantic!" Avery enthused, forgetting her original purpose in coming over. "How can I help?"

"Do you have time? I don't want to get in the way of your work schedule. But, if you could help that would be great. We've only got a few days to pull this off."

"What do you want me to do?"

"Well, I think we really should approach this in the way we would a reenactment," Joanie said after a moment. "Which means we need to find as much documentation as possible before we do anything."

"How do we do that without the wedding pictures?"

"Could you go up into the attic and poke around in some of my files? Who knows? I might have one or two pictures tucked away somewhere. And it wouldn't surprise me if you ran across some of my original lists and notes. You know me, I don't eat breakfast without making a plan first."

"And you never throw *anything* away," Avery said, thinking about the last time Joanie sent her up to the attic, in search of the Thanksgiving turkey platter, and the stacks of filing boxes she'd seen lined up against the walls. So many boxes.

"Nope, I never do," Joanie replied proudly, as if her sister had just paid her the highest of compliments. "I've still got the original pattern for Meg's wedding dress, along with swatches of the fabrics I used to make it. I'd better start sewing the new one right away. So much to do!" she exclaimed happily, then pulled a whisk from a crock on the counter and started beating the bowl of eggs. "Food, cake, music, flowers, dress . . . After I get this banana bread into the oven, I'll hop in the car and go to the fabric store to see if I can find some satin and lace to match the original."

The mention of Joanie's car reminded Avery of why she was here. "Oh, yeah . . . Before you do that, I need to go downtown. Can I borrow your car?"

Joanie dumped some flour into the egg mixture and kept stirring. "Okay, but can it wait until later this afternoon? I really want to start working on the dress."

"Um . . . Not really. I have to pick somebody up at the train station in a little while," she said, hoping this would satisfy her sister's curiosity even though she knew that would just be delaying the inevitable.

Joanie stopped stirring the bread batter. "Who?"

Avery took a deep breath.

"Minerva."

"What?"

The expression on Joanie's face was so blank and the tone of her voice so even that at first Avery couldn't tell if Joanie hadn't heard her or didn't believe her.

"Minerva sent me a text last night. I didn't see it until after we got home from Meg's house. She's arriving in Seattle today and asked me to pick her up at the train station."

Joanie looked at her with that same silent, blank expression that felt more like a denunciation than any words she could have spoken.

"I couldn't say no or tell her not to come," Avery said. "She was already on the train. And she's got nowhere else to go. Her boyfriend died a few months ago and his kids made her get out of the house two days later. They wouldn't even let her go to the funeral.

"She got an apartment and a job as a restaurant hostess, but you know how expensive it is in LA. She couldn't keep up with the bills and was evicted from her apartment. When she came home from work, the door was padlocked. She finally was able to get in and get her clothes, but she ended up giving the landlord all her furniture to settle up on the back rent. Everything she owns is packed into two suitcases and is on the train to Seattle."

Avery spread out her hands helplessly. "She's my mother. She asked me to come and get her. What was I supposed to do?"

Joanie shook her head with a slow, almost imperceptible movement. "How do you even know all this?"

Avery squared her shoulders. "Because I've been talking to her. On the phone. Not all the time, but on and off for the last three years. She's my mother," Avery repeated in a tone that begged her sister to understand. "And yours. Maybe not the best mother in the world, but the only one we've got. And the fact that she doesn't get to talk to us is just breaking her heart. And she's never even met her grandchildren. How would you feel if—"

"I don't care how she feels!" Joanie barked. "I am not letting her within ten thousand miles of my son. You *know* what she's like, Avery."

"I do. Maybe better than you. I lived with her for seven years after the book came out, Joanie. Losing us changed her. I'm not saying she was suddenly transformed into a normal mother— Minerva is always going to be Minerva. But what's so great about being normal? Normal is boring."

"She's not quirky, Avery. She's toxic. She scarred us."

"Is that what you think we are? Scarred?"

"You think we're not?" Joanie scoffed.

"No. Maybe a little . . . dented. But that's what makes us interesting! And Minerva is part of that. Not only did she let me fly my freak flag, she encouraged it."

"It wasn't a freak flag," Joanie spat. "It was a freak show. She exploited us, Avery. She used us to feed her own need for attention, she engineered us, tried to make us be what she couldn't."

"How do you know that?"

Joanie scowled. "What do you mean how do I know? I lived through it. I know what she did. So do you."

"But do you know why she did it? Did you ask her?"

"What are you talking about?"

"We were kids when the wheels came off the bus. We were impacted by the choices she made, but do we really understand why she made them? Maybe there were things going on that we didn't understand. Maybe she was doing what she thought she had to do. Did you ever ask her?"

"I don't need to ask her. I don't want to know."

"But I do."

The sound of that deep, familiar voice made

them both turn around. Walt was standing in the doorway. He was so tall and broad, with the shoulders and voice of a man. But at that moment, he had the pleading eyes of a child.

"Walt," Joanie said quietly. "You don't . . . you can't understand—"

"I know. But I want to. If you don't give me a chance to figure it out, I never will. I've been researching the character I'm going to interpret at Fort Nisqually over the summer, Lawrence Aloysius McCormick. He died more than two hundred years ago. Do you realize that I know more about his family and ancestors than I do my own?

"There are so many blanks in my history, and yours. So many things we never talk about. I don't know who my own dad is, let alone my paternal grandparents. And your dad was just some anonymous sperm donor. But now, the only grandmother I might actually have a chance to talk to is coming to Seattle. You might not want to hear what she has to say, but I do. I'm tired of knowing the history of strangers better than my own family.

"Remember when I was little and you explained to me that you and my aunts were test tube babies? You were afraid that somebody at school was going to tell me before you did. I didn't really get it. For a long time, I pictured faceless people in lab coats mixing up some potion in a big glass beaker, stirring until it started to smoke and spark. When the smoke cleared, there was a baby in the beaker. I thought it was the same for me. Even then I realized that wasn't how other people came into the world, but in a way, it kind of made sense for us. We weren't like other families. I thought that was why. But there's more to us, isn't there? We're not just some sort of collective chemical reaction.

"There's a history to all this, Mom, and it's more than you're telling me. Maybe it's more than you know. But whatever it is, I want to understand it. I want to understand *us*. Don't you?"

Chapter 36

Having spent most of the morning rehearsing ways to bring Joanie around to the idea of resuming filming, Hal was more than a little surprised when she opened her front door and announced, "I'm ready for you to bring the camera back. Under certain conditions. Well, really only one condition. No crew. I want only one camera and you're the only one behind it."

"Absolutely," he replied. "Whatever you're comfortable with."

One camera and no crew would make his job tougher, but if that was what it took to get production back under way, so be it.

"What made you change your mind?"

"Minerva's coming for a visit," she said, setting her lips into a line.

"You're kidding," he said. "Minerva is coming here? To Seattle?"

"Her train arrives in about an hour. Avery and Walt just left for the station. They're going to swing by and get Trina along the way. Apparently, Walt's not the only one who's eager to meet his notorious grandmother. I hope they don't end up regretting it," she said in a voice that made Hal think she meant the opposite.

He was disappointed to have just missed Avery and Walt. Film of Minerva meeting her grandchildren for the very first time would have been documentary gold. For a moment he toyed with the idea of hopping into his car and going down to King Street Station to capture the moment. But in the face of her mother's impending arrival, Joanie had a lot on her mind as well and with the house empty, Hal knew she needed to talk. The only problem was, he didn't have his camera with him.

As he was about to say he needed to run back to the apartment and pick up his equipment, Joanie said, "Hungry? I just pulled a loaf of banana bread out of the oven. I put in extra walnuts, just for you." He followed her into the kitchen.

This would be the last time, he promised himself, their last undocumented conversation. From here on out, everything Joanie and her sisters said or did would be recorded on tape, fodder for his film. But anxious as he was to get to the red meat of this movie, he knew he was going to miss these talks. Just as he knew that their relationship was about to change.

Lynn was right. No more softballs. He had a movie to make, a job to do. If Joanie and the others got hurt in the process of him doing it . . . Well, that's what they signed up for. Joanie understood the risks involved and she'd cashed his checks anyway. But why the sudden change of heart?

"Because of Walt," she said, handing him a plate with two thick slices of warm, crumbly banana bread slathered with melting butter. "He wants to know his grandmother, to understand where he comes from. Can I deny him that opportunity? If I tried, he'd only come to resent me for it. He's not a baby anymore. I can't shield him from every-thing, can I?

"But if Minerva insists on coming here, invading my territory and disrupting our lives, then I want it all on film. I'm not going to give her a chance to lie, rewrite history, or try to take it all back later."

"Fair enough. Cameras don't lie," Hal said, and shoved another piece of the warm banana bread into his mouth. "Hey, as long as we're telling the truth, why is this stuff so good?" he asked, licking melting butter from his fingers. "What do you put in it? It's like some kind of banana bread crack."

"Sour cream. Makes it moist. And I put in a little extra cinnamon, too, plus some ground cardamom."

"Well, it's incredible. Why aren't you having any?"

"I'm dieting." He gave her a look and she said, "No, really. I'm serious this time. I've got to fit into my wedding dress."

"Your what?"

Hal choked on surprise and a chunk of walnut. Joanie grabbed a glass from the cupboard, quickly filling it with water.

"I'm okay," he rasped, his eyes watering as he waved off her attempts to pound his back. "Went down the wrong pipe. Now, what was it you were saying? Your wedding dress?"

"Not *my* wedding dress. Just the dress I want to wear to the wedding."

"Who's getting married?"

"Meg," she said distractedly, putting the bread knife into the sink and brushing crumbs from the countertop. "And Asher. They're going to renew their vows during the Memorial Day barbecue, reenact everything as close to the original ceremony as possible. Didn't I tell you?"

He shook his head.

"Guess I've got a lot on my mind. And so much to do before the wedding. That reminds me; could I get your help with something?"

. . .

The attic, entered via a sharply angled ladder that pulled out of the upstairs ceiling, smelled like paper, dust, and mothballs and was so dark Hal could barely see his hand in front of his face.

"The light pull is in the middle of the room," Joanie advised, calling up to him from the bottom of the ladder. "Just walk about five steps straight ahead and you should find it."

Hal took a tentative step forward, feeling his way with the toe of his shoe. "Hey, are there mice up here?"

"No."

"Good. Hate mice." He took another step forward, searching for the light pull, his hands sweeping and groping through the darkness like he was playing blind man's bluff.

"Definitely no mice," she assured him. "Maybe a few spiders."

"Hate those too."

The light pull, a single piece of string that felt a lot like a spider web, hit Hal in the face. He let out a startled yawp and flapped his hands in front of his face.

"Found it," he said, ignoring the sound of Joanie's laughter. He tugged on the string, illuminating the attic, which was a lot roomier than he'd supposed.

"You are a deeply disturbed woman," Hal said when Joanie's head popped through the hole in the floor. "Even your attic is organized. Look at this!"

He spread out his hands to encompass the rows of matching and neatly stacked boxes, arranged according to size, and various pieces of furniture, artwork, and equipment, all shrouded by white dust covers.

"When you take down your Christmas decorations, I bet you test every string of lights, replace the missing bulbs, and coil them into neat little bundles before you put them away, don't you?"

"That way they're all ready to use the next year." Joanie climbed off the ladder and dusted off the legs of her jeans.

"Okay, you are never allowed to come to my apartment. Ever. So," he said, clapping his hands together, "what are we looking for?"

"Pictures. All of Meg and Asher's photo albums were lost in their house fire, so they don't have any pictures of their wedding. I'm hoping there might be a couple of shots up here somewhere, anything I can use to help re-create the original bouquet, the table decorations, and the food— that kind of thing."

She walked to the center of the room and put her hands on her hips, frowning. "I haven't been up here for years, Walt always brings down the Christmas stuff for me, but I think the pre-2000 boxes are over in that corner."

"You mean you didn't label them by individual years?"

"Not until 2006. Wish I'd thought of it sooner. What?" she asked when he shook his head. "I have a system."

He lifted his hands. "Not saying a thing. Systems are good."

"Darn straight they are," she grumbled.

Hal pulled the upper boxes from the stacks and set them on the floor so Joanie could start searching through them. For all her declarations about being in a hurry, when Joanie opened the first box and found it filled with Walt's old baby clothes, Hal realized this might take some time.

"Oh!" she exclaimed, holding up a teeny pair of red corduroy bib overalls. "I'd almost forgotten! Can you believe Walt actually used to fit into these? Sixteen years . . . Seems more like sixteen minutes." She sighed, folded the overalls, and put them back into the box. "Those were the first clothes I ever made for him."

"Who taught you to sew anyway?" Hal asked. "That doesn't seem like it would have been Minerva's thing."

"I taught myself. When I bought the house the old owner left behind a sewing machine and cabinet, a 1948 Singer—"

"That old-fashioned black one you have in the corner of your sewing room?"

"That's right. For three months, I used it as a sofa table—I didn't know there was a machine inside. But I was rearranging furniture and I realized it was pretty heavy for a table that size. I opened the lid and found the machine inside, still working perfectly. The timing was perfect too. I had a houseful of naked windows and no money to buy drapes. I found ten yards of blue gingham in a bin at the thrift store and made curtains out of it. Until that moment, I'd never so much as sewn on a button. Couldn't have been simpler— I stitched a hem on the bottom, folded over the top, and stitched that to make a rod pocket—but you wouldn't believe how many times I ripped out the seams. But when I finally hung them up I was so proud. Silly." She laughed softly. "I felt like I'd really accomplished something."

"But you did," Hal countered. "You taught yourself something completely new and you stuck with it even though it was hard. Now you're such an expert that you can make your living sewing. Not a lot of people have that kind of determination."

"Maybe." She shrugged. "It might just have been my perfectionist streak kicking in. Or because Minerva practically stenciled the words 'failure is not an option' on my nursery room walls. Or, I might just be stubborn."

"You are that," Hal said, pulling another box from the stack. "I've never had anybody tell me no so many times and with such conviction. You're better at setting boundaries than anybody I know."

Joanie opened another box and pulled out a

stack of three-ring binders. "Well. Maybe there's a silver lining to everything. Even having Minerva for a mother."

"Has it ever occurred to you that you wouldn't be who you are today if not for Minerva."

"Yeah? And what's so great about that?" she quipped, flipping through one of the binders.

Watching her face, Hal had to fight back the urge to say, *Everything.*

"Tax returns from 1998 to 2004," she mused, unaware of his gaze. "Complete with copies of every single receipt arranged by date. *Pfft.* Think we can probably get rid of these." She closed up the box and tilted her head toward him. "Don't say it. I already know. I'm a total whack job."

He swallowed the witty retort that came to his mind, reminding himself that his mission was to uncover the facts, not flirt with Joanie, and put the box on the floor next to her.

"How do you feel about Minerva's showing up after all this time? Are you even a little bit glad to see her?"

Joanie shoved the box aside. "Not an atom's worth of glad. I'm only doing this for Walt. Hey, do you mind going through the boxes over in that corner?" she asked, pointing. "If you find any-thing besides pictures, just close it back up and don't tell me. If I keep taking trips down Memory Lane every time I uncover another artifact we'll never get out of here."

She opened another box.

"Oh! Will you look at this? The macaroni necklace Walt made for me in kindergarten. He painted the noodles blue because it's my favorite color. Aww . . . He was such a sweetie. I should have had ten more just like him."

"Why didn't you?" Hal asked, tearing the tape from a box that turned out to be filled with old sheet music.

"Have more kids? It's not easy raising even one child when you're single, let alone two or three. For all her faults, I really don't know how Minerva did it."

"You could have gotten married. Didn't you ever want to?"

"I have Walt. He's all I need."

He recognized that clipped tone she hadn't used with him for some time, the one that signaled the raising of invisible barricades. A few days before, even as recently as yesterday, he'd have backed off. Now he couldn't.

"What about Walt's dad? Why didn't you ask him for help?"

"Because I didn't know who the father was. I told you before. I was seeing a couple of different guys."

"Okay, but a couple isn't the same as an army—there couldn't have been that many candidates. You could have gotten a paternity test, forced him to help pay the bills."

"I decided we'd be better off on our own."

"Like Minerva?"

Tearing the tape from another box, he paused to look at her, expecting to see that familiar flash of anger in her eyes. What he saw instead was disappointment. Whether with herself or with him he couldn't say, but he knew he'd wounded her and that burned more deeply than her anger ever could.

"I'm sorry . . . I only meant . . . You're both strong women. You did what you had to do."

"It's not the same. Minerva planned it, every minute of our lives from conception on, because she wanted to be in control. I was trying to make up for the one time in my life when things went out of control. I did what I did so that everyone, that Walt could live as happy and normal a life as possible." She stood up, looking down at him. The betrayal he saw in her eyes pierced him.

"It's *not* the same."

She walked to the ladder and climbed quickly down, ignoring his apology and disappearing into the hole in the attic floor. Hal stood up and called her name, starting after her. Stepping across the box he'd just opened, he glanced down and noticed there were pictures inside. He squatted down on the floor, folded back the box flaps, and began rifling through the contents. With any luck, he might locate a couple of snapshots from Meg

371

and Asher's wedding that he could use as a peace offering to Joanie.

Luck was with him.

Near the bottom of the box he found three photos. The first showed Meg and Asher standing behind a table and cutting into a three-tier cake topped by fresh pink roses instead of the traditional bride and groom figurines. The second was of Meg and Joanie together, arms around each other's waists as Joanie triumphantly waved a bouquet of pink roses and ivory sweet peas over her head—had Joanie caught the bridal bouquet? The third was of the ceremony itself and showed Meg and Asher from the back, looking toward the blue-suited minister—or perhaps a justice of the peace?—while Joanie, in silhouette and holding a single pink rose, stood witness to her sister's vows.

He laid the picture in the flat of his hand, careful not to leave fingerprints. Joanie was younger, no doubt about it. Her hair was longer and she was a little thinner—though not as much as all her moaning about the need to lose weight would have led Hal to believe. Time and troubles hadn't yet etched that little indentation that appeared between her brows when she was bothered into a permanent line.

She was pretty. But, to Hal, the Joanie he knew now was even more attractive than the girl in the picture. Those few extra pounds and the accompanying curves suited her. So did that line between her brows. It meant she'd lived, and learned. She was a survivor. And, he thought to himself with a smile, as stubborn as the day is long. But that was one of the things he liked about her. One of the many.

He placed the pictures carefully on the floor and searched through the rest of the box. At the very bottom, he was rewarded once again.

The photo, black and white, four inches by six, showed a close-up of a very much younger Minerva, lying propped up in a hospital bed and holding a newborn in her arms. Hal slipped it into his back pocket, then snapped off the light and climbed down the ladder, holding the other pictures in his hand.

Chapter 37

When they told her about the plan to renew their vows, Trina was over the moon.

"Really? That's *so* cool! Can I be a bridesmaid?"

"I was kind of hoping you'd be the maid of honor," Meg said.

"Awesome. That means I'm in charge of the bachelorette party, right? How about a Nerd Girl theme? We could go to the Science Center for an IMAX marathon and then to the Pie Bar for strawberry rhubarb crumble. Or maybe the skate park at the Seattle Center? I'm up for anything. As long as it doesn't involve finger paint."

Meg laughed and put her arms around her daughter.

Appointing Trina maid of honor was a deviation from the plan to adhere as closely as possible to their original wedding, but Meg wouldn't have had it any other way. She knew it wouldn't be possible to perfectly re-create one moment in time anyway. So many things had changed.

The justice of the peace who had married them the first time had retired to Puerto Vallarta. Asher wanted a real minister this time and suggested his childhood friend Matt, who was a pastor at a small community church in Ballard.

That's where they were when Avery called with the news of Minerva's imminent arrival. Asher drove them down to the King Street Station as fast as he could. They arrived five minutes late and ran from the parking lot into the depot, searching for Avery, Walt, and Trina, only to learn that the train would be delayed fifteen minutes.

Now there was nothing for Meg to do but wait. Wait, cling to Asher's hand, and try to breathe normally. She couldn't understand why her heart was pounding so hard or why her chest felt so tight. Meg didn't remember her mother any more than she had the rest of the family. Why should she feel anxious about meeting her?

The status on the electronic reader board changed

from "Delayed" to "Arrived" at the exact moment a voice came over the loudspeaker, announcing the Coast Starlight was now arriving on track two. Other people who had come to meet the train, lounging and loitering in distant corners and scattered benches, now consolidated near the entry doors, searching the faces of arriving passengers.

Avery and the kids surged to the front of the crowd. Meg, still holding Asher's hand, hung back. Even so she spotted her mother before the others did, outside the windows, walking toward the door of the station, tidy and perfectly coiffed in the middle of a clutch of more disheveled disembarking passengers. Had she never seen a photo of Minerva in her life, she still would have known who she was.

Her features were an oil-and-vinegar blend of her three daughters, flavors that complement but never combine completely, with Joanie's searching eyes, Avery's full lips, and Meg's short, slightly upturned nose, looking just like her girls but, at the same time, entirely like herself.

She wore a light tan skirt and jacket, trim at the waist, made from a fabric that looked like linen but either didn't wrinkle or hadn't yet. It looked expensive, but not as expensive as the diamond tennis bracelet she wore on her right arm. She carried a bouquet of yellow carnations, wrapped in green paper and tied with a white ribbon, laid long across her left forearm, held lightly, like a tribute for visiting royalty or a prima donna from the Paris Opera.

It seemed strange to Meg that she would exit the train with flowers. People generally brought flowers to the train, not from it. Didn't they? But then, seeing the anxious darting of her mother's eyes as she attempted to look over and around her fellow travelers for a familiar face, Meg understood. The flowers were a prop, something she could hold on to, giving herself courage and the appearance of being wanted and welcomed even if neither turned out to be true and no one came to meet her.

It was a ridiculous ploy, comical and simultaneously sad. Still, Meg couldn't help but feel a grudging respect for this strange woman who worked so hard at playing the part, determined to land on her feet no matter how far she fell.

When she saw her mother nearing the door, Avery's delighted squeal reverberated off the enormous barrel-shaped ceiling of the great hall. Minerva flung her arms wide. Avery ran into them and Minerva embraced her, now clutching the carnations in one hand so they stood straight up, looking like they were growing out of Avery's head. The two of them stood that way for a long moment, heedless of the fact that they were blocking the doorway, drawing some scowls and some smiles from the passengers who had to wend their way around them.

When Minerva released her at last, Avery grabbed her mother by the arm and steered her toward Walt and Trina, who, though searching eagerly for their grandmother before, suddenly appeared shy and uncertain of what to say. Minerva either didn't notice or didn't care.

Ignoring Walt's extended hand, she opened her arms just as she had for Avery and hugged him as close as she could, her fingertips several inches from meeting on his back and her head no higher than his chest. He hugged her back, patting her shoulders awkwardly.

"Look at you!" Minerva exclaimed when she finally released him, hinging her neck all the way back so she could see his face, like she was gazing into the upper branches of a mighty oak. "You're enormous! And so handsome. You look like an outdoorsman and philosopher, a young John Muir."

Walt's face split into a goofy grin. She couldn't have picked a compliment that would have pleased him more. Muir, the naturalist and writer known as the "Father of National Parks," was one of Walt's heroes.

"And you," she said, clasping a hand to her breast and making her voice softer as she turned to Trina, who seemed a bit more reticent than her cousin. "Those eyes. Such a deep and beautiful brown with those little golden flecks. Thoughtful and so intelligent. You remind me of Nancy

Roman. Do you know that I met her once? Back in 2015."

Trina's beautiful, intelligent eyes went wide.

"You met Nancy Roman? The first Chief of Astronomy at NASA? The one who headed the Hubble telescope committee?"

"None other," Minerva replied. "The California Science Center held an event marking her ninetieth birthday. I brought a postcard with a picture of the Hubble and asked her to sign it for you, hoping that someday, I would finally get to meet you. And now, at last, I have." Minerva opened her arms once again and Trina stepped willingly into her embrace.

Through all of this, Meg stayed back and close to Asher, watching from the fringes. Now Minerva walked toward them.

Closing the distance, Minerva dropped the arm that encircled Trina's waist, placed her hands on Meg's shoulders, and searched her face for a long, silent moment before collapsing into tears and her daughter's arms.

Meg held her, dry-eyed. When Minerva's sobs finally began to subside, Asher tapped her on the shoulder and gently suggested they collect the luggage. At that point, Avery, whose eyes were as red as her mother's, stepped in and took charge, explaining that Minerva would be staying with her for the duration of her stay.

"In your tiny house? The one Asher built?"

Minerva asked, smiling wetly at the two of them.

"Not quite," Asher corrected. "The one Avery built with my help."

"With a lot of your help," Avery laughed.

"How wonderful. I can't wait to see it."

Minerva's entourage moved on with Avery leading the charge and Meg and Asher bringing up the rear, but slowly. When the others were out of earshot, Asher leaned closer to Meg.

"I'll say one thing for her—she knows how to make an entrance. Do you remember her now?"

"No, I don't think so."

"Ah," he said, sounding a little disappointed. "Well, maybe in a day or two."

She took his hand and longer steps, trying to keep pace with her husband and outdistance the lie she'd just told.

Chapter 38

As they neared the door of the bookstore, Avery placed her hand flat over Hal's camera lens.

"Cut! That's as far as you go. I told you before, Adam doesn't want cameras following me around the shop. He says it would disrupt the customers."

"Come on. It's just me. I won't be in the way."

Hal moved his head to one side, looking at her

around the end of the camera he held perched on his shoulder. Avery shook her head and Hal pretended to pout.

"You know what I think? I think Adam just wants to keep you to himself."

"Right. Like he'd ever be interested in somebody like me."

"Why would you say that? What's wrong with you?"

"Nothing. But, aside from loving books, we've got nothing in common. He came from this totally regular, all-American family—Mom and Dad, still married, sister, family dog, church picnics, Sunday night supper with the grandparents—and I was conceived in a lab."

"So you're going to hold that against him? Don't be such a snob, Avery. It's not his fault he's normal."

"Very funny. You know what I mean. I'm not his type. And I'm not sure he's mine either. Adam is so . . . so white bread. If he was just a little weirder—"

"You want him to be weirder?" Hal snorted out a laugh.

"No," Avery protested, then reversed herself. "Well, yes. I mean, not *weird* weird. I'm not looking for somebody who wears tinfoil hats or anything. Just interesting weird—quirky. Crazy, but in a good way. You know what I mean?"

Hal shook his head. "I do not know. Not about

you or any other woman. You're all impossible to make sense of. But look, all I need is fifteen minutes of you doing your bookseller thing. Ten," he said, lowering his offer when he saw her immovable expression. "And I'll buy you a cupcake."

"Now that I'm working I can buy my own cupcakes. But, hey, you've got a front-row seat for my mermaid shoot down at the pier. I asked the producer if it would be okay and he was all for it. Apparently, he's a big fan of your work."

"Well, then that makes him a member of a small and exclusive group. One that's getting smaller by the minute."

"Why? Does Joanie hate you now that you're behind the camera again?"

"No, we've negotiated a truce. She's even letting me come to the big family dinner next weekend. As an observer, not a guest. Unlike some people," he said, giving her a pointed look, "Joanie understands I have a job to do."

"Hey, if it wasn't for me there wouldn't be a family dinner next weekend. I'm the one who talked her into it. We had to have at least one group activity while Minerva is here, right?"

Hal lifted the camera from his shoulder. "Not even five minutes? Seriously, I'll be the least disruptive man on the planet. I'll be wallpaper."

"Can't do it. Besides, I thought you were supposed to be wallpaper over at Joanie's?"

He shook his head. "Nope, I was supposed to be at Meg's, interviewing her while she's working, but she blew me off. Said she was coming down with something. It's all right; I've got some research to do anyway. Can I get some time with you and Minerva together? Maybe at your place?"

"Sure," she shrugged, "if you can find her. She spends every spare moment with Trina and Walt, playing tourist. So far, they've gone to the aquarium, Pike Place Market, the Space Needle, the EMP Museum. Trying to corrupt the next generation, I guess. The current one being such a disappointment." Avery smiled, but it wasn't very convincing. Hal reached out to touch her on the shoulder.

"Hey. It's only natural that she'd want to spend time getting to know her grandkids. Don't let it bother you."

"I'm not jealous of the kids. I want them to have a chance to get to know her. If anything, it's kind of a relief to have her point her laser at somebody else for a while."

"Point her laser? What's that supposed to mean?"

"Nothing," she said, waving him off. He craned his neck and followed her eyes, refusing to be put off. "Really. It's just Minerva being Minerva. It took less than a day for her to let me know, without quite coming right out and saying so, that a minimum wage job selling books isn't quite what she had in mind for her daughter. She called it betrayal of my talent, which is another way of saying I'm a disappointment."

Hal's jaw clenched tighter and tighter as Avery was speaking, his eyes like two smoldering coals. When she finished, he unleashed a string of oaths that practically turned the air blue.

"Whoa!" she exclaimed. "Calm down. Where did that come from?"

"Sorry," he muttered darkly. "But I mean it; screw Minerva! First off, you're not making minimum wage. You got a raise."

"True. A whole seventy-five cents an hour."

"Yes, because you got a promotion, less than two weeks after you were hired. You're on your way up. You're a manager. Which is more than I can say for Minerva. Where does she get off—"

Hal stopped in midsentence and started to pace, two steps to the left and then two to the right, trying to walk off his anger. It didn't seem to be working. Avery watched him. She didn't quite understand why he should be so angry on her behalf, but she couldn't say it didn't please her.

"What right does she have to be disappointed in anybody?" He fisted the air and then spun around to face Avery. "Let me ask you something—are you disappointed in you?"

Avery lifted her brows, a little surprised by the question. She mulled it over, thinking about where she'd been four months ago and where she was today, thinking about her growing little cadre of customers, the mom who sought her out just the week before and thanked her for helping her son find books he really enjoyed, crediting her for helping turn him into a "reader."

"No," she said honestly. "Actually, I'm kind of proud of me."

"Good!" Hal said, the anger in his voice becoming more like a simmering defiance. "Because that's all that matters."

Hal didn't say that he was proud of her, too, but he didn't have to. Avery knew it was true. That pleased her too. Hal bent down to retrieve his camera and hefted it back onto his shoulder.

"Not even five minutes, eh?"

She laughed at his pathetic expression.

"Not even. But that was a good speech."

Avery was reorganizing the middle-grade fiction shelves when Adam came up and stood next to her.

"So. Uh . . . I was wondering. How do you feel about baseball?"

"How do I *feel* about it? Fine, I guess. I mean, I like it all right. I don't know much about it."

Baseball? Was he suggesting she do something with a sports theme for the next Saturday Shenanigans? She'd been thinking about a Fractured Fairytales theme—there were lots of fun titles with twisted takes on classic folktales. But, Adam was the boss. If he wanted baseball . . .

"But I'm sure I could figure it out."

"Great. See, I'm shooting this show down in Tacoma next weekend. I thought you might want to go with me."

Avery's brow furrowed. "Shooting a show? In Tacoma? Where in Tacoma and why? I'm not following."

"Sorry. I didn't explain that very well," he said, reaching up and pushing the hair out of his eyes. "The Tacoma Rainiers—a farm team for the Seattle Mariners—has a home game next weekend. Afterward, there's going to be a fireworks show and I'm going to help shoot it. I'm a licensed pyrotechnician. Anyway, I thought you might want to come to the game with me and then stay to see the fireworks."

Avery laughed. "A licensed pyrotechnician? Really? Is that something else you picked up to impress girls? I mean, besides balloon animals?"

"Nah, just something I do because it's completely awesome," he said, his eyes sparking with boyish enthusiasm as his face split into that adorably goofy grin of his. "My family thinks it's crazy—my mom is always worried I'm going to blow off my hand or something. But what the heck. Everybody needs a little crazy in their life, right? It'd be pretty boring otherwise."

"So true," Avery said, matching his grin with her own.

"So, would you like to come with me?"

"Oh, Adam, I'd love to. But I can't. My mom is in town and there's a big family dinner."

"Sure," he said, the bow in his lips flattening a little. "I just thought we might have fun. Maybe I shouldn't have asked you, since we're working together and everything."

"No, no," she rushed to assure him. "I'm really glad you did. Are you busy on Memorial Day weekend? There's a barbecue at my sister's house. . . ."

She blurted this out without thinking, anxious for him to know she was sincerely interested in him, but then, remembering Owen's reaction to her prior invitation, immediately wished she'd kept her mouth shut. If Owen thought she was trying to move too fast by inviting him to a family barbecue a couple weeks into what she had thought was a serious relationship, then what would Adam think about being invited to a family event—a wedding, no less—right off the bat?

"A barbecue at your sister's," he said, prodding her to go on.

"Right . . . well, it's actually kind of a wedding. My sister Meg and her husband, Asher, are going to renew their vows. You probably wouldn't want to come. I mean, I'm sure you've got better things to do—"

"Sounds great," Adam interrupted. "What time should I be there?"

Chapter 39

Joanie placed her hands on her sister's shoulders, then turned her around 180 degrees, so Meg was facing forward.

"You can look now."

Meg lowered her hands from her eyes and stared into the mirror. Seeing her expression, Joanie's face fell.

"You don't like it."

Meg examined her reflection, eyes traveling from the double ruffle hem, to the wide waist sash that tied into a bow at the back, to the scoop neck bodice with the three-quarter-length sleeves, gathered into puffs at the shoulders.

"It's not that I don't like it. It's just . . . It's not me."

"But it is! It's exactly like the first one, a perfect replica. I used the same pattern, just made it a little bigger."

"No, I get that part. You did a beautiful job, Joanie. The dress is exactly the same. But the thing is, I'm not."

Meg turned around to face her sister, an apology in her eyes.

"I'm not a nineteen-year-old girl discovering life and the first breathless blush of romance anymore. And if I *ever* thought Laura Ashley looked good on me"—Meg grabbed two fistfuls of white taffeta and held the enormous skirt out even wider—"I was tragically mistaken."

Joanie frowned. "It does have a kind of Bo Peep vibe going, doesn't it? Maybe we could lose the sash? And get rid of the puffed sleeves. I know!" she said, her face brightening. "We could lose the sleeves altogether."

"I think it's going to take more than that. I'm a different person than I was seventeen years ago. We all are. I think it's time we acknowledged that. Sit down."

"You're making me nervous," Joanie said, taking a seat. "No good conversation ever begins with somebody telling you to sit down."

Meg lowered herself onto a nearby ottoman. The dress poofed into taffeta clouds around her waist. "Don't worry. It's nothing bad. But the thing is, ever since Mom showed up—"

"What did she say to you?" Joanie snapped. "I told her not to—"

"Let me finish," Meg said, raising her hands to interrupt her sister's interruption. "Minerva didn't say anything to me. She's been so busy running all over Seattle with Trina and Walt that I've barely had a chance to speak to her. It isn't anything she says, it's more what she does. Who she is when she thinks nobody is watching. It's made me think about . . . well, a lot of things. And at the top of the list is that this wedding reenactment is a bad idea."

"What!" Joanie gasped. "Oh, Meg. Don't say that."

"I didn't say I don't want to go through with the ceremony. I just don't want to reenact it. You know why? Because even if I wear the same dress, and carry the same flowers, and eat the same wedding cake—it won't be the same. It can't. Too much has changed.

"Remember when I told you that only my happy memories were returning? That wasn't really true. As soon as I came home from the hospital, I started to remember that I was unhappy before the accident. Hurt. I couldn't remember why. I still don't. But I remembered how it felt and that it had something to do with Asher. That's why I tried to keep him at a distance at first, because remembering hurt too much.

"But then I started to spend time with him and . . ." Meg looked down at her dress, smoothed out one of the taffeta poofs with her hand, smiling. "And I fell in love. Again. How could I not? He's Asher.

"But that's where the problem started. Things were so good between us. Too good, really. We had great fun, great sex, a great daughter. Every-thing was perfect. Why would I want to mess with that?

"Only one reason . . . Sometimes in life, we experience perfect moments and think, 'I wish I could freeze it, preserve it, like a picture in a frame. I wish it could always be like this.' But that's all it is: a wish. Blow on the dandelion and the seeds scatter to the wind. Trying to make a life out of perfect moments is like trying to paint a picture with only one color. It might be absolutely beautiful, your favorite, but if it's the only one you're willing to use, there's no contrast, no shading, or shape, or image. You can paint with that color for the rest of your life and it will never mean anything.

"That's what I was trying to do when it came to Asher, paint with only the colors I liked, the happy colors, the safe ones. It took the fear of losing him completely for me to figure it out, but I finally did. I love Asher, with all my heart. There are still things I don't remember about our life before, maybe some that I never will, but what I know about our life going forward is that I'm willing to use all the colors, the full spectrum, dark as night to bright as dawn and everything in between.

"When I married Asher, I thought our life together would be perfect. I thought *he* was perfect. I couldn't imagine that he could ever, ever do anything that might hurt me. Now I know better. And that's why I can't repeat the vows I made to him back then, Joanie. That moment has passed. But I can *renew* my vows to Asher. I'm ready to do that. And I want to, so much."

Meg looked at her lap and shook her head.

"But *not* in this dress."

Joanie started to laugh. So did Meg. Before long, they were wiping tears from their eyes.

"Fair enough," Joanie said, grabbing her measuring tape from a nearby table. "How about a sheath? Maybe with a crocheted lace overlay?"

"Better. But before we worry about dresses, there's something else I wanted to say, about Minerva."

Joanie lowered herself slowly back into her chair, the measuring tape hanging loose in her fist.

"The accident was a kind of a rebirth for me," Meg said. "I hadn't painted in years and I was deeply unhappy. Then I woke up, and that was all gone, I didn't remember anything or anyone. It was like the first day of my life.

"When I started to paint, it was like some sort of instinct kicking in. And I was so happy doing it. I didn't worry about technique, or style, or whether what I was doing was good or not, I just poured everything out on the canvas for the sheer joy of doing it. I wasn't trying to impress anybody. I just wanted to create. I had to. It felt like that was the reason I was born."

"Well, I think that's true," Joanie commented. "You're doing the best work of your life. You were born to be an artist."

"Yeah, but you know something?" Meg said urgently, leaning far forward on the ottoman so she could lay her hand on Joanie's knee. "I think *everybody* is born to be an artist. Creativity is as natural to the human condition as respiration, but people spend their whole lives holding their breath. Why? Fear. Fear of failure. Of judgment. Fear of disappointing ourselves and others.

"The day after Minerva showed up, I went to my studio after lunch like I always do, but I couldn't paint. I was second-guessing myself with every brushstroke, worrying about the end result instead of just enjoying the process and pouring myself out onto the canvas. It was the same thing the next day.

"I told myself it was better that way because I should be spending my time helping Asher with the business. Nobody was paying me to paint. What right did I have to waste time on some silly hobby when we have so many bills? I spent the whole next day in the office, didn't even try to paint. But by the end of the day, I was starting to snap at Asher, taking out my frustration on him.

"When I woke up the next day, another one of my memories returned, something that happened right before the accident. I was in the car, talking to Minerva on the phone. I was so, so angry. I don't remember why, but I do remember Minerva saying I should start painting and that the reason I hadn't was because I was creatively blocked."

Joanie, unable to contain herself, started in on Minerva and the value of her opinions, as well as Avery and the disloyalty of double agents.

"Stop," Meg said. "Don't go picking on Avery. Or Minerva. It's not her fault I couldn't paint, then or now. I know you hate hearing it, but she was right. I was creatively blocked. As soon as I remembered that she'd said it, I knew it was true. So I went looking for the source of that block and I found it. On the Internet."

Meg reached down and picked up her purse, which she'd left sitting on the floor next to the ottoman, then reached inside, took out a folded piece of paper, and started reading aloud.

In her new exhibition, Periphery, which opened at the Clairmont Gallery on Friday, Meghan Promise failed to live up to her name. Her brush-work is clumsy, and her themes and perspective uninspired. Her attempts at artistic irony, particularly in the series Dog and Bison, are kitschy rather than clever, highlighting the immaturity of a painter whose reputation as a prodigy is pure hype and wholly undeserved.

Promise, one of the subjects of the 1996 book The Promise Girls, penned by her mother, a woman whose emotional instability would be revealed within weeks of the book's publication, created a momentary sensation in the public imagination and those who had little connection with or understanding of the art world. Though a handful of critics lauded her, the remainder were less impressed and divided into two camps: those who said it was too soon to tell if hints of the teen's promise would someday be fulfilled, and those who dismissed her as a talented amateur, the product of a slick marketing campaign and shameless promotion by a Machiavellian mother.

On Friday, the question was settled once and for all.

The world loves an underdog. And when that underdog is a child who, through no fault of her own, suffered hardships at the hands of her own mother and as a result of undeserved public attention, the artistically unschooled cannot help but cheer. However, much as we might wish it were otherwise, when it comes to painting, talented amateur is the descriptive that can be most accurately ascribed to this formerly famous flash in the pan.

If Meghan Promise's first solo exhibition turns out to be her last, the professional art world shall suffer no loss.

"Oh, Meg . . ." Joanie said. "Why did you go looking for that? It was so long ago."

Meg nodded. "Seventeen years ago. I moved up here to escape Minerva, but I was also trying to outrun that review. Even though I kept painting after we got married, it was just a matter of time. I used Asher, and motherhood, and the business as excuses, but there was only one reason I stopped painting—fear. I was afraid that the reviewer was right, that I was nothing more than a talented amateur. Poor me! How tragic!"

Meg clapped a hand to her breast and heaved an exaggerated sigh, her actions bringing a confused smile to her sister's lips.

"Do you know what amateur means?" Meg asked.

"Well . . ." Joanie responded slowly. "A nonprofessional, I guess."

"Exactly. Some people, like snotty art critics, use the word *amateur* as a slam, a shorthand term for second-rate, a dabbler. But all it really means is someone who does something without being paid; the word itself carries no implication of quality or lack of it. Amateur is taken from the Latin word *amator*, meaning 'lover.' An amateur is somebody who does something purely for the love of it, because doing so brings them joy.

"Sure, I'd love to impress the professional art world and see my work hanging in galleries and museums. There's nothing wrong with wanting more. But if that never happens and the worst thing anybody can say about me is that I love to paint so much I'd do it for free, bring it on!" Meg laughed. "The reviewer was right. I love to paint so much I'd do it for free. What's not right is letting fear stand in the way, of anything.

"And so I've made up my mind," she said emphatically, hopping to her feet, taffeta folds falling in a soft whoosh to her ankles. "Today, I proudly declare my status as a talented amateur, a passionately dedicated lover of art, of Asher, of my family, and my life."

Joanie jumped to her feet and started clapping her hands. "Good for you, Meg! Bravo! That's brilliant."

Meg grabbed her skirt and dipped in a quick curtsy. "I thought so. And to think, all it took was a skull fracture and thirty thousand dollars in medical bills for me to figure it out."

"Worth every dime," Joanie said.

"Thank you. I'm glad you feel that way. But since I can't arrange a car crash for you—even if we could afford the hospital bills—I guess it's up to me to give you the knock in the head you so desperately need."

Meg spun around, back to her sister.

"Undo these buttons, will you? We're going on a field trip and I'm not going dressed like this."

Chapter 40

"What are we doing here?" Joanie asked when Meg parked the car in front of Capitol Hill Consignment, a store that sold used furniture, mostly from the modern era, but with an occasional antique thrown into the mix.

"You'll see," Meg said, grabbing her sister by the arm and dragging her through the door.

"Ah, you're back. And you brought your sister. Good," said Mrs. Levitt, the owner, when she saw them. "Someone else was looking at it after lunch. But, I said I would hold it for you until five and I kept my promise. Right this way."

Joanie mouthed a silent question to her sister, but Meg shook her off and followed along after Mrs. Levitt, gesturing for Joanie to do the same.

They wended their way through a maze of over-stuffed chairs, polished dining room sets, bed-frames arranged according to size, reproduction Tiffany lamps, and a large and somewhat alarming display of mounted deer antlers. Joanie kept looking left and right, wondering why Meg insisted on bringing her here. There wasn't room for so much as a coatrack in Meg and Asher's house. Joanie didn't need any furniture either. Even if she had, she couldn't afford it. For the next few years, every spare dime had to go to Walt's college fund.

But as they rounded the corner of an enormous oak armoire, Joanie knew what Meg wanted to show her.

"Here it is," Mrs. Levitt announced, sweeping her arm through the air like a game-show spokesmodel. "A 1908 R. S. Howard upright grand piano. Oak satin stain. Perfect condition. As you can see, though it doesn't take up any additional floor space, it's taller than a standard upright. This allows for greater reverberation, giv—"

"Giving them a richer sound, comparable to a grand piano," Joanie said, finishing Mrs. Levitt's sentence before turning to her sister.

"No, Meg. No, I don't play anymore. I haven't for years."

"I know. And I didn't paint anymore. But now I do. And it's given me my life back. Sit," she commanded, pushing Joanie down onto the bench.

Meg lifted the piano's honey-colored lid. Joanie spotted the price tag: $2,500.

"Meg, listen to me. I'm not in the market for a piano. Even if I was, I don't have twenty-five hundred dollars."

"Neither do I. But Mrs. Levitt and I have come to an arrangement. I'm giving her four of my paintings, the rhododendron series, and she's giving me the piano, which I'm giving to you."

"Yes," Mrs. Levitt confirmed. "It's a good arrangement for everyone. Your sister is a beautiful painter—a true artist."

"No," Joanie protested. "I'm not letting you give away your work just to get me a piano that I don't want and can't play. It's too much!"

"But it's not like I'm being all that generous. There's something in it for me, too, you know. Remember how I said I want this wedding to be different from the first one? One of the things I'd like to change is the music. No guitars. I want you."

"I am not going to play for your wedding."

"Fine. Then play for yourself. For the sheer joy of it, for love. Like you used to. And you did love to play, Joanie, once upon a time. I remember. I've been watching you for these last weeks, ever since Hal came. You'd barely even listen to the radio before he came. Now you've always got music playing—Beethoven, Bach, Rachmaninoff, Liszt. And sometimes, when you don't think anyone is watching, I see this look on your face. It's like you've been completely transported. It's still in you, Joanie. That love. You can bury it, but you can't kill it."

Joanie shut her eyes tight, like she was wincing in pain, trying to block out her sister's words.

"I can't."

"Yes, you can. Try. Please? Do it for me. No, do it for yourself."

Joanie didn't open her eyes, but didn't move either. Gradually, the pained look faded from her face. She took several slow, deep breaths, relaxing her shoulders, calming her heart, then moved her feet to the pedals, testing them with her toes. She lifted her arms and arched her hands, leading from the wrist, hands hovering, then slowly lowering them to the board, feeling ivory against her fingertips, satin and slick.

"Go ahead," Mrs. Levitt urged. "It's a wonderful

instrument, you'll see. The keyboard has a nice action still. Don't be afraid. I played as a girl, for six years. But I took it up again a few years ago. Now that my children are gone, I have a little more time. I was surprised how much I remembered, even after all this time, but—"

Joanie tuned her out. She refused to hear anything, not Mrs. Levitt or those long-ago voices that lived on in her head, Minerva's voice, the director at the Curtis Institute, her own.

She pressed her fingers against the keys, playing the first two bars so softly that Mrs. Levitt didn't hear her at first and kept talking. Meg clutched at the older woman's arm, silencing her.

The opening section of the Liebestraum was to be played *poco allegro*, a little quickly, but Joanie had always favored a slightly more languorous interpretation and she did so now, partly because she loved this section so much and found the fluid, repetitive slurring of the right hand so calming, but also because she was feeling tentative and needed time to find her footing.

It didn't take long. Ten measures in, she forgot to think and surrendered herself to the music completely, swaying slightly as she reached and stretched her hands, caressing the keys, finding the heart of the piece, finding that part of herself she'd abandoned half a lifetime before and thought never to reclaim again. And yet, it was the sweetest of reunions, with no apologies, penance, or repercussions, only the rediscovery and resurrection of a lost love. She remembered every note, chord, and rest, or rather, her fingers did. She didn't need to think, only to release her fear and let the music flow from her.

And it did. Even in the cadenzas, the more animated, passionate, and technically challenging sections, she played flawlessly, simply letting go, like a rider letting loose the reins and giving a horse its head. The music filled every part of her, flooding into her empty spaces, salving the aches she had ignored for so long that aching had begun to feel like her natural state. It was not.

She was not meant to live simply to endure, but to thrive, to create, and in doing so reflect the glory of creation itself, and the Creator who had fashioned her for this purpose.

Before Joanie touched her fingers to the keys she'd forgotten this essential truth, this tenet that defined her. By the time the final notes faded from her hearing, she remembered. She knew. So did everyone else.

Joanie wilted at the keyboard, drained. Her shoulders drooped and her head dropped forward, chin to her chest, and her breath came in shallow gasps, as if she'd reached the end of a race and the limits of her stamina.

Mrs. Levitt's hand went to her mouth.

"Oh . . . I didn't know. Forgive my chattering, I had no idea. No idea," she murmured to the back of Joanie's bowed head. She turned toward Meg. "She's like you, an artist, a true artist. Are you all like this? The whole family?"

Meg smiled at the woman.

"We are," she said, coming up behind her sister, bowing her body over Joanie's curved back, sheltering her, wrapping her arms around her shoulders. She lowered her head and whispered in Joanie's ear.

"We are. But sometimes the hardest part to play is yourself."

Chapter 41

The crew call for Avery's commercial shoot was set for eight o'clock that morning. Hal set his alarm a half hour earlier than usual to give himself plenty of time to get down to the pier and set up his equipment. When his cell phone rang exactly at seven, Hal didn't even look at the screen. Only one person could be calling him this early.

"Lynn, could you possibly wait until after I've had my first cup of coffee before you call and tell me I'm going broke?"

"Don't be so snippy. I'm not calling about bills. This is important. Is your computer on? I just sent you an e-mail."

"Hang on." He sat down at his desk and clicked on his in-box. While it was loading, he said, "This isn't going to take long, is it? I've got to be out of here in fifteen minutes."

"Just give me five. Trust me, you want to see this."

"Well, what is it?" he asked, frowning at the laptop screen. "The computer must need coffee too. This is taking forever."

"All right. Remember the pictures you sent me? The ones from Joanie's attic? I was looking through them and noticed something interesting about Joanie's newborn picture, the one in Minerva's hospital bed. Minerva is wearing a white bracelet in the picture, one of those identification wristbands.

"I wanted to see what it said, but the print was too tiny. I tried scanning the picture into my computer, then zooming in and enlarging that one spot, but it was so blurry I couldn't read it. Not surprising since the picture was taken in the pre-digital era. The resolution of older pictures is a lot lower than for modern photos, so if you try to blow them up it just makes for a larger, blurry image."

Hal glanced at the clock in the corner of his computer screen. "Hey, Inspector Gadget, is there a point to this story? I'm supposed to be at the pier in forty-five minutes."

"Hang on. I'm getting to it. Anyway, I did a little research and found this software that can enlarge any kind of photo, even older, low-resolution prints, and still make them look clear. It's actually pretty cool. The program eliminates the relationship between pixels and resolution and an algorithm turns it into a mathematically encoded image."

"Lynn. I'm growing old here."

"Fine. As a former math guy I thought you'd be interested. Anyway, the software basically gets rid of the pixels and then uses fractal technology to intuit what the image should look like. So even if you are isolating one tiny section of it, like a hospital ID bracelet, you can see it."

"Hold on. The computer's finally working."

Hal clicked on Lynn's e-mail message, subject line: "I'm so good you should give me a raise," and then on the attachment. Immediately, a fairly sharp photo of a woman's wrist, encircled by a band of white, appeared on the screen. The print on the band was surprisingly clear and read:

Northside Hospital, Atlanta, GA
Melanie Anne Weldon
12/22/1978

"Whoa," Hal murmured, leaning closer to the computer screen. "So this isn't Joanie's baby picture and your source was right. Minerva had another child in Atlanta, before Joanie was born. Which means there's a fourth Promise sister."

"No, there's not," Lynn corrected. "Do the math. The first test tube baby was born in the UK in July of 1978. According to Minerva, she went to England shortly after because she wanted to have a baby using the new IVF technology and it wasn't yet available in the States; also because part of her plan to raise a baby artist was to expose them to fine art and European culture from an early age.

"But that had to be a lie. She can't have given birth to one child in Georgia in December, then go to England, enter an IVF program, and give birth to Joanie in August of '79. That's only eight months. Even if she flew to Europe the next day, there's no way she gets enrolled in an IVF program, has a successful procedure, and punches out a baby eight months later. There is no fourth sibling, Hal.

"Joanie told you that was her baby picture and it's true. But everything else about it is a lie."

"Coffee?" Evan, the director for the restaurant commercial, who couldn't have been more than twenty-five, handed a cup to Hal. The two men stood leaning against a wall drinking coffee while the production crew set up lights and uncoiled cables.

Hal was grateful for the coffee. He'd spent so much time on the phone, arguing with Lynn about their next move, that he hadn't had time for breakfast. He had to confront Minerva; on that they were in agreement. Hopefully, the photo would convince her to finally come clean about her past.

"Hit her with it when she least expects it and in a public setting," Lynn said. "She'll be so flustered she won't have time to think. If you show her your hand, you're only giving her an opportunity to invent new lies. You can't afford to let that happen. This story is gold, Hal. And right now, you need all the gold you can get."

He understood what Lynn meant, but what she was suggesting didn't sit right with him. It felt a lot more like tabloid journalism than making a documentary. Who did she think he was anyway —Geraldo? Ambushing Minerva at the shoot was out; he wouldn't spoil Avery's big day. Doing it at the dinner wouldn't be quite as bad, but still . . . Minerva wouldn't be the only one getting ambushed. What about the rest of the family? What about Joanie?

"You know," Evan said after a moment, "I scheduled an early call because the pier is always loaded with tourists this time of year and I didn't want a bunch of gawkers hanging around, making noise. But Avery invited enough friends and family on set that I don't know why I bothered.

"Oh, I didn't mean you," he added quickly, clarifying his comments as if he'd just realized how they might sound to Hal. "I just meant the rest of them—the kid, the sisters, and now the mother. But how could I say no? I mean, you've been filming her for weeks now, right? Is she hot or what?"

Evan ducked his head to take another slurp of coffee. Hal shot him a look and was about to say something, but reminded himself that: (a) he wasn't Avery's father, uncle, or big brother, and therefore wasn't in charge of defending her honor; (b) when he was twenty-five he'd have said the exact same thing; and (c) Evan didn't seem like a bad guy.

"Anyway," Evan continued, "I was pretty pumped when Avery said you wanted to come. I mean, I've seen your work. I was at Sundance a couple of years ago and managed to score a ticket for *Spells the End*. Loved it."

"Thanks."

"Seriously, man. Great stuff." Evan scratched his beard, shuffled his feet. "Listen, about today, if you have any suggestions or anything—I know this is just a local commercial, but it's only my third directing job."

"Nothing wrong with shooting commercials," Hal said. "That's where I started. You learn a lot, figuring out how to tell a story in sixty seconds."

"Yeah, I'm trying to get some experience here and then move to LA in a couple of years. Say, if you know anybody down there . . ."

"Sure," said Hal, reaching into his back pocket for a business card. "Shoot me an e-mail before you go and I'll give you some names."

"Thanks! Appreciate that."

Evan put the card in his own pocket. Someone folded back the flap of the tent where the cast was getting into costumes and makeup. Avery, sitting in a wheelchair, dressed in her mermaid tail and a pushup bikini top that made her breasts look like two mounds of rising bread dough, was wheeled through the opening by one of the costume people.

"Looks like we're ready to roll," Evan said, grinning as the crewmember wheeled Avery toward them. "How you doing, sweetheart? Ready to shoot this thing?"

Evan bent down, ready to kiss her on the cheek. Avery, fully in character as well as costume and makeup, froze him with a look.

"Oh, I *really* wouldn't if I were you, sailor. It's not safe."

Before the young director could respond, the costume mistress jerked her head toward the tent. "The pirates were getting into a fight over her so I brought her outside. I think you'd better get in there. They brought their own wardrobe. A couple of them are carrying real daggers."

"Crap." Evan let out a disgusted sigh and followed the costume mistress to the tent, mumbling something about keelhauling.

Hal looked down at Avery and frowned.

"What happened to your shell top?"

"A last-minute wardrobe alteration. The director's idea."

She cast a dangerous glare toward Evan, who had entered the tent and could be heard yelling, "Put that away! I'm serious! You pirates have got to start getting along!"

Avery sniffed. "If they knew how to get along they wouldn't be pirates, would they?"

Hal took off his denim jacket. "Here. Put this on."

"Your gallantry is appreciated, Captain, but I'm not cold."

"No, I know. You're hot. So put this on before I have to fistfight somebody."

He draped the jacket over her, tucking it up to her chin, and looked toward the far end of the pier. Joanie, Meg, Minerva, and Trina were walking toward them. A moment later, Lilly Margolis, dressed in the mermaid tail that Avery made for her, came around the corner as well, her wheelchair pushed by her mother.

"Your public has arrived," he said to Avery, then hefted his camera onto his shoulder and dropped back quietly, doing what he did so well, blending in, being wallpaper.

He filmed them all: Joanie and Meg kissing their sister on the cheek and wishing her luck; Trina, who was interested in the camera setup; and Minerva, who clucked and gushed over her daughter like a proud mother hen.

It was the first time Hal ever had a chance to film the whole family at the same time, Minerva as well as her daughters, and he was trying his best to keep them all in the frame. But he also worked on getting some close-ups of Minerva, not sure when he might have another opportunity. It was hard to keep his mind focused on getting the shots, knowing what he knew about her, and also what he didn't know. Was Lynn right? Should he just shout out what he knew in front of everybody and let her twist in the wind while the camera rolled?

He captured a close-up conversation between Lilly and Avery. It was great stuff. As the girl wheeled closer, Avery pushed Hal's jacket away, resplendent in all her mermaid finery, and beamed at her little protégé, admiring her beautiful tail, the glitter in her hair.

"We're sisters now," Avery told the little one. "Daughters of Poseidon."

Lilly beamed a smile, displaying a gap left by a recently lost tooth. What a doll. No matter what, this moment had to stay in the film.

A disgruntled Evan came out of the wardrobe tent tailed by a band of six pirates, two of whom were still glaring at each other. "Okay," he shouted, clapping his hands, "let's get rolling, people. Avery, you ready? Your guests need to find a place to stand that's out of the way. I don't have time to deal with civilians tripping over cables or getting into the shot."

Before Avery could respond, Minerva approached

the director and flashed her most charming smile. "Thank you so much for letting us watch. It's such an impressive setup, like something out of a movie. Four cameras! We certainly don't want to be in the way. Would it be all right if we stood over there? Near the tent?"

"Sure," Evan replied, his tone somewhat more conciliatory. "That'd be fine. There's some coffee over there, if you want to get a cup before we start. But once we're rolling, no one can move or talk. Not even whisper. Understand?"

Avery sat up a little higher and pulled her shoulders back just slightly. "Oh, Captain. Can I ask you a favor?"

Watching her through the camera lens, Hal smiled to himself. She was Minerva's daughter all right. Evan didn't know it yet, but he was about to say yes to whatever Avery asked.

"My sister mermaid is onshore for a visit," she said, motioning toward Lilly. Would it be possible to find a spot for her closer to the action? It's so hard to see sitting in a chair."

Avery smiled sweetly. Evan smiled at her, then at Lilly.

"C'mon, kid. I'll find you and your mom a front-row seat."

The premise of the commercial was that the pirates, sick of hardtack and grog, were trying to catch some fish for their dinner. Using a rope and pulley system, they hauled a huge net up over the side of their boat and, to their delight and amid much cheering and jeering, discovered that their catch included a winsome, buxom mermaid—Avery. The final shot would show the ship's captain, sporting a lobster bib, enjoying a dinner served by the lovely mermaid, who stroked his hair while feeding him bits of butter-dipped lobster as an off-camera voice said, "Salty Dog Seafood. The freshest, best-tasting, best-*looking* seafood in Seattle."

It was a painfully simple plot. Also somewhat nonsensical. Presumably the audience wouldn't notice that the pirates were fishing with a cargo net that had holes big enough to allow the escape of a fifteen-pound salmon. And probably they wouldn't. They'd be too busy looking at Avery. No matter the commodity, from seafood to sealing wax, sex sells.

But though the plot was simple, the filming was not. There were technical difficulties, first with the net—the pulleys got stuck—and then with one of the microphones, which somehow fell from the boom and nearly ended up in the water. Then there were problems with the talent. The pirate captain had only one line—

"Stand away, ye lubbers! I saw her first!"—but kept flubbing it, saying "lovers" instead of "lubbers."

Hal, still holding the camera, was beginning to

think they might lose the light—and possibly the audience—before they got a decent take. The adults were still paying attention, but the kids were getting bored. Trina was sitting cross-legged on the ground with her chin in her hand, staring at her phone. Lilly, her wheelchair parked behind the camera and near the edge of the pier where she had a good view of Avery, was fidgety and restless, fiddling with the scales on her mermaid tail.

On the eleventh take, it looked like they were finally going to get it. When the pirates hauled the net to its highest point, leaving Avery suspended over the water, the pirate captain said his line perfectly, only to be interrupted by a loud splash and then the sound of screaming.

Hal instinctively turned the camera toward the sound. He saw an empty wheelchair and Mrs. Margolis, screaming hysterically in a mixture of English and Spanish. Lilly's disappearance into the cold waters of the Elliott Bay was so sudden and unexpected that it took a few seconds for everyone, including Hal, to grasp what had happened. But those seconds felt more like minutes. Every word and movement that followed seemed like a separate image and action, freeze-framed stills flipping one to the next, like a movie in an old-fashioned nickelodeon.

There was shouting, screeches of horror and calls for 911, mixed with the anguished mother's cries. Men shouting and calling out, "Can you see her? Can you see her?"

Hal, still carrying his camera, ran toward the edge of the pier, kicking off his shoes along the way, prepared to go in after Lilly.

From high above the water, a silver turquoise flash of color flew through the air. Avery, arms extended like an arrow point above her head, dove backward from the cargo net, pierced the murky skin of the water, and disappeared beneath the silver black surface.

There were more shouts, more cries from Mrs. Margolis, and then silence as anxious eyes and Hal's camera focused on the surface of the water. Once again, the passage of time was brief, but it felt like an eon. The ripples left in Avery's wake faded to flat calm. Hal kicked off his second shoe.

Just as he was about to lift the camera from his shoulder and dive in, Avery burst forth from the black, springing to the surface like a porpoise at play with Lilly in her arms. There were more shouts, triumphant ones this time, and cheers from the pirates. Avery swam for the pier, using one arm to hold the child and one to swim, relying on the undulating movements of the turquoise tail to propel them both to the pier and the dozens of arms reaching down to raise them to safety.

The EMTs arrived on the scene shortly after Avery resurfaced, checked out both mermaids, and said they were fine.

"I held my breath a long time," Lilly announced. "Mermaids are good at that."

"But remember how I told you that mermaids have to learn how to be mermaids?" Avery asked solemnly. "That goes for swimming too. No more going into the water until you have swimming lessons. And even then, you have to talk to your mom first, okay? Promise me you'll never do that again."

"That goes for you too," Minerva said, addressing her daughter. "If you ever pull a stunt like that again, I'll ground you for a year!"

Avery laughed. "Very funny, Mom."

Minerva looked like she wanted to say something else, but couldn't get the words out. Despite Avery's sopping swimsuit top and bedraggled hair, she threw her arms around her daughter. "Don't you ever do that again, Avery. Ever! I was so scared."

Avery patted her mother on the back, shushing her. "It's okay, Mom. I'm fine. Everything is fine."

Watching the emotional scene, Joanie, Meg, and Trina started to cry. Even a couple of the pirates started to sniffle and dab at their eyes. Evan, too, looked like he was ready to break down, but for a different reason.

"Well, I guess that's a wrap," he said. "We've only got permits to use the pier until three. Guess we'll have to reschedule it for another day."

Avery looked at him. "Why? It's only two o'clock."

"Yeah, but by the time we dry your hair, fix your makeup, and set up again, we'll barely have time for one take."

"Well, then I guess we'd better get it in one." She looked toward the pirates. "What do you say, gentlemen? Shall we try again?"

The captain called for all hands on deck. The pirates cheered. Avery patted her mother on the shoulder and told her she had to go, accepted yet another hug from Mrs. Margolis, kissed Lilly, and waved good-bye to her sisters and niece as she was wheeled off to the makeup tent.

Mrs. Margolis had to get to work so she left with Lilly. Meg had to take Trina to a workshop at the Science Center so they left as well. Minerva wanted to watch the rest of the shoot, but Joanie had promised Allison that she'd come over and advise her on a home decorating project.

"I've canceled on her twice already," Joanie told Minerva. "I can't do it again."

"I can take Minerva home," Hal said. "I already told Avery I'd give her a lift back to the house and there's plenty of room in my car."

"Are you sure?" Minerva asked. "I hate to put you to any trouble."

"You're not at all," Hal replied, smiling. "I was hoping we could find some time to talk."

Chapter 42

Joanie sat cross-legged on the floor of Allison's bedroom, surrounded by swatches of cotton duck decorator fabrics.

"I like that one too," Joanie said, pointing to a spa blue, yellow, and gray ikat floral on an ivory background. "But if you're going to use it for the duvet, then you go with a solid for the drapes. Otherwise it'll just be too busy in here."

Allison picked up the floral swatch from the floor and considered it for a moment. "Yeah, I think you're right. This for the bed, light gray for the window shades. Okay, good. Decorating disaster averted. Now let's get back to you." She put down the fabric and looked Joanie in the eye. "Are you sure you want to do this?"

"Want to?" Joanie let out a hollow laugh. "Definitely not. But I'm starting to think I have to. What do you think?"

"Doesn't matter what I think. This is one you've got to decide for yourself, Joanie. So talk it out. Tell me the reasons for and against."

"Well, the reasons against are pretty straightforward—there's a very good chance that just about everybody in my family, including my son, will end up hating me and won't speak to me for the rest of my life."

"I think the rest of your life is probably taking it a little too far, but there's definitely some risk involved. On the other hand, how much more upset will they be if you *don't* tell them and someday they find out? That would be worse, wouldn't it?"

"Probably." Joanie raised her gaze to the ceiling, staring at the light fixture with glazed eyes. "And it just doesn't seem fair, especially to Walt. When he came in that day and told me how much it bothered him, knowing less about his own history than he does about some stranger who died two hundred years ago, I suddenly realized . . . I'm just like my mother."

Allison clucked her tongue. "You are not 'just like' your mother. You made some hard choices because you thought it was the best way to protect your family."

"But what if I've been kidding myself? Walt has always been such a mellow, happy kid. Nothing ruffles his feathers, he just goes with the flow—Asher's influence, I think. But when I saw his face that day . . . This has caused him real pain. And it's my fault." Joanie looked at Allison again.

"Maybe I didn't plan everything out the way Minerva did, but the results are the same, aren't they? I cheated my son out of half his heritage, I denied him the opportunity of knowing and having a relationship with his father, the same way that Minerva cheated me, Meg, and Avery.

Maybe it's a little less awful that I was responding to an accident, a mistake I'd give anything to take back instead of engineering the whole thing, but I don't know. At least she owned up to it. I lied to everybody. Maybe even myself. Sure, I told myself I was doing it to protect Walt and the others, but wasn't I protecting myself too? I'm starting to wonder if I haven't been a little too hard on Minerva."

Allison's eyebrows popped into arches. "Too hard on Minerva? Now those are words I never thought I'd hear coming out of your mouth."

"Me either. But I saw her face when Avery dove in to rescue Lilly; she was terrified. And then, when she broke down after the two of them were pulled out of the water . . ." Joanie shook her head. "It was the first time in my life that I felt like I understood exactly what she was thinking and feeling. At that moment, she wasn't Minerva. She was just a mother. Maybe we have more in common than I thought."

Joanie started picking up the fabric swatches one by one, laying them in a stack on her knees, making sure all the edges were even. Allison sat quietly, watching Joanie's hands.

"So? What do you want to do? Come out with the truth or keep on going like you have been and just hope nobody finds out?"

Joanie's chin dropped to her chest. She rested her hand flat on top of the pile of fabric. "Tell the truth," she said after a long moment. "That's what I should have done all along." Joanie lifted her head. "But if my entire family disowns me, you'll still speak to me, right?"

"Speak to you? Heck, I'll adopt you. Or you can adopt me. It might be fun to be a Promise sister."

"Not as much fun as you think; trust me. But it does have its moments."

"At least you're not boring," Allison said with a smile. "So? How are you going to do this? You're not going to wait until the dinner tomorrow and spring it on them all at once, are you?" Joanie shook her head. "Then who do you start with?"

"Asher."

Chapter 43

Joanie came into the dining room, two black oven mitts on her hands, carrying a pan of lasagna. Hal stood in the corner, looking at his camera and tripod.

He wasn't fiddling around with it the way he usually did, fussing with lenses or lighting or whatever. Instead he was staring at the camera with a slight frown on his face, as if he couldn't quite remember why it was there. Joanie set the hot pan on the trivet in the middle of the table and took off the mitts.

"Something wrong? Dead battery? Bad light?"

Hal moved his head from left to right, the movement so small and imperceptible that Joanie wondered if he'd heard her. He lifted his head and blinked a couple of times, like he was trying to bring her into focus.

"Hal? Are you feeling all right?"

"Yeah, I just . . ."

Once again, he looked toward the camera, then back to her, but when he did he seemed more like himself, less distracted and more present.

"I'm going to take the night off," he said briskly, then started loosening the knob on the tripod prior to lifting the camera from the base. "Think I'd rather be a guest tonight."

Joanie frowned. He couldn't be serious, could he? After all the money and time he'd invested in making this film, the wheedling and cajoling he'd used to talk her into allowing him and his camera access to their lives, *tonight* he didn't want to film? If he had any clue about what was about to go down, even the slightest inclination . . .

She wasn't any happier about being forced back into the limelight than she'd ever been, but she'd made a deal, and after all she'd put him through she intended to live up to her end of the bargain. She'd overheard some of the conversations between him and Lynn and understood that his financial position was, if not dire, then at least shaky. Now, after heaven knew how many scores of hours of filming her and the rest of the family involved in the most mundane activities, he finally had the chance to film something genuinely dramatic, a revelation.

"Are you sure? How long have you been hoping to get footage of the whole family at the same time? Now's your chance."

He wasn't listening. Instead, he was putting the camera back in the case, folding up the tripod. She walked up behind him, talking to his bent back.

"Hal, I mean it. I really think you should film tonight. You'll regret it if you don't."

Hal closed the metal buckles on the camera case with a decisive snap, then stood up to face her.

"Uh-uh," he said. "I'll regret it if I do. I have violated the first commandment of a good documentarian—film the story, don't become part of it. In other words, be an objective observer, don't get emotionally involved. Too late. I'm already involved. I was from the first moment I laid eyes on you, in the green room of the talk show. Avery was right, I never got over it. Or you. So I'm calling it a wrap."

Joanie shook her head; she couldn't be hearing him right.

"Wait. You're not going to make the movie? When did you decide that?"

"For sure? About ten seconds ago."

"But, Hal, you've got so much riding on this. You sold your house to finance this film. Now you're just going to walk away?"

He bobbed his head. "I know. Crazy, right? I had Lynn on speakerphone during the drive over here and she said the same thing, but with a lot more swear words. You know what I said?

"I said I didn't give a fistful of sweaty nickels for any of it—the money, the movie, the business. None of that is as important to me as the Promise sisters, the entire, screwed-up, batshit crazy bunch of you. Kids, cousins, and in-laws included. And you more than all the rest put together."

He took a step closer. Joanie felt her heart begin to pound in a way that it hadn't for many years, so long that it might as well have been completely new. It *was* new. Whatever it was she was feeling, she knew she'd never felt it before. Hal reached up, pushed a strand of hair from her face, and locked her eyes with his.

"It's a done thing, Joanie. I broke the rule. I got involved. What else can I do? Except this."

He kissed her. She knew he was going to, had known as soon as he stepped toward her. And that pounding in her heart? It was hope—hope that she was right and he was going to kiss her— and yet, when he put his mouth on hers she was surprised because his lips were so soft, and his kiss so sweet, and she couldn't recall being kissed like that ever before, because she hadn't.

It was one of those moments when time stands still. She felt the way she had when Avery dove in after Lilly and she was waiting for her to reappear. It was as if the seconds elongated into some new dimension that was simultaneously so fast that it was hard to comprehend exactly what was happening, but so slow that you could examine every frame and moment, breath by breath.

At the moment Joanie's brain caught up with her body and she thought, *Yes,* and started to kiss him back, raising her arms, exploring the blades of his shoulders with her hands, the dining room door swung open and Avery walked in, carrying a big wooden salad bowl.

"Oh," she said, sounding surprised but not as surprised as Joanie would have thought. And then, "Hi, Hal. I didn't know you were in here."

Hal lifted his hand. "Hi, Avery."

"Yeah, so . . . everybody's here. Walt's getting the door." She put the salad down on the table and smiled. "I guess you didn't hear the bell."

Avery went back into the kitchen. Joanie dropped her hands to her sides and started to say something, but Hal shook his head to stop her.

"It's okay," he said. "We don't have to talk about this now. Or ever. Unless you want to. Right now you need to focus on your family. You've got a long, tough night ahead of you."

Joanie could hear the sound of voices in the

foyer. She nodded and headed toward the door, smoothing her hair, her brain so overloaded with all that had happened and all that would or might happen before the night was through, that she didn't think to ask how he already knew what kind of night it was going to be.

The lasagna could have used more oregano, but that didn't stop Walt from taking a third helping. Avery had seconds and even Trina, who was normally such a picky eater, ate a double portion of the vegetarian lasagna Joanie had prepared for her. The three younger members of the family did most of the eating and the talking, still excited about Avery's heroic rescue of little Lilly. The others were more subdued, but Joanie was so busy thinking about what she was going to say, and when she should bring it up, that she didn't notice.

"You should have been there," Trina told her cousin. "Avery was awesome!"

"Yeah, it sounds pretty cool. But Hal got it all on tape so I can see it later, right? Uncle Asher and I had a great time. We're going back for the three-day encampment in August. I'm going to bring my rifle."

Minerva, without consulting Joanie, had given Walt a present—a reproduction 1859 Sharps Infantry model rifle, something he'd been wanting for a long time. She'd given Trina a similarly expensive gift, registration at a week-long summer astronomy camp at the Kitts Peak National Observatory in Arizona.

Joanie was too distracted to be irritated at her mother for buying Walt a gun without asking permission, and Walt was so thrilled that she wouldn't have said anything anyway. She did wonder where her supposedly destitute mother had found the money to buy such expensive gifts. Then she noticed that the diamond tennis bracelet Minerva always wore was missing from her wrist.

It was getting late. Joanie glanced at Asher, who gave her a tiny nod, which she returned. Joanie cleared her throat.

"Is everybody finished?"

Walt looked toward her, the expectant look on his face saying he hoped she was about to announce dessert. But for once in her life, Joanie hadn't made dessert. When she had everyone's attention, she took a deep breath.

"There's something I want to talk to you about. It affects everybody in the family," she said, looking around the table, from Minerva, to Meg, to Asher, to Avery, to Hal—who was giving her a curious frown—and then back to the kids. "But the greatest impact is going to be on you, Walt.

"First, I want to say that I'm very, very sorry for not telling you the truth before tonight. Looking back, I realize that I've made a lot of really stupid choices. It's time I owned up to that and took responsibility and—"

"Wait," Asher said, cutting her off. "This isn't all on you, Joanie. Meg and I discussed it and we think this is a conversation we all need to participate in." Meg nodded, confirming his statement.

"Like Joanie said, this impacts all of us, the whole family. Yes, there were some really bad choices made that brought us to this point, but you weren't the only one who made them. This whole thing started with me. Actually," he said, frowning as he reconsidered his statement, "it started farther back than that—with me and my dad.

"You all know that I grew up outside of Spokane, that my mom died seventeen years ago, just before I met Meg, and that my dad and I don't speak anymore. That started even before Mom passed. Even when I was growing up, my father was a very angry, very controlling man. I don't pretend to know the reasons why; it just was what it was.

"My mom was the peacemaker in the family, the only one who could get around Dad. The only times I saw him smile was when he was looking at her. Mom said he loved us boys, but just didn't know how to show it. If that was true, I never saw any sign of it. For some reason, I seemed to get under his skin more than my brothers put together. If I had a nickel for every time he yelled at me, 'Wipe that smile off your face!' I'd be a rich man. Sometimes I'd smile just to spite him but, inside, I was seething—just as frustrated and furious as he was. Maybe more.

"During my senior year of high school, we had a fight. I didn't fill up his car after I borrowed it and when he drove to work the next day he ran out of gas. He was mad and I don't blame him, but he wouldn't listen to my apology. When he hit me, I hit him back. We rolled around on the floor, pounded on each other for a while. Then Dad went into his room, brought out his pistol, and told me to get out of his house.

"Seemed like a good time to move," Asher said with a sarcastic shrug. "My friend Scott's family took me in so I could finish school. Dad wouldn't speak to me and told Mom not to either, but she'd sneak over sometimes when he was at work. When I graduated, she gave me an envelope with almost five thousand dollars inside. She said I should move to the city, make something of myself.

"I moved to Seattle, found an apartment, two roommates, and started working and going to school part-time. I always knew I wanted to make my living as a carpenter, that was one thing that my dad and I actually had in common. Studying English was something I did just because I loved books. I was an okay student, not a great one. I'm convinced some of my professors gave me passing grades for pure enthusiasm. But when I got to the point where I was going to have to take out some big loans to finish, I left college and started working construction full-time.

"That's about the time Joanie and I met and became friends, good friends," he said, smiling at her. "I came over here on Saturdays to fix up her creaky old house, and she fed me really great meals. We'd talk for hours about all kinds of things. Pretty soon, this house started to feel like home to me. For a guy who had been rejected by his family, that was huge.

"When I was twenty-two, my mom died of a cerebral aneurysm. She was only forty-five. Nobody expected it. My little brother, Noah, called and told me what happened. I drove to Spokane, but Dad wouldn't let me in the house, and when I tried to go to the funeral, he blocked the door of the church," Asher said, his voice becoming hoarse as he choked out the words. "He wouldn't even let me say good-bye."

Meg, her eyes brimming with tears, reached out her hand and stroked her husband's arm. Asher took a moment to compose himself, then went on with his story.

"I drove back to Seattle and then straight to the liquor store. I'd never done much drinking, but that night I drank like a frat boy on spring break. I showed up on Joanie's doorstep three sheets to the wind and carrying a case of beer. She let me in, let me drink, let me cry. I wanted to drive myself home, but Joanie took my keys and put me to bed in the guest room. But when she tried to leave, I started sobbing. Joanie sat down on the edge of the bed to comfort me and I . . . I just didn't let go."

Asher put one elbow on the table and his forehead in his hand, his face pained, as if he couldn't bring himself to look them in the eye, especially Walt, who had been listening intently, connecting the dots, filling in the details Asher was too ashamed to speak of.

"So you're my dad," Walt said, his tone falling somewhere between a statement and a question, as if he understood intellectually, but hadn't quite convinced himself to accept it. "Why didn't you tell me?"

Walt looked to his mother.

"Why didn't you?"

"I should have, a long time ago. But, back then, I thought it would be better for everyone if I kept it a secret."

"Did you love him?"

"I did," Joanie said. "But the way you love a friend. When Asher said that he wouldn't let go of me, that's true. But I didn't push him away either. There was nothing passionate about it, not in the romantic sense. My friend was suffering, in agony. I comforted him. I'm not saying it was right because it wasn't. But that's the way it was.

"Asher had so much to drink. Until I talked to

him, he didn't realize how far things had gone. He remembered me helping him walk to the guest room, but nothing after that. I didn't say anything the next day. I thought it would be awkward for both of us and, anyway, I was excited because Meg called that morning and said she was moving to Seattle.

"A week later, Asher and Meg met for the first time." Joanie flashed a smile in her sister and brother in-law's direction. "And sparks flew. It was obvious where they were headed and I was thrilled. They were young, but I couldn't have wished anyone better for my sister. I knew Asher was a good man who would do anything he could to make her happy. Which was a lot more than you could say about the guys I'd been dating.

"A couple of weeks before the wedding, I realized I was pregnant with Asher's baby. I didn't know what to do and there was no one I could talk to, especially not Meg or Asher. The counselor I saw told me to think about having an abortion and I did. For about five seconds, probably less. When Meg and Asher got back from their honeymoon I told them I was pregnant and that one of the guys I'd been dating was the father. Since Asher didn't remember what happened when he came home from Spokane, they had no reason not to believe me.

"When I saw that counselor, you were barely the size of a walnut," Joanie said, tilting her head and addressing her son with a tender smile. "But you were already my baby. And I wanted you. I've made so many mistakes and bad decisions—but having you wasn't one of them. Being your mom is the best thing that's ever happened to me."

Walt's forehead creased as he tried to digest all that he'd just heard.

"Wow."

"I know," Joanie said. "It's a lot to absorb. I'm sure you're going to have a lot of questions after it all sinks in and that's okay. You can ask me anything you want."

"Or me," Asher added. "Anytime you want to talk, I'm here for you, buddy."

"I know," Walt said. "You always have been, for as long as I can remember. When I was little and you'd take me and Trina to play in the park, or out for ice cream, I'd pretend you were my dad. And, in a way, this all kind of makes sense because that's how I always thought of you.

"But in another way . . . Wow," he repeated, in a slightly dazed voice, looking from Joanie to Asher. "This is just really weird. You're my mother. And you're my father."

"And you're my brother?" Trina asked, sounding nearly as stunned as Walt and looking at him with an expression that fell midway between horror and disbelief.

Walt pivoted his head sharply to the right, gazing at Trina with an almost identical expression. The two former cousins regarded each other for a long, long moment and then, at exactly the same time, burst into laughter, breaking the tension for everyone.

"It *is* so weird," Trina said emphatically, wrinkling her nose, calmer but still laughing.

"Yeah," Walt confirmed, "I mean, sure, I finally have a father and, lucky for me he's a great guy. But, still . . . look at the downside. It wasn't bad enough to be taking my cousin to the prom, now I'm taking my sister. How sad is that?"

Walt grinned and Trina bopped him on the shoulder with her fist. "Jerk."

Joanie felt her shoulders unknot, relieved of the burden of secrecy she had carried for so long, grateful that revealing the truth had not been as awful as she had feared and that she hadn't had to do it alone. She looked across the table at her brother-in-law and sister, mouthed the words, "Thank you," and received looks of love and absolution in return.

"Man!" Avery exclaimed. "And here I thought I was going to win the prize for most dramatic story of the weekend, rescuing a drowning child. But, no. Here I finally do something cool and Joanie has to come along and upstage me. Thanks a lot," she said to her sister in a teasingly sarcastic tone. "I guess you win."

Minerva, the only member of the family who wasn't laughing by this time, took a sip from her water glass and then set it down on the table.

"Just a minute, Avery. Before we hand out any prizes and as long as we're making confessions, there's something I have to say. To all of you."

Chapter 44

Minerva pushed her chair back from the dining table and rose to her feet. *As if she were making a speech,* Joanie thought to herself.

As it turned out, she was.

"This is a complicated story and not an easy one to tell, so I'm going to ask you not to interrupt me or ask any questions until I'm finished.

"I told the three of you," she said, looking at her daughters, "and the world, that you were 'test tube babies,' as they used to be called. I said that I had you all by choice, choosing three sperm donors who were highly accomplished in their respective fields—music, art, and literature—because I wanted my daughters to lead remarkable lives, and fulfill the artistic promise that was your birthright.

"I did have you all by choice. Your births were all wanted, at least by me, and planned. And I did want you to lead remarkable lives. But everything else was a lie.

"You were conceived in the usual way and you all had the same father: Karl Gregory Altendorf."

Meg and Asher exchanged a look as Minerva made the announcement and Asher put his arm around her shoulders. Avery's face was frozen into an expression that was almost comical, as if she was sure this all had to be a joke and was just waiting for the punchline. Joanie was shocked, too, partly because that name—Karl Gregory Altendorf—sounded so familiar. She'd heard of this man, she was certain. But when and why? The answer was on the tip of her tongue, but Minerva said it first.

"He was the conductor of the Atlanta Symphony Orchestra. He was also married and a father of five. And from the time I was sixteen until he died, a year after Avery was born, I was his mistress."

From the moment Minerva rose to her feet and began to speak, her voice had been calm, measured, her demeanor and expression resolute, almost haughty, as if she had decided beforehand that her listeners would despise her and was daring them to do it. Now Joanie could see doubt in her eyes, a crack in that steadfast veneer.

Minerva reached for her water glass and took a drink. Her hands were shaking.

"I'm sure you want to know the what, why, and how of all this. There's much more to it than I can tell in one night, so I'll just try to give you the highlights," she said wryly.

"I was born and raised in a small town in south

Georgia. My mother was unmarried and I was a bastard. And everyone in town knew it.

"Momma was a waitress, but we couldn't survive on what she made in tips alone, so she supplemented her income with gifts from gentlemen callers, as she referred to them. None of them were gentlemen. All of them were married. Momma had her pride, though. She didn't go in for one-night stands and she wouldn't accept money. That would have been low class," Minerva said with a mirthless little laugh.

"She took on lovers one at a time, sometimes for a few weeks, sometimes for a few months, until they tired of her. They showed their devotion with tangible goods—clothes, food, sometimes even with gas for our car. One man, a grocer from another county, gave her an eighteen-pound Virginia ham. We lived on it for weeks. I've never eaten ham since," she said, and took another sip of water, as if to wash the taste from her mouth.

"My mother never stood a chance in that town, nobody did. I had more to work with than Momma —more brains, more ambition. I was prettier too. When she died, I got out of there.

"Momma said that when the doctor slapped my behind I opened my mouth and started wailing an aria. That was a funny thing about Momma. She loved opera. One of her first gentlemen callers gave her a record player. For some God-knows-what reason, Momma got herself a record of Maria Callas singing Puccini.

"I swear," Minerva said with a nostalgic smile, unconsciously slipping into the accent of her youth, "she just about wore through the vinyl playing that thing. I grew up listening to it and singing along. I had a good voice. Untrained, but good. Momma thought music might be my ticket to a better life. So did I.

"Some of the bigger towns—Columbus and Albany—had concert associations. Whenever she could afford it, Momma and I would go to the classical concerts. That's how we met Karl. He was only an associate conductor at the symphony back then and would make extra money by guest conducting at regional concerts throughout the South. The first time we saw him, as luck would have it, he was conducting a small-scale production of *La Bohème*. Of course, we knew the music. Momma sat listening with tears rolling down her face the whole time. When it was over she grabbed my hand, dragged me down two flights of stairs from the upper balcony, and all but ambushed poor Karl. He was awfully sweet about it. After everyone left he played the piano accompaniment while I sang for him. '*O Mio Babbino Caro.*' I was nervous and not in the best voice, plus I was only thirteen. But he was encouraging, said I had promise, told me to work hard in school and keep singing. I'm sure he was just being kind, but Momma took his words to mean I had a great future in music. And I have to say, at the time, I thought so too.

"Momma and I saw him conduct three more times after that. I didn't sing for him again, but he remembered us and was always kind, asking how my studies were coming along. It was all very innocent. He was a sort of a grandfatherly figure to me.

"When Momma died of heart failure, I was put into a foster home and it was terrible, terrible. Of all the things that have happened to me, the worst was seeing the three of you taken from me and put in the same situation. I never wanted that for you."

Minerva's placid, almost flat expression turned stormy. Joanie felt that familiar pang of guilt that always came when she thought about their family being torn apart and how she had been the catalyst for all of it.

Had it been her turn to speak, Joanie would have echoed her mother's words. But if there was anything she had learned in the last weeks, it was that the past was indelible. No amount of wishful thinking could change it. A lifetime of guilt and regret would not alter it in the least degree. You could, possibly, confess it, learn from it, and thereby alter the future, make it better for everyone. This was her hope. Perhaps it was Minerva's as well.

"There was to be another concert that summer with Karl as conductor," Minerva continued. "I slipped out the bedroom window of my foster home and caught a Greyhound bus to Columbus. At the end of the concert, when Karl greeted me and asked where my mother was, I started to sob. He took me backstage, comforted me, said he'd drive me home. Before we got into the car, I threw my arms around him and kissed him. He kissed me back.

"That's how it began. I was sixteen. He was nearly sixty.

"He set me up in an apartment in midtown Atlanta so he could see me before or after rehearsals. He wouldn't let me go to concerts in case someone should find out about us—that was always his great fear. He discouraged me from making friends or working too. He did arrange for me to take voice lessons with Cornelia Armstedt, but she was old and very ill so that didn't last long. It was a very lonely life and at times I was very depressed, thinking that I had turned out exactly like Momma, a thing I had sworn would never happen. I could have left anytime, but I didn't. I was in love with him.

"Karl was a remarkable man. Remarkable," she said again, her voice dropping to a reverent hush. "He should have been conducting in New York or London, not Atlanta. But it was a matter of timing. And politics. The musical world is far more political than people realize. But I adored Karl. I would have done anything for him.

"Of course, I wanted him to marry me and he said he would after the last of his children were grown. He was deeply devoted to his children. That was part of the reason I started pressuring him to give me a baby. Karl was resistant at first, but eventually warmed up to the idea. I'm not sure that would have been the case had he known that only two months after Joanie was born, he would be promoted to Music Director and Principal Conductor of the Atlanta Symphony Orchestra.

"The experience of going from associate conductor to the principal is akin to a one-term congressman from a small state suddenly being appointed president. Karl was on the fringes before, but overnight he became the center of everything. Everyone knew him. He was interviewed in the press, recognized on the street. It should have been a wonderful time in his life, but it wasn't. He was more afraid than ever that someone would find out about me, about us," she said, looking to Joanie, "and that it would all be taken away from him.

"In addition to more money and more prestige, his new position gave him friends in high places, men of discretion who had the power to do all kinds of things, alter birth certificates, erase identities, create new ones. I was moved across the country and told to pick a new name. For my first name I chose Minerva, goddess of wisdom and the arts. For the last, Promise, because that's what Karl said he saw in me when we first met and because I hoped he would see the same thing in you," she said, looking at Joanie, then at the other girls. "In all of you.

"I liked Los Angeles. I wasn't able to see Karl as frequently, but for the first time in years, I had a purpose, a happiness that wasn't centered on Karl, a baby to love, then two. Until Joanie was about three and a half and started to call him Papa, he would come to the house. After that, he thought it was too risky, so we met in hotels.

"He was very involved in your education. Avery, when you were born, he sent an entire library worth of storybooks. Meg, when you took my lipsticks and drew on the wall, I wanted to spank you, but Karl just laughed. The next day, he sent a set of finger paints and five huge pads of butcher paper. From then on, you were never without paints, brushes, canvases, or art books.

"Joanie, he bought your piano and gave you your very first lessons. Later, he called his old friend Gerhardt Boehm and asked him to give you an audition. Boehm would never have taken you if you didn't have the talent, but it was your father who brought you to his notice. And that picture over there," she said, pointing to the photograph that had formerly hung on the wall of Boehm's studio, "do you see me, far, far in the background? The man I am talking to is your father. He stood in the wings to listen to you play. I tried to convince him to stay, and to let me introduce you. But he left. I was very upset. I convinced myself that had you won a gold medal instead of bronze, it might have been different and he might have acknowledged you at last. It was a lie. But when you tell so many lies to so many people, even yourself, you start to believe them.

"Joanie . . ." she said tenderly. "A bronze in your first major competition—what an accomplishment! It should have been a wonderful day for you, a triumphant day, but I spoiled it for you because I bought my life with lies and made you pay the price. I am truly sorry."

Minerva looked at Joanie in a way that was so raw that Joanie felt like she was seeing her mother for the first time. She felt something loosen inside her, loosen and release.

"I encouraged your talent," Minerva went on, widening her gaze to encompass all three of her daughters, "and often I pushed you, too hard, because your creativity pleased him so much. I hoped he would become so attached to you that he would finally make us a real family. But that wasn't the only reason I pushed. I wanted you to have the opportunities I couldn't. It was the same wish my mother had for me. The difference was, you had the talent to make it come true.

"Keeping your paternity a secret was still tricky," she said, "especially as you were getting older. The first test tube baby was born in England in 1978 and the first American baby in 1981. Before long, it was quite a common procedure, so I came up with the idea of telling people that you were conceived using in vitro. It was a little complicated to pull off. For one thing we had to alter Joanie's birthday—I'm sorry, sweetheart, but you're thirty-nine, not thirty-eight. We altered my age as well, so if anyone ever did find out about Karl and me, at least he wouldn't have had a mistress who was underage. But that makes the news better for me—I'm actually fifty-eight, not sixty-three. We also had to invent an intricate story about me going to England to have the first two babies.

"Once again, Karl contacted his friends in high places to take care of the paperwork. And I soon discovered, embellishing a story with additional details, no matter how far-fetched they may seem, actually made it more convincing. People love stories, the more fantastic the better. They want to believe. No one bothers to check and see if they're true. Almost no one," she said, shifting her eyes toward Hal.

"As time went on, I started adding more details to the story, telling people that I had chosen accomplished artists as sperm donors. Not because I was ever planning to write a book, just because it made the tale more interesting. You see, Avery?" She smiled wanly. "Some of your talent comes from my side of the family.

"When Karl's youngest child finally left home, I realized he was never going to marry me. But he promised always to take care of us, said he'd made provisions in his will. When he died, a year after Avery was born, I discovered that had been a lie too.

"His attorney gave me a check for forty thousand dollars but, in order to cash it, I had to sign papers swearing I would never reveal your paternity to anyone or make any claim against his estate. Otherwise, we'd get nothing. What could I do? I couldn't afford to hire a lawyer and if I tried to sue, I would be up against those powerful friends who had eliminated my identity once before. I took the money. It bought me some time.

"I met a reporter for the *LA Times* who was writing an article about families who had babies conceived through in vitro. The part about us was only a few paragraphs in a much larger article. Next thing I knew, a literary agent called and asked if I might be interested in writing a book. She said publishers might be willing to pay a lot for a book like that, six figures at least. The forty thousand was nearly gone. I had no education, no job experience, and three daughters to feed and clothe. I said yes.

"And so," she said, and let out a sigh, "now you know who you are. And who I am—a liar. Of course, if I knew then what I know now, I would have done many things differently. Many, many things. But life isn't like that. We make the choices we make, at the time we make them, and we have to live with them—and suffer the consequences. Which I am prepared to do," she said, sitting down at last, looking more resolute than ever, but suddenly smaller and older.

"Like Walt, I'm sure you have a lot of questions. If so, ask them now because I'm sure that after tonight, you'll never want to see me again."

Chapter 45

Avery and Joanie did have questions, quite a few of them, but Meg just sat there, holding Asher's hand, feeling . . . she had to think about it for a while before coming up with the word. She felt whole.

Everything lost had been recovered and made whole, her memories, her family, her joy, her love of art, of herself, of her daughter, of the man she would have married all over again.

And she would marry him again, in a week's time. Not because she couldn't remember what the first time had been like—it had all come back to her now—but because she wanted to celebrate and reaffirm the goodness of their life together. Also because Joanie had gone to so much trouble to make the dress. And bake the cake. And do the flowers.

But that was good. It was all good.

She smiled, so content and quiet that finally her mother looked at her and said, "Meg, isn't there anything that you want to ask me? You're the only one who doesn't seem all that shocked by any of this."

"I'm not," Meg said. "I knew about it before."

The others, all except Asher, looked at her with surprise and disbelief.

"Well, not the details, but the broad principles," she clarified. "The fact that my sisters and I have the same father. Trust me, it was shocking at the time. So shocking, and infuriating, that I drove my car into a concrete wall. In retrospect, it seems like an overreaction."

"What?" Joanie's mouth fell open. "How could you have known that?"

"Oh, I not only knew that," Meg said casually, enjoying the stir she was making, "I also knew that Asher was Walt's father. But for a while, I didn't know that I knew. The memories seeped out of the crack in my skull. But now they're back. All of them."

She tilted her head back against Asher's shoulder so she could see his face. He kissed her lightly on the forehead.

"You're saying you knew even before the accident?" Avery asked.

"Uh-huh. I started to suspect that Walt was Asher's son a long time before that, almost three years ago, when he had his first big growth spurt. In the course of a few months, he went from stubby and scrawny to big and burly. Walt, you just got so huge!" she exclaimed. "You're a mountain of a man, just like your father."

Walt grinned. "We stood back to back at the encampment; I'm a half an inch taller than he is."

"See? How many guys in Seattle are six foot six and have shoulders like a redwood beam? There were other things I noticed too. You have Asher's walk, his temperament—easygoing, always happy. And you're studious like he is too. You love reading, working with your hands, doing things the old-fashioned way." She tilted her head so she could see Asher again. "Does anybody on earth have a bigger collection of hand planes than you?" she asked him.

"It's much more satisfying to plane and smooth wood by hand," Asher said. "And you get a better result. Totally worth the effort."

"Again," Meg said, spreading her hands, "my point is made for me. So I had suspected for a while. But the older Walt got, the more certain I became. Asher and Walt just look so much alike."

"And that's why you were so depressed," Joanie said, making a statement rather than asking a question. "Because you thought that I . . . that we . . ."

"I wasn't depressed about that, Joanie. I could do the math; I knew that whatever might have happened between you and Asher occurred before he met me. What upset me was that you didn't tell me about it. It made me feel like you didn't trust me. Also, I hated the idea that you might have sacrificed your own happiness for mine. For all I knew, it was a case of unrequited love and you stepped aside, never even mentioned that you were pregnant, because you didn't want to get in our way. I mean, you never married, and never showed any interest in getting married."

"Is that why you were always trying to sign me up for those online dating sites?" Joanie asked. "Listen, the reason I didn't want to get married was because all the guys I met were jerks. I don't have anything against marriage in principle," she said, her eyes shifting quickly toward Hal.

"And, as far as Asher and unrequited love . . . He's not really my type," she said, glancing toward Hal once again. "No offense, Asher."

"None taken."

"Still," Meg said, "suspecting is one thing and knowing is another. I didn't want to say anything until I was certain and the only way I could be certain was to get a DNA test. Don't you remember?" she prodded Joanie. "A couple of months before the accident we were all having dinner and I talked everybody into spitting into those little vials you get from the genealogy Web sites. I said it would be fun, especially to know about the ethnic background of our three different fathers. I made everybody do it because I thought it would look too suspicious if I only wanted to test Asher and Walt."

"But Walt wasn't even there," Joanie countered. "How could you know his paternity if he didn't take the test?"

"I got his sample later. I told him I was working on a family tree project, a Christmas present for you and Avery."

"Why didn't you tell me?" Joanie asked, giving her son an exasperated look.

"She said it was a secret," Walt said defensively. "I didn't think it was that big a deal. You three are always coming up with some weird project or other. I quit asking questions a long time ago." Walt looked to Asher for support. "Better to just go along with what they want, right?"

"Son, I predict you will have a long and happy marriage."

Asher and Walt bumped fists. Meg shot them both a look and went on with her story.

"Anyway, the results came in on the day of the accident and confirmed my suspicions: Asher was Walt's father. I'd been expecting it, but it was still a lot to wrap my brain around. When I scrolled down, read the rest of the report, and realized that the *three* of us all had the same father, I thought my head would explode. It felt like my entire life was a lie.

"Then you called me in the car," she said, addressing Minerva, "pushing for the three of us to make a documentary perpetuating that lie, and that's basically what happened. My head did explode.

"I do have one question. Actually, I have two—why were you so dead set on doing the documentary anyway? After everything that had happened, why not let it rest?"

"Maybe I should have," Minerva conceded. "But from my vantage point it looked like the three of you were wasting your lives and talents—you weren't painting, Joanie wasn't playing, and Avery wasn't really doing anything. I thought that doing the documentary might reignite the creative spark. I told you that I wanted the three of you to live remarkable, interesting, meaningful lives. My mistake was in not realizing that you're already doing that." Minerva's gaze moved from left to right, resting briefly upon each of her daughters in turn. "I am so enormously proud of you."

Until that moment, Meg hadn't realized how she'd longed to hear her mother say those words. Catching sight of her sisters' faces, she understood that they'd longed for the same thing.

"You said that after tonight you were sure we'd

never want to see you again. Why do you think that?" Meg asked.

Minerva let out a derisive little laugh. "Be serious. Now that you know the truth about what I did, you'll be glad to see the back of me. I'm moving into a motel first thing in the morning. But don't worry about me. I found a job. A small cruise ship company needed waitstaff and stewards for the summer season. I'll sail from Seattle to Juneau and back every two weeks until September. I've always wanted to see Alaska. Who knows? I might meet a rich, music-loving widower who's in the market for a second or third wife. It could happen," she said with a smile.

"Mom, if that's what you want, then I'm happy for you," Avery said. "But you don't need to move into a motel. I don't see any reason why you should leave. Do you?" she asked, addressing the rest of the family.

One by one, they all confirmed their desire for Minerva's continued presence among them, until it came down to Joanie, who looked straight at her mother.

"I could really use your help with the wedding. There's still much to do before next week. Please, Mom. I'd like you to stay."

"And the formal is the next day," Trina added. "You've got to stay for that too. You don't want to miss seeing Walt in a tuxedo. Biggest penguin on the face of the planet," she said, tossing a teasing glance to her brother, who responded with an oh-very-funny sort of expression.

Minerva shook her head. "I'm supposed to fly to Alaska and meet the ship on Tuesday. I'm so sorry. I'll hate to miss all that."

"I could take some videos," Hal offered.

Joanie looked at him. "You're not going back to California right away?"

"Seattle has grown on me. I'm thinking about moving up here permanently."

"Oh."

Asher glanced at Meg, his eyes asking if she'd seen the look that passed between Hal and her big sister. Meg just smiled.

"Mom, are you sure they won't let you join the crew in Seattle?" she asked. "It's only a few days later, isn't it?"

"I'm not sure. But I guess I could ask. If you really want me to."

"I do. We all do. And when the sailing season ends, if you want to, you can come back here and move into the tiny house. I don't need it anymore."

"But that's your studio. And I . . ."

"I can paint inside the house."

She smiled and Asher squeezed his arm closer around her shoulders.

Minerva's face was solemn. "Are you sure?"

"We're sure," Asher said, answering for everyone. "It's good to have you here, Minerva. Good to have the family together again."

• • •

The party was over. Asher, Meg, and Trina went home. Minerva went back to Avery's house, and Walt went upstairs to work on his homework. When Avery went into the kitchen to wash the dishes, Hal offered to help Joanie clear the table.

"Were you serious?" Joanie asked, stacking plates. "I mean about moving to Seattle."

"One hundred percent."

"But what about your business? Are you really just going to walk away?"

"At this point," he said, gathering up the silverware, "there's not all that much left to walk away from. I got enough to pay my debts and give Lynn a reasonable severance with a little bit left for me to move, find an apartment, and make a fresh start. Sure, I could keep the company going for another few months, but I'd just be running out the clock."

"But what will you do?"

"In Seattle? I'm not one hundred percent sure yet. Might look for a job. Might start another business. One thing I know for sure," he said as he dumped a fistful of forks onto the top plate in Joanie's stack, "is that I'm going to spend a lot of time aggressively pursuing you and trying to convince you that there is at least one guy in the world who isn't a jerk.

"In pursuit of this goal, and you," he said, moving closer, his voice low, confident, and measured, "there is almost nothing I'm not prepared to do—take you dancing, weed your garden, charm your family, be a second dad to your son, cook for you. You didn't know that I make a grilled teriyaki steak so good it'll bring you to tears, did you?"

Joanie, already close to tears, shook her head.

"I'll even take up reenacting, dress up as a Union general and grow a mustache to go with it. And if that doesn't work—you never did give me a chance to tell you about the Euler line. It's pretty impressive. Bottom line is, I'm willing to do whatever it takes to win you, Joanie. I won't give up until I do."

"Hal, stop. After tonight, knowing how I lied to everybody . . . How can you say that?"

Her eyes brimmed over. He took another step and wrapped her in his arms.

"Because I love you. Since the first day I saw you, I've never felt about anyone the way I feel about you. And after hearing your story, I finally understand why. Every single thing you did, you did out of love. As far as I'm concerned, that only proves what I thought all along—that you're perfect, Joanie. Or damn close to it."

"But, Hal. You don't realize all the—"

"Okay, you're not quite perfect," he said with a laugh, pulling her closer. "You've got only one flaw. You talk too much," he said, and then he kissed her.

· · ·

A few minutes later, Avery, in search of the dirty plates, opened the door of the dining room and saw Joanie and Hal once again entwined in a passionate embrace.

She quietly closed the door, snapped off the lights in the kitchen, and left through the back door. The dishes could wait until morning.

Chapter 46

As it turned out, apart from it involving the original bride and groom, almost nothing about the reenactment of Meg and Asher's wedding resembled the original ceremony.

Gone was the Bo-Peep wedding gown, replaced by a simple knee-length white sheath dress with a bit of beading around the neckline. Instead of the borrowed suit that had made him look so uncomfortable in the original wedding pictures, Asher wore stone-colored khakis and a white button-down shirt, both crisply pressed. Walt, in his role as best man, wore the same color pants as his dad, but with a lavender shirt that matched the dress worn by maid of honor, Trina.

The lavender accents were a last-minute change suggested by Minerva who, after a teary call to the human resources department about not wanting to miss her daughter's wedding, neglecting to mention that the ceremony was a reenactment, got permission to embark in Seattle, a week later than originally planned. Minerva took charge of all the flowers and managed to get a very good deal on late-season lilacs, creating bouquets, boutonnieres, and table decorations herself. She also got Asher to quickly knock together a latticed archway, which she decorated with masses of purple and white lilacs and green vines. It made a lovely backdrop for the ceremony and for the pictures afterward.

Joanie was more than happy to turn the flowers over to her mother and Avery so she could spend some time at her new piano, practicing the processional, the "Air" movement from Handel's Water Music. It wasn't a terribly difficult piece, but she wanted it to be perfect, so she memorized the score.

That turned out to be a good thing because as soon as the radiantly beautiful Meg began walking down the aisle toward her beloved Asher, Joanie's eyes swam with happy tears and she couldn't see the sheet music. She recovered in time to play the exit music, an upbeat modern piece called "Deep Blue," then gave her sister and brother-in-law a congratulatory kiss before scurrying off to the kitchen.

Hal wasn't kidding about how good his teriyaki steak was. People devoured every mouthful, along with the maple and mustard glazed salmon he cooked on the grill. Avery and Adam took charge of the bar. Allison insisted on helping Joanie and Minerva serve the side dishes they'd made the previous day—green, potato, vegetable, noodle, and fruit salads—along with an assortment of homemade rolls. Allison supplied a bowl of her infamous lime Jell-O salad as well.

As they were placing the bowls down on the long tables that also held the three-tiered cake Joanie had stayed up until midnight to decorate, Allison looked toward the grill and Hal, who was flipping an enormous flank steak.

"If that tastes even half as good as it smells . . ."

"It does," Joanie replied. "I wouldn't let him hijack my menu until he auditioned the dishes first. It's incredible. So is the salmon."

"Really. Coming from the queen of all food snobs, that is high praise indeed. But what's that purple thing he's got on?" she asked, squinting in Hal's direction.

"A grill apron that Joanie sewed," Minerva answered. "And it's not purple, it's lavender. Joanie got a little carried away with the color scheme."

"And he actually agreed to *wear* it," Allison said, clearly impressed. "Man. He wasn't kidding when he said he'd do whatever it takes, was he? You know something, Joanie? Hal might be just weird enough to fit in with this family."

The next day was the formal.

An hour before the dance was set to begin, Joanie, Meg, and Minerva were on their knees, pinning the hem of Trina's new dress—at the last minute, Trina decided it needed to be shorter. Avery was looking on, making sure they were pinning it evenly. Asher was in the kitchen, rooting around Joanie's refrigerator for wedding leftovers.

Hal, who had gone into the dining room to take a call, walked into the sewing room, looking slightly dazed, holding his phone in one hand, his arm limp at his side. Joanie took the pins out of her mouth.

"What?" she asked "Is something wrong?"

"No," Hal replied, moving his head back and forth so slowly it almost looked like he was underwater. "Actually, something is really, really right. Or it might be. Depending on how Avery feels about it."

"About what?"

"About being the star of my next movie."

"What!"

Immediately, Hal was bombarded by questions from all three of the sisters, plus Trina and Minerva. The cacophony of female voices seemed to bring Hal back to himself.

"Okay, okay," he said, grinning and holding up both his hands. "Calm down and let me talk, will you?

"Lynn just called. I figured she wasn't speaking

to me, but it turns out, she was working. She pulled together some of the footage that we shot of Avery, including the rescue last week, and put it together into a nine-minute sizzle reel."

"What's a sizzle reel?" Avery asked.

"A short video used to pitch an idea. Usually, they're used to sell networks on possible TV shows. Lynn had an idea of doing a documentary centered just on Avery's mermaid persona, titled, *The Siren's Song*. She put together a sizzle reel. The very first potential investor who saw it loved it. He's ready to fund the whole thing.

"But, Avery," he said calmly, tempering his enthusiasm, "it's really up to you. We've got a good start, but I'd have to shoot some more film and interviews to make this work. If you're not up for that, it's fine. I completely understand."

"Are you kidding?" Avery laughed. "I'd love to do it! Who wouldn't?"

"Well. If you're sure," Hal said, his smile returning, "it looks like Stunted Genius Productions is back in business."

Avery squealed and threw her arms around Hal. Asher came into the room, carrying a platter of food, and asked what all the commotion was about. After they filled him in, he pumped Hal's hand. "That's great, buddy. Good for you."

"And for me," Avery said, preening and shaking her long locks. "I'm going to be a movie star."

"I always knew it would happen someday,"

Minerva said matter-of-factly. "You're a born performer, Avery. An artist. It was just a matter of time until the world figured it out."

"Oh. So now I'm a performer?" Avery asked with a teasing smirk. "And here all this time I thought you'd said I was a born writer."

"Don't be so literal," Minerva said, flipping her hand. "Six of one, half dozen of the other. The point is, I always knew you had potential. And now you're going to get a chance to fulfill it. Just like your sisters have."

The sisters exchanged a look, their eyes saying that their mother hadn't—and wouldn't—change. Ever.

"It's wonderful news," Joanie said, walking toward Hal with an outstretched hand and a smile that didn't quite reach her eyes. "I'm so happy for you."

Hal frowned, dipped his head lower, until he was practically nose-to-nose with Joanie.

"What's with the face? Oh, wait," he said, smiling again. "You think that being back in business means being back in business in LA."

"Doesn't it?"

He reached into his pocket, pulled out a key, and handed it to her.

"What's this?"

"The key to my new office. I took out a lease yesterday, two years. Can't get out of it. Don't want to. And before you ask, Lynn is moving to

Seattle too." He put his hands on her shoulders. "When are you going to get it through your head that I'm not going anywhere? You couldn't get rid of me if you tried."

Before Joanie could answer, the sound of elephant feet tromping on wood came from the stairway.

"Mom!" Walt bellowed. "Mom!"

Joanie rolled her eyes.

"We're in here!"

Walt appeared, wearing his tuxedo and looking very unhappy.

"What?"

He turned around. Joanie gasped. The tuxedo jacket was torn from his shoulders to waist, Walt's white shirt showing through the gaping hole.

"It's too tight," he said miserably, looking over his shoulder. "Everywhere. My arms are stuffed into the sleeves like sausages. When I reached up to fix my tie, the whole back popped open."

"Oh no," Joanie murmured, examining the burst seam.

"Can't you fix it?" Trina asked anxiously.

Joanie shook her head. "It would only pop open again. The rental place must have sent the wrong size."

"The guy at the shop said it was the biggest they had," Walt replied.

Trina started to cry. Meg and the aunts tried to comfort her.

"What if Walt wore something else?" Asher suggested. "The clothes he wore to the wedding?"

Trina shook her head, sniffling. "It's formal. The guys have to wear a jacket or they won't let them in."

"Hang on a second," Walt said. "I've got an idea."

Eight minutes later, Walt came back downstairs, dressed in his Union general uniform, complete with hat, gold-fringed shoulder boards, and a matching gold sash.

"What do you think?" he said, spreading his arms out wide and turning in a circle.

Trina looked at him doubtfully.

"Doesn't get a lot more formal than that," Meg offered, putting her arm over Avery's shoulders.

Trina still wasn't convinced. "Can you dance in that thing?"

"Of course." Walt tipped his hat.

"Well . . . Just do me a favor and try to act like a normal person, would you?"

"My dear sister," he said, bowing low, "would you do me the great honor of helping me lead the opening reel?"

A slow smile spread across Trina's face, even as she was shaking her head.

"Never mind. It's no use. And what's so great about being normal anyway?"

"Nothing," her mother and aunts replied, almost in unison.

Walt offered Trina his arm and she took it. "Okay, General. Let's go bust a move."

On Tuesday, the entire clan, including Hal, who by unspoken but unanimous agreement was now considered, if not literally part of the family, certain to become so before long, piled into cars and drove to the pier to see Minerva off.

The men were dry-eyed and smiling, but the women, including Minerva, were teary, not from regret but from the knowledge that something very important and difficult and good had passed between them in the last few days and that from here on out their lives would be, not radically changed, but made better because of it.

Minerva hugged them all in turn, clinging to each of her daughters for a long time. When she finally let loose and said she'd better board, Walt presented her with a farewell gift, chosen by Trina—a portable, three-pound telescope.

"Thank you!" Minerva exclaimed, squashing her grandchildren in her arms one more time. "I love it! Remind me, which direction do I point it to see Cassiopeia?"

Finally, Minerva walked up the gangplank and disappeared inside the belly of the ship. For a time there was nothing much to see beyond dockhands hefting lines and returning crew members jogging up the plank with plastic bags in their hands, having taken advantage of a few hours ashore to do some shopping. Asher and Hal dropped back from the others a bit, chatted together, discussing the possibility of taking Walt on a camping and windsurfing trip down to Hood River, Oregon, sometime during the summer. They didn't think of suggesting that they might as well leave, under-standing that, until the ship pulled away from the pier, none of the women were going to budge.

Long minutes later, Minerva appeared on the deck and stood at the railing, leaning as far out as she could without tumbling over. A deep, bass-toned horn blasted from the bridge, signaling the imminent departure of the *Wilderness Discoverer*.

Minerva lifted her arm high over her head, waving her arm back and forth like a banner, calling out to each of her daughters in turn.

"I love you, Avery! I love you, Meg! I love you, Joanie! I love you all so, so much!"

And the Promise Girls, standing in a line on the dock with their arms about each other's waists, looked up toward the bright blue sky and the face of their very difficult, sometimes toxic, never to be changed, and entirely devoted mother and called back as one, "We love you, too, Mom!"

Chapter 47

June is the month when Seattle finally makes good on its promises.

Should you come to visit then, see the pink and red rhododendrons blooming in an unabashed, almost giddy celebration of summer's arrival, smell the hint of salt and brine and fish wafting from the waters as the seafood purveyors toss glittering, freshly caught salmon through the air at the Pike Place Market, feel the soft summer breeze caress your cheek and turn your face to catch its kiss, then bare your arms to let the warm sun work its way into your winter-weary muscles, the odds that you will start looking at flyers advertising homes for sale posted in the windows of realty offices and possibly end up buying one are better than half.

But if you already live in Seattle, June is the month when you forget about the gray, and the rain, and the times you got stuck in traffic, forgive everything and fall in love with your city all over again because you realize that it's all worth it, a small price to pay for something so singular and so lovely.

On a late afternoon in early June, Meg and Avery and all the rest go for a picnic at Gas

Works Park. But Joanie begs off and stays behind, saying she has work to do, which is not true.

After they are gone, she goes into the living room and opens the windows on the north and west sides of the house so the breeze can come through. She sits down at her piano, lifts the lid, and begins to play. The sound of the music floats through the windows and out onto the sidewalk until it reaches the ears of Mr. Teasdale, who is going out to get his mail without his walker for the first time since his stroke and, hearing it, smiles.

Joanie sits in her house, in her home, in this place and moment and city that is hers alone, and plays.

And it is enough. And more than enough. It is everything it should be, or could be, or is meant to be.

So is she.

Dear Reader,

Thank you for joining me on this armchair journey into the lives and world of Joanie, Meg, and Avery, the Promise Girls.

This book is incredibly special to me, one of the rare instances in my life as an author when I finished the final manuscript and felt entirely, completely, incandescently happy with my work. I hope that you've enjoyed the reading as much as I've enjoyed the writing. If so, please consider recommending *The Promise Girls* to a friend (or five). Word of mouth from passionate readers is still the very best form of advertising and the greatest compliment that any author can receive.

I do love hearing from readers. If you have a moment, drop me an e-mail at marie@marie bostwick.com or contact me by regular mail by writing to:

Marie Bostwick
P.O. Box 488
Thomaston, CT 06787

I read all of your e-mails and notes personally and every note gets a response. I look forward to hearing from you.

Social media makes it easier than ever for

me to stay connected with readers. You can find me on Facebook at https://www.facebook.com /mariebostwick/, and on Twitter, Pinterest, and Instagram by searching @mariebostwick.

Also, please take some time to visit my Web site: www.mariebostwick.com. While you're there you can sign up for my monthly newsletter, read my blog, enter the monthly reader giveaway, and download free recipes and quilt patterns created exclusively for the personal use of my readers. To find them, go to the Quilt Central tab on my Web site and choose Patterns and Recipes from the pulldown menu. (Please note, these patterns and recipes are for your personal use only and may not be copied to share with others or published by any means, either print or electronic.)

The Promise Girls is the first book I've written in some time that doesn't use quilting as part of the story, but fear not, quilt-loving readers! There will be a new, free, Promise Girls–inspired quilt pattern for you to download on or near publication day. I'm still working on some ideas for this project, but I feel pretty confident there will be some sort of mermaid connection.

For my food-loving readers (which is everybody, right?), I will have a couple of Joanie's favorite family recipes for you to try. Lasagna, anyone? How about some banana bread?

Finally, whether this is the first of my books

that you've read or the sixteenth, please know how much I appreciate the fact that you've chosen to spend this time with me and with my characters. In spite of the fact that words are my business, I cannot find any strong enough to express how much that means to me.

And so I simply say, with all my heart, thank you.

Marie Bostwick

With Many Thanks to . . .

My friend and fellow writer Lauren Lipton, who, on a hot summer day that feels like a lifetime ago, listened patiently as I stammered my way through some disconnected thoughts for some characters I wanted to write about, without rolling her eyes when I said the words "mermaid" and "memory loss." Thank you, Lauren, for asking questions, pushing back in the right sort of way, helping me talk through those jumbled thoughts and turn them into the beginnings of a plot, the most ambitious of my career. Had you responded in any other way, I'm not sure I'd have had the guts to go on with it.

Martin Biro, my editor, who is always so positive, professional, and "for" things. Thank you, Martin, for granting me space and freedom to test myself, for your willingness to take a chance on new ideas, for never letting me slip into the passive voice (or passive *anything*), for giving me confidence, and for taking perfect care of all of the important aspects of book creation so that I can rest easy and can focus my full attention on the writing. That is an enormous gift.

Liza Dawson, my agent, for that most precious of commodities—your time. How much of that valuable currency did you spend on this one,

Liza? Adding up brainstorming, critiquing, counseling, cheerleading, read-throughs, line edits, notes, intermittent fielding of my panicked e-mails—how much? Being a writer, I can't count that high. But I know that if not for that generous investment and your profound expertise, *The Promise Girls* would not have become what it is—a book we can both be so proud of. Thank you, Liza.

To the people at Kensington Publishing who have made the last dozen years of my career an adventure, a pleasure, and a possibility. With particular thanks to Steven Zacharius, Lynn Cully, Adam Zacharius, Vida Engstrand, Alexandra Nicolajsen, and Paula Reedy. But also to every single member of the Kensington family—from the people who ship the books and answer the phones, to those who sell the stock and the sub-rights. Though I may never meet some of you in person, I am keenly aware of and grateful for the important role you play in helping good books get into the hands of eager readers.

Betty Walsh, my sister, and John Walsh, my brother-in-law, for another round of very speedy and insightful first-round copyediting. I am so grateful to you both for your willingness to drop everything and get the text into readable shape in short order. And, though they might not realize it without seeing the mess my manuscript was in when I sent it your way, my readers are grateful too.

Lisa Olsen, my Sparkly Assistant, for her copyediting help and input, as well as for her faithfulness, good humor, optimism, organizational skills, and all-around ability to make life more fun and interesting. You are a bright light in my world, Sparkly Lisa.

Adam Johnson, Artistic Director of the Northern Lights Symphony Orchestra, for helping me to gain a deeper insight into the mind-set of a young piano prodigy. Adam, I was only able to scratch the surface of the knowledge you so generously shared, but your input was crucial in helping turn Joanie into a richer, more authentic, and more vibrant character. Thank you.

To James Crook, for letting me borrow a bit of your prodigious IQ (not to mention your "Brown Dwarf" science fair idea) so that Trina had a chance to look as smart as you are. Or pretty close to it. Keep being cool, kid.

And, of course—first, last, and always—to the readers. Thank you for doing what you love to do so that I can continue to do what I love to do. You've made my dreams come true.

Discussion Questions

1. *The Promise Girls* tells the story of three sisters, Joanie, Meg, and Avery, whose personalities broadly conform to somewhat familiar patterns regarding birth order— bossy, hyper-responsible first-born; shy, peacemaker middle child; and the flighty, irresponsible baby of the family. If you have siblings, do you think birth order has played a part in forming your personality and influencing the relationship dynamics in your family? If you are an only child, how has that influenced your personality?

2. Though Joanie is devoted to her sisters, she values her relationship with her friend Allison because "she cared about Allison, but didn't feel responsible for her" and could share things with Allison that she could never share with her sisters and do so without fear of judgment. Do you find it easier to be honest with friends than family? Or do you feel secure that you can tell your family members anything and know that they will continue to love and accept you as you are?

3. Meg Promise Hayes was a painting prodigy. However, after her marriage she gave up

painting entirely to help Asher in his home construction business, becoming his book-keeper, office manager, scheduler, and co-designer. What did you think about Meg's decision to put aside her creative vocation in favor of the family business? Was she being practical and selfless? Or did you think she had hidden motives for putting aside her career as a painter?

4. Avery, the youngest Promise sister, has a vivid imagination that she fosters intentionally. Did you admire that quality in Avery? Or, like Joanie, did you find yourself wondering when Avery would ever grow up? Did you believe that Avery was as carefree as she claimed to be? Why or why not?

5. Meg and Asher met when they were just nineteen and twenty-two and were married six weeks later. Hal first laid eyes on Joanie when they were both seventeen and never really got over her. Do you believe in young love? Love at first sight? Can it last over the long haul? Or do you think the slow and steady burn of love is preferable to a quickly sparked flame of passion?

6. Many characters in *The Promise Girls* experience a major career change at some

point in their lives, and statistics tell us that most Americans will experience five to seven career changes over the course of a lifetime. Do you see that as a positive or negative aspect of modern American life? Have you undergone a major career shift in your own life? If so, was it by choice or necessity? What positive or negative impacts has that had on you?

7. Considering career shifts—if finances were no object, what would your fantasy career be? What is it that you find appealing about that career? Do you think that this is something you could ever make happen? If so, what steps would you need to take to turn your fantasy job into a real-world career? Or if a career shift is just impractical now, are there hobbies or volunteer opportunities you could pursue in that field?

8. Asher and Meg's construction company specializes in Not So Big houses, well-built and efficiently designed small homes. Avery lives in a tiny house with just a little over 200 square feet. Have you ever considered downsizing to a Not So Big home? What about a tiny house? What would be the plusses and minuses of such a move? Just for fun, get some graph paper and pencils and sketch out a floor plan for your perfect, compact-sized dream house.

9. Personal creativity is one of the major themes of *The Promise Girls*. Meg believes that "inside every person there is an artist waiting to get out, that all human beings are born with a natural talent and urge to express themselves through art." Do you think this is true? If so, what do you think prevents people from expressing their artistic side? What can people do to help knock down those creative blocks and live a more creative life?

10. When it comes to spiritual matters, Avery is vocal about her faith and the reasons behind it, some coming from personal experiences, some from her observations of the natural world, including the fact that there are two thousand different species of starfish. Whether you profess a personal faith or not, what experiences or observations give you a sense of something greater than the here and now of this world? What wonders of nature inspire you with awe and make you think about the bigger questions of creation, God, and human existence?

11. A scathing review that referred to her as a "talented amateur" was part of the reason Meg gave up painting. As we learned in the story, the word *amateur* is taken from the Latin word *amator*, meaning "lover," so an

amateur is somebody who does something for the love of it. What things do you enjoy doing, artistic or otherwise, purely for the love of it? What might you want to try in the future? What step can you take to make that happen?

12. For personal reflection: Minerva's arrival in Seattle stirs up strong emotions in her daughters, especially Joanie. As the story unfolds, Joanie learns that Minerva's motivation for the decisions she made, while still hurtful, were more complicated than she realized. Most of us carry some childhood hurts into adulthood. If you were able to have an adult conversation with someone who caused you pain in childhood, what would you want to know about the circumstances and reasons surrounding that situation?

13. When Meg loses her memory, she and Asher start from square one getting to know each other again, spending several weeks "dating." Why do you think Meg found that situation so appealing? Why was she afraid to recommit herself to her marriage? If you're married or in a long-term, committed relationship, does a month of "dating" your beloved sound like a fabulous fantasy? Or way too much work? If your relationship could use a bit of reviving, what are some steps you could take to rekindle the love you knew early on?

14. "Sometimes the hardest part to play is yourself." Is this true? Why or why not? What gets in the way of you being yourself? What could you do to make it easier?

Center Point Large Print
600 Brooks Road / PO Box 1
Thorndike, ME 04986-0001 USA

(207) 568-3717

US & Canada:
1 800 929-9108
www.centerpointlargeprint.com